A Serpent in t

A former journalist, Howard Linskey's works include crime series and standalones set in the north-east, including the DC Ian Bradshaw series published by Penguin, and two espionage novels. He also writes historical fiction and non-fiction. His books have been published in nine countries. Originally from County Durham, he lives in Herts with his wife and daughter.

Also by Howard Linskey

The Drop
The Damage
The Dead
No Name Lane
Behind Dead Eyes
The Search
The Chosen Ones
Don't Let Him In
Alice Teale Is Missing
The Inheritance
Ungentlemanly Warfare
Hunting The Hangman

William Shakespeare Mysteries

A Serpent in the Garden

HOWARD LINSKEY

A Serpent in the Garden

CANELO

First published in the United Kingdom in 2025 by

Canelo
Unit 9, 5th Floor
Cargo Works, 1–2 Hatfields
London SE1 9PG
United Kingdom

A CIP catalogue record for this book is available from the British Library.

Print ISBN 978 1 80436 877 0
Ebook ISBN 978 1 80436 879 4

This book is a work of fiction. Names, characters, businesses, organizations, places and events are either the product of the author's imagination or are used fictitiously. Any resemblance to actual persons, living or dead, events or locales is entirely coincidental.

Cover design by Head Design

Cover images © Shutterstock, Alamy

Look for more great books at www.canelo.co

Printed and bound in Great Britain by Clays Ltd, Elcograf S.p.A.

1

For Erin & Alison with love

'When a man's verses cannot be understood...
...it strikes a man more dead than
a great reckoning in a little room.'

As You Like It

Quod me nutrit me destruit.
That which nourishes me destroys me.

Motto on the portrait of Christopher Marlowe, 1585

Preface

Nothing is known about the life of William Shakespeare between 1585 and 1592: his 'lost years'. The son of a glove maker and disgraced wool merchant who had fallen on hard times, Will left Stratford, aged twenty-one, with no prospects. His wife and three young children remained there. Will's next recorded location was London, seven years later.

Somehow, in the interim, he managed to amass a large enough sum of money to buy a partnership in a theatre company. No one knows how he did this.

A Recollection

When Will looked back on it, as he often did in his later years, he realised the tale had everything. There was a murder – more than one, in fact – but there was also love of a deep and lasting kind and, it had to be admitted, a fair portion of lust. Fortunes changed hands, men were elevated and some fell. There was conspiracy, intrigue and betrayal. It had its lighter, more comedic moments, when misunderstandings and mistaken identities set the course of incredible events in motion, and the stakes were almost always far too high. There was justice, of a kind, for some but not all. By God, if you threw in a shipwreck, it would have had all the makings of a damn good play. Not that he could ever have written a word of it, for he was sworn to secrecy and would take the events of that year to his grave, or be in it sooner than he planned. In any case, who would ever have believed him?

Prologue

London, 1592

Hic Incipit Pestis
Here Begins the Plague

It was a shrill and piercing scream and it cut through the din of the streets. The click-clack of horses' hooves, the rumble of wooden cartwheels bearing heavy loads along uneven roads, the shouts of hawkers, beggars and Bible-men were drowned out for an instant. The scream was loud enough to command the attention of all and they turned to her, as one. A young, dark-haired, slender woman, of perhaps twenty years, had burst suddenly from the building, as if fleeing from the devil's house, but all who heard her could tell this was no cry of alarm or appeal for help. This was a wail born of unbearable grief.

The woman's hair was wild, her eyes nearly blind with tears and her face reddened with an anger that seemed directed at God himself. Her second cry moved all who heard it. She fell to her knees, tilted her head back and her features contorted in agony as she cried, 'My lady is dead!'

Chapter One

'Fetch me my rapier, boy.'
— Romeo and Juliet

The first thrust nearly cost him an eye. The second, Will managed to parry at the very last moment, and the third forced him desperately backwards but too swiftly to maintain his balance. The movement almost sent him tumbling over, as he fought to avoid the rapier's point.

His attacker paused for an instant to survey Will but a second later the next thrust came, aimed at his midriff. Will swiped at the blade, a defensive movement across his body that managed to block the blow. It was but a temporary respite, however, and the next thrust from his opponent might have sliced through him if Will had been closer to his attacker. He stepped quickly to one side and tried to get around his assailant but was soon closed in again. For a second time, as he tried to dodge the thrust of the sword, he almost fell.

'This is no sport! Come at me!' his attacker urged, beckoning him with his free hand as he jabbed at Will with the other. Will stepped to one side so quickly he collided with a wall and it knocked the wind out of him. His pride was injured more than his body and the taunts continued. He was slow, he was ungainly, he was very far from being a warrior.

'I was not ready!' he called back, aware that it was a weak objection to the first thrust, which had come a dozen blows earlier. He had been on the defensive ever since.

'My sword cares not whether you are ready! Yours sleeps in your hand.'

'There is no balance to this blade,' Will protested, and he wiggled the sword out in front of him, regarding it suspiciously.

His adversary would hear nothing of this. 'What is the purpose of a rapier if you know not how to use it?'

'I know how to use it.'

'Are you sure? It is not just part of your apparel. This is your weapon. Do you even remember the moves?' The other man was scornful.

'I remember them well enough.' It was said through gritted teeth. 'Remember your own, Richard.'

'Ready then?' And, without waiting for an answer, Richard Burbage launched himself at Will, thrusting out the rapier once more, calling out the moves as if he was the other man's dance partner, while Will tried frantically to parry them. His friend stopped, stepped back and immediately urged Will to 'now thrust and lunge'.

This he managed to do, though not well enough to satisfy Burbage, who swatted his sword thrusts aside contemptuously. 'Convince me, Will. Make it real or at least make it seem so. *Convince me*,' his fellow actor repeated, 'or you will not convince the audience.'

Will would have rallied then, eager as he was to show his friend he was a better man than evidenced by his ungainly part in this feeble duel. Before he could do so, they were prevented from further combat by a familiar voice that roared up at them. It came from the space before the stage where the groundlings stood during a performance. Though it was now empty, it barely contained the older man's fury.

'William Shakespeare! If you break my scenery, you will pay for it, by God!' Then the theatre owner turned his attention to the other man, 'Or my son shall!' James Burbage regarded Richard scornfully, with the contempt a father reserves for a son he genuinely fears will come to naught.

Richard tried to calm his father's temper with a smile. 'There's no damage...' Then he looked more closely at the piece of lopsided scenery that had been displaced by Will's collision with the wall, adding, '...that cannot easily be fixed.'

His father joined them on the stage to survey the dislodged emblem of a carved Lancashire Rose that had been placed there some weeks ago, for a performance of *Henry VI*. This was William Shakespeare's first and, as yet, only play as writer as well as actor and, by the look of fury on James Burbage's ruddy face, it might well prove to be his last.

'What in God's name are you doing?' he demanded.

'Rehearsing,' said Richard.

'Our theatre is closed,' the exasperated man reminded his son, 'or haven't you noticed?' He flailed his arms at the empty benches around them.

'And one day it will open again. Better for us to master a stage fight before it is needed, and we thought we might put on an exhibition beforehand to lure our audience in. It has worked before.'

His father was not placated. 'While laying waste to my stage?'

'Arses on seats.' Richard used one of his father's favoured expressions to justify the chaos.

The older Burbage looked as if he wanted to continue the argument until his tone suddenly softened, his curiosity getting the better of his temper. 'Why do you say our theatre will open again? What have you heard?'

'I say it will reopen for it always does,' Richard explained. 'They are never shut overlong, not for a riot.' He said this as if a riot was a trivial thing.

'So, you have heard nothing.'

'I heard something,' Will offered and the theatre owner gave him an inquisitorial look. 'I was told the queen herself had enquired as to when the theatre might be reopened for her subjects.'

'Where did you hear this?' In truth, Will hadn't heard it but he wanted the argument changed from one about wrecked scenery to another about the timing of opened theatres, the better to placate James Burbage.

'From Marlowe,' he said doubtfully. 'I think, or was it Kyd?'

'There!' proclaimed the younger Burbage, as if Will had proven an argument with a quote from the Good Book and not simply conjured the names of two fellow playmakers, albeit ones far more established than himself.

His father shook his head. 'They will not reopen us,' he said, and the younger men exchanged glances. Will was surprised by the lack of hope in his voice. There had been a riot, certainly, and it had begun during only the fifth performance of his first play, enacted by their troupe at this very theatre. Burbage seemed to be surveying the octagonal amphitheatre with resignation now. He had built it with his own hands, using his skills as a trained carpenter, named it The Theatre, and drawn huge crowds to this spot just off Curtain Road in Shoreditch. The open-air arena where the groundlings paid a penny to stand and watch a performance was called the pit. The stage projected out into the pit and there were three tiers of roofed galleries with balconies beyond, which overlooked the stage. The more affluent audience members paid twopence to sit there.

No one knew why the riot had started and it was doubtful that the content of the play, which was neither seditious nor heretical, had prompted it. More likely, the whole thing had begun with a shove or a trodden-on foot, causing an escalation of anger amongst the groundlings who were packed tightly into the pit, like fish in a net. If one man suddenly struck another, he could not help but bring several more into the fight. Then roaring boys would set about each other in a melee that soon became loud enough to drown out the actors on the stage.

Some were hurt in the fighting, other innocents trampled during a panicked exit of the crowd, and one man lay dead from a stab to the heart. The company was blamed for the affray and the theatre shut immediately.

Surely it would not stay closed forever, though? London crowds loved the theatre, even at the risk of a few cracked heads or broken limbs, and would demand its swift return. Each of the players now standing idle expected this, following a suitable period of penance from the company.

Not so, it seemed.

'Why will they not reopen us, Father?' asked Richard.

When James Burbage replied, it was with a heavy heart. 'Plague is in London.'

Chapter Two

'What other pleasure can the world afford?
I'll make my heaven in a lady's lap'
— Henry VI

'They have been counting the dead using the parish registers,' James Burbage explained. 'Once they reach thirty a week, all public assembly will be stopped. We live in most uncertain times. How can a man prosper when his theatre can be closed on the whim of the Privy Council? They shut us down because of a riot but will keep us closed for the plague.'

'Is plague here for certain?' asked Will. 'There was talk of it months ago when a gentlewoman died of it.'

'Lady Celia Vernon,' James answered.

'You knew her?' asked his son.

'I did not know her but knew *of* her.'

Will recalled the general alarm at the time. To think that plague could reach the centre of London so suddenly, taking a gentlewoman's life into the bargain? 'Then it abated,' he said, 'and none more perished for a while.'

'Not at first,' James agreed. 'There were some new cases on the edge of the city, following that lady's death. They tried to contain it by nailing up the doors of any family with infection. I heard most perished but it stopped the spread for a time. Plague is a persistent malady though, and they do say it loves London, so it will always find a way in.'

'Churchmen say the plague is God's judgement for lewdness, drinking and whoring. And who encourages this?' asked Richard Burbage rhetorically. 'Why, it is the actors of course, playing at murder and displaying lustful acts, leading good Christian men from the right

7

path. The minute the crowd departs, it heads to the taverns and brothels, so shut them too and blame the plague!'

If Richard was trying to console his father, he may have chosen the wrong method. 'A pox on the plague!' he cried out before exiting to the rear of the stage.

'Did he just wish a pox on a plague?'

Richard smiled. 'My father is a man of many moods. Today he most resembles an angry bear. Best exit now.'

'Good then and timely,' said Will, and when Richard seemed not to understand, he added, 'you have not forgotten our meeting?'

Richard thought for a time then said uncertainly, 'With the fair Lady... *Katherine*?' The look on Will's face showed his disappointment.

'I did forget,' admitted Richard. 'It is today? When?'

'We should leave for the river soon.'

'Very well.'

But when Will made to leave, Richard placed a restraining hand upon his arm. 'You are sure she brings her friend?'

'The lady did assure me she would.' This was not quite the same as being sure of it. The fair Lady Katherine had indeed promised to bring a companion to walk with Richard Burbage, while she strolled with Will.

Richard halted him once more, squeezing the same spot on his arm. 'And this friend is fair?'

'I am sure she is.' Though he had never set eyes upon her. A woman as fair as Katherine must surely have friends of equal beauty, but he was hardly going to insist upon it, though Will did not want to give his friend any reason to remove himself from this liaison he had spent so much time arranging. They would meet on the north bank of the river at London Bridge, where merchants sold all manner of things of interest to even the most noble of women. They would then walk together for a time, their afternoon full of possibilities.

While Richard practised his easy charm on the other girl, Will would look to bring the long courtship he had conducted with the Lady Katherine to a happy conclusion. If Richard's fair looks distracted the other lady, might it even be possible for Will to bring Katherine back to his rooms? She had virtue but not so much that she felt unable to meet him unchaperoned, except for a friend Richard could keep occupied.

Will first met Katherine after a performance of *Henry VI*, when she had made her way to the rear of the stage to tell him how much she enjoyed the theatre and his play. Since that day, he had penned many words to her, expressing his admiration for her beauty, elegance, wit, gentle nature and, of course, virtue, while quietly hoping she might one day choose to surrender it to him.

–

It took a little over a quarter of an hour to walk from Holywell Lane in Shoreditch down to London Bridge. On their walk to the river, the two men discussed a familiar topic.

'I had hoped to God we would avoid a full reckoning with the plague,' said Richard. 'It has been weeks since those first victims were identified.'

'The men off that French ship, or was it from the lowlands?' Will tried to recall. 'Ten of them, I believe.'

'Yet it did not spread from the docks to the streets as we once feared. Most likely because the ship was quarantined in time.'

'There was that lady who was stricken down.' He reminded Richard of their conversation with his father.

'I recall the fear that spread upon her passing. There is nothing strikes terror in the lowly more than hearing that even the prosperous can die suddenly of some sickness or another. Plague being the worst of them all.'

'And yet no epidemic followed,' said Will, 'until now. When was that? Two, three months since?'

'The ship or the lady?'

'Both.'

'One was within days of the other,' Richard recalled. 'There has been much discussion on cures since then.'

'There is no cure for the plague,' Will asserted, 'nor any trusted method of prevention.'

'I hear of new methods to prevent the plague every day,' Richard countered.

'Which only proves the previous day's miraculous cure a failure.'

Undeterred, Richard continued. 'I have a friend who has an apothecary for his neighbour. He says you should grind up live swallow chicks with a pestle and take that.'

'Must you pluck their feathers off first, or eat them too?' he asked with some scepticism.

'You have to get them when they are newborn, before they gain their feathers.'

'I will note that,' he said, knowing the prospect was an unlikely one.

'Urine is good too, for it contains healing properties.'

'Must you drink it or bathe in it?'

'Either,' said Richard, 'or both.'

'I am not sure I could produce enough.'

'They say you can pay men to collect sufficient to bathe in.'

This also seemed unlikely. 'Have you ever met one of these urine collectors?'

'I have not but then I have never met a witch, though I know they exist and walk among us.' Will could not refute the logic of this but instead argued the plague was too melancholy a subject to discuss while on their way to meet fair ladies and Richard agreed.

The imposing structure of London Bridge came into view then. It always amazed Will how such a thing could still stand without its many buildings being swept away by the surging tidal river. There was a chapel jutting out from it and a drawbridge tower, which sometimes displayed traitors' heads as a warning to others. A large number of shops and spacious houses hung precariously over the edges, some as much as four storeys high. These tall buildings overhung the centre of the bridge, making it feel like a tunnel when you crossed it. Movement was always slow, thanks to the crowds of people who bought items from traders, and carts sometimes blocked the way. There were armourers, goldsmiths and jewellers here, as well as haberdashers and glove makers, drapers and tailors, but the bridge was too narrow for street traders selling food and they were forced to stay on the banks of the river. Will considered London Bridge to be a wonder of the world and felt sure it would be a charming distraction for the ladies he now spotted walking towards them.

'There they are.' Will held up an arm to attract their attention.

'By God, she is fair,' muttered Richard approvingly. 'They both are. Which of them is mine?'

They were close enough now to be overheard but Will whispered, 'the left,' to indicate the woman Richard would distract, while he staged a performance of his own with the other.

Like every good actor, Will had rehearsed his opening line. 'Fair Lady Katherine, I have long yearned for this day. Come, let us walk and talk of love…' He paused dramatically then smiled as he added, '…in poetry.'

She did not respond to this but Will doubted he had offended her. The verses he had written to her had been far more daring. Was it because he paid no attention to her friend and neglected to introduce his own, even though she must know who Richard was, having seen him upon the stage in leading roles? He turned to the other lady now. 'Might I present Richard Burbage, finest actor in the land, and you must be…?' He was hoping one of them would enlighten him but neither spoke, so he admitted, 'Forgive me, I do not yet know your name.'

'Portia,' the other woman answered without warmth.

'A most excellent, fine and fair name.' He thought for a moment. 'Portia, meaning offering or gift, I believe. I shall use it in a play!'

He expected the usual protestations of modesty but knew vanity would make her weaken in the end, for almost everyone wanted to be famous these days. But she said nothing, so he returned to Lady Katherine.

'Fair Katherine, and thou art most fair. Shall I compare thee to a—'

'No,' she interrupted him. 'Thou shalt not.' She glanced towards Portia then. 'We must be going.'

'How say you?' He could not imagine how they had caused the ladies offence. 'We are not late?' He turned to the other woman, who simply stared back at him. 'I understood we were free to walk this afternoon and talk of poetry?' If they had to leave so soon then why come at all?

'And I understood you were unmarried, Master Shakespeare.' Her eyes were cold and her words pierced him like a blade. 'Why don't you go home and talk of poetry… with your wife?' Then she turned to her friend. 'Come, Portia, let us exeunt this scene.'

He had to admit it was a good line. This must have been her sole reason for attending their meeting. Like an actor, she wanted to have her say then leave the scene, and Katherine had just brought the curtain down on this one.

Chapter Three

'For what is wedlock forced but a hell,
An age of discord and continual strife?'
— Henry VI

Katherine and Portia swept past them and were gone without another word, before Will could think of anything to say to redeem himself.

'Did you tell them?' he demanded of Richard.

'About your wife? How could I?'

'Who then?'

'I have no idea but 'twas not I. I have never met either of them before now.'

'I do have enemies,' Will admitted.

'We all have those, Will. Though, in fairness to that enemy, this was no slander. You *do* have a wife.'

'And *you* do not need to remind me of that.'

'Really? For I thought you had forgotten her.' The two friends started to trudge back the way they had come, stepping round a man intent on selling them 'hot pies' from a basket he was carrying.

'This Katherine?' asked Richard. 'You have not known her over long?' Was he trying to make light of Will's humiliation, by inferring she was but a passing fancy?

'I have known her long enough.' Will's unsuccessful pursuit of her had occupied too much of his time.

'Was she the dark lady you told me of?' asked Richard. 'The one you write about in sonnets?'

Will shook his head. There was not one specific woman Will used as a muse for his sonnets, no singular former lover, nor current fancy he looked to as his ideal. Instead, he drew inspiration from splintered memories of a number of women he had known over the years. The first was a girl whose parents visited his friend's family when Will was still a child. He had seen her leave just as he arrived there. She was taller than Will, though the same age, and extraordinarily pretty. He had instantly decided she had to be the most beautiful girl in the world and he would surely never be able to live another day without her. She walked past him haughtily then, without a glance in his direction, and Will never saw her again but always remembered her, or more truthfully the effect she had on him. It was the first of many lightning bolts that had struck him since. There were a number of pretty tavern girls, and his own wife, Anne, of course, when he first saw her and had been filled with longing. More recently, there was the Lady Katherine, for whom he had held such hopes until they were cruelly dashed.

There was one other woman who could perhaps lay claim to being the root of Will's present passions and the inspiration for the fictional dark lady he wrote about more and more these days, yet he did not even know her name. Will had met her but once and in the strangest of circumstances, when he accidentally walked in on her in a state of near undress. The sight of her like that had momentarily robbed him of words, bar a mumbled apology, before he retreated from the room. She had been such a beauty he could not force himself to forget her. Will's mind continually wandered back to that day when he sought inspiration to describe a fair maid or a hopeless passion for one.

Richard pressed him further about Katherine. 'Why pursue a lady and risk bringing ruin upon her and yourself? Why not spend time in the company of' – he searched for the right phrase – 'lesser women?'

'Whores, you mean?'

'Where's the harm in it?'

'There'll be harm in it when I get the pox and take that home to my wife.'

'Then bring her down here!' Richard was becoming exasperated with his friend.

'Anne will not come.'

'She will if you command it.'

'I am her husband so she must obey me,' he conceded, 'but Anne will not like it here, nor will she settle. Then my life will be filled with petty quarrels disguised as reluctant obedience. You know how men are confounded by strong-minded women and what fools they make of us. I would get no writing done.'

'Leave her there then, if she can't bear to remove herself from tiny Stratford. How many souls are there? A thousand?'

'Two.'

'Two thousand and here in London there are two *hundred* thousand. We live in the city of the world, Will! It's filled with actors, writers, whores and spies, and that's only the best people.' Will laughed at that. 'Add in the soldiers, merchants, apothecaries, scriveners, printers, lawyers, courtiers, fishermen and tavern owners and you have the whole of England to write about. What better place is there than here, with or without a wife?' Then he reminded him, 'When you first came from Stratford, what did you think of London?'

'That I did love every foul-smelling yard of it,' he conceded. 'But it's no matter to you, Richard, for you have no wife.'

'I plan to, perhaps, one day,' he said distractedly as he watched a gentlewoman walk by, her pretty, pale face whitened with ceruse, 'when I have tired of all that London has to offer.'

'Then that day will never come. But if it should, you will better understand my problem.'

'Oh no,' he said casually, 'it's different for actors.' And when Will did not appear to understand, he added, 'Come now Will, everyone knows that. It's allowed, like an exemption from a tax.'

'You claim actors have an exemption from the laws of God and marriage?'

He at least had the decency to look shamefaced then. 'When on tour, yes. What's a man to do? Tup a sheep? Some of those tours last weeks, months even. I'd be clogged up and unable to express myself upon the stage. No, I'm certain of it. God averts his eye to an actor's—'

'Sins?'

'Follies, I was about to say. They are of no consequence when set against the noble act of bringing entertainment to the masses.'

'You think the plays enrich Englishmen who see them?'

'Undoubtedly. You do not?'

'Oh, I do. I think he is enriched, educated and presented with a far wider view of the world than the tiny corner of it that he never leaves, and learns better morals from the message within the play...'

'There then!' said Richard.

'Which he can reflect upon afterwards in the tavern, while the actor is tupping his wife… or daughters.'

Richard groaned in exasperation. 'Always thinking too much on the act, as ever, Will. That's an advantage when you are writing your plays but no way to live your life. Can't you just say "hang it" for one day and follow your gut?' He jabbed his friend in the belly with his finger. 'Or some lesser organ of the body. If you are embarrassed someone might see you, take yourself over the water. There are one hundred bawdy houses there and barely an alehouse in Southwark that doesn't double as a stew. At the Cardinal's Cap, you could have twenty minutes with a moll of medium looks for sixpence.'

'It could cost you far more than that,' observed Will. 'No, I cannot imagine it.'

'And yet you can usually imagine all manner of things, Will. Come, let us drink our way back to Shoreditch.'

'Must we go so far for ale?'

'When the ale is free, yes.'

'What mad man is serving free ale?'

'The owner of the Four Swans. He is honouring Christopher Marlowe today with free drinks for the man and his friends. *We* are his friends,' Richard reminded him.

They were indeed and it seemed to Will that all men were drawn to Kit Marlowe. It was something about the way he conducted himself, as if everything mattered to him but nothing too much. They all wanted to be with him, some yearned to *be* him, and Will himself had felt that envy for his more esteemed friend and rival. But it was hard to resent the man, such was his good humour in a tavern. He had enemies, but none to speak of among his fellow writers or players, and was as interested in your thoughts as he was the words of a noble. There were times when he could make you believe that you alone among men mattered most to him, before leaving you to bathe in that feeling, and moving on to another, who would doubtless feel themselves just as blessed as you were from a little touch of Marlowe in the night.

'Well, if the ale is free,' said Will, 'then it is worth the walk.'

'And we can call into taverns along the way, though I know you do not like to spend money.'

'The expense of a tavern is most necessary,' Will countered. 'I've learned more from sitting in an alehouse than ever I did in a school-room. I can observe all manner of men, using them as fuel for my writing; the way they stand or speak, jest or quarrel, all of it ends up in a play. But I demonstrate thrift in everything else. I keep back every penny I make that does not go towards either my lodgings or food and ale.'

'But why save the rest of your money, Will? I know you run two households. Is that the reason?'

'It is *a* reason,' Will admitted, 'but not *the* reason.'

'So, why do you need money?'

'I am an ambitious man, Richard, and would very much like one day to be more than I am now.'

'What is so wrong with being an actor and a writer?'

'Nothing, but it would be better to be actor-writer-partner.'

'And who has offered you this opportunity?' Richard was imme-diately suspicious, clearly fearing he might lose his friend to another company.

'You know there is talk at court of a new company, to be formed by the Lord Chamberlain. Your father has been approached and he told me other partners might be welcomed, if they have money.'

'How much?'

'Fifty pounds.'

'Fifty pounds?' asked Richard in disbelief. 'Do you have anything like fifty pounds, Will? You can't have.'

'I am as yet some way from that amount but one day perhaps...' His words trailed away, as if he did not truly believe this himself.

'But it would take a man like you a lifetime to save such a sum. How can you possibly even hope to raise it?'

'All men should live in hope, Richard,' said Will, though he sounded disconsolate.

'Aye, all men should.' Will could tell Richard believed there was as much a chance of him becoming the next Duke of Northumberland as of making fifty pounds.

'I have amassed a goodly sum,' said Will. 'I simply need more.'

'How much of a goodly sum?'

'Six pounds,' he said, with forced conviction.

'Six pounds?' repeated Richard, in a tone that suggested Will was liable to die of old age before he was even halfway to the total, but then he offered. 'You know, a generous patron would add to it, in return for sonnets or a piece of poetry they can declaim to their friends as having been written in their honour. The easiest way to prise money out of a wealthy patron is to appeal to their vanity. You should ask Marlowe how he does it.' He reflected on this. 'Though having thought on it, perhaps you should not.'

'Why not ask Marlowe?'

'I think the fair and pretty Marlowe trades more than just poetry for his patronage.'

Will understood well enough what that meant. Christopher Marlowe had never been secretive about his desires nor shy about his appetites, claiming more than once that only a fool would not love 'tobacco and boys'.

'I am not good at prising money from rich men's purses, Richard.'

'Have you tried?'

'I spoke to Lord Strange after the first performance of *Henry VI*, when he did seem to like my play. I explained I could write more if my thoughts were not always filled with worry about the cost of victuals and living in London. He said hungry men make better artists.'

Richard scoffed. 'When has our patron ever been hungry? Are you sure he understood your meaning?'

'He either understood and chose to ignore the request or knew what I was about and thought it an impudence, so the failing was mine.'

'I would urge you to ask him again but my father has heard he may be out of the queen's favour and might withdraw his patronage from us altogether, or be commanded to.'

'How is Lord Strange out of favour? He is not against Her Majesty.'

Richard Burbage lowered his voice so that only Will could possibly hear him in the busy street. 'He has a claim to the throne.' This seemed incredible to Will. 'His mother is a descendant of Mary, younger sister of King Henry, the queen's father.'

'But that is no claim compared to Henry's daughter,' Will argued, 'who has been on the throne for thirty-four years.'

'Even after all this time, there are those who still question the legitimacy of the Protestant daughter of a queen who was a second wife and executed for high treason. For any plot against Queen Elizabeth to succeed, it needs a claimant. Who better than one who can trace his lineage to King Harry?'

'Is Lord Strange in danger then? I cannot see how a kingdom that generally stands firmly with the queen would ever rally behind a lord who is yet to even become an earl.'

'The queen considers his father, Lord Stanley, a loyal and faithful servant and, while he lives, Lord Strange is protected. But the Earl of Derby is past sixty years and, should he die…'

'Lord Strange will be unprotected?'

'That is the sum of it.'

'No wonder there is talk of founding a new company under the Lord Chamberlain. Is your father worried?'

'He clings to the hope that the queen has been entertained enough by us, so will be again. He wants us to perform her Christmas play and thinks much will rest upon it.'

'These are dangerous times,' conceded Will.

'The more reason to secure a patron for yourself.'

'Who then?'

'Marlowe told me that Henry Wriothesley might call in tonight. The Earl of Southampton,' he added, when Will did not seem to recognise the name.

'An earl in a tavern?'

'He is a young, fair and vain man, who enjoys the baser company of writers and actors. He likes to pretend to play the scoundrel. Wriothesley has an interest in earthly pleasures and is a generous supporter of artistic pursuits.'

'He has money?'

'More than he can ever spend.'

'You think he could prove a generous patron?'

'He already is, Will,' said Richard. 'Just not to you… yet.'

Chapter Four

'We know what we are, but know not what we may be.'
— *Hamlet*

They were the first of Marlowe's friends to reach the tavern, arriving before the man himself.

Richard asked, 'What will it be, Will? A Dragon's Brew or a Mad Dog?'

'Today I need stronger ale.' He was still feeling melancholy following his failed attempt to woo Lady Katherine.

Richard took the waiting girl gently by the arm. 'We want two Left Legs.'

'Then you'll likely fall over,' she teased.

'We likely shall,' he said with a laugh, 'if we drink enough of it.'

The serving girl was more than ordinarily fair and, despite his earlier disappointment, Will could not help himself. When she returned with their drinks, he asked her, 'What is your name, girl?'

'Cordelia, my lord.'

'I am no lord, though I might like to be yours one day.' He smiled at her and she blushed. 'Cordelia is a fair name. Do you know its meaning?'

'No, my lord.'

'Light,' he told her. 'I find it apt because your smile brings light into the world.'

'My friend here is the finest playmaker in London,' Richard told her. 'Let him borrow your name and he will put it in a play.'

'Then I will lend it gladly, my lord.'

'And I shall return here once it is written, to tell you more of it,' he assured her before she left them with another smile that seemed full of promise.

'How is it that you can remember the meaning of every name?' asked Richard when she was gone.

'I cannot.'

'Then how is it you can remember the meaning of every *woman's* name?'

'Because they are charmed by it – usually.' For it had not worked on Portia, with her prior knowledge of his marital state. 'You have your charms, Richard. I lack a fair face, so I use this feat of memory and sometimes... well, I can't always remember,' he admitted, 'so I make it up. At times, it is politic to do so. *Portia*, for example comes from the Latin *porcus*, which more commonly means pig or hog.'

'I can see why you might shield a woman from that truth.' Then he mimicked Will: 'What a fine and fair name you have there, girl! Portia, meaning pig!' and they both laughed heartily.

'Why do you do it anyway, Will? Is it worth the trouble it brings you after you've tupped them? You have a wife, and the theatre is closed, so go and see her, instead of that serving girl.'

'It is three days' ride to Stratford and I cannot spare the time.'

'And you won't bring her here,' recalled Richard, before he asked Will the question only a close friend would dare. 'Did you love her ever?'

When Will answered there was a trace of sadness in his voice. 'I did love her once. When I was but a boy, who knew nothing of the world, Anne seemed all of it to me and everything in it.'

'But now?'

'My love for her is like a fire untended. It glows but faintly. She is my wife and has given me three children. For that I am of course grateful but she was older when I met her and seems more so to me now. Am I not still in my prime, Richard? I owe Anne a home, a living and some station, all of which I am happy to provide, but must I give her my entire heart? I fear I have no real love left for Anne.'

'If she was older and you still young back then, why did you wed?'

Will spoke quietly. 'I was but eighteen. I took something from her and though she gave it freely, she gave me something in return.'

'The pox?'

'Not the pox! A daughter. A wedding was the natural outcome of *that* natural outcome.'

'You *had* to marry her.'

'Or ruin her and the baby.'

'Then you did your duty, Will, and still provide for them.'

'And our twins, who followed within two years. I sometimes think Anne willed it that way, so I never had cause to bother her again.' He held out his hands apologetically. 'I jest.'

'It is the modern way of things,' said Richard. 'You, the husband, are away, working hard to provide for your family. Your wife would not expect you to go without victuals for sustenance, nor ale to drink. How then would she expect you to go without that other thing all men need?'

'We have never talked about this. It did not seem proper.'

'Of course, it's not proper to *talk* about it. Good God, man, you can't make a fool of your wife! It's not what is said but what is left unsaid. You are a man, you have been away for some considerable time. She knows what fools men become in the close company of women. She, of all people, is aware of this or you would not have had cause to marry her in the first place.'

'I took vows before man and God and considered them sacred,' Will assured his friend. 'Only the Lord knows how badly I feel when I break them.'

'I'm sure it gives you great pain,' Richard said solemnly.

'It does,' agreed Will. 'Every time.'

'Then drink,' said Richard, 'for ale dulls pain.'

–

They'd consumed several ales by the time Christopher Marlowe finally entered the tavern, to accept the accolades of all there and claim his celebratory drinks. He was accompanied by a man far more recognisable than even the great writer himself: none other than Edward Alleyn, London's most renowned actor who, upon the stage of the Curtain, just two hundred yards from their own theatre, had become the living embodiment of Marlowe's finest creations: Barabas, Faustus and Tamburlaine. The owner of the tavern advanced upon them both expectantly, as if he had been waiting excitedly for their arrival and feared they might not come. He commanded a serving girl to fetch them the best ale but Marlowe demanded wine instead and received it without argument. He spotted Richard Burbage and Will then, approached them cordially and ordered more ale for them.

'How was *Doctor Faustus* today?' asked Richard.

'Rather better than normal. Twelve hundred arses this afternoon.'

'Twelve hundred? It is to be expected with our theatre closed. You took our groundlings.'

'Art is never a contest,' said Marlowe lightly, 'merely a choice, but today the crowds chose *Faustus* and were not disappointed, thanks to this fellow.' He slapped Alleyn on the back. 'And all men now agree there is no finer actor in England than Edward Alleyn, the Prince of the Admiral's Men.' Marlowe stated this as if it were fact and Alleyn took the compliment as his due, with a slight bow.

'Have all men been asked?' replied Richard. 'I must have been elsewhere at the time. On our stage rehearsing, perhaps.'

'And you are a very fine actor too, Master Burbage,' demurred Marlowe. 'Just not quite the best in England. One day, perhaps.'

Will had been silent, but now Marlowe addressed him directly. 'Master Shakespeare. How is it with you?'

It was a question Will had been dreading, even from a man he respected above all others, perhaps more so because of this. 'Good... I am well... I have been working on... something.' He knew how hesitant he sounded and hated himself for it.

Marlowe appeared interested. 'Can I read it?'

'You *could* read it of course but should you? I think no good would come of that.'

'You think I will steal your ideas?' asked Marlowe, immediately affronted.

'Lord, no. I think you would be unimpressed. My words are stopped.'

'All writers suffer from that.' Marlowe was dismissive.

'It's a crude, unfinished work. I have no ending, scarcely a beginning and the middle is wretched.'

'A work in progress, then.' Marlowe placed a consoling hand on Will's shoulder. 'Come and see me when it has progressed further.'

'What Will needs is a patron,' said Richard quickly before Marlowe could leave them. 'Then he would not fret so over the importance of each word and they would come more freely.'

'They may,' admitted Marlowe.

'I hear the Earl of Southampton might grace us with his presence this very night?' Richard continued.

'He might.'

'The earl is Kit's patron, Richard,' Will cautioned.

'I understand he has a very deep purse?' Richard replied, turning it into a question for Marlowe.

'He does.' Marlowe seemed taken aback by Richard's bluntness, even though he was far from shy himself. 'I will mention you, Will.'

'Thank you, Kit.'

'But that is all I can promise to do.'

'I understand.'

'If he takes a liking to you, then...' He spread his palms as if to say all will be well. 'But if he has no interest, then I cannot compel my lord to accommodate you.'

Marlowe bowed then steered Edward Alleyn away to a table that commanded the best view of the room, ensuring all who entered could not fail to see the two great men sitting there together.

When he was gone, Will asked Richard, 'Do you think he will mention me?'

'No,' said Richard bluntly.

'I think he holds onto the earl's purse strings as if they were his own,' Will concluded.

'Why sell yourself so cheaply, Will?' Richard demanded then. 'If you do not elevate the value of your work, no one else will.'

'That's Marlowe.' He pointed. 'Marlowe, mark you. *The* Marlowe.'

'I know who he is.'

'The great Marlowe.'

'Stop saying his name. It serves no purpose. If he is so great and men think him so, then why not tell him your next work is your masterpiece and let him say this to others, convincing them in the process.'

Will thought on that. 'Do you think people care what writers say of other writers? Would that really convince them to part with their money? I think not.'

'If they like Marlowe's plays, they will love yours. I do not know why you become so diminished in front of him. Is it because he went to Cambridge? Lots of men went to Cambridge.'

'Did you?'

'You know I did not. Nor Tamburlaine either.' Richard cited the name of the man immortalised in Marlowe's famous play. 'He was a shepherd yet conquered half the world.'

'He didn't have Marlowe peering over his shoulder asking him how it was going, did he? I suspect that, if Alexander the Great urged Tamburlaine to reveal his battle plan to him, he might have found his tongue tied.'

'It is not the same.'

'They say Marlowe conjures up the devil every day on that stage.'

'In *Faustus*? I know you do not believe that,' challenged Richard. 'You've seen how we cause distractions using trap doors and smoke.'

'*I* do not believe it,' Will said, 'but the audience does. They faint in droves during *Faustus* and sometimes flee the theatre, trampling others underfoot. I cannot disguise my envy. There is such a deep truth in Marlowe's words. Words I truly fear I may never be able to equal. He was the first to write in blank verse and tell of things men sense but keep hidden deep in their hearts. He has trod that path to show the rest of us the way.'

'Then follow him, Will.'

'Marlowe is undeniably the first man in London and you're suggesting I let him read my rough-hewn words?'

'Aye, and what makes you say they are rough-hewn?'

'Because they take so much coaxing from me.'

'Perchance, they are better than you think. But if they be coarse indeed, perhaps the master will provide instruction on how to smooth their edges. *Tamburlaine* is blank verse, *Doctor Faustus* is blank verse. Marlowe is of the new world, like yourself. Who better to guide you than he?'

'Your father is still against blank verse.'

'My father will bend when he hears how Marlowe had twelve hundred arses at a penny a pop.'

'*Marlowe had twelve hundred arses?* Now there is a line I can use.'

They laughed at that, then regarded the man sitting across the room from them. 'Marlowe's a handsome bastard,' admitted Richard. 'He probably *has* had twelve hundred arses. For *now*, he is the first man in London, Will, just as Alleyn is the finest actor. But don't try to imitate

Marlowe and be the poorer for it. Be Will! Be Shakespeare and write me great parts so that I can be Burbage, better than Alleyn one day and by far.'

'I shall my friend. I promise.'

Chapter Five

'Hide not thy poison with such sugar'd words'
— Henry VI

As the tavern filled with playmakers and actors there was an air of celebration. Free ale helped, of course, putting all in good spirits, but it was more than that. For some, especially those from Will's own company, there had been little cause for merriment of late. Some had not seen each other in a while and were glad to be back within the company of men of a similar mind. Threat of the plague in London and the prospect of death, as well as the curtailment of all entertainments, including plays and even drinking in taverns, spurred them on to enjoy this while they still could, and they drank deeply.

Not everyone there was an actor or playmaker. A company of actors always attracts its fair share of low characters seeking to profit from an association with the stage, and actors have always drunk with vagabonds. Will considered this now when Poley, Skeres and Frizer walked into the tavern together. Marlowe immediately rose to warmly greet three of the biggest scoundrels in London.

Kit met them close to Will's table and Will took a sudden interest in the contents of his cup to avoid catching the eyes of the newcomers. It was a warm night but Robert Poley still wore a jerkin over his doublet. The leather might not be strong enough to prevent a forceful lunge from a rapier; but if a dagger were thrust at him from an angle, it might not make it through, particularly if the man who stabbed him was nervous and his hand shook, which it surely would if he was going to take on Poley. His infamous reputation as a ruthless agent of the crown, as well as a crook, somehow preceded him, though it was supposed to be a secret. It would explain why he always wore the jerkin, even at the height of summer.

Ingram Frizer left Poley and walked up to Will then. 'I have a mind to do you a service, Master Shakespeare.' Frizer was a merchant who dealt in all manner of things, yet Will had never met a man who had prospered from involvement in a trade with Ingram, nor any other who had spoken well of him afterwards. 'I have heard, and believe it to be true, that you are in need of coin… for some enterprise or other,' he concluded vaguely.

'And who has informed you of this?'

'Oh, I heard it somewhere, from someone,' he said airily. 'You tell it to one man, he tells it to another, before long word will always reach me.'

'What I am actually in need of is a patron,' Will deflected. 'Someone who will reward the writing of a play or be content with being named as the inspiration for a sonnet.'

'In exchange for coin?' Frizer frowned at such a strange notion. 'A rare man indeed. But what if you do not find such a creature? Where would that leave your plans, eh? In ruins,' he said, nodding sagely. 'But I can help you.'

Will glanced at Marlowe, who said nothing. He was merely watching Frizer with curiosity. 'And how will you do that?'

'By allowing you to invest in a most precious commodity. My good self.' He grinned broadly. 'And my partner, Master Nicholas Skeres.' He indicated that same man, who was standing off from him but regarding their conversation with interest.

'I do not—' Will began.

'Hear me to the end,' demanded Frizer. 'I have a head for trading and a talent for turning a profit. I could let you in on my plans, in return for a small consideration.'

'You want me to give you a sum of money, which you will invest in… what exactly?'

'A number of ventures with members of the merchant class. Each more profitable than the last.'

Marlowe interrupted him. 'I wonder why you might need Will's investment, if you have such a talent for profit yourself?'

'Stay out of this, Kit,' Frizer warned him, in a voice noticeably harsher in tone than the one he had used to address Will, who he turned back to now. 'Every penny you trust unto me will be returned, along with another fifth.'

'A fifth? Would there be a contract stating this?' Will asked, as if genuinely considering it.

'What need is there of a contract between gentlemen? We would shake hands and have done with it.'

'There is every need,' said Marlowe, and Frizer shot him a warning look.

'What say you?' Frizer asked Will, offering his hand.

'He says no,' Marlowe responded before Will could ask about this scheme further.

'I told you to stay out of this!' hissed Frizer.

'Alas, I cannot. You are a friend, Ingram, but then so is Will, and I do hate it when friends steal from other friends.'

'I am no thief!'

'And yet your partner is Nicholas Skeres,' Marlowe observed, 'who is a proven one, though he did not swing.' He turned to Will. 'Like Frizer here, he has friends in low places.'

'Nicholas was a deceiver once,' countered Frizer, 'but he has done good service since then and I believe every man deserves redemption.'

'Then do you guarantee here, in front of witnesses, that the sum you will return to Will is to be paid in coin?'

Frizer looked as if he had been caught in the act of something that might see him hanged for it. 'What mean you by that?'

Marlowe told Will, 'Frizer and Skeres will take your money, but when the time comes to return it, they will give you goods instead: wool, wine, cheese, guns, it matters not. You will be expected to sell it all to realise your investment. What will be beyond doubt, however, is that you will not make half the value Frizer claims it to be worth.'

'That is a slander!' Frizer's hand flew to the handle of his dagger.

'It would be,' agreed Marlowe, 'if it were not true. Now, say it is not so and call me liar?' He placed a hand on his own dagger and the two men stared at one another.

Nicholas Skeres appeared then and restrained Frizer with a hand pressed firmly on his shoulder. Frizer stared malevolently at Marlowe but must have thought better of challenging him. 'It is as well I think of you as a friend, Kit,' he said without warmth, before turning away.

'Thank you,' said Will when Frizer was gone, 'though I would not have given him money and I am sorry you quarrelled.'

'It will be forgot by morning.' Marlowe was calm again now. 'Frizer is a friend... of sorts. But only because I have a taste for vermin.' He smiled at Will then. 'They are better drinking companions.'

He laughed at this, but Will had spotted something Kit had not. Ingram Frizer was now standing in the opposite corner of the tavern, being consoled by Skeres and Poley, staring back at Will and Kit with a vengeful look on his face.

Chapter Six

'...for the very substance of the ambitious is merely the shadow of a dream.'
— Hamlet

There seemed no end to the free ale. The revellers drank more and grew steadily louder. The only break in the shouting and raucous laughter came when the tavern door was pushed forcibly open and four large men, dressed in the same livery, stepped inside, but it was not their imposing presence that quieted the assembly. Instead, all eyes turned to the young man they were guarding.

'Who is this?' asked someone aloud of the fair youth who had now entered the tavern. The young man was exquisitely attired, in such finery as Will had never seen outside of court. Two of the large, rough-looking men who accompanied him moved ahead and surveyed the room for any threat, while the other two flanked him as he walked into the tavern, to ensure there could be no attack upon his person. He needed these men, thought Will, or he'd be killed for the value of his doublet alone. A fifth, much smaller man arrived last and stayed close to his master's side, likely a steward of some kind.

That young master was tall, with long dark hair that fell to his shoulders. His face had a wisp of a moustache and the beginnings of a beard he had not long grown into. This had to be the Earl of Southampton. Who else could afford such finery, as well as acolytes dressed in his livery? He was as fair as Richard Burbage had said, fairer even than young Ed from their company, who played the parts of women and girls upon the stage and was renowned as possibly the most handsome boy in London.

Marlowe was up out of his seat already and striding to the youth. The four large men watched Kit warily but did not stop him. Will wondered if they recognised Kit or had been ordered to allow him to draw near to Henry Wriothesley, the young, fair and vain Earl of Southampton Richard had told him about. Marlowe was quoting his own lines aloud in greeting as he advanced on the earl, arms outstretched as if to embrace him.

'*Was this the face that launched a thousand ships, and burnt the topless towers of Ileum?*'

The smiling Earl of Southampton replied exuberantly with lines from another of Marlowe's poems: '*Who ever loved that loved not at first sight?*'

They embraced like brothers then, with no formality or recognition of the earl's far superior status. Marlowe ushered him away from the main group to a corner table and sat down next to Henry Wriothesley, the earl's ever-watchful guards about them. To be so familiar with a man who far outranked him in station showed that Marlowe was clearly a favourite. Will watched enviously as they talked excitedly together and laughed at one another's observations, while wine was poured for them both by the tavern owner himself.

'You see?' whispered Richard. 'You must flatter the young earl if you wish to make him your patron, Will.'

'Not all men enjoy flattery.'

'It seems to work for Marlowe. The earl is not yet twenty. He is green and still new to the world, known for nothing more than fair looks and the patronage of a handful of poets who write sweet verses about him. Do you remember John Clapham's poem, "Narcissus"?'

'I know of it. Written a year or more ago?'

'But did you know it was dedicated to Henry Wriothesley?'

'I did not.'

'Some would have taken a poem warning against the dangers of self-love as a rebuke, but the young earl took it as a compliment and favoured Clapham generously thereafter.'

'Then I accept your counsel,' said Will, 'and shall write the earl a sonnet that will have him reaching deep into his purse.'

'Flatter him then flatter him some more and flatter him well. He could be the end to all of your problems.'

Or the beginning of them, thought Will, as he surveyed the devilishly handsome young man at the other end of the room, who was now looking straight back at him. Will did not at that moment see salvation in those eyes, only danger.

–

Will watched as Marlowe and the earl continued in deep conversation together. From time to time, Marlowe would glance over at Will, giving nothing away with a look or gesture. Occasionally the earl himself would give Will an appraising look but the meat of their conversation remained a mystery to him.

Presently, Marlowe left the earl's side and came to Will. 'He wants you.'

'Wants me?' *What did that mean?*

'Go to him now,' Marlowe urged, 'before he is distracted.'

Will got to his feet and followed Marlowe back to the earl, who greeted him with a smile.

'This is William Shakespeare, a fine poet,' announced Marlowe, 'and the writer of *Henry VI*. He is the coming man.'

'The honour is mine, my lord,' said Will and bowed deeply. The earl did not dispute this.

'I have heard of you, and did see your play.'

'I had no idea.'

'I prefer to come to the theatre disguised as a lesser man,' Henry Wriothesley explained. 'It is not fair on the actors if the eyes of the audience wander from the stage.' Did he truly believe himself to be so much of a distraction? Narcissus indeed.

'Will is working on a new play,' said Marlowe.

'What a pity it will not be shown,' said the earl. 'The theatres will all close soon because of plague. The queen shall command it.' The earl glanced at Marlowe then. 'Leave us, Kit.'

Marlowe seemed to half expect this command and he joined other revellers a discreet distance from them.

'Kit speaks well of you, Master Shakespeare,' said the earl. Then he asked, 'How old are you?'

'Twenty-eight.'

'Hardly a young man yet scarcely settled in the world. Not a university man either,' he observed, having presumably gleaned this information from Kit. 'Are you in London on your father's coin?'

'My father was a wool trader and glove maker. He had money once but lost it.'

'How careless of him. You had some schooling, though? You must have.'

'No more than grammar school.'

'Kit tells me you have a wife and children in a separate household. Money must matter to you.'

'Money matters to most men. If it does not matter to you then you are blessed, Your Grace.'

'And you are a poet too, as well as a playmaker?'

'I flatter myself that I am.'

'Then compose me a sonnet.' At first Will thought he was being offered patronage but then it dawned on him that the earl meant for him to do it that very minute, right there in the tavern, without even a quill or parchment to assist him.

'Now?'

'Is there a better time?'

'No, Your Grace.'

'Then...' The earl waved a hand to make him commence and Will took a breath to try to compose himself. Before he could, the earl clapped his hands together and ordered, 'Quiet!'

If that command had come from any other man in the room, it would have been ignored or might even have started a brawl, but all of those close to the earl instantly ceased their chatter. This silence spread quickly, once other men realised who had called for it and they too obeyed the command.

'Master Shakespeare will compose a sonnet for our entertainment,' Henry Wriothesley announced. The eyes of everyone in the tavern were on Will now. How in hell could he dream up a sonnet on command like this? But if he did not, the earl would instantly lose interest in him. Haltingly, he began to place some words together while the earl listened intently.

'*When, in disgrace... with fortune and men's eyes,*' Will began, '*I all alone beweep my outcast state.*' Will was conscious of nothing now but the silence around him, and the eyes that seemed to burn into his back. He kept his own eyes locked on the earl's, blotting out everybody else, fearing their presence would distract him. This was far more difficult than acting on the stage. At least then he had learned his lines in advance.

'That is a pleasant start. Go on,' Wriothesley urged.

And Will did go on, screwing up his eyes in concentration as he spoke, a man forced to create art upon demand by someone who had little understanding of the manner of its invention. He paused after every line to give himself time to compose the next.

> *'And trouble deaf heaven with my bootless cries,*
> *And look upon myself... and curse my fate,*
> *Wishing me like to one... more rich in hope,*
> *Featured like him, like him with friends possessed,*
> *Desiring this man's art and that man's scope,*
> *With what I most enjoy contented least;*
> *Yet in these thoughts myself almost despising,*
> *Haply I think on thee, and then my state,*
> *Like to the lark at break of day arising*
> *From sullen earth, sings hymns at heaven's gate;*
> *For thy sweet love remembered such wealth brings*
> *That then I scorn to change my state with kings.'*

Will bowed slightly to show that he was done. There was an awkward moment when all remained silent in the room, for no man dared speak until the earl had delivered his verdict.

The Earl clapped his hands together once, then he did it a second time, then a third. The sound of his hands coming together seemed to fill the room. 'Bravo!' he cried with glee. 'A sonnet well-composed and well-spoken, indeed!' The room instantly relaxed, and Will along with it. There were murmurs of approval from the assembled actors and poets and a smattering of applause, some of it for the sonnet but most perhaps for the improvisation needed to compose it under such difficult circumstances. 'A talent such as yours is wondrous rare, Master Shakespeare! Wondrous rare! You must come and visit me at my home,

Place House in Titchfield. See to it,' he ordered his steward, who bowed to the earl and gave a slightly stiffer bow towards Will.

'I shall make use of you, Master Shakespeare,' the earl told him. Then he smiled archly and added, 'Though perhaps not in the way you might imagine.' Before Will could ask the earl what he meant, he became distracted, as Marlowe had said he might, by the smile of a fair youth who had walked in with the cast of Thomas Kyd's latest play. 'You and I will talk again,' he said absent-mindedly to Will by way of dismissal, and he beckoned the boy towards him.

Will rejoined Richard Burbage at his table. 'Well done, Will,' Richard said, then lowered his voice to little more than a whisper. 'That *was* an old one?' For he had not been entirely fooled by Will's pauses after every line nor his feigned concentration. Richard knew acting when he saw it.

'Not an old one,' Will answered from the corner of his mouth, to avoid being overheard. 'I wrote it scarcely a month ago and have been worrying away at it since, taking out a word here, another there. I cannot do it on demand,' he explained, 'despite what the earl thinks. A good sonnet takes a week or more.'

'And yet you made it look easy.'

'That was my intention. I know not why but few men appreciate the fruits of great labour when it comes to art. They want it to fall easily into their laps, like an apple from a tree that's scarcely shaken by a breeze.'

'Now he thinks you a genius. Did he offer to become your patron?'

'Not as yet,' admitted Will. 'Though he did invite me to his home.'

'Did he, by God?' Richard laughed at the possible reason for this invitation, leaving Will a little less optimistic than before.

–

They were drunk on their way home and shouting at each other, as if the near-empty streets were as loud as the inside of the bustling tavern.

'Do you believe Edward Alleyn to be the best actor in England?' demanded Richard.

'Today, he was not even the best actor in that tavern' – Will stabbed a finger exuberantly back towards the alehouse they had just left – 'and I do not include myself.'

'You think I am better than he, really?' Richard seemed cheered at the thought but only for a moment. 'Of course, I know I am not, but maybe one day I will be worthy of the comparison.' Then he thought for a moment. 'But *you* do think I'm better? You are my friend of course, Will, so more likely to scorn him and elevate me.'

'I do scorn him but not because of our friendship.'

'How so? Tell me plain.'

'He saws the air too much with his hands.' And Will waved his own hands around as he spoke, to illustrate his point.

'He does do that. I have noticed it.'

'And he does not project, he bellows.' Will mimicked the man as a shouty ham of an actor. 'I mean to be a terror to the *world*!'

Richard chuckled. 'That does sound like him.'

'And he has no ear for the lines in *Tamburlaine*. It's not "I mean to be a terror to the *world*!" It's "I mean to be a *terror* to the world." Or you could even have "I *mean* to be a terror to the world!" No,' he corrected himself, 'it's definitely "I mean to be a *terror* to the world!"'

'There is a difference and your way is best,' agreed Richard. 'One day you will write me a part like that. Better even.'

'But it won't be *Richard III*.'

They had been over this before and Richard was impatient with his friend. 'Why can you not get the measure of the man? You've written him already.'

'He was but a lesser character in *Henry VI*. I cannot find his voice.'

'Simply write more of what you gave us before. My father demands it, Will. I would caution you not to forget he has already given you half your fee in coin, for a great play about King Richard.'

'Then I must inform him I am unable to write one.' Richard shot him a look of drunken alarm. 'Something else then,' offered Will, 'about a ship, wrecked in a storm, or a forbidden love?' When Richard looked unimpressed, he offered instead 'a prince whose murdered father visits his son from beyond the grave to demand he take vengeance—'

'No, no, no! Unless that prince is one of those poor innocents foully murdered in the Tower by King Richard. My father, who is not known for his mild manner or forgiving nature, has given you a pound on the understanding that you will give him a play. Do not trifle with the man and his violent temperament by delivering him anything else. If you do not bring him King Richard, I tell thee plain, it will not end well.'

'Then that is lamentable,' admitted Will, 'for I fear I cannot.'

Chapter Seven

'Marry, he must have a long spoon that must eat with the devil.'
— *The Comedy of Errors*

Because of the need to learn his lines, rehearse plays in the morning, then perform them in the afternoon, Will had been forced to do much of his writing in the evening and he went through more tallow candles than a church. They were made of animal fat, always gave off a foul smell as they burned and he was forever trimming their wicks. Their soot stained his walls, his rooms always stank a little of them and the flickering light they gave off made writing hard, but then writing was always hard these days, as Will seemed to have lost all inspiration.

Still, with Richard Burbage's words from the night before still fresh in his mind, he had to try. He owed James Burbage a play and it had to be about Richard III. So, *go to, Will,* he told himself, *go to.*

He placed another tallow candle into a brass candlestick and lit it. His quill pen was new and fashioned from a goose feather. Will took time to sharpen it to the perfect angle, before dipping it into his ink. He held it over the paper, poised to begin. But when he needed words most, none came. He had known what he was going to write but now he hesitated, for he had already begun to doubt that which seemed so apt only moments ago. It was always the same with this play and he knew why.

Will always began by placing himself in the mind of the character whose words he was fashioning. He would ask himself what they might say about the scene he had placed them in and how they would argue their case convincingly to another, for no man ever thought of himself as the villain in the play of his own life. This method had worked well until now, when he was finally confronted with a character so odious there could be no justification for his vile acts. King Richard III had, it was generally agreed, taken his own nephews into his care, then murdered them to clear his way to the throne. What manner of man could even contemplate killing his brother's sons without immediately recoiling from the thought, lest he be damned forever? Surely even a monster's resolve would be stopped by thinking on it, and how could he then enjoy the fruits of that unholy labour once he became king? Would guilt not torment him? It seemed to have not troubled Richard. He valued the crown far more than their young lives and, with his unnatural ambition, he confounded Will, who could never understand him, so could not give him words.

After several minutes staring at a blank piece of paper, Will sighed and gave up, then went back to the new sonnet he had been composing. *James Burbage will murder me*, he thought, *but at least then my worries will be at an end.*

—

Will spent much of the next day writing but not a word was about King Richard. He felt reborn as a writer following his meeting with the Earl of Southampton, a man who, though dangerous due to his rank and impetuous youth, might just prove to be Will's salvation. With the earl as a patron, he could be freed from constant worry over money, time and recognition. If he could charm and flatter the earl further at his home, then all would improve.

The earl's Steward of Matters Domestical had given Will the day, date and time of his forthcoming visit to Place House in Titchfield. He told Will not to concern himself with plans for travel. He would be venturing there with his fellow playmakers, Christopher Marlowe and Thomas Nashe, and all else would be arranged.

Will now had to write a new sonnet for the occasion but was already overthinking every word, for much rested upon them.

It was getting dark when he finally gave up and ventured out, as he did most evenings, to meet Richard Burbage for supper at a tavern a few streets from his rooms.

Will had gone only yards when, to his alarm, a man stepped out of the shadows in front of him with his dagger drawn. Before he could do anything about it, Will was manhandled by this larger assailant, spun round and his face pushed hard against a wall, the dagger's blade pressed against his side.

'Cry out and I'll stick this knife in you,' hissed Robert Poley, who must have been waiting for Will to come out. Did the man think Will had wronged him or was this revenge for the belittling of Poley's friend, Ingram Frizer, by Marlowe in the tavern? Will instinctively tried to struggle free but Poley's grip was too strong and he pressed the knife point harder against him. 'Stop squirming, Shakespeare, or I'll gut you here in the alley.'

Will ceased his struggles and, though he was still afraid of the blade, he reasoned that if Poley had wanted him dead, he would have killed him by now.

'How easy it would be to say you came at me with your dagger drawn, so I had no choice but to plunge my own into your throat. They would see me pardoned for it too.' He seemed very sure about that and Will did not doubt it.

'What do you want with me, Poley? I have no money about me.'

'I don't want your money,' snarled Poley. 'You are coming with me.' And with that, he led Will away at knife point, his blade concealed by a cloak carried over his arm.

'Where are we going?'

'You'll know that when it is time for you to know that.'

–

Poley led Will along a number of narrow streets. They passed few people at this hour and Will was not foolish enough to try and enlist help from strangers in London. They would hardly become involved in another man's quarrel. He had already decided against trying to break free. Poley was far bigger and stronger than Will and was known to have killed before, sometimes in the service of the crown. Will's best hope lay in playing the obedient prisoner, while hoping he would be released soon enough. Was Poley taking Will to Frizer? Would he be beaten because of the events of the previous night? Surely Poley was not dragging him across London for that? He could have given Will a beating in the alley outside his rooms.

They reached the front door of a house that showed no signs of life. Poley opened it and shoved Will inside. It was dark, except for a single lamp glowing in a corner. Poley put away his dagger and picked up the lamp, then pushed Will in the back and ordered him to walk towards another door.

Will stumbled through and into a much larger room lit by candle-light. At first he thought it was empty, but then noticed a single large chair by the fire at the opposite end of the room. He could just make out a seated figure, its face concealed in the darkness and partly obscured by the wooden frame of the chair. With the seat turned to one side it acted as a canopy and hid him from view.

'Go on,' urged Poley and Will received another firm push in the shoulder. He wanted to ask who this man was but suspected the question might anger Poley. So, instead, he walked silently and gingerly forward.

As he drew nearer, all Will could see of the man was his boots, which were richly made, with scarcely a mark on them. He must have been brought here by carriage to avoid the filth in London's streets. Moving closer he could make out the man's arm, which lay on the side of the chair. Will could see the sleeve of his tunic in the dim light from the fire's embers. It was made of a fine material, and there were two large gold rings on his fingers, with precious stones set in them. There was wealth here, and power too, if he could command a man like Poley to drag Will across London to meet him.

He raised the hand with the rings on, a signal to prevent Will from drawing near enough to see his face. Will noticed there was a second chair between them in the otherwise bare room and, as he reached it, an authoritative voice called for him to sit. He obeyed, glancing back towards Poley as he did so, who was still in the doorway keeping a watchful eye on Will.

'Master Shakespeare,' the disembodied voice began. 'What is your business with the Earl of Southampton?'

So that was what this was about. Will could have challenged the man then, he could have asked him what business was it of his, or demanded to know his identity, but he strongly sensed that would not end well for him. He reasoned he was in the presence of authority and tried to sound humble. 'I have no business, as yet. The earl is a patron of poets and the theatre. He expressed an interest in my new play.'

'Your play? Are you a playmaker or an actor?'

'I humbly call myself both, if it pleases Your Grace.' Since Will had not been informed of the rank of the man opposite him, he chose the loftiest form of address.

'All writers are natural spies and thieves. They steal from the lives of others. This I have observed.' Will thought it best not to contradict him on this point, even though he felt it both inaccurate and unfair. 'Continue.'

'The earl said my next play would not be shown, as the theatres would close because of plague.'

'They shall.'

'The earl had heard I have a modest talent and thought to commission poetry from me.'

'That is all?'

'That is everything.'

'Really?' The tone of the man's voice expressed his strong doubts. 'He did not invite you to his home?'

Poley must have overheard this invitation in the tavern, then informed his inquisitor. Was that why he had been summoned here?

'He did extend that invitation, Your Grace.'

'A Catholic and a known recusant, a man who has been close to the queen, invites you to his home and you wish to keep this from me?'

'I did not think a man such as yourself would think it important.'

'A man such as myself?' It sounded to Will as if he was deciding whether to take offence at this.

'Forgive me, Your Grace, for you did not permit me to know your name, but you are obviously of rank and have station.'

'I am merely an agent of the state,' he replied, 'and humble servant of the queen. Your invitation from Henry Wriothesley is no trifling matter but you claim there is no business between you?'

'He seemed to be of a mind to commission a sonnet but I await his command still.'

'Is this why he has ordered you to visit his home?'

'I think so, yes.'

'And Marlowe attends too?' he asked. 'Nashe as well? Raleigh, of course.'

'You are better informed than I, Your Grace.'

'You know Marlowe?'

'I know Marlowe,' he admitted.

'And Raleigh? You have met the man?'

'I... have *seen* Sir Walter at court but do not know the man.'

'But you do know Marlowe.' He said this again, thoughtfully. 'They are rumoured to be of one mind.'

'Upon what, Your Grace?'

'On the existence of God, they doubt it and do deny him.'

'I think Kit jests when he—'

'Proclaims himself an atheist?' He raised his voice to interrupt and Will took this as a warning and ceased the defence of his friend. 'To deny God is to deny the queen's anointment by him, directly challenging her authority on earth as our sovereign. That is treason, is it not?' Will stayed silent and hoped it would be seen as acquiescence. He had no wish to damn his friend further, but nor did he want to defy his interrogator. 'Answer me. Is this treason or no?'

'I am not learned enough to decide the magnitude of a man's crimes, but if Your Grace, in his wisdom, deems this treason, then it must be so.' A combination of flattery and deference, along with an admission of ignorance in important matters such as these, seemed the best way to wriggle from the hook.

'It is said Marlowe and Raleigh are members of the School of Atheists. When they speak together and with Wriothesley, I do think they commit treason.'

'Can a man be a traitor with words alone?' Will's own words were out before he had time to suppress them.

'Treason is in the deed but before the deed is the word. Treachery begins in the very thoughts of men.'

'But how can we truly know a man's thoughts?' Again Will could not help himself, even though he knew it would likely do him no good to question his captor.

'There are methods proven to bring them out. Bring me your new master Henry Wriothesley's secrets. Deliver them to me. Or...'

'Die?' Will asked, almost disbelievingly.

'Nothing so...' The ringed hand waved vaguely.

'Brutal?'

'Merciful.'

Chapter Eight

'Foul deeds will rise'
— Hamlet

Will wondered at first if the man was joking but, if he was, he gave no indication of it. It took him a moment to compose himself enough to ask, 'What does my Lord wish to know about the earl?'

'Everything. I want to know all that you see and hear.' Will must have appeared confused by such a general command, for the man continued, 'He is a Ganymede.' It was said contemptuously. Ganymede had lived thousands of years ago in Troy and was said to have been so beautiful, Zeus himself became infatuated with the boy and took him away to become a cupbearer to the gods. Nowadays, his name was a byword for unmanly or degenerate behaviour. Will's inquisitor clearly viewed the youthful, handsome and vain Earl of Southampton in a similar fashion. 'I believe Henry Wriothesley is a sodomite. A practice that has been punishable by death for ten years now. Are you a sodomite, Master Shakespeare?'

'I am not.'

'I have heard it said that all actors are. Is this not so?'

'Many actors are married or have...' – what safe word could he use to describe a lover or mistress to this God-fearing, judgemental man? – 'favoured ladies that they woo.'

'If I was a sodomite, I would marry too,' he said almost matter-of-factly, 'the better to hide my depravity from the world.'

'It would be hard to hide it from a wife.'

'Yes,' he admitted, 'I suppose it would. What is your view on *mos Graecorum?*'

'The Greeks were known for their philosophy and their learning,' Will began, before he was cut short.

'You know what I am referring to. *Mos Graecorum* is in common enough usage these days and describes acts of love between two men.'

'I do know the phrase but think it is likely misunderstood or mistranslated.'

'Doesn't everyone now accept that, for all their learning, the Greeks committed most unnatural acts upon one another, to the exclusion of women?'

'The Greeks often talked of platonic love, friendship born out of affectionate regard for another man without involving...' Will searched for the right phrase.

'Sodomy? Those platonic friendships almost always seemed to be between an older man and a younger one.'

'Your Grace is more learned than I on the matter.'

He had not meant it to sound as impertinent as it did, even to his own ear, and the tone of the disembodied voice changed then. 'What if I were to command Poley here to lop off an ear?' And he leaned forward ever so slightly, while jabbing a finger towards the door where Poley still lurked. As he did so, Will was afforded a brief glimpse of the man's face in the firelight and those features were burned into his mind in an instant, before his interrogator leant back and was shrouded in darkness once more. 'He would do it on my command and remove your nose as well, if I asked him. Tell me, would it be harder for you to make your way onto a stage then?' Will was too afraid to answer him and cursed his careless tongue. 'There is impudence within you and, I think, criminality. I've heard the story of the poaching on Sir Thomas Lucy's land. They say that is why you left Stratford. It is not true though, is it? Or you'd be arrested when you returned to visit your wife.' He clearly knew a lot about Will, who said nothing. Would it be better to be accused of poaching by this man or something worse? 'That's not why you fell foul of the sheriff. It was implication in a Catholic plot, was it not?'

'There was no plot, Catholic or otherwise.' Will found his voice again to protest. 'I left Stratford to make my life into something. If I was trying to evade the queen's authority, London would be a strange choice.'

'It would be simple enough for a wanted man to disappear among two hundred thousand others.'

'Unless he was foolish enough to climb upon a stage,' Will reminded him. 'If I really was wanted, it would be a poor choice of profession.'

The man could not refute the logic of that, so instead asked, 'Are you loyal, Master Shakespeare?'

'To the crown? I am.'

'I hear your father misses church.' Did this man know everything about Will and his family?

'Through debt. He owes money and is shamed to come.'

'That's a common enough lie these days, from recusants.'

'If your men know he misses church, they will know how real his debts are.'

He seemed to accept this. 'He painted the walls of the church at least.' Will recalled his father being tasked with covering forbidden icons of the old religion with whitewash, which he duly did but only to avoid suspicion.

His interrogator might seem to know everything about Will but he still had to guess, which proved he was no mind reader. Will had been in a company of players for years now and, like everyone else in that relatively small but close band, had told others his story, or at least the fragments of it he was willing to reveal. He would not normally have shared the lasting shame of his father's disgrace with anyone, but there were nights when, with his guard lowered from excess of ale, he had confessed a desire to restore his family name by making his own life more of a success than his father's. John Shakespeare was a man of low means and reduced circumstance, forced to resign from public office and scorned in his home town as a debtor. He had, in many ways, fallen from grace. Details like these could have been passed on to the queen's men from anyone in the company.

'Wriothesley is a Catholic,' the interrogator reminded Will, 'and none can be trusted.'

'The queen trusts him,' said Will hopefully. 'She allows him at court and grants him favour. This is known to all.'

'It is not for the queen to uncover the numerous plots against her divine majesty. It is the Privy Council who are tasked with this. She will show favour to those at court until they are revealed as her enemies. The queen's favour can change too, and often does.' Then abruptly he changed direction again. 'Tell me, Master Shakespeare. Do you love God?'

'Of course.'

'Do you not love the queen?'

'I do love the queen, as my sovereign ruler.'

'And who do you love most: God or queen?'

Will knew this was a trap. If he said he loved the queen more than God, it would be considered a blasphemy, but if he admitted to loving God above the queen, it might brand him a papist.

'I love them both in equal measure, for I know that God placed our queen upon the throne and anointed her. To love God is to love the queen, to love the queen is to love God, for she is His instrument upon earth.'

Will's answer must have satisfied the noble. 'I hear Wriothesley has *symposiums* after dinner.' He made the word symposiums sound disgusting. 'I wish to know what is discussed in them. Some say it is heresy, even atheism. Bring me proof of it.'

'I could say that I heard something but how can I prove it was said?'

'Your word will be sufficient for me to approach the queen with fears for her safety. She will allow me to press him and others on the matter.'

To press him? What a delicate way to describe torture. He must have seen reticence in Will then. 'Do you think yourself the first player who has been paid for secrets? We have spies in every company and audience. How else can we keep a watch on you? If you wish to agitate one man you must speak with him often, over time, to win him to your cause. A man in a pulpit can persuade twenty, perhaps forty at a time to rebel. If you wish to agitate a thousand men then you can do it in an afternoon, with a play.'

'The words of the plays are examined before they are performed, my lord, by the Master of the Revels.'

'I know that, Shakespeare, but the Master of the Revels does not always recognise the disguised messages in poetry, nor fully understand that, when ancient scenes are depicted in a certain way, they give a nod to our world that hints at insurrection, even treason. Moreover, like all officials, he can be bought.'

'Are you suggesting bribes have been offered to the Master of the Revels?' Will hoped he sounded shocked enough.

'Offered, taken and spent. That's clear enough when he lives far better than he should.'

'Then why…?'

'Keep him in office? Dismiss him and it ends a minor corruption. Keep him in place and I might learn who corrupts him and to what end. If a company of players pays the Master of the Revels to keep seditious lines in a play, I need look no further than their patron to see the cause. Then I will know the queen's enemies. Some, at any rate, for she has many. Plots abound against Her Majesty.'

'How can I report to you when I know not how to find you?'

'Master Poley will bring you to me when I desire it. Be mindful; you cannot hide anything from me. Not even your thoughts. I see everything. I hear *everything*.'

'Your Grace,' he murmured.

'And now you may go.' Will rose gratefully. 'But we shall meet again soon, then you will tell me all that you know about Henry Wriothesley, holding back nothing, as a most loyal servant of the crown is obliged to.'

Will managed a little bow, which he hoped would be taken as acquiescence, then left as quickly as he could without actually breaking into a run.

Poley met him by the door and, as he left the house, Will turned to the man who had abducted him. 'Who was that noble lord?'

'One great enough to whisper in the queen's ear,' said Poley. 'If he says it should be so, she will most likely command it.' Then he added, 'A word of warning. If you ever lie to him, he will know it.' And in case Will was in any doubt about the seriousness of his position, he said, 'You are his creature now.'

Chapter Nine

'This sickness doth infect
The very life-blood of our enterprise'
— Henry IV

Though his inquisitor was unlikely to summon Will again until he had visited the Earl of Southampton's country home, he was eager to avoid happening upon Robert Poley in the street, even by chance, so he stayed away from his rooms during the day. Instead, he went to the theatre, where there was a certain safety to be had behind its walls and in the company of its players.

'I fell asleep while writing,' Will explained his failure to arrive for supper with Richard the night before. 'I was trying to compose a sonnet for the Earl of Southampton.'

'Then write it quickly, Will,' Richard cautioned, 'and turn your attention to the play my father paid you for.'

Will was pleased Richard took so little offence at his missing of supper but wished he would cease hounding him over the play. 'I will do that as soon as I have found the right words to address the earl. I will flatter him, as you counselled, yet do not wish to leave him confused upon the matter.'

'Confused about what?'

'The level of my affection for him.'

Richard laughed at that. 'You are worried he might think you are in love with him? Take advice from a fellow actor, Will. Always play to the gallery and give your audience exactly what they want to hear.'

'You mean I should make it appear as if his affection for me could be returned?'

'Write your sonnet for the earl as if you were writing it for the Lady Katherine.'

'You are sure he would like this?' Will recalled looking over at Henry Wriothesley and Marlowe sharing a joke in the tavern together. Abruptly, their laughter had ceased and the way the two men looked at each other then had reminded Will of lovers. Richard must have seen it too, for he said, 'I know he will.'

–

Will took himself away to re-read some of his writing for an hour, stationing himself on one of the closest seats to the stage. Though he had promised to think further on the play about King Richard, he went over the lines of his sonnet again and again.

Richard's father came up to Will and without even a greeting asked, 'What did that man want with you last night?'

'What man?' Will quickly put down his work, making sure James Burbage could not see the words of his sonnet.

'One of our company told me he saw you walking through the streets with Robert Poley. He did not greet you, considering it no business of his.'

'Which it is not.'

'Perhaps, but he did think it might be mine,' James Burbage warned him.

'He is an admirer of my play.' It was the best Will could come up with under the older man's accusing glare.

'Really, Will? You claim that Robert Poley, an agent of the crown, was merely interested in discussing your play.'

'You know the man?' Was there anyone with even the slightest link to court that James Burbage did not know? 'And you say he is an agent of the crown? Aren't spies meant to keep their actions secret?'

'His actions brought him a certain infamy, for he helped to uncover the Babington Conspiracy, a plot to kill the queen. That man Poley, in part, condemned the Queen of the Scots,' explained James, 'and now he takes an interest in a member of my company? You will understand why that concerns me. Are you his man, Will? Out with it.'

'God, no!'

'And now you feign surprise. Always the actor but only a convincing one upon the stage. Perhaps you should persist with the writing after all.'

'Go to hell and damn your impudence!'

'Better, but you need to work on the pitch of your voice.' Always directing his actors, thought Will. 'An angry denial should be higher in tone if your audience is to be convinced.'

'They should be convinced. *You* should be convinced. I am not Robert Poley's man.'

'Whose then?'

'No one's.'

'You swear? On your honour?'

Will was careful to choose the right words to respond to James Burbage's accusation. He did not want to lose his honour by swearing to a lie. 'I am sided with no man and pledged to no cause nor involved in any plot or conspiracy.' This was at best a partial truth and Will felt guilty stating it in such a manner. Poley had reminded him of the power of his mysterious inquisitor, but Will told himself he was not the man's 'creature' and still had some free will in the matter. He might even outwit this mysterious noble by providing him with nothing damning on Henry Wriothesley.

James Burbage did not say whether he believed Will or not. 'These are most dangerous times,' he warned, 'and everything is heightened. Men see plots everywhere.' Then, with some portent, he announced, 'And now the queen will leave London.'

'Are you sure?' Richard overheard this and came towards them.

'It is all anyone is talking of.' He meant at court. Burbage had his contacts there, some of whom were paid to provide him with information pertinent to his predicament, as the owner of a closed-down theatre with an idle company. 'She leaves Greenwich for Oxford by the end of the week.'

The court moved often enough and only stayed in the same spot until the drains could no longer cope, but the queen did not usually take it away from London, preferring her palaces at Greenwich, Richmond and Whitehall.

'The queen has left London before,' offered Will tentatively, 'for Windsor Castle.'

'It is not the leaving,' James told him, ' 'tis the manner of the leaving. She quits London in haste because of the plague, which means it is getting worse. Members of the court are fleeing, though they will not admit this. The story put about is that she is to visit her old champion, Sir Henry Lee, at his estate in Ditchley, near Oxford, more than fifty miles from London. She is to sit for a portrait commissioned by her loyal knight. There will be rich entertainments, yet no actors have been summoned to appear. Are we all so out of favour with her now?' Burbage concluded, the disagreement with Will seemingly forgotten thanks to this greater concern. 'This is very bad.' And in case they did not fully grasp the seriousness of the situation, he added, 'For all of us.'

Chapter Ten

'And live we how we can, yet die we must.'
— Henry VI

They waited expectantly for the queen and her retinue to pass by, standing amidst a sizeable crowd which lined the streets waiting for her.

'Have you never witnessed a Royal Progress?' Richard asked him and Will was surprised to hear the excitement in his voice. 'It is something to behold. They need two thousand horses to move the court.' He looked about him then. 'All of London stands here to watch the queen go by, for she is still loved by all.'

Not all, thought Will, judging by the words of his inquisitor, who saw plots against her everywhere. He hoped that, if he stood patiently enough, waiting for the men of the court to pass, he might eventually recognise the face of the noble who had questioned him. He had been afforded only a momentary glimpse of the man but the image of that hard face had been burned into Will's memory.

The streets had started to fill early that morning thanks to the enticing prospect of a sight of the queen and despite the risk of infection from the miasma. Surely the foul air could not infect everyone with plague. Like gamblers playing dice, the people of London felt the odds would be in their favour. Others maintained that the presence of the queen, who must surely be favoured by God, would deter the plague, as it would not dare to infect a monarch.

Will and Richard stood off to one side, set back slightly from the crowd and standing in a raised position, thanks to the slope of the side street behind them. They had a good view of the road down which the queen and her courtiers would pass on their progress. While they waited, Will sought his friend's opinion on something that had been troubling him.

'Do you believe there is a power in words?' he asked, genuinely wondering if he did have a responsibility to do more than simply charm a crowd, which had until now been the limit of his intention. 'Do you ever worry that we might be the unwitting cause of insurrection? Treason even?'

'You cannot turn an honest man into a traitor by putting on a play for him,' scoffed Richard. 'And you are not responsible for your audience.'

'There was a riot during the last performance of my play,' Will reminded him.

'The cause of the riot wasn't the play! It was the groundlings. Though my father will never admit it, we let far too many in that day. They pushed and jostled to get a better view. A shove led to a blow, which started a brawl that became a riot. That is why they closed us, Will, or would you rather believe your words caused it?'

'I would not.'

'Are you sure? To be the man whose oratory holds such power it makes the masses rise up?'

'That would be a short and dangerous occupation.'

'But think of the glory!'

'You mock me.'

'I do.'

There was another matter preying on Will's mind. 'Your father was angry with me,' he recalled. 'Someone saw me the other night when I was supposed to be at supper with you.'

'You told me you fell asleep while writing.'

'I did tell you that,' Will admitted, 'and am ashamed of the lie but thought to protect you from the truth.'

'Which is?'

'That I was abducted.'

Richard started to laugh at the very notion but then realised Will was serious. 'Abducted? By whom? And why?'

'By Robert Poley.'

'By Jesu, Will. What have you done?' His alarm was clearly genuine. Will decided it would be best to tell all then and spared his friend no detail. When he was done, Richard said, 'I can see why you did not tell my father of it.'

'You think I am in danger?'

'I think we all are. You were dragged at knife point to meet a man you cannot identify, though you reason he must be powerful, perhaps even a close servant of the queen. Next, you say he wishes to bring down the Earl of Southampton, no less, and use you as his device? Have you any idea of how much peril this places you in?'

'I believe I have.' Though hearing Richard's alarm increased his own.

'And what if either of those powerful men becomes displeased with you? Our company could be broken up, our friends placed in chains and your life forfeit.'

'Which is why I am telling you of it now and could not bring myself to confess it to your father before.'

'What will you do?'

Will wanted to answer truthfully but also to offer up a plan that might calm his friend's rising fears, let alone his own, but he could not. 'I tell you plainly, Richard, I have no idea.'

–

The Royal Progress was indeed something to behold. The lines of men on horseback stretched back far beyond the road they stood by. The air was filled with the sound of rattling carts and hundreds of horses' hooves clopping down London's streets in unison, while onlookers were pushed back by liveried yeomen armed with pikes, who shouted for them to move. There were cries of 'God save the queen!' and 'Long live Her Majesty!' from the crowd as the procession reached them and loyal cheers greeted her at every stage of her journey. At the head of the column rode more armed men who stared firmly back at the people, looking for anyone who might be tempted to mount an attack upon the queen's person from the anonymity of the crowd. Gentlemen of the court, dressed in finery, rode next. Will craned his neck and strained his eyes looking for a familiar face amongst them but he saw no one who resembled his inquisitor. The queen's own arrival was announced by raucous cheers from the crowd. She rode by, flanked by the very closest members of her court. As she came into view, even Will found he was holding his breath.

Will had seen the queen before, close enough for Her Majesty to hear every word when he had acted before her with the rest of the company, and had never been more nervous during a performance. This time, though she was further away, she somehow managed to seem even more regal. Her face was completely white, her red hair pinned back above a high forehead, and her dress was made of cloth of gold adorned with jewels, which shone in the sunlight. The queen stood out easily, even among a long line of courtiers riding three abreast before and behind her, their rich clothes barely noticeable when set against her finery. The spectacle seemed designed to show Elizabeth's magnificence to her subjects and remind them of her power over them all.

It was then that Will's eyes were drawn to a slight but familiar figure who rode directly behind the queen. The hard, unsmiling face was the same, his proximity to Her Majesty surely an indication of his exalted rank at court. Here was Will's interrogator. He was sure of it.

Will leaned towards Richard and asked him urgently, 'Who rides behind the queen?' At this point Will did not even dare point towards the man, in case the gesture was seen by him.

'Besides the queen? That's Cecil,' answered Richard, who had misheard him in the noisy crowd. 'Lord Burleigh. The queen listens to him first and considers his counsel above all others. It is he who convinced our sovereign to execute her cousin Mary, Queen of the Scots.'

'No,' said Will, '*behind* her, not *beside* her.'

'That is his son, Robert Cecil.' Then Richard realised why Will might be asking the question. 'Tell me he is not your inquisitor?' he pleaded, with alarm in his voice, and when Will could find no words to placate him, Richard uttered a short prayer, heartfelt enough to increase Will's alarm tenfold.

'He is to be feared then?' He knew the answer already but needed his worst fears to be confirmed.

'Feared? Will, that man's father killed a queen,' hissed Richard. 'What do you suppose he would do to you?'

Robert Cecil rode by them at that point. He turned slightly in the saddle and seemed to stare right at them both and, though he did not acknowledge Will, it was as if he knew they were talking about him.

When he had passed, Richard whispered, 'He could not have heard that?'

'No.' But Will remembered his warning then.

You cannot hide anything from me. Not even your thoughts. I see everything. I hear everything.

Chapter Eleven

'*Golden lads and girls all must,*
As chimney-sweepers, come to dust.'
— *Cymbeline*

'We have to tell my father,' Richard urged him once the Queen's Progress was done.

'Must we?'

'Of course we must! Will, I thought our situation dangerous, now I believe it grave. I reasoned you had fallen foul of some ambitious lord with a quarrel against the Earl of Southampton, but Robert Cecil might be the most powerful man in England one day, if he has not already attained that position. My father knows people at court who might be of help to us. I take no joy in telling him any of this, for it will surely anger and grieve him, but not telling him puts us all in greater peril.'

It seemed there was nothing else for it. 'All right then.'

-

With the theatre closed, there was little for the members of the company to do with their afternoons but drink, and this they did, with an enthusiasm born from both a love of ale and an understanding of the fragility of life now that plague had reached their city. Why save what little money you had when you could be gone in a week?

That night, the actors from two theatrical companies met in a tavern to drink together and share stories of plays ended early, more theatres rumoured to be closing soon, and men they knew who had recently died whether from violence, plague or through drink. Toasts were drunk by the Admiral's Men, led by Marlowe and Edward Alleyn; and by Will's company, Lord Strange's Men, with Will and Richard Burbage drinking deeply that night in the hope of finding courage at the bottom of their cups. They had reached the stage of the evening where men had to shout above the din of other drinkers to be heard in the packed tavern.

'I enjoyed your *Henry VI*,' Marlowe told Will, 'even though I recognised a line or two.'

Will blushed at that. 'I meant it more in tribute than in theft.' He had in fact taken a couple of lines verbatim from Marlowe's work, a common enough practice among playmakers influenced by one another and working at speed.

Marlowe smiled. 'Writers never steal, Will. They borrow, then they adapt. We all take from Ovid and Plutarch and where would we get our stories without Holinshed's chronicles?' Warming to his theme, he added, 'Writers mine their own lives too and those of others. Be proud of being a magpie. *Henry VI* was a hit, a palpable hit. How many arses? Come on, tell me.'

'Eight hundred,' Will answered, 'on its second night.' That had been the peak of London's interest in his first play, and a moment Will did not get to enjoy for long before the theatre was closed, following the riot.

'That's good, Will,' said Marlowe, 'though not as good as *Tamburlaine*' – and he smiled mischievously – 'or *Faustus*. But it really is not bad, you know, for a first play.'

–

The gathering became more boisterous with the arrival of Thomas Kyd, another playmaker Will envied, second only to Marlowe in acclaim, thanks to a series of plays that included the hugely popular *The Spanish Tragedy*. He was far better known in London than Will, another handsome bastard to boot and already quite drunk. This made Kyd all the keener to regale the assembled poets and actors with stories of his rivals, living or dead, keeping them entertained with tales of oafishness, lewdness or plain ill luck, which the throng enjoyed, while competing with each other to throw in embellishments they claimed to have witnessed with their own eyes. Kyd had to ever raise his voice further to drown them out.

'They say Robert Greene tried to buy a coat of arms once,' and there was some mirth at this pricking of his late rival's pomposity. 'Imagine him forfeiting twenty pounds for a piece of heraldry that wouldn't change a single man's opinion of his low worth.'

Richard noticed Will was the only one not laughing, which puzzled him as Will had been a target of Greene's barbs, until he said quietly, 'I would like a coat of arms one day.'

'Whatever for?' asked Kyd. 'Why, they are a device entirely designed to remove money from fools and make them feel better about their base origins.'

'Then I plead guilty to being such a fool, for it would make me feel better.'

Unfortunately, Kyd was too drunk to notice how seriously Will meant this, and he continued with his mocking.

'What would you have on your escutcheon, Will? Let us consider it, shall we?' Kyd pretended to do just that, with a hand against his chin. 'Instead of an iron gauntlet, a pair of folded gloves.' There was some laughter from the men around him, for they all knew Will's father's profession. 'And in place of a sword, a sheep!' Will's father had also dealt in wool before he lost his money. 'A damn fine and fair-looking one at that!' And Kyd mimed a vulgar gesture of tupping that same ewe.

The laughter was raucous now and Kyd revelled in it, until Will rose angrily to his feet. 'Enough!'

A hand was pressed against his arm then by Richard, while Kyd looked alarmed. 'Calm yourself,' Richard cautioned.

'You can all laugh,' growled Will, 'since none of you ever watched a father brought so low he was shamed by it.'

'I meant nothing by it, friend,' said Kyd, who looked genuinely worried now. 'It was a jest.'

'You hear that, Will?' said Richard. ' 'Twas but a jest.' Then he leaned in closer and murmured, 'Remember Knell?' and the mention of a man they both knew, who had given his life up cheaply in an argument begun in a tavern, seemed to take some of the heat from Will then. He waved a hand dismissively at Kyd but it was a gesture that meant he realised he had overreacted to the slight.

'Sit down, Will,' suggested Marlowe. 'You have naught but friends here. My own father was a shoemaker, so I will have buskins on my escutcheon and the arse of a cow.' There was grateful laughter at Marlowe making light of it all.

Will did sit down then. 'You're a Cambridge man,' Will reminded Marlowe. 'And do not need a coat of arms to give you standing.'

'I was only at Cambridge thanks to a scholarship and can scarcely lay claim to being a gentleman at all.'

'Then what do you lay claim to being?'

He flourished his hand and dipped his head, like an actor taking a bow. 'Marlowe.'

'A part you are at least used to playing.'

'And it is a part,' Marlowe agreed, 'which is most adaptable, depending on the audience. I may be a writer but I am always a player. It is all pretence, Will.'

'And yet you navigate those waters, between the worlds of theatre and court, more naturally than all others.' In Will's limited experience of the court, during appearances in plays put on before the queen, he had deliberately kept his mouth closed except when performing and had avoided eye contact with his monarch, while witnessing the humbling effect she had on other, far nobler men than he, as they cowed before her.

'I do not try as hard as they do,' explained Marlowe. 'They give off an odour in front of the queen, a stench of fear or desperation. The waters at court are still treacherous but I try to wade into them as if I don't give a damn whether I drown or not.'

'But you do give a damn?'

'Of course, and when I see the queen, I do what all men do.'

'And that is?'

'Shit themselves,' Marlowe said, and Will laughed. 'The woman has the power to end all our lives with a short, spoken word. Most men are too frightened to say anything to her, for fear of ending up on the rack or in a gibbet.'

'But not you, Kit. Does she favour you?'

Marlowe didn't answer at first. 'I interest her,' he allowed then. 'At least I did.' Then he added vaguely, 'I was able to do her some service once.' He was both enigmatic and guarded but the inference was not lost on Will. 'Perhaps I still interest her and will gain advantage from it, shamelessly. There goes Marlowe,' he intoned in the voice of another, 'the queen's favourite, her creature, and she is his muse.' He seemed amused by this notion.

Will wasn't sure quite why he felt the need to urge caution then, but he did. 'Be careful the queen does not take too much of an interest in your words and deeds, Kit. There is danger in that.'

'*Quod me nutrit me destruit.*' Marlowe responded.

'That which nourishes me destroys me.' Will pondered its meaning with a definite sense of foreboding.

–

At what they hoped to be the right moment, Richard and Will led James Burbage away from the main body of revellers to tell him of Will's encounter with Sir Robert Cecil. They had chosen a public place in the hope it would contain his fury. As he talked, Will wondered if James had consumed enough ale to blunt his senses.

James Burbage took the news about as calmly as a man can when it has just been explained to him that, through no fault of his own, his life and livelihood, and those of his family and entire company, were now in peril thanks to the actions of another. At first, he stared at Will in something like disbelief, then he sat down heavily to finish hearing him out. When Will was done, he went for a while without saying anything until Richard and Will could bear his silence no more.

'Father?' urged Richard, to bring the elder Burbage out of his trance.

'My God, Will,' James said at last, 'you might have just killed us all. Robert Cecil is quite possibly the most dangerous man in the kingdom, apart from his father. I'd say he is even more dangerous in fact, having not yet achieved the status he believes his by right, so he will be in a hurry to attain it. It is said that the queen listens to none but him now. You must mark everything he says and be mindful of other meanings. His questions are never innocent and he will almost always know the answers to them already. He sets traps with his mind and baits them with words.'

'He sounds like a devil,' said Will.

'The devil waits forbearingly to greet you in the next life. Cecil will send you early to him from this one.' James explained how Cecil's father had trapped Mary, Queen of the Scots, with a plan of his own making, to prove her treachery to the queen. Then he persuaded Elizabeth to cut off her own cousin's head. 'Still, even our dread sovereign's hand trembled when she signed the death warrant. The thought of killing another queen anointed by God gave her pause, so she entrusted the warrant to a member of the Privy Council to delay carrying out the sentence. But William Cecil did not hesitate. When he discovered the warrant had been signed, he took it upon himself to see the execution through. Mary was killed that day on his word, not the queen's. Her Majesty was furious and Cecil might have followed Mary to the block but was only cast out of court to do penance instead, until such a time as the queen was in peril again and needed him back. It did not take long.'

James Burbage believed that Robert Cecil had been trained by his father since birth, with Francis Walsingham, the queen's late spymaster, and the most ruthless man in England as his other tutor. 'Do you honestly believe your life means anything at all to Robert Cecil? Your worth lies only in what you can do for him.'

'Then what must I do?' Will asked helplessly.

'He asked you about the Earl of Southampton, did he not? The bigger the man he brings down, the more favour the queen will bestow upon him. This is a strategy he learned from his father. Elizabeth more greatly fears an enemy who has land or money enough to raise an army against her, and so she should.'

'But I am of low birth and no consequence to him.'

'You have lately commanded the attention of the earl, and Cecil asked you about Marlowe whose influence over the masses I think he fears.'

'Most of the groundlings don't understand that plays are written, let alone remember the writer's name,' said Will. 'They think the actors make up their lines on the spot.'

'That was once so,' James countered, 'but there are more companies now and the audience has a choice. They wish to know who wrote this or that play. Was it the man who wrote *Tamburlaine* or the one who brought us *The Spanish Tragedy*? That is how the multitude makes its choices these days.'

'Ask your son and he will tell you it is the actor that is the draw.'

'He would say that. He is an actor, whereas you are—'

'A writer, for the most part. No one wants to clasp a writer's hand when the play is done or perch upon his knee in a tavern then whisper how warm his words made them. They applaud the musician, not the lute.'

'A woman might, but Robert Cecil does not overlook the writer of the play. He knows words have power. If he dislikes what is written, he will silence the writer.' There was a burst of laughter then, and Will turned back towards the noise and his laughing friends.

'Kyd and Marlowe are loud and bend to no one, and Nashe is impudent,' said James. 'They will not have escaped the notice of a man like Cecil and nor shall you.'

Will thought for a while before confiding, 'I think Kit might have done service for Cecil. How long ago I know not, but he still goes abroad.'

'On whose service does he do that now?' wondered James. 'The queen's or some other power?'

'Kit is no traitor nor an agent for another power. He is outspoken when at his wine and oft proclaims there is no God, but for sport, I think, or perhaps to uncover men who concur.'

'So he can denounce them?' asked James. 'Or join them?'

'Is it not a clever way to draw secrets from a man's heart,' argued Will, 'by acting as if you share them?'

'That is a dangerous game. Kit could easily lose his life at the hands of those same men, or others who want them dead.'

'Then likely I am wrong,' Will concluded, 'for Kit is no fool.'

'What exactly does Robert Cecil want from you, Will?'

'He wishes for me to spy on the Earl of Southampton.'

'And what does the earl expect from you?'

'I can only think a play or a sonnet,' he replied while privately recalling the earl's exact words: *'I shall make use of you Master Shakespeare, though perhaps not in the way you imagine.'*

'He is a generous patron,' admitted James, 'but this earl has been linked to Catholic plots, albeit without proof. He is a known recusant, yet still liked by the queen, though I believe he has of late fallen out of her good favour.'

'What if this great lord wishes you to spy for him too, Will?' asked Richard. 'In exchange for his patronage?'

'I would refuse his entreaty.'

'Just as you refused the great Robert Cecil,' James retorted.

'That was different. Cecil is an agent of the crown.'

'You did not know who he was,' James reminded him. 'He merely *said* that he was the queen's agent.'

'Then we saw him ride behind her on the progress. He is who he claimed to be.'

'Whatever the Earl of Southampton asks of you, it will place you in danger,' James continued. 'That danger is doubled now that Cecil has asked you to spy on the earl. Either man could cut you down.'

'What then can I do about it?'

'A man cannot have two masters. You must choose one,' James told Will, 'and hope that he destroys the other.'

'But which one should I choose?'

His answer was immediate. 'The strongest.'

Chapter Twelve

'Life is as tedious as a twice-told tale,
Vexing the dull ear of a drowsy man'
— King John

Three of them rode in the carriage. Marlowe was there of course, and Thomas Nashe, who Will knew less well, though they had spoken once of collaborating on a play. Marlowe and Nashe had visited the Earl of Southampton before and spent a good part of the journey regaling Will with tales of his legendary hospitality. 'Eat your fill,' said Marlowe, 'and you won't have to buy any more food for a week.'

'Eat it?' said Nashe. 'I brought sacks full home with me and you should do the same. A poet needs sustenance and the earl provides it.'

'And are you both providing payment,' asked Will, 'in the form of poetry?'

Marlowe shook his head. 'Last time I gave him "The Passionate Shepherd to His Love". I am told that someone, I know not who has the impertinence, has prepared a reply to it.' He snorted at the temerity of someone picking up that gauntlet while possessing only a fraction of his talent. Then he turned to Nashe. 'It isn't you?'

'Not I,' Nashe laughed at the notion.

'Nor I,' Will assured Kit, before asking Nashe, 'Then what will you give him?'

'A trifle.' Nashe was evasive.

'And what will this trifle involve?' Will had increasingly begun to doubt the quality of his new sonnet and sought to discover if Nashe was more confident about his own work.

'A restless youth's infatuation,' he said vaguely.

'With?'

'The object of that infatuation.'

'A love poem then?'

But Nashe feigned boredom at this point. He turned to look out of the carriage to end Will's questions. 'We shall not get much further before nightfall.' Will took his hint and asked no more.

The carriage had been provided for them by the earl and Will wondered how many of his guests would have been afforded such an honour. 'We are not the only ones,' Marlowe had assured him. 'Carriages will have been sent out to collect anyone the earl deems amusing.'

'Imagine being able to do such a thing.'

'It is as nothing to the earl,' Marlowe replied. 'They say the income from his land alone is worth a thousand a year.'

Will could hardly conceive of such a sum, but it crossed his mind that the fifty pounds he needed to become a partner in the new company might be something the earl would barely miss.

–

An hour passed and the rocking of the carriage sent Nashe off to sleep. Will fell gloomily silent and Marlowe noticed. 'What ails thee, Will? You seem discouraged.'

Will had been so before his appointment with Robert Cecil and now had even greater concerns. He could recall every threatening word of Cecil's, as well as the dire warnings about the man from James Burbage, but could reveal none of this to his friend.

'In truth, you are the worst man to ask me that.'

'I am the worst man?'

'For you are the best man,' Will explained, 'in this carriage, this county or on this sceptred isle.'

'Mmmm.' Marlowe thought on this. 'Sceptred isle is good.'

'I might use it. Lately though, I cannot find the words, and that is why I say to you, most clumsily, that you are the worst man to ask what ails me.'

'The words won't come?'

'They did. They used to, easily. I spent months writing lines or parts of scenes with others, while trying to convince James Burbage I could pen a whole play for him one day and, when finally he allowed it, the words tumbled from me and fell upon the page.'

'Your *Henry VI*?'

'The very same.'

'Old Burbage speaks well of it.'

'Does he? Not to me.'

'Well, he would not,' Marlowe said. 'Because he bought it from you and, if he wants another, can never admit its merits. If James Burbage inflates your worth, he drives up your price. So, instead, when you have completed your next play, he will tell you that it is rough and unfinished, needing many changes, till you begin to doubt every word of it. Then, with some reluctance, he will offer you the same sum as he did for your previous play, as if helping you to survive because he likes you.'

'He has said much the same to me already, before reading even a word of it. He has told me I am but a boy in the theatre and it takes a man of experience to mould plays into a shape that's pleasing to an audience.'

'And yet you know Burbage to be no fool. Do you think he would really buy a bad play from a poor writer then spend weeks moulding it? Privately, he told me your *Henry VI* was good enough to rival even the great Christopher Marlowe.' They both laughed easily at this.

'Did James Burbage really say that or do you jest?'

'He said it and more. Might that help you summon the words you need, Will?'

'In truth, I know not. That first play came in a mighty rush of words, yet this time they have to be dragged from me, as if surrendering reluctantly one at a time. When they do, I am not close to happy with any of them.'

Marlowe was not remotely surprised. 'It is always thus for a second play. It was the same for me. Ask Nashe when he wakes. Ask Thomas Kyd too, and he will tell you his second play was the hardest of under-takings.'

'Surely the first ought to be the hardest; then, having done it before—'

'Expectation,' Marlowe said. 'There is none for a first play. You write it knowing it might never be completed, much less performed. People expect a first-time playmaker to fail or, if they do impress, then to do it lightly. Now they have seen what you can do, Will, they will want more of the same and that is when you begin to doubt yourself. Your first play was born of passion, crafted during leisure time, written with the good humour and confidence of a tavern drinker. The second time it becomes a different thing entirely.'

'What does it become?'

'Work. You have been commissioned to deliver a play, the days seem to run out as quickly as grains of sand slipping through the hourglass, and yet...'

'And yet?'

'You are not writing, and what's more, you know not why you are not writing.'

'That is the truth of it.' Will's sigh was one of relief, for Marlowe understood him and it seemed he was not alone in being affected by this heightened expectation. 'Every day I rise with the lark to commence writing and say I will not stop until a pretty pile of pages lies before me. But then I cannot start until I have eaten bread and drunk small beer. Then I tell myself I might walk the streets while thinking on the play and learning what news there is abroad. By the time I have paused to greet friends and talk with them, the morning is gone. So, I return to my rooms vowing to spend the afternoon with a quill in my hand, but then I stare at the window, as if I will find words written there upon the glass. I'll wager you have never done that.'

'I have, many times, and will again. 'Tis common.'

'Then how do you complete your plays?'

'In a great flurry of crude words, written in haste,' admitted Marlowe. 'Then I spend hours forging them into something worthy enough for an actor like Alleyn to spew upon the stage.'

'Dear God, I thought I was the only one.'

'Being a writer, a poet, a playmaker, is not, as many believe, to be visited daily by some gentle muse, who whispers fine words into your ear, nor to channel the voice of God and scratch his words upon the parchment as if they were commandments. You have to search for those words, Will, and you alone will find them. You can break your fast then walk, greet friends, drink in taverns. But in the end, you must sit in your rooms alone and write. It is the only remedy. There, somehow, you must fashion a world and people it with characters who will convince nobles and peasants alike that they are real. You must give them words to say that will leave an audience breathless with love or longing, sadness, hate, jealousy or rage, and keep the groundlings so in thrall that they will talk of nothing else afterwards but *William Shakespeare!*'

'That's not easy, Kit.'

'Nor should it be, else everyone would do it. Immortality must be earned, Will.'

'Immortality? Do you really think we will be remembered after we are gone?'

'For a year or more, perhaps.' He shrugged. 'If the men that come after us are cut from lesser cloth, then maybe the memory of our plays will survive as long as the lives of some of those who saw them and were entertained. After that, all is dust.'

'Then perhaps I should not care about it so much.'

'Oh, you should care. Treat every word as if it matters more than anything. But, here's the thing.' He held up a finger. 'To give yourself the freedom to write, you must also tell yourself they are naught but a folly, then you will be released from the prison of caring overmuch.'

'So, I must think the play matters greatly yet not at all, at one and the same time?'

'That is the writer's lot and the reason why we pull out our hair and tear the very pages we write upon into pieces. It is also why wine was invented.'

Will smiled at Marlowe then. 'Even though my problems are far from ended, they seem lesser from knowing you recognise them.'

'And share them, as do all writers. When I wrote my first play, it felt as if the quill would dart across the paper of its own accord. I was merely its servant not its master. But then I read it over and over, changing a word here and removing another there, often putting them back in again later. I was never happier with it than at the point when I thought it finished but before I was about to show it to another. If I could have timed my death exactly then, I would have died the happiest man in England.'

'I do know that feeling.'

'People liked it, which was a relief and a joy, but then came the second play: an interminable work, every word wrenched from my being. My mortal enemy was the date on which I had promised to deliver the thing. The money I secured in advance had already been drunk, eaten, gambled or whored away, and every blank page mocked me with its unsullied purity.'

'And yet, somehow you finished it.'

'In the end, I did. And so shall you, my friend.'

Chapter Thirteen

'...be not afraid of greatness: some are born great, some achieve greatness, and some have greatness thrust upon 'em.'
— *Twelfth Night*

Will had acted in front of Her Majesty at court and seen its opulence and grandeur, so he was not as easily impressed by a mansion as some might be, but Place House was truly magnificent. Marlowe explained it had been built by Thomas Wriothesley, Henry's grandfather, on the site of the old Titchfield Abbey, which had stood there for three hundred years until Henry VIII's dissolution of the monasteries. With the abbot and monks expelled, Thomas Wriothesley was able to seize it for himself and chose a master mason, Thomas Bartewe, to tear down parts of the abbey and its tower, before turning what was left of the building into a splendid home. There was a gatehouse with four turrets, which they passed through into a huge courtyard with an impressive fountain. Dozens of servants moved swiftly in and out of the enormous building, preparing Place House for a sizeable number of visitors.

Inside the mansion was a Great Hall for banqueting and even an indoor theatre. Will and his companions were shown their rooms, which contained fine beds with feather mattresses, before being ushered downstairs once more so they could join the guests who had already arrived. Food was laid out on tables to be picked at by hungry travellers, and a steward brought them all glasses filled with wine. Will drank but not too deeply, the better to understand the earl's true intentions for him.

I shall make use of you.

He needed to stay undiminished by wine so he could deliver the sonnet he had been sweating over for a week or more now, then decide upon the best course of action thereafter, once he knew the earl's true desires. Unlike Marlowe, Will had never been intimate with a boy. The earl laid a good claim to being the fairest youth in the land, with almost womanly features and a coquettish way about him that Will could not deny was more than a little appealing. Would lying with this boy be a duty to be endured or a pleasure to be savoured? Would he find himself going along with the seduction only to be repelled at the final moment, angering the earl and shaming himself in the process, while ruining any hoped-for chance of patronage?

When the earl himself appeared, he was greeted by more than a dozen men, exclaiming gratitude for their invitations. They praised his grand house, fine clothes and impeccable taste as a patron of their art. Will began to worry then because he had not rehearsed any kind of fawning greeting. He need not have concerned himself. When the earl reached Will, he was the first to speak.

'Walk with me, Shakespeare.'

—

'This is a fine house, my lord,' Will offered when the earl initially said nothing as they walked its perimeter, 'built on… fine land.' Nervousness had robbed Will of the one thing he could usually rely on: words. His were clumsy and he knew it, as did the earl.

'Yes, it is indeed… fine,' he said blandly. It was a form of rebuke. Will took it to mean he should be wary of boring him again.

Perhaps he should abandon the talk of homes and land and instead ask outright what was on the earl's mind. He thanked Henry Wriothesley for his invitation, then asked, 'How might I be of most service to my lord?'

The earl thought for a moment. 'I am sure you know I am a patron of writers who doth please me.'

Will smiled. 'Then how may I please my lord?'

'Your sonnet was a good beginning.'

'I have prepared a new sonnet and think it a better one. I was impertinent enough to dedicate it to you, if it pleases my lord?' The earl shot Will a look that was hard to decipher. Did it indicate pleasure at being flattered in such a way by a new writer, or did he agree that it was an impertinence to dedicate a sonnet to him without permission? Had Will already gone too far?

'You shall deliver it tonight, as part of our entertainments,' said the earl. 'Then we shall see if it is worthy of our name.'

Two more carriages approached the house then. Will was surprised to witness a dozen young, fair and seemingly well-born women emerge from it. They looked to be in high spirits and, from their dress and bearing, appeared to be guests not servants. These ladies seemed to know the mansion too, since none of them stood gawping at the fountain, turrets or high walls of Place House and needed no ushering into the house. Once inside, their arrival caused something of an uproar. Will could hear the bawdy shouts of men in the Great Hall as they went by.

The earl spoke then. 'I have always preferred the company of men,' he confessed. 'Women are a mystery to me. They are like spies.'

'How so, my lord?'

'Women are trained, almost from birth, to never reveal their true natures nor speak of anything of import, lest it offend a man,' he observed. 'But what goes on inside, I wonder?' He tapped his head to show he meant their minds.

'I have wondered this too,' said Will. 'When I write the part of a woman, it cannot be the same as when I write a man.'

'Of course,' said the earl. 'You have no knowledge of what it is like to be a woman and can only imagine it.'

'It is not just that. I too have wondered about the thoughts hidden by women and what they really think of us. What secrets must they keep from their fathers and husbands?'

'Now that is worthy of exploration in a play.'

'Indeed, my lord.'

Wriothesley's brow furrowed then. 'It is not required for you to end every sentence with "my lord". We shall take your understanding of my position as assumed from now on.'

Will had to stop himself from saying 'my lord' in reply. Instead, he gave a very slight bow of acknowledgement, then their eyes were drawn to a fine-looking girl who had re-emerged from the mansion on her own and was now walking, as swiftly as convention would allow, back to the carriage where she had presumably left something. They saw her retrieve a bag and head back into the house. She noticed them for the first time and curtsied.

When she was gone, Henry Wriothesley told Will, 'I am to be married.' This was not a surprise, because even a man who shared Marlowe's less conventional appetites would bow to society on such a matter, especially one in so lofty a position and in need of an heir. Before Will could offer his congratulations, he added, 'But I like her not.'

'Marriage is often a duty, especially for one so exalted.'

'I will not see it through.'

Will wondered how he would get out of the arrangement, which like all such marriages must have been approved by the queen, but apparently the earl had plans to persuade her to dissolve the contract.

'This weekend will be my last here, before I join the queen at Oxford, where I will petition or woo her, or both. She is a woman after all and they have their favourites. But before I leave to play the loyal courtier, there will be one last series of revels.' Will realised that, if he was unable to convince the queen, they could be his last as an unmarried man. 'And I have a special role in mind for you, Will Shakespeare. I rather think you are the man for it.'

Two servants walked round the side of the building then, each carrying one end of a deer carcass that was suspended upside down from a wooden pole ready to be roasted over a fire somewhere. As they passed, the earl asked, 'Do you like meat or fish, Master Shakespeare? Most gentlemen prefer one or the other. I enjoy both.'

Was this what it was like to be a woman, Will wondered? To be courted by a man who, perhaps unsure of his subject's affections, preferred to hint at his interest, or was Henry Wriothesley the kind of man who always liked to play games?

'I will take what I am offered when hungry.'

The earl smiled at Will then, as if they were both of similar mind and had reached an understanding. He put out a hand and placed it gently against Will's cheek. 'I should imagine you were passably fair, once,' he told Will impishly, but then broke from the conversation when he noticed a bright-eyed, pale-skinned boy, dressed in the earl's livery, who had emerged from the house and was standing off to one side, waiting patiently for his master's pleasure. 'We will talk more, later.'

Chapter Fourteen

'Even so quickly may one catch the plague?'
— *Twelfth Night*

The festivities at the home of Henry Wriothesley, Earl of Southampton, were lengthy. They were also the grandest Will had ever witnessed, even at court. The food was rich and expensive, the tables in the banqueting hall so overladen they groaned and threatened to collapse under the weight of it all. There was far too much of everything and this was surely deliberate. The earl watched over it all like a king staging a feast for his courtiers.

There was every kind of boiled or roasted meat you could name, including beef, lamb, venison and a large number of roasted chickens, as well as quail, lark and swan, along with sweet meats and all manner of pies. There were huge platters of fried fish too. When the men had eaten their fill of that, enormous puddings were brought in, flavoured with sugar, honey, ginger, oranges or cinnamon. These were carried by some of the women Will had seen that morning and, to his astonishment and the accompaniment of loud cheers from the men, they wore feathered headdresses and all of them were bare-breasted. The women returned again and again with jugs of wine, and poured them into glasses that were never less than half empty, so that no one could possibly know how much they had drunk. The girls were nimble at avoiding the pawing of the drunker men, and they needed to be.

'And now for our evening's revels!' Wriothesley announced when the feast was done. 'Who will be first?'

Nashe rose to his feet and boomed, 'I will be first! While I can still stand!' There was an outburst of laughter at this. Nashe was clearly a popular guest and the earl indulged him. Nashe waited for his audience to become silent, which they did by and by. Only then did he commence speaking.

'My lords,' he began, 'my ladies' – he dipped his head to acknowledge the bare-chested women in the room, causing a murmur of humorous appreciation from the men, then finally added – 'my gentlemen.' And he bowed theatrically before them. '"The Choice of Valentines",' he declared, 'is a sonnet to the Lord S.' He nodded towards his patron, who smiled his approval. 'I will circulate it in its entirety later in manuscript form. For now, as time is brief, so shall I be. I give you tonight not the bones of the sonnet but the *flesh.*' His teasing pronunciation of the word set the men stamping their feet in appreciation for what was to come. 'This is the tale of Tomalin, a young man who, on St Valentine's Day, does visit a brothel' – this scandalous notion set off a great roar of appreciation from his audience – 'where his lover, Mistress Frances, is its most famous resident.' More laughter and braying at the very notion. 'Tomalin pays the sum of ten gold pieces for Mistress Frances's time and her favours!' More braying at the word 'favours', which they were all now presumably imagining. Nashe raised a hand then extended a forefinger to command silence before he commenced his poem, from memory, at the point when young Tomalin had already begun his amorous advances towards Mistress Frances.

'*And make me happy, stealing by degrees. / First bare her legs, then creep up to her knees.*'

The next lines were lost to Will's ears because of the noise of the laughter and the stamping of feet in approval. Nashe had to speak louder in order to be heard.

'*Oh heaven, and paradise are all but toys,*' he said. '*Compared with this sight, I now behold,*' and he lowered his gaze to what would surely have been the level of Tomalin's mistress's cunny. '*Which well might keep a man from being old.*'

They loved that idea and Will lost another line or two because of their laughter. Nashe was still describing the woman's nethers when he could be heard once more:

'*It makes the fruits of love eft soon be ripe / And pleasure plucked too timely from the stem / To die ere it hath seen Jerusalem.*'

With that, Nashe's audience lost collective control of itself, at the image of the unfortunate Tomalin, having paid all of that gold, only to become 'spent' before enjoying the act he had paid so much to complete. This was a tragedy and comedy combined. They laughed so hard and joyously, some of them were in tears, and once again Nashe had to wait for their humour to subside, for he had saved the best till last.

'*Unhappy me, quoth she, and wilt not stand?*' Nashe mimicked the devastated face of Mistress Frances at the spectacle of this spent force before her. He completed the picture by holding up his little finger then bending it until it drooped low.

'*Come, let me rub and chafe it with my hand! / Perhaps the silly worm is laboured sore, / And wearied that it can done no more.*'

More lines followed in which poor Tomalin's quill was brought temporarily back to life, until he himself admitted that '*The well is dry that should refresh.*'

The look on Nashe's face was intended to convey Mistress Frances's lack of satisfaction at this state of affairs, at which point Nashe reached into the bag around his neck and drew something out. Will was not the only one to crane his neck to see what it was. Nashe was now holding a good-sized wooden phallus of a sturdy nature.

He carried on as Frances in a higher pitch.

'*My little dildo shall supply their kind,*' he explained to uproarious applause from all assembled, not least the earl, who was clapping and rocking back and forth in his chair with undisguised glee now.

'*That bendeth not, nor foldeth any deal, / But stands as stiff as he were made of steel.*'

He placed it between his legs and pretended to be a woman, and finally Will realised to his horror that he had completely misread both the room and occasion. Christ, he was meant to have conjured up something obscene, for the entertainment of men who had seen a bit of life. What did he have to offer them instead? Flattering words to an earl, in a sonnet he would soon be forced to recite before an audience who were heartily laughing at a fellow poet who was ending his own sonnet by pretending to penetrate himself with a wooden dildo? If Will could have quit the room now and ridden back to London without serious recrimination, he would have done so and resolved never to see the earl or his comrades again, but he was trapped.

The laughter and applause that signalled the end of Nashe's poem finally subsided and Will was plucked from his thoughts by the words of the young earl.

'Master Shakespeare!' he called. 'Come, for you are next! What now will you give us?'

Will walked out into the middle of the room with the reluctance of a man approaching the gallows. The assembled gentlefolk regarded him with guarded curiosity, presumably wondering how this newcomer could follow such hilarious entertainment from a well-regarded vulgarian like Nashe?

'It is a love poem for my lord—' Will corrected himself hastily, '*dedicated* to my lord.'

The earl seemed to find this misstep amusing. 'And what is it called?'

'Venus and Adonis.'

'A good title. Will you read the whole?'

'It is eleven hundred lines.' And that elicited groans from his audience. 'I thought to read but a line or two, then present the whole to my lord thereafter.'

'Proceed then.'

Will took a breath and his lips felt dry. The assembled fellows were watching him intently, some frowning at this unhappy-looking interloper, as if he was unworthy of their attention. What in God's name was he doing here, pretending to be a poet?

'I said proceed.' The impatient words from the earl made him lurch into the verse.

'*Touch but my lips with those fair lips of thine…*'

'Can't hear!' someone called from the rear of the gathering.

Will died a little, cleared his throat and called louder and more clearly: '*Touch but my lips with those fair lips of thine!*' His words seemed to echo in that room, reaching the ears of everyone within it. He had their attention now and continued.

'*Though mine be not so fair, yet are they red. / The kiss shall be thine own as well as mine. / What seest thou in the ground? hold up thy head: / Look in mine eye-balls, there thy beauty lies; / Then why not lips on lips, since eyes in eyes?*'

The end of those lines was greeted with complete silence and Will wanted to disappear.

'A good sonnet.' Henry Wriothesley dipped his head to acknowledge the quality of the writing. 'Though perhaps wasted on this fine company.' His smile told the audience they were being teased and they laughed along. 'And dedicated to me, you say?' he asked this as if it was both a surprise and also of not too much importance to him.

'None other.'

'Good then.' He nodded in recognition and seemed quite moved for a moment before saying dismissively, 'we shall talk more on it later.' Then he called out, 'Who is next?'

'It is I, Raleigh!' a voice boomed from the back of the room. 'To restore some good humour to this affair!' That was a slight on Will but he already felt bad enough without taking further insult from the great adventurer. It turned out that Walter Raleigh was the man to deliver a riposte to Marlowe's 'The Passionate Shepherd to His Love', with his own 'The Nymph's Reply to the Shepherd', which made the shepherd sound like a naïve boy who thought lovers could survive by living off little more than air. The scornful nymph had a more realistic view of love and sent him on his way. Marlowe took its good reception well or at least pretended to and applauded along with the rest.

There were more entertainments provided by poets of varying quality. Most of them chose a bawdy tone and even the least proficient were greeted with less hostility than the sonnet Will had slaved over for days. When the final verse was read, the party dispersed, splitting into smaller groups, served by the half-naked girls. Some of the girls led men away from the banqueting hall, taking them to rooms elsewhere. Others allowed men to pull them onto their knees to be kissed and fondled in plain view. Will knew they were paid to do this and marvelled at their ability to act as if they were delighted to be groped. Some of the men found it amusing to fondle their most intimate parts in full view. This is what an excess of wine or sack does, thought Will.

At that point, Raleigh, Marlowe, Lord Strange and their host, the Earl of Southampton, left by a side door, along with a handful of others, including Nashe and the Earl of Northumberland. This seemed to be a pre-planned exit, hinting at a clandestine meeting to which Will and most of the other men were not invited. But what was its purpose?

Pleasure perhaps, of a more private or debauched nature, or something darker, such as the atheistic symposiums Robert Cecil spoke of, where even revolt might be discussed. Will knew he had to follow them and at least attempt to see or overhear what was discussed, or feel the wrath of Robert Cecil. He left quietly through a different door, knowing he would not be missed while the girls were keeping the other men so royally entertained.

Will had deliberately taken off in the opposite direction to the earl and his followers, making sure he moved quicker than their unhurried pace, hoping to catch up with them by making a circuit of the ground floor until he chanced upon their meeting place. He opened the doors to several rooms along his way, but none had been set up for a symposium. Finally, he came upon a spacious one that contained a long table with chairs and had been lit by candelabras. This looked promising. He entered and searched for a hiding place.

'Where are we to be?' came a voice from the corridor outside.

'The small hall.' Will recognised the earl's voice: Henry Wriothesley was close and had probably just mentioned the room he was standing in. Hide then, he told himself, but where? The fireplace? It was unlit and he could perhaps climb up it and try to wedge himself there, but what if they lit that fire beneath him? What if he fell and crashed to the floor in front of everyone? How could he explain his presence there in any other role but spy? They would run him through.

The voices were getting closer and he could hear their footsteps in the corridor. They would soon be in the room and he had no excuse for being there. He noticed the arras at the other end of the room. At court these huge tapestries usually concealed a rarely used exit. If Will were bold enough to hide behind this one, he could possibly hear what was said without being seen and then report back to Sir Robert. It was a risk, though. If one of the men chose to use this for an exit instead of the door they were about to walk through then he would be finished. He quickly walked the length of the room, pulled back the arras and got behind it before straightening it to conceal his presence. Behind him was another unoccupied room that was dimly lit by a few candles.

Soon the Small Hall was filled with the sound of scraping chairs and animated voices. Henry Wriothesley spoke then, asking his honoured guests to give the room their thoughts on the subjects of God, monarchy, duty, loyalty and what did or did not constitute heresy in this new and more enlightened age.

'Are we not scholars?' A man's voice questioned the gathering and Will recognised it as Walter Raleigh's. 'Should we not question everything?'

'Even God?' A new voice this time and it sounded incredulous.

'I speak no blasphemy,' Raleigh told him, 'though many will say I do. No, I believe there is a God, a creator of the earth and all things in it, but is He that very same God revealed to us in the scriptures? That I do question.'

'You doubt the holy word of the Bible. This is heresy and you will offend God by it.'

'I doubt I will offend God,' countered Raleigh. 'The queen, perhaps.' And there was some amusement at that. 'So it is best she never knows of it,' he warned lightly and there were murmurs of agreement. 'No, I ask only that we be prepared to question God in the way a child might question his father, when he asks him why the world is so and what he thinks can be done to make it better. A stern father might rebuke that child but a gentle one would concede the boy was right. Are we not supposed to improve the world with each new generation? Has England not become a little more magnificent since the Romans left us?' That amused the men too. 'Or were we supposed to keep all as is and stay barbarians? The world changes with each passing year. Perhaps our understanding of God might change with it.'

'What if there is no God at all?' Will recognised this new and confident voice. It was Kit Marlowe, speaking undeniable heresy and shocking some of the men in the process. 'Or there once was a God but He is dead.'

'I will not stand for this!' The shouted protestation of one man was drowned out by the groans and catcalls of others, then there was the sound of a door slamming as someone quit the room in disgust.

'Go after him,' Henry Wriothesley ordered someone, 'and make it known I will take it badly if he speaks of what he heard.' Then he said, 'I think your words are too much even for us, Kit.'

'Nothing should ever be too much for the School of Atheists,' Marlowe chided him good-naturedly.

'Is that what they call us now? What a tiresome name. A handful of men engaged in a little scholarly talk after dinner and they would burn us. Whatever next?' There was more laughter at their host's dismissiveness. 'I think all men should be free to question God and the world, as long as they do not use this as reason to bring down the queen.' No one contradicted him. 'Her advisors, however? Well, that is a different matter.' And there was hearty agreement. It seemed almost everyone here distrusted or despised the queen's counsellors, and Sir Robert Cecil was one of her closest.

Will would have stayed longer to hear more but, at that moment, a door opened behind him and he was discovered. 'My lord?' The voice was soft and low but loud enough to be heard by Will and, more importantly, the men on the other side of the arras. Will spun round and was greeted by the sight of a young woman, her breasts still bare. Even in his panic, he assumed she was looking for someone else. 'What do you seek?' Her eyes went to the arras he was hiding behind, as if she was wondering what could be beyond it.

Will was already walking away from the tapestry and heading towards her, his arms outstretched, a smile painted firmly upon his face. As he drew nearer, he said, 'Why, it was you I sought!' and held his arms wider, as if to embrace her. 'And now I have found you!' He was deliberately loud because he could hear men in the next room questioning what they had heard. Soon someone would investigate.

'My lord?' She seemed to doubt him but smiled at his interest in her.

Will did not break stride. He scooped the girl up in his arms, causing her to let out a little cry of surprise, followed by a laugh. Will turned back the way he had come just as the arras was pulled back and his presence revealed to those in the other room. They had ceased their debating to look for an intruder and now they had found one. Will was standing there with a young, barely dressed woman in his arms, hoping he looked as if he were about to carry her off to bed. With a sea of suspicious faces before him, Will used his actor's skill to fake surprise. 'Forgive me. The room is already in use.' And he hoisted the young woman higher and she obligingly laughed as he spun her round and said, 'Come, Mistress…' Foolish of him to say it, for he had not yet learned her name.

'Doll Tearsheet,' she told him in a whisper.

'…Tearsheet. We shall adjourn to another.' And without looking back, Will crossed the room and urged Doll to open the door as his hands were full of her. As he went through it, still carrying his prize, he glanced back. He was unable to read the composed faces of the men who continued to watch him leave. Did they really believe this was a chance encounter, or would he wake in the morning with a dagger at his throat, or perhaps not wake at all?

Will decided to get very drunk then, the better to make his act of being discovered in the wrong place with Doll more plausible. This would serve a double purpose by quelling his very real fear that the men in that symposium might have him killed in the night. He carried Doll back to the banqueting hall where they rejoined a scene of complete debauchery. Will was not easily shocked, having spent years in the company of players who were not known for their morals, but this was something quite different to behold. Men were not bothering to go to a bed but were mounting their women openly in dark corners of the room. The hall was filled with the sounds of moans from lovers who had met but an hour or two before and were now coupling publicly. Will could just about stand the spectacle but would not be performing himself and had no intention of taking Doll to his bed. Instead, they drank then drank some more. Both partook of a colossal amount of wine and sack until he became quite accustomed to the scenes around him. He even found it amusing when one man finished with a woman and she stayed in position, to cheerfully allow a second to mount her and carry on much like the first. He did not recall a great deal after that and certainly had no remembrance of heading for his bed but he must have done, for he woke there suddenly.

Chapter Fifteen

'To tell thee plain, I aim to lie with thee.'
— *Henry VI*

'Wake, Master Shakespeare! Wake!' Will did so and with a jolt. A drunken Henry Wriothesley was kneeling by his bed, shaking him quite violently, and at first he wondered if someone had been murdered or if the manor house was on fire. Even in his startled, half-aware state, Will could tell the first light of morning had arrived but Henry Wriothesley had obviously not been to his bed. 'Wake, damn you,' he ordered, before scolding Will, 'Is this what it is to grow old?' as if Will was in his dotage and not two years shy of thirty.

Will sat up in his bed, wondering if he was about to be seduced by the drunken earl or even taken by force by him. How could he prevent that without ruining everything? Before he could think on this overlong, Henry Wriothesley said, 'Meet me in the Great Hall.' And he quit the bedroom, leaving Will more baffled than before.

The earl had woken Will from a vivid dream filled with lustful thoughts. In this dream, Will was on that same bed and Doll Tearsheet was with him. They were unclothed and pawing at each other, with the kind of abandon only the drunk could muster. Doll was encouraging him with base, low words he would not have expected from one such as her, for this courtesan had an aura that suggested she, along with the other women brought here to entertain them, would have cost Henry Wriothesley a pretty penny. The earl was there too in Will's dream, sprawled on a pillow at the head of the bed, watching Doll and Will, encouraging them to commit ever more lustful acts together. Then he had pulled his shirt from his body to reveal a fair and lean figure. Groggily, Will became aware of his closer presence, as Henry Wriothesley leaned in, first to kiss Doll on her lips and then Will on his.

It was a most unusual dream but now that he was awake Will suddenly realised he was not alone.

Next to him lay Doll, face down and naked, breathing deeply in an exhausted sleep. Had he actually taken her to bed and not just dreamed it? He must have done, but they had consumed so much sack he could not be entirely sure of it, even with the evidence lying beside him.

A thought struck him then. Had Henry Wriothesley been there too, calling out encouragement for their lewd and lecherous acts? Had they touched each other, embraced one another, gone farther along than that one kiss?

Doll stirred then and opened her eyes. 'Good morrow to you,' she said, with a warm smile and an approving gaze upon him.

'Stay here and rest a while,' he encouraged her, for he was trying to avoid recalling the events of the night before and needed to catch up with the earl.

'I will,' she agreed sleepily, 'but make sure you return to me and tell me about that play.'

'Which play?'

'The one you promised to write me into.' Will had no recollection of this. 'But make sure your Doll Tearsheet is a wanton woman.'

'Would you really want me to name such a woman after you?' he asked.

She laughed at that. 'I would not mind it,' she told him. ' 'Tis not my real name.'

'And what is your real name?'

She laughed again. 'You would have to marry me to find that out.'

–

There were men passed out on benches in the Great Hall and even on the floor. It was clear the revelry had not long ceased and the earl was one of its last remaining survivors. Everyone else was spent.

Wriothesley was sitting alone now at a bench, chewing on some food left over from the night before. He already seemed more lucid than he had been moments earlier in Will's room, when he was barking at him to get up. It was as if the young earl had managed to simply shrug off his drunkenness – or perhaps he had drunk himself sober by now.

'Sit. Eat,' he commanded, 'while you hear my wishes.'

Will did sit but he did not eat. He felt the sluggishness of a man who had gone to bed very late and risen early. Wriothesley, in contrast, seemed almost as fresh and energetic now as when he had begun drinking, nearly twenty hours ago.

'I need the services of a common man,' he explained. 'One who can mix with the lowest and most base without causing suspicion or alarm.' He pointed his finger at Will. 'You are just such a man.' The earl seemed neither to mean this as a compliment nor an insult.

'I am your servant.' Will always felt he had a knack with the common man, from years of drinking in taverns and mixing with a company of players, some from the lowliest of upbringings.

'But if it was known that you are my man,' Wriothesley said lightly, 'then your life would likely be forfeit.'

'It's dangerous work? Then why choose me for it and not some rougher man?'

'You have an actor's manner and a writer's eye. Who better to pass unnoticed yet observe all? You were not known to me until most recently or associated with my household, nor are you anyone of note. Do this service for me and you will be amply rewarded. Then we shall talk more of these poems of yours.'

The offer of patronage seemed to hang in the air. Will wanted to grasp it but, for now, it would remain out of reach, at least until he had granted his new master's wishes.

'You will have heard of Lady Celia Vernon?' he asked Will. 'A gentlewoman. She was the first to die of plague in London.'

'Yes, I remember.'

'There were no other victims of the disease of note at that point, only talk that plague was back in the city, carried by foreigners disembarked from ships on the Thames.'

'I had heard she was the first to fall.' Will wondered why this was of any interest to the earl.

'Celia was my kin. She was a Wriothesley.' He paused to allow Will to digest this information, before adding, 'I value family above all, save for my own name and its honour.' Will stayed silent while he explained. 'When I was a young boy, Celia was the only girl I knew. My father was betrayed by my mother, or so he always claimed, and he banished her from our home. He then swore to allow me no female influence while growing up. Even the servants were forbidden to speak to me. Celia was the exception, because she was young and still innocent. To me, she seemed an exotic creature, though back then she was more of a boy than a girl. She was a playmate and fellow conspirator in the avoidance of my lessons. She would open a window and leave it for me to climb out, then I would escape with her for a time and those hours of truancy were always worth the whipping they caused.

'Celia was my cousin. Not a first cousin but family still. Her father and my father were related but his estate was not so grand. Whatever prosperity her mother thought she was marrying into was largely gone by the time I knew Celia, but she was, I think, unaware of her meagre prospects, at least at that age. Her father died when we were very young and in the summer she would stay with us. This was a form of charity though it was never discussed. I took to Celia and she to me.'

In the recounting of his story to Will, the earl seemed to be lost in a reverie of his younger days. 'I do not think I even considered her a girl, though she dressed as one. She climbed trees, could ride a horse and was always running. She could keep up with me when we raced across the fields. We would read together in the library, sharing a love of poetry even at that tender age. Celia was deemed a suitable companion to keep me out of my father's way. He was rarely at home and died when I was but eight years old. The summer visits were permitted to continue during my wardship, until I was sent to Cambridge when I was twelve. She was approaching marriageable age by then and it was no longer proper for her to be alone with me, though I never had any interest in her in that way, you understand?'

Meat and fish. Perhaps the Earl of Southampton did not actually care for both.

'I graduated at sixteen, by which time she was engaged to Sir Thomas Vernon, of whom I knew little. Celia had to be wed if she was to avoid a life of low means, but I missed her and thought of her from time to time. I come to London often, to do my duty at court and see the plays. I learned my cousin lived in Shoreditch.'

'As do I, my lord.'

'I know.' The reply was withering, and Will decided to interrupt no further. How did the earl know where he lived? From Marlowe perhaps…

'I asked for an account of my cousin's new life and learned a thing or two about the man she married. This caused me to pay other men to find out more. Sir Thomas is seen in taverns most nights. He plays at dice, losing often. He frequents brothels but not theatres, is a former soldier and now a merchant of sorts who involves himself in trade. He spends like… well, like an earl. Vernon is one of those men who have few gifts or advantages yet waste the ones they are given. I also learned that he beat Celia regularly. That is of course a man's own business,' the earl conceded lightly, 'but there should at least be some cause.'

'And there was none?'

'They had but few servants in their house. The one my man spoke to talked of heavy blows when drink was taken.'

He leaned back in his chair and stared across the room. Will could see the regret in his eyes. 'Even then I told myself I could not interfere. They were joined together by God, and no man could change that. Then word reached me that Celia was dead.' Wriothesley looked like a sad little boy then. He shook his head, as if to clear it. 'It was blamed on the plague but I do not believe it.'

'You made further enquiries?'

'I would have done, but the man I entrusted with them was discovered. He made his interest in Sir Thomas too obvious and for that he too was beaten.' He said this almost in passing but it was clear to Will that the beating had been severe enough to ensure his man was in no position to ask further questions. It seemed Henry Wriothesley wished Will to take the injured man's place and ask those questions for him, a prospect that did not fill him with delight.

While the earl had been telling the story of his younger life, his kinship to Celia and her troubled marriage and death, men had begun to stir around them. Some woke from benches or the floor and sloped off to bed so they could sleep more soundly, while other more sensible men who had retired earlier came down to the hall seeking sustenance, recounting stories of the previous evening's revels. One or two even began drinking again, including Christopher Marlowe. The earl's eye roamed the room and settled on Marlowe, who was loudly proclaiming an opinion to a small group of attentive friends, drawing even more attention to himself.

'I thought to give this commission to Marlowe once.'

'He is perhaps more suited to the task,' admitted Will.

'Because he is a spy?' Will was surprised to hear the rumour acknowledged by a man of such prominence. 'Many have said it, even Kit himself, though I know not why.' Then he fixed those hypnotic eyes on Will. 'Perhaps he is not a spy,' he said, 'but wishes everyone to think he is. Or he *is* one but likes to make a game of it by shouting the truth in taverns.'

'Until no one believes it to be true, thereby averting suspicion?' offered Will.

'Marlowe is a great poet and a formidable man,' said the earl. 'He is fair but perhaps too fair to go unnoticed. And vain. Kit is a peacock, and they are loud birds. Have you heard their cry?' Will conceded he had not. 'I admire his talents and am proud to be his patron, but he is a vulgar and gaudy man. He flaunts his tiny wealth, yet forgets his position and is quarrelsome. It is said he could start a duel in a church on Sunday, though I hear he frequents them less often these days. At any rate, he is far from subtle and subtlety is what I need, Shakespeare.'

He seemed to be appraising Will's person now. 'I require a man with the common touch. One with no golden threads upon his doublet. If I commanded Marlowe to ask questions about Celia, it would be noticed immediately.' As if on a prompt, there was more raucous laughter from Marlowe's group. 'But you are different, Will. You are such an ordinary man.' It was not spoken as an insult, but the contrast made between the gilded star Marlowe and the dullness of himself in his plain brown doublet still shamed Will.

'Celia died by God's hand or man's. I must know which. Put yourself near to those who were close to her, until one of them allows the truth to slip. Then bring me proof. Do you understand your commission?'

'I do.' It was a reluctant admission. Will knew this to be a dangerous task but realised it could also be the solution to all of his problems. 'You suspect Sir Thomas Vernon is responsible for the death of your cousin?'

'Vernon is a rough and ungodly man, who bought his title but does not live up to it, in neither his manner nor bearing, but that does not prove him a killer. There are many vile men in London but they do not all murder their wives.'

'Did he mourn her?'

'Outwardly, I am told that he did.'

'Would he gain anything from his wife's death?'

'You ask the right question, though the answer appears to be nothing. All of her land and property, goods and plate became his on the day of their wedding. I can see no reason why he might kill her, but that is not the same as believing him innocent.'

'Was the marriage happy?' The fact that he beat his wife would seem to indicate not.

'I need you to discover that. In any case, show me a happy marriage and I will show you an ill match. Marry for love and lose position.'

'And did Celia marry for love or position?'

'Neither. The match was arranged by her mother but she was a Wriothesley.' He seemed aggrieved that Will needed to be reminded of this. 'I told you.'

'I meant, was it Sir Thomas's position that was the consideration here?'

'Of course,' said the earl, as if a child could have worked this out for himself. 'There was some land and a little money in the dowry but Sir Thomas would have been elevated at court by his marriage into my family.'

'Undoubtedly, my lord,' Will agreed quickly. 'Was there anyone else who might profit from her death, in her household or beyond?'

'What know I of her household, man?' His exasperation told Will it would be his task to look deeper into that. 'I am concerned with the manner of her death. I need you to examine it further and discover whether Celia had an enemy, either in her household or beyond it.' Then he added intriguingly, 'She kept more company than usual for a married woman.' But he did not elaborate and Will felt unable to probe further.

Will now understood what the earl wanted but was at a loss as to how to fulfil the task. 'But how do I—' He was about to say *disguise myself in order to approach her household.*

'Go about this in whatever manner you see fit. I simply require truth and justice.'

'You wish to bring Celia's killer before the law?'

'That might be possible, if you were to bring me proof, but there is more than one form of justice. If all the facts are known, it can be secured by a trial and settled with a hangman's noose. If they are not and there is still a damning suspicion but naught can be proved, what then? That's the kind of grievance that can only be settled in the dark, by rough men with clubs and cudgels.'

'But who decides upon it?'

'Someone who has control over such men,' he said simply, surely meaning himself. 'If you succeed, I will look kindly upon you and your work. I am known to be a generous patron.' And before that cheerful seed had even been planted in Will's mind, he added, 'Fail and I will overlook you.'

So, there it was. The Earl of Southampton's generous patronage was available to Will but it would come at a price. This would be a dangerous game and the spectre of Sir Robert Cecil still hung over any pact he might make with the lord he was meant to be spying on. With the theatre closed, his play about King Richard unfinished and likely to remain so, almost all of Will's hopes were dependent upon a patron. What choice did he have, then? If he wanted patronage from Henry Wriothesley there was no way around this.

'Then I readily accept.'

'Good, then it is agreed. One final thing. If you are found out, you cannot use my name to avoid a reckoning. I will deny you. I must. Like all great men, I have enemies at court. They will say I am become justice itself, that I have set myself up too grand, above even the queen, so we shall only speak of this between ourselves and involve none other.'

'I understand.'

'I hope you do, Master Shakespeare, for if you were ever to betray me, you would find I am a vengeful lord. It would be a pity to deny London the flower of your talent ere it blooms.'

Chapter Sixteen

'I was adored once too.'
— Twelfth Night

Will spent much of the journey back to London wondering how he could begin to find out what had happened to Lady Celia Vernon when he knew so little of her.

As he understood it, plague was usually brought into the city by outsiders: foreign sailors on board a ship or travellers who walked into London from the countryside carrying it. A man seeking his fortune there might be the unwitting cause of its near collapse, as tens of thousands died during an epidemic. So, Celia had been unlucky then, unless Henry Wriothesley was right to be suspicious and she was killed by another, perhaps even her own husband. How could Will possibly discover the truth of the matter, let alone gain proof? He would need to learn more about Celia and her household, but he could hardly march up to their door, knock upon it and demand to question them. He lacked even the earl's authority, as Wriothesley said he would deny him, much less the queen's. He would have to be cautious in his enquiries then, but who would know about Celia's household that was not still a member of it? Somebody who made a living trading with the servants who bought and prepared the food there, possibly? A certain someone who seemed to know everything that happened in their small corner of London would be useful, especially since that someone was also well known to Will.

–

'Lewdness!' shouted the man and he pointed at Will as he walked by. 'Depravity!' This proclamation, which was aimed at him alone in a marketplace that held perhaps a dozen others buying goods from its stalls, was disconcerting to Will and he walked faster to escape the sermon. 'The cause of plagues is sin!' the preacher shouted after him. 'And the cause of sin is plays! You, sir' – he pointed at Will again – 'are engaged in the devil's work!'

Had it come to this already? Plague had taken a bite out of London, so preachers were blaming sin as its cause, and the theatre for encouraging wickedness in the population. Thousands went to plays but few raped or murdered on their way home. Were Will and his troupe to be blamed for every crime in the capital? He hurried on.

Gertrude could have been any age between fifty and seventy. She hardly left the marketplace, except to sleep at night before returning there the next morning to sell more of her wares, but always seemed to know everything about everyone. Perhaps it was because everybody came to her. She certainly knew more about Will than he had ever told her. Here was the right place to start with his questions.

'Cheese, butter and milk, Master Shakespeare?' She said it easily, as if his order would not vary because it never had before. Their conversation would go easier if there was coin in it for her, so he kept her busy, asking for a little of this and a little of that, while he pretended to pass the time conversing with her, which he often did. Will liked to make a study of people of all stations, the better to recreate their speech and manner convincingly in a play. He wrote about beggars and soldiers almost as much as generals and kings, and prided himself he could pass time amiably with every kind of man.

Will commented on the coldness of the day as a reason for the lack of people in the market. Gertrude snorted. ' 'Tis the plague that keeps everyone indoors. When they do come out they buy more to last longer then scuttle home and bolt their doors behind them, until the next time they have to venture out for more.'

'Plague is a terrible thing and they say it will surely take hold here again.'

'It already has. I saw more dead lying in the street this past week. Most of us will be gone before it's passed.' She said this in the same tone she had used to price his cheese.

'What know ye of that gentle young woman who died of plague?' he asked, as if he had suddenly thought upon her.

'The first one, you mean, apart from foreigners?'

'Aye.'

'Lady Celia Vernon?'

'The very same.'

She shrugged. 'She was young and fair, or that's what they all said about her, though I thought her little more than skin and bone myself. She did have a pleasant enough manner for a lady and so did her companion.'

'She had a companion?'

The woman nodded. 'Rosalind, one of those who came with her from her mother's household. They were often together. I think her husband did not permit her to roam alone.'

'Her husband?' Will pretended not to know of the man.

'Sir Thomas Vernon, a knight of the realm,' she said scornfully, 'though no more a gentleman than I am.'

'You know him?'

'Half of London does.'

'And what do they know of him?' He had perhaps been too eager and detected a faint flicker of suspicion in her eye, but she continued anyway.

'A man of ill temper, who is most quick to anger. He makes his money from trade... for the most part.' This hinted that some of Sir Thomas's gains were more ill-gotten.

Will chuckled. 'And how does he make the rest?'

'Only he and God know that,' she affirmed. 'Or the devil.'

'A rogue then, and yet God took his poor, fair young wife instead of him. He does move in the most mysterious of ways.'

'Who are we to question God?' she berated him sharply.

Will pretended to agree most heartily. 'We are but His humble servants in this life and the next. Tell me, does anyone know how she contracted plague?'

'You seem most interested in the Lady Celia, and don't tell me you are going to put her in a play, for I shan't believe it.'

He had to come up with something to allay her suspicions. 'I was affected by her passing, though I never laid eyes on the lady. For a gentlewoman to die like that, suddenly and alone, why 'tis wondrous indeed.'

'It was,' she agreed, her suspicions seemingly forgotten, 'but it was in the air.'

'Wouldn't more have died of it then?'

'Some did,' she countered, 'but none more from her household.'

'How is that possible?'

'I heard they kept her away from the others. All but Rosalind, who tended her till she passed.'

'The companion you spoke of as being oft in her company? And yet she did not succumb. Where is she now?'

'Sir Thomas threw her out.'

'What cause did he have?'

'None,' she said assuredly. 'He never took to her by all accounts.'

'He dealt harshly with her then?'

'I'm not the only one would say so. Now he tells people he suspected her a witch.'

This was the first time witchcraft had been mentioned. If Sir Thomas really thought Rosalind had practised it in his household, then this was serious indeed. 'What made him say so?'

She was dismissive. 'She had a great knowledge of herbs, tinctures and unctions from her time outside the city. She could cure most things that could be cured and was sometimes called to help deliver a child.'

'That does not make her a witch.'

'There were mutterings about Vernon putting a young woman out to starve, so soon after her mistress's death. Only then did he talk of witches.'

'Know you where she went?'

'I do not… Why do you care?'

'I care for all gentlewomen with no roof over their heads. We all know what can become of them.'

'Aye, we do,' she said archly, 'when men prey upon them.' And he realised she was beginning to think he might be one of those men.

'What was this Rosalind's family name?'

'Rivere.'

'You have no clue to her whereabouts then?'

'I have none,' she said firmly and he wondered if she was lying about that. She folded her arms to show he should cease his questioning on the matter.

'Was there anyone else left from before?' he asked. 'One of the others who came from Lady Celia's old household perhaps.'

'There was a big oak of a man who never spoke. Isaac was his name. He used to go around with Sir Thomas, who threatened to unleash him on anyone he quarrelled with. I only ever saw him from afar and that was enough to prevent me from drawing nearer. He has gone too.'

'He left with Rosalind?'

'Before, I think.' She thought for a moment. 'There was a teacher as well. His name was Daniel.'

'What need was there of a teacher in that house?'

'That was an odd one. Lady Celia brought him with her as part of the marriage contract, though there were no children yet and she had no need for more learning now she was married. It was most unusual.' Her tone made it clear she also considered it improper.

'I'll wager it was spoken about.'

'There *was* talk.'

'What kind of talk?'

'Of horns,' she said with a twinkle in her eye.

'That the teacher made a cuckold of Sir Thomas?' He tried to sound gleeful at hearing naughty gossip from her.

'He *was* young and handsome. There was even talk that they were secretly wed before her marriage to Thomas Vernon, or at least promised to one another. Others said she was married to someone else. I never paid much heed to any of it and the teacher did not last long in the household. He was put out even before Lady Celia passed.'

'For being over familiar?' he asked, while wondering about these claims of a pre-marriage contract between them. That was common enough, especially when two people wanted to lie with one another before marrying later.

'Thomas Vernon said it was for his impudence, whatever that means. He went but not quietly. There was a brawl in the street and it ended badly for the teacher. Half his face is missing. Not even a whore would touch him now, let alone a lady.'

In Will's experience, people often exaggerated when retelling the tale of a fight, particularly if they themselves had not witnessed it. A cut would become a gaping wound, a severed limb was really only a gash, half a face missing might actually just mean a scar. 'If Thomas

Vernon did that, then he must have believed his wife had sinned with the fellow?'

'Perhaps. She was seen at your theatre once with a man.' She gave him a confiding wink, as if he and his fellow players were responsible for this. 'And it wasn't her husband.'

'What man? Was it this teacher?'

'Them that did the seeing did not see much. They did not recognise the man but they had not seen the teacher's face before neither. Nor will they ever now, since much of it is gone.'

'So, the man she was with remains a mystery but, whoever it was, he took her to see our play.'

'I reckon it was likely her teacher. It was your *Henry VI* I'm told, and when the play was done and most of the audience gone, he kissed her.'

'In full view of all?' Will was astonished that any man would attempt such a thing, especially if the woman was already wed to another.

'Not in full view,' she corrected him, 'but tucked away in some dark corner of a balcony, where they thought no one could see. But they *were* seen and God judged them both for it. Now she is gone and he has no face.' She said this as if justice had been done, though she was surely exaggerating the attack on the teacher. From half a face to no face in a matter of moments, he thought.

'Why do you want to know of her, Will? She is dead and gone.'

'The theatre must stay closed because of the plague.' He said it confidingly, knowing this would be of interest to her, for she dealt in knowledge as much as goods. 'It made me think on her, who was first carried off by it.'

'It did begin with her,' said the old woman, 'but many more will be taken before this is over.' She handed him his cheese. 'Soon they will not be able to dig the plague pits quick enough. I was here thirty years ago when twenty thousand died.'

'Was it so many?'

'It was one in four back then.' If the plague took a quarter of its current citizens this time, then fifty thousand were doomed to die of it. 'Those that can, flee for the country.'

'Yet you stay?'

'Where would I go? I'll put myself in God's hands.' Gertrude chuckled. 'If He wants me, He knows where to find me. Besides, if I leave, you'd have to go elsewhere for your cheese.' She gave him a gummy smile, then she said, 'I know a woman who lives across the way from Sir Thomas Vernon's house. Miranda is her name.' She told him the address. 'She would enjoy a visitor, I think, and has seen things from her window that might interest a playmaker.'

'Then perhaps I will call upon her, for I am currently at a loss as to what to put in my next one.'

'You can put me in it, Master Shakespeare,' she said happily, 'so I can live on for a time after I have died.'

'Gertrude…' He spoke her name aloud. 'Which means the strength of a spear.' She liked this. 'And what would you be?' he asked. 'Mother, sister, daughter, lover?'

She cackled at that.

'Make me a witch,' she commanded. 'Some people already call me one. Or mark me down as a queen, as long as she is wicked and full of sin.'

Chapter Seventeen

'The devil can cite Scripture for his purpose.'
— The Merchant of Venice

The widow Miranda lived alone at the top of a tall house that leaned to one side. Her high window overlooked Sir Thomas Vernon's much larger home and she could see into his yard, or so she told Will, whose visit she welcomed as if someone had prescribed it as a cure for her loneliness. She could watch the stable boy putting away his horse from her vantage point and had seen Sir Thomas coming and going at all hours of the day and night. Then she lowered her voice, leaned in conspiratorially and told Will how she had most recently seen the ghost of Lady Celia Vernon.

Will had heard tales of tormented spirits haunting those they had grievances against but had not seen one himself. On occasions, drunk, mad or overly superstitious souls had told him ridiculous tales of wraiths, but Miranda appeared sober, sane, God-fearing and not prone to excitement. So, when she swore she had seen a ghost, Will took notice of it.

'You have seen Lady Celia returned from the dead?'

'Standing by her window, looking mournfully down upon the street below,' she recalled, 'and I have seen her pace the courtyard, a restless and tormented spirit who haunts that house still.'

'You saw a woman. Why do you think it the ghost of Celia Vernon?'

'This was a lady who, in death, wore the same clothes she wore in life. I recognised her shawl, her bonnet and the hooded cloak she wore, while she paced the yard, her head bowed as if in prayer, a lost and tragic soul, trapped somewhere between this life and the next.'

'Upon what time of the day was this?'

'She was at the window in the evening. I saw her face and was so afraid I bowed my head then crossed myself and, when I glanced up again, she had gone. Her ghost was banished when I uttered a prayer. Her spirit was driven away by God's hand.'

'But it returned,' he said, 'and you saw her again in the courtyard?'

'Very early one day, as the sun rose. Her cloak was a fine blue, the colour of the sky in springtime, and it drew my eye.'

Will reached for his purse, drew out a coin and handed it to the woman. 'Show me.'

Miranda had not lied about the view from her window, which overlooked the roof of Sir Thomas Vernon's substantial house and his yard, which was empty. It was possible to see into his upper windows but there was no one there either.

'I see no ghost,' Will informed her.

' 'Tis the wrong hour,' she replied. 'Too early for the window and too late for the yard.'

His eye was drawn to a new figure who had just ridden into the yard. 'Is that Sir Thomas?'

The woman leaned forward and peered down. 'The very same.'

Will watched as a groom took the horse and Sir Thomas got down from it. Even from here, he looked to be a big man, towering over the young groom. Strong too, Will guessed, as he watched him dismount then march purposefully into his home.

Chapter Eighteen

'Ay, but I fear you speak upon the rack,
Where men enforced do speak anything.'
— The Merchant of Venice

Robert Poley was waiting impatiently outside his rooms, so Will realised he was about to have another appointment with the queen's inquisitor, who must be back in London, even though the queen was not.

'Don't keep him waiting,' Poley cautioned.

'Are we to the same house?' asked Will.

Poley smiled, though there was no humour in it. 'I am taking you to a bigger one.'

It was only when they drew quite near that Will realised what Poley meant by a bigger house and fear began to grip him. He even thought of trying to break free but knew that would be folly. The cause of his terror was the most notorious building in London, the whole of England, in fact. Will had never met anybody who had been imprisoned in the Tower of London and lived to talk of the ordeal. Most of its stories involved agonising torture on the rack, which stretched the limbs, or the Scavenger's Daughter, which compressed them.

'No need to shake so.' Poley must have seen the fear in Will's eyes. 'He wants to hear what you have to say. That is all. Unless you lie to him.' As they were admitted to the Tower, Will understood that this was both a warning and a demonstration of Cecil's power. He would only have to say the word and Will would never leave here.

This time, Robert Cecil did not bother to hide himself or mask his appearance in darkness. He was working away at papers of state in a comfortably furnished room, several floors above the cells and dungeons. When he rose, it was clear he was a man far greater than his physical stature, being little more than five feet three inches in height.

Will was a good four inches taller than his interrogator but no less cowed by him. A small man might enjoy exerting dominance over larger ones. When Cecil moved towards him, Will noticed something else that had been hidden from his view while he watched Cecil from a distance. His back was crooked and one of his shoulders noticeably higher than the other. Will realised he would have been cruelly mocked for this affliction since he was a boy, with many assuming it a punishment from God.

'I saw you by the side of the road, Master Shakespeare, during the Royal Progress.' So he had noticed Will, from within a crowd of hundreds that lined the street that day. 'By now, you must know who I am.'

Was there any point in lying? 'I do, my lord.'

'Then you also know the peril you are in.' Will decided silence was the best answer. 'But then we all are, in this state. Do you know what this is?' He reached down, passed Will a case and urged him to open it. Inside were two short metal candlesticks, a chalice, a rosary and a Bible.

It was obvious what this was. Will knew Cecil would not take kindly to a lie but he did not want to seem overly familiar with its contents. 'They are used in the old religion,' he offered tentatively.

'It is a secret mass kit,' confirmed Cecil. 'Catholic priests use these, though they are forbidden to, on pain of death. They move from house to house, administering the unlawful sacrament to some of the oldest families in the land, right under our noses. My men watch and they listen. It is not uncommon for good, God-fearing English men, and even women, to come to them and say, 'My master has a papist hidden in his house', and so we search those houses and do you know what we find?'

'Priests?'

'Nothing. There are no priests, no signs of mass, no relics or icons, nor any forbidden books. At first, my men used to punish those who had wrongly claimed the presence of heretics in their masters' households, but I asked myself, why would they lie? One or two ungrateful servants perhaps, but not all of them, surely? So I ordered a more thorough search of a noble house and that is when we found something truly shocking. Hidden behind wood panels on a false wall was a secret room.' He seemed newly affronted as he described the scene. 'This mass kit was laid out on a small table and there, quivering and shaking before my men, was a priest. As they dragged him out, knowing he faced his doom, he wished death upon the queen. He called her a heretic and the bastard daughter of a whore, with no more right to life than she has to the throne.' He shook his head at the depravity of the captured man. 'And so we burned him, as he deserved, but he is one of many. Most of Europe is against us and do you know why?

'In 1570, the Bishop of Rome issued a Papal Bull, excommunicating Her Majesty.' Will noted he did not use the word Pope to describe this Bishop of Rome. 'He called her the pretended Queen of England and the servant of crime, telling her Catholic subjects they should do everything in their power to remove her. Thousands think it no sin to murder the Queen of England and that God will even look kindly upon them in the next life if they do. When we catch assassins and they die in deserved agony, some even welcome it as martyrdom. I see it as preparing them for the pain of an eternity in hell. You look shocked, Master Shakespeare. Do not imagine I enjoy this work, but I assure you it is necessary.'

'I am shocked to learn Her Majesty has so many enemies.'

'I want to make England into an Eden,' Cecil continued. 'A perfect isle, beyond whose borders foreigners will continue to damn their own souls. But not here. England will be a garden without weeds or thorns, a place where an Englishman can be proud of himself and the land into which he was born. God Himself will smile down upon us.' He sighed. 'But my work here is far from over. There is a serpent in the garden, Master Shakespeare, and I intend to cut off its head.'

'A serpent?'

'The old religion. Only when we rid ourselves of every last icon, priest and blasphemous Catholic word can we ascend to our true state as a great nation, anointed by God. Until then, we need be ever vigilant, and where we discover the serpent, we must strike and strike hard. We cannot afford to be merciful to God's enemies. They fear only our strength.'

'I understand, Your Grace.'

'Good, because I asked you to watch the recusant Earl of Southampton so I may have proof of his treachery. Now tell me, did your patron speak of religion to you?'

Will had no desire to implicate Henry Wriothesley and rob himself of the prospect of patronage. 'No, my lord.'

'Never?'

'Not once, my lord.'

'What of the queen?'

'Only in the most brief and respectful terms.' This was not entirely true. The earl had indeed spoken briefly of her but only to infer that she could be won over by him, so he could wriggle out of his intended marriage.

'And yet he is a Catholic,' he reminded Will. 'Her Majesty fears regicide every day and always at the hands of Catholics.' Cecil tried another tactic. 'If I were to ask you to judge Henry Wriothesley, what would you say of him?'

'When I think of others, I try to remember Matthew,' Will said. 'Judge not that ye be not judged.'

'A message of tolerance.' Robert Cecil leaned forward. 'I can only imagine Matthew wrote it at a time of peace, but in this kingdom, at this hour, we do not have the luxury of tolerance.' He spat the word, as if it were a sin even to say it. 'If my father has taught me one thing, it is this. A state can never be in safety where there is a toleration of two religions. They that differ in the service of their God can never agree in the service of their country. Is that not so?'

Will calculated that disagreeing would almost certainly see him branded as a recusant by Cecil. 'Indeed.'

'So, give me your true opinion of Henry Wriothesley.'

Will knew Cecil wanted him to damn the earl, but perhaps he could accuse him of lesser crimes than treachery. 'He is somewhat vain,' he offered.

'That he is.' Cecil nodded his head in agreement. 'In a way that is most unmanly.'

'And he does enjoy the company of some questionable gentlemen.'

'You can judge a man by the company he keeps.'

'He drinks and feasts to a degree that nods towards gluttony.'

'One of the capital vices, gluttony.' Cecil was beginning to relish Will's words now, as if they might naturally lead to more serious revelations.

'I think he is no stranger to other vices,' Will suggested, 'though I did not see this with my own eyes.'

'What kind of vices?'

'Lust, perhaps.'

'With boys?' He was eager for Will to confirm this.

'I know not. There were women at Place House,' he added, in case Cecil thought every man there to be only interested in boys, 'who had been brought in for reasons of entertainment.'

'His proclivities are well known.' Cecil was dismissive of the notion of women being in any way to Henry Wriothesley's liking. 'As are Marlowe's and other of his friends I could mention. They are all Ganymedes, though you claim you are not.'

'I am not.'

'Good then. So, you do not share your lord's appetites, urges or religion,' he confirmed, 'and therefore have no loyalty to him. Tell me what was said in his symposium. What did Wriothesley tell the members of the School of Atheists and how did they answer him? What blasphemies were spoken?'

'I know not, my lord.'

Cecil's face hardened. 'Did I not command you to bring evidence of Henry Wriothesley's treasons and atheism to me?'

'You did.'

'And?'

'I was not permitted to attend the symposium, only the larger gathering that preceded it.' This was a partial truth. Will explained how he, Thomas Nashe and Walter Raleigh had begun the night with verse, then Wriothesley retreated to a private room with those closest to him, leaving out the part where he followed them and overheard blasphemous talk, as well as their obvious hatred of the queen's advisors.

'Who were his closest men?' asked Cecil. 'If I find you left anyone out, it will be the worse for you. I know your friend Marlowe is a member of the School of Atheists, as is Lord Strange. Also, the Duke of Northumberland, who is known as "The Wizard Earl" for his interest in science. I have heard he practises alchemy. They were all present that night?'

Will did not want to incriminate the men but it seemed Cecil already knew of their guilt, if that was the right word for merely attending the symposium. 'They were there, my lord.' And he felt the sting of guilt at betraying them, even with little choice.

'And Walter Raleigh too, of course?'

'Him too.' Will nodded his assent.

'Did you recognise anyone else?'

'I did not.'

'Did you overhear anything spoken at the symposium?'

He hesitated for a second before deciding to lie his way out of incriminating the earl further. His patronage depended on it.

'No.'

'Did you even try?'

'They left swiftly, the house is large and I had no way of knowing which room...'

'So you followed them,' Cecil suggested amiably, 'to see where this gathering took place? You positioned yourself by a window or hid behind a curtain?'

'No.'

'I instructed you to gather evidence against a man who, even now, might be plotting to assassinate our beloved queen. Were you too scared?'

'It all happened very quickly and I...' He saw the look of disapproval in Cecil's eyes and finished, 'I was scared, yes.'

'More scared of this Ganymede than of me?' Cecil acted as if he could not believe it. 'Come then, it is time you met the Duke of Exeter's daughter.'

–

Poley led Will down several flights of stone steps. The three men reached a grim, bare, windowless room dimly lit by candles. Here, Robert Cecil showed Will the rack. 'They call it the Duke of Exeter's daughter,' Cecil explained, 'after John Holland, the second duke, who fought with Henry V at Agincourt. He is said to have invented it when he was Constable of the Tower. It is still the most efficient method I know of for coaxing the truth from papists.'

Will was forced to look at this imposing device, a sturdy wooden frame raised from the ground that could easily accommodate even the largest of men. There was a solid wooden roller at each end, with lengths of rope tied to them. The wrists and ankles would be bound to these. A handle would then be inserted to turn the rollers during the interrogation, tightening the ropes and gradually increasing the strain on the accused's joints and tendons until finally they snapped. Word of the barbarity of the rack's torture had reached men in every corner of the kingdom.

'Imagine the pain,' Cecil goaded him. 'But of course, you can imagine it, can't you, Shakespeare? You are a writer. That is what you do.' Then he said, 'Get me what I want or you will imagine it no more. Next time, report every word of the earl's symposium to me, or I promise you will feel the daughter's warm embrace.'

Then Cecil said something that stayed with Will long beyond that night. 'Be careful, Master Shakespeare. You are a leaf blowing in a storm.'

Chapter Nineteen

'Play judge and executioner all himself'
— *Cymbeline*

Will realised that, of late, he had considered death far more often than usual. It now seemed he was more likely to perish at the hand of the queen's inquisitor as by any other method, unless the plague took him first.

When next in the theatre, he confided the details of his latest encounter with Poley and Cecil to James and Richard Burbage. The older man asked him, 'Does he want you to become magistrate and hangman too, since your word alone must condemn a man to death?'

James then asked Will what the Earl of Southampton wanted from him in return for patronage. He decided to let them both into his confidence then, informing them of the earl's interest in the fate of Lady Celia Vernon and the role played in this by her husband, Sir Thomas Vernon.

James Burbage shook his head in wonderment that Will could have inadvertently placed himself between two such powerful courtiers. 'Give both men what they need,' he urged.

'To do that, I must tell the Earl of Southampton his cousin was murdered by her husband, whether that be true or not. Then Sir Thomas will die for it. If I am to please Robert Cecil too, I must tell him Henry Wriothesley is a heretic who wishes the downfall of the queen, then he will die also. If I plot the course you advise, two innocent men will be killed.'

'Neither of those men is innocent, Will,' James counselled him. 'Considering them so reveals you to be the innocent, as well as the one most likely to end up dead. They would not hesitate if the roles were reversed and nor would I.'

Will could not decide if he was shocked by James Burbage's ruthlessness or admired him for it but knew one thing for sure. He could not emulate him. 'I fear I cannot do that.'

James looked as if he was dealing with a foolish child. He sat down heavily next to Will and Richard. 'They burned a woman once, for heresy,' he told them. 'My father brought me to see it, though I must have been no more than fifteen years old.'

'Why would he do that?' asked Richard.

'To show me the end of the path for sinners. He did it to frighten me and was most successful. I will never forget the face of the woman they burned that day nor the sound of her screams, even after all these years. Usually, it was an accepted mercy that the executioner would strangle the condemned with a garotte as soon as the fire was lit. Her crime being heresy, a stronger example had to be made to dissuade those who might be tempted to repeat her words, for she was that most dangerous of things.' And when Will questioned James with a look, he told him: 'A poet.'

Will understood immediately. 'You watched Anne Askew burn?'

'The very same. It happened at Smithfield more than forty years ago but I remember it as clear as any act I ever witnessed. Though she was a woman, they still put her on the rack first, tearing her so badly she had to be carried to the stake chained to a chair, for she could not walk nor even stand. I think by then she would have welcomed death, if it had not been by fire.'

He continued, 'A crowd will more than likely cheer a hanging, even while the condemned man still kicks at the air, but a burning? That's too strong for most. When the flames caught hold she screamed as if the devil himself was dragging her down to hell. The crowd called out as one to kill her then, for pity's sake, but it was too late. The executioner could not get close enough to grant that mercy even if he had wanted to, so we had to listen to her screams until they were finally choked by the flames. If I could banish one second of any memory from my mind and keep all others, however grim, I would choose that one.'

'Then why relive it now?' Will asked.

'Because, Will, there were points along the path she took to that burning when Anne Askew could have saved herself. By confessing, repenting or recanting her words, by pleading for the king's mercy before she was racked but, most of all, by not setting out on that path at all. You, more than most, know the power of words, so be careful how you use them and never give men of real power reason to burn you for them.'

'I thank you for your care but I am a poet, not a Gospeller like Anne Askew, and will bend with the wind if it threatens to blow me over.'

'One more thing,' James said. 'I told you she was racked but the Constable of the Tower refused to do this to a woman. The king granted him permission to withdraw from the terrible work, so the Lord Chancellor turned the wheel himself, with such a keenness that her shoulders and hips were torn from their sockets, her knees and elbows dislocated. I cannot imagine such cruelty.' Then he added quietly, 'It was Thomas Wriothesley who so enjoyed his work that day, the 1st Earl of Southampton, your new patron's grandfather. You will have seen his portrait on the walls when you visited Place House in Titchfield, for he was the man who built it. Now you know what that family is capable of.'

James Burbage stood up and walked away then, telling his son, 'You counsel him further. I cannot.'

Richard had no words of comfort for Will. 'Do not ask me how you can free yourself from this, because it is beyond my understanding.' Then he spoke to his friend in exasperation. 'You do not even wear a sword, Will, when daily you find yourself in peril from the likes of Robert Poley?'

'You think carrying a rapier would prevent Poley from abducting me when his master calls for it?'

'It might give him pause at least.' Richard almost always wore his sword, while Will carried only a dagger. Both of the blades they had used in their stage fight belonged to Richard, who owned several. 'You act as if you fear the rapier, when you should treat it as your servant, your friend and protector.'

'I do fear the rapier. I believe that one day I will die on its point.'

Richard snorted. 'Why fear that death more than any other? You are as likely to drown or die of plague… or hang for some capital crime or other.'

'I think it could be my destiny.'

'To die by the sword? Why would you imagine that?'

'Because of Knell,' he said solemnly.

Richard clearly did not understand. 'Why should your fate mirror his?'

'Don't you see?' asked Will, as if it was obvious. 'I joined the company following his death and only because of it. His passing created a space and I filled it. If Knell had lived but a few days more, the company would have still had him when you reached Stratford and I would not be here with you now.'

'I don't understand what that has to do with—'

Will grew impatient. 'Because I stole his life.'

'That's madness, Will. You didn't take his life. That was John Towne and he had cause. William Knell chased him with his blade drawn. Towne was defending himself when he ran Knell through the neck, which was why Towne didn't swing for it. It was a sad affair and drink was much involved but you were not even there. If anyone took Knell's life, it was Towne.'

'I did not say *took*, I said *stole*.' Will's frustration turned to sadness. 'Sometimes, I feel I am walking in the footsteps of a dead man, an imposter who did not earn his place in the company.'

'Maybe you didn't,' said Richard – and Will shot him a hurt look – 'back then, but you have since, a thousand times. Will, you have done every job there is in the theatre and all of them well, or at least passably so. You used to hold horses for gentlemen outside the building. Now look at you! You have written a play those same gentle folks paid to see and have acted in too many others to recount. If anyone has earned the right to fill the gap left by Knell's untimely end, it is you.'

'Perhaps.' Will felt a little happier for hearing this.

'And we all feel like imposters.'

'Do you?'

'Every day, before I walk upon the stage.'

'I did not know that.'

'A man does not like to admit to his doubts,' said Richard, 'or his fears. It took you this long to admit yours to me. Do you really think the tormented spirit of William Knell roams the earth still?' Richard asked Will, as if he was a child who was afraid of the dark.

'No, but...'

Richard raised a finger to silence Will. 'And if it did? Do you think he would blame you for his death and not, say, the man who actually stabbed him?'

'In truth, no,' Will admitted, feeling foolish now.

'I knew William Knell. He was a young and roaring boy, with a rage as hot as his talent. If he could come back to life long enough to blame anyone, it would be himself, for getting drunk and taking too much offence from so small a slight, then drawing his sword on Towne. It was likely to lead to the death of one or both of them and what a waste of a good actor it was, but you are not cursed by the event.'

'Did you witness the fight between Knell and Towne?' asked Will. 'Sometimes at night, in my mind's eye, I see Knell thrust his sword at Towne, before he loses his step then stumbles, just as Towne jabs at him with his rapier and it slices through Knell's throat. Why do I see it so vividly?'

'You imagined it, Will, just as you imagined the events of the play you wrote, without ever having witnessed any of them. You have the writer's gift. You see things others cannot.'

'Sometimes it is a curse.'

'Is Knell the reason you never wear a sword? Because, I tell you plain, you are more likely to die at the point of a rapier if you walk the streets of London without one.'

'I do not own a sword. Only a dagger.' And he placed his hand on the inadequate weapon he carried. 'Because of the expense. I need money for other necessities: goose feather quills and many candles, for I write late into the night, and thick, coarse paper is not cheap.'

'Wait here anon,' Richard told him before he disappeared behind the stage.

When he returned, he was clutching an old sword that was still in fine condition. 'Take this. No gentleman can walk the streets without a sword. There are a hundred thousand men in London and one in ten of them would slit our throats for a penny. When a man has ten thousand enemies, he must take up a sword.'

'I cannot,' Will protested, 'unless I buy it from you.'

'But you have naught to buy it with, save for money set aside for a greater purpose.'

'Then it shall remain yours.'

Richard shook his head dismissively. 'It's not my best sword and I have several. I know I can never use more than one at a time, yet I like to own them nonetheless. My father tells me I am a fool. Perhaps he is right.'

'All fathers tell their sons that, forgetting they were once young and foolish too.'

'You see, Will, that is why I enjoy your company. You understand everything. Now take the damn sword. If only to calm my father. It will be one less thing for him to berate me over.'

'Not without payment.'

'Then pay me in ale! 'Tis fair? Now clasp hands and say it is a bargain.'

Will reluctantly shook his friend's hand, then took the sword.

Chapter Twenty

'What, has this thing appear'd again tonight?'
— *Hamlet*

Once he had put on his new sword, Will told Richard he would walk a while and his friend offered to accompany him, which had not been Will's wish. He would have to part company with Richard before long as he had something important to do, but hoped his friend would let him leave without asking too many questions.

There seemed to be a bonfire lit on every corner of London these days, as the smoke was said to purify the air and ward off the plague. The evidence of the streets outside the theatre told them the lie of that. Three bodies had been put out here since morning, to be collected later by the death carts. This was now a common enough sight for neither of them to be unduly alarmed by it, though they still kept their distance. At least these bodies were not feasted upon by rats.

'They say a man was caught stealing from plague victims,' Richard told him as they walked, his mind clearly on the bodies too.

'What did they do to him?'

'Threw him into a plague pit.'

Will could not imagine anything more horrible. Victims of the plague were wheeled in carts to the pits by labourers who had to be well paid for their gruesome and dangerous work. All of them were given plenty of ale too, to increase their courage, but many succumbed to the disease afterwards and likely joined those they carried into the same pits.

'It was twenty feet deep and already half full of dead. They called after him to take whatever he found there, then buried him alive with his bounty.'

Will shuddered at the thought. 'Is that true?'

'It's not the first terrible tale I have heard of plague this week. A family not three streets from here was nailed into their house. By the time it was discovered there was no plague there, they had died anyway, starved to death before anyone realised the error.'

'Why didn't they have food pulled up to them in baskets?'

'They had no money to pay the men of the watch, and no way to earn any, since they were all locked in.'

They halted on a corner then and Will explained he had to leave his friend for now to head in a different direction.

'Where are you going?' Richard was suspicious. 'I must ask, afore you make another powerful enemy. You do it so easily when we let you out alone.'

'A woman's house. She wishes to show me something.'

'Does she by gad? And what will she show you, Will?'

'A ghost.'

–

By the time he had been at the woman's house for nigh on thirty minutes, Will had begun to consider it an entirely foolish errand. Then, just as he was contemplating asking Miranda if she had imagined the spectre at Sir Thomas Vernon's window, he finally saw her, the apparition.

Instinctively, Will crossed himself and mumbled a prayer, as he gazed down upon a slight hooded figure wearing those same clothes his host had described as belonging to Celia, clothes that were too fine to have ever belonged to a servant.

The poor spirit went about its pacing for a time, up and down, from one end of the yard to the other and back again. It did this perhaps a dozen times or more. Will was peering at it so fixedly that he forgot to show care and, before he could tear his eyes away from the ghost, it suddenly raised its head and seemed to stare right back at him. Will started and pulled away from the window. Only when he had composed himself did he dare to lean forward to glance carefully out once more, but the spirit was gone.

Shaken and trembling, Will left the room, walked back down the stairs and was immediately questioned by Miranda. 'You saw her?' she asked, for she could see it in his face. 'You saw the ghost of Lady Celia Vernon?' She needed him to confirm it to her exactly. 'It is her spirit, which haunts that house?'

'I did,' he admitted, his voice cracking, 'and do believe it so.'

–

That night they dined with Marlowe but, even in such brilliant company, it was hard for Will to banish all of his troubles. His appointment with Sir Robert Cecil and the forbidding sight of the Earl of Exeter's daughter stayed with him. A hundred times already he had imagined how it would stretch and tear him. Now he had seen the tormented spirit of Lady Celia Vernon with his own eyes and the world was no longer the familiar place it had once been.

'Are you ever scared, Kit?' he asked Marlowe. 'When you travel abroad, do you ever fear you might not return?'

'Since death must happen to us all,' replied Marlowe, 'why fear it?'

'Yet I hear it said that you do not believe in God, so surely you cannot believe in heaven nor hell?'

'No man knows what waits for us in death,' Marlowe explained, 'nor has anyone ever looked upon the face of God and returned to describe the experience. How then can any man tell another there is a heaven or hell?'

'Because he has learned it from the scriptures?' Will offered. 'Been told of it in church?'

'By an old man, who was told it by another old man, who was told it by a third, long ago, who also had never seen what happens upon death. I do not fear what I cannot know.'

'But you embrace danger, Kit. You march towards it and greet it like a familiar friend.'

'None of us knows how our days are numbered, Will, nor what waits for us at the end of them. The biggest sin comes not in leading a wild or ungodly life but in living no life at all.'

Those words, though they were not necessarily aimed at him, preyed on Will's mind, and when Marlowe was gone, he asked his friend, 'Do you think I do not live a life, Richard?'

'What do you mean?'

'I rise early and write, I learn the words I must perform in a play, I rehearse them, I walk the stage and act upon it. Then, when the play is over, I eat and drink, then write more before sleeping. Is that a full life? Is that any life at all, in fact?'

'Fuller than toiling in the fields all day and falling into an exhausted sleep come sunset.'

'My father calls it scratching,' said Will. '*You are always scratching that quill upon the parchment. It's no life for a man.* Until now, I paid him no heed. You know, I am the only one of my family who can even write their own name. My mother and father must make a mark. Anne is the same.'

'Anne cannot read your plays?'

'Not a word.'

'Nor see them performed, unless we bring one to Stratford. There is some irony in that. Will Shakespeare's own love will never know his genius.'

'I am so very far from genius, Richard.'

'You're closer than you think.'

Chapter Twenty-One

'If this were played upon a stage now, I could
condemn it as an improbable fiction.'
— Twelfth Night

Before they left the tavern, Richard Burbage asked Will how he had been dividing his time of late, for he had seen him less often since his return from Place House.

Will explained that when he was thinking about Celia Vernon, he was ridden with guilt for not writing, but when he was writing, he felt he should instead be searching for an answer to the mystery of her death, 'the better to honour her memory and gain my patronage, which would enable me to write more. You see how I am conflicted?'

'But how does the earl expect you to explain the death of a woman who was said to have died of plague. If all believed it to be true, then is it not so?'

Will admitted that he was equally confounded by that notion and could never hope to understand what truly happened to Lady Celia, unless he could speak to members of her household. 'Especially those who came with Celia from her mother's home when she was wed. One of them is the teacher, Daniel, who was mutilated by her husband.'

'I heard of that most barbarous act,' said Richard.

'He has disappeared and I have no way to find him.'

'Who else then?'

'There is another man, who also left the household, but he is mute. Even if I could discover him now, he would be able to tell me naught. Still a third is also beyond my reach, having been cast out by Thomas Vernon, and I have no way to find her either.'

Richard thought on this for a moment. 'What is her name? If it be a common one then you will be searching forever in London. If not, then perhaps someone has heard what happened to her. They lived in Shoreditch too. It is a kind of village.'

Richard was right about that. It was not impossible that somebody in Shoreditch might know someone who knew the person he was looking for. 'I should put her name about,' Will agreed. 'It is Rosalind, with a family name of Rivere.'

'What?' Richard almost laughed in recognition. 'It is Rosalind Rivere that you seek?'

'The very same. You know of her?'

'I have met her,' he told Will, then smirked. 'You have too.'

'Not I,' Will protested, but his friend seemed sure of it. 'When? And where?'

'Early one morning,' said Richard, who was clearly enjoying this, 'in the attiring room.'

It took a moment for Will to realise what Richard meant. Could this be true? The fair maid he had glimpsed half-naked in the theatre's attiring room was the very woman he sought? '*That* was Rosalind?'

'The very same.'

Will had walked into the attiring room that morning in a state of nervous excitement, looking for James Burbage. He had heard the theatre might be closed because of the riot and there would be no more performances of his play. He had to find out if it was true. Will had expected to find James backstage. He did not imagine he would walk in on a beautiful, raven-haired young woman in a state of undress. She was standing by a small basin of water, with a wet rag in her hand, wearing only a thin cotton shift and, though it covered her body, it was rendered immodest by the water that had fallen onto it from the wash cloth and a bright, low, morning sun from the window behind her, making it almost transparent. This was as naked a state as a man could expect to see a gentlewoman in, without actually becoming her lover or husband, and Will froze. The moment was burned into his mind in that instant. The woman looked up, surprised by the intrusion, but she neither moved nor tried to cover herself. Instead, she met his gaze defiantly and said nothing. Will stammered an apology and backed out of the room.

He finally met James Burbage on the way out and was unable to hide his jealousy. 'I saw your new mistress.'

'She is not mine,' scoffed James. 'That poor lady is allowed to lie backstage for she has nowhere else. It is an act of charity and she is safe here. From everyone,' he said, adding pointedly, 'except poets who respect nothing, even the hour.'

Will was embarrassed enough by this rebuke to mention the lady no more, nor enquire of her name. 'Is it true?' he blurted instead, changing the subject. 'Will the theatre close?'

'I have heard it to be so,' said James, and that was the moment when all of their troubles began.

Will had confided his embarrassment to Richard back then. Not only had he walked in on the young woman when she was near-naked, he compounded the sin by falsely accusing James Burbage of keeping a young mistress in the attiring room. Now, Will looked closely at his friend to see if he was jesting but it appeared he was not. 'You are sure that was Rosalind Rivere?'

'The same. She works as our seamstress and makes costumes.'

'Then why did you not tell me?'

'I did not realise she was of the unfortunate Lady Celia's household.'

Will could not believe his good fortune. The woman he could have wasted months searching all over London for without success was not only known to Richard Burbage and his father, but she was also the woman he had spent so much time thinking of. Could this really be the same Rosalind or was he deceived? It was the kind of coincidence normally reserved for the plot of a play. If it truly was her, then this was surely a sign from God.

Rosalind was as much his dark lady as any other woman who could lay claim to the title across the years. But where was she now? Richard had no idea, so Will left the tavern and immediately sought out James Burbage, who was watching a rehearsal, while occasionally calling out to one of his actors.

'I can hear you, just, but I am standing in the pit. What if I were in the upper gallery? I would have to guess at your words since you mouth them so inadequately.' The actor continued with a raised voice and James Burbage left him practising his speech to attend to Will.

'You remember some weeks past,' Will asked him, 'when you offered sanctuary to a young woman who slept in the attiring room?'

'I do.'

'Where will I find this Rosalind?'

'I know not.' Will failed to hide his irritation and the older man smiled. 'But I know where she will be the morrow.'

'Where?'

'Here. She brings yards of cloth to show me. I have asked her to make more costumes for when the plague lifts and we reopen, which will take her a while, so she had best get started.' Then he sighed. 'And she wishes to talk to me about make-up. I do have a mind to get her to make up Master Ed. If she can make him fairer, I will pay for the make-up and for Rosalind to apply it when we reopen. The prettier he is as a lady, the more arses on seats there shall be.'

'Do you think we will reopen soon?'

'Perhaps these reports of the plague are exaggerated.' It seemed as if James Burbage was trying to convince himself. 'How can they close the whole of London in any case? It's not possible. There would be no markets or apothecaries, nor any way to earn a living, and is there a point to life without a tavern in it?'

'None that I can see. But are you not too busy to meet a woman to talk of cloth and make-up? Permit me the task. I can be a good judge of whether young Ed is fairer after her work.'

'I shall permit it, if you explain why you wish to see her *again*?' James was suspicious. 'I recall you walked in on her once. Be warned, Will, Rosalind is most fair but too wise to be led into disgrace by a man like you, and I have no wish to lose my costume maker if she falls by your hand.'

Clearly, Will had to convince James his intentions were honourable. 'My interest in Rosalind is confined to herbs and tinctures. I have heard it said she has more knowledge than an apothecary. I must write of poisons in my next play.'

'You think the princes in the tower were poisoned?' James asked excitedly.

'I do,' he agreed quickly, 'at that evil, hunchbacked villain's hands. But it must be lethal yet tasteless, so those poor children drink it down unknowingly before meeting their doom.'

'I can imagine the scene!' James was both moved and engaged with the idea. 'There will be tears at that. Do it then and use Rosalind's knowledge of things rank and foul in nature to concoct your stage poison. Then we will have a play to present before the queen at Christmas, if she but gives us the chance.'

Chapter Twenty-Two

'I can add colours to the chameleon'
— Henry VI

The next morning, Will approached the attiring room cautiously, for he did not wish to be accused of violating the young woman's privacy for a second time. He even coughed to announce his presence at the doorway before entering. Rosalind looked up and all doubt left him when her eyes met his. The woman he sought from Celia's household was indeed the most fair, dark lady he had thought so much on of late. They were one and the same.

'Lady Rosalind,' he called, 'I am Will Shakespeare, sent by James Burbage to examine the make-up and yards of cloth you told him of. I write his plays,' he said, even though he had written just one.

Young Ed was already sitting in a chair, eagerly awaiting her ministrations. Rosalind herself, dressed far more modestly than on their first meeting, had laid out a number of brushes and bottles, powders and lotions on a table, as well as a blonde wig for the actor to try.

She glanced at Will before looking away. 'We have already met,' she said archly, 'but were not introduced.' It was a private rebuke without Ed becoming any the wiser.

'I recall and do beg your pardon. I did not realise you were lodging in the attiring room. I sought James Burbage.'

'But found me instead.'

He wished she would talk of other things. It did not seem to bother her much, except as a device to taunt him with now.

'You are about to make up young Ed,' he said, to divert her from the subject.

'Master Burbage asked me to improve the appearance of your Joan, the Maid of Orleans, for when the theatre reopens.'

'He was not satisfied before?'

'With your play? Yes, and with the performance of young Ed here, most definitely. He makes a very fine young maid, but I can turn him into a better girl.' And Rosalind placed her hand under the boy's chin, smiled at him impishly and raised his head to examine it more closely. She reached for a horsehair brush, which she dipped into a pale liquid then began to paint his face. The young actor was tickled by its touch and giggled.

'And how do you change a boy into a girl?' asked Will.

'We start with egg whites, to tighten the skin.' And she drew the brush across his face until it coated the boy's cheeks and he giggled again.

Will picked up a stool and drew it near so he could see more closely. Rosalind did not look at him, concentrating instead upon the task in hand while gazing at the boy's features. Will watched her work but was able to steal occasional glances at Rosalind's own face, while she remained intent on transforming Ed's appearance. By God, but she was as beautiful as he had recalled and truly the dark lady of his imaginings.

'Close your eyes,' she commanded and the boy did so, before she added a second layer. 'Now we wait,' she told him, 'for no more than a quarter of an hour, then I remove it.'

She used that interval to show Will the cloth she had brought and describe the costumes she planned for James Burbage, while assuring Will the cost would not be too rich for him. Will agreed the costumes sounded fine enough but advised Rosalind to agree a final price with James. He knew the theatre owner would not be held to a bargain made by one of his actors.

Rosalind took a linen cloth and soaked it in water scented with rose petals to wash the boy's face. Once the egg white had been removed, his skin looked tighter and Rosalind used another substance she had already prepared in a little dish.

'Venetian ceruse,' she told them. 'The queen uses it to banish the signs of age. We must apply it thickly to the face' – she dabbed the boy there – 'the neck' – another giggle as the horsehair brush tickled him – 'and the breast.' The boy laughed when her brush moved lower and touched his breastbone, beneath the feminine shift he wore.

Will waited patiently as she painted Ed until he was covered with a thick white mask. She surveyed her handiwork and seemed satisfied.

'Now we pluck and arch the eyebrows.' And when she had done that, she brushed Ed's hair back from his eyes and kept it in place with a pin. 'We want a high forehead, the better to see my lady's beauty.' And the boy loved that.

'Now we line the eyes with black kohl.'

Will watched fascinated as she transformed the boy's eyes into a maiden's. He was more girl than boy now, but Rosalind was not finished. She reached for a dropper and Ed leaned back. 'Drops of belladonna, to make the eyes appear bigger.' The boy blinked after the drops had gone in but seemed happy enough to receive this treatment, if it made him more beautiful.

'And a small mouth makes the eyes look bigger.' She concealed a portion of his lips with another paste. 'There,' she said, 'like rosebuds.'

'The final application is crushed madder root with beeswax' – she dipped a new brush into yet another bowl – 'which will make my lady blush.' She added circles of pale red onto the white mask of Venetian ceruse. Finally, she placed the wig on him.

'All done,' she announced, 'and my maid is transformed.' She handed the boy a mirror and he stared into it, seemingly lost in silent contemplation of his new-found beauty. He had been plucked and shaped, painted, dyed and bewigged. Now he looked every inch the girl. Both he and Rosalind seemed pleased with her handiwork.

'Tell me, Master Shakespeare, has there ever been a fairer lady in this theatre?' She meant the boy of course, but when Will answered, he was looking at Rosalind.

'Never,' he told her.

Chapter Twenty-Three

'I had rather hear my dog bark at a crow than a man swear he loves me.'
— Much Ado About Nothing

Will suggested young Ed show the other members of the company how fair he looked. It would be better for Rosalind if they could bear witness to James Burbage of her skills.

'Mind they don't ravish you,' he called and Ed left the room laughing.

Now Will was alone with Rosalind but for how long? He guessed it might be a while before the young actor grew tired of showing everyone how he looked but he had to use this interlude.

'Rosalind is a good name for a girl. It means pretty rose,' he told her, but she did not react to that. 'I am told your family name is Rivere?'

'Not a family name. I was given it when I was very small. They found me by the road not far from the river, so Rivere,' she explained. 'I was taken away on horseback, so someone named me Rosalind, from *Hros*, the old German for horse. I haven't thought on it but I suppose my name means horse-river, not *pretty rose*.'

'Perhaps I will use Rosalind one day in a play, if you will permit it?'

'Don't make me famous,' she said quickly. Ordinary folk usually welcomed fame, some even longed for it. When they discovered he was a poet and writer of plays, women often begged Will to name a heroine after them or even a villain, but not Rosalind.

'I do not think it will make you famous,' he countered. 'A good play might be performed no more than a dozen times and is soon forgot, but I won't if it offends you.'

'I don't own the name, so can't prevent it. There are other Rosalinds.'

'But surely none more fair.' He expected her to blush at the compliment, perhaps even mock protest, but instead she laughed at him.

'Do women usually believe such nonsense from you, Master Shakespeare?'

He felt foolish now but did not answer. Instead, Will told her of his play about King Richard III and how he needed a poison that might be administered to the princes in the tower without them suspecting.

'Hemlock perhaps,' she suggested. 'Or belladonna?'

'The same belladonna you put into young Ed's eyes this very morning?'

'In much smaller quantity,' she assured him.

'And how did you acquire this knowledge of lethal substances?'

'I have known of nature's darker properties since I was a child. I was always with other women and they passed their knowledge to me.'

'You were with other *women*? You lived in a great house then?' He asked as if he had no knowledge of it.

'Grand enough.' It was said almost defensively but he already knew the state of Celia's family's fortunes.

'What brought you to London?'

'I came with my lady when she was married.'

'And now you have your own money? From the work you do for James Burbage?'

She scoffed at that. 'You don't know how much he pays me. I should say, how little.'

'I do not, though I can imagine.'

'I am his seamstress,' she explained, 'repairing the costumes he's used a hundred times already. Now, I hope he will have me make something new.'

'And you paint faces?'

'I make unctions that add years to a man's face, so that young Richard Burbage can say the words of an old man. I make beards and paint them grey, to create the illusion of age. Sometimes, even death.'

'How do you do that?'

'I can make a face turn so pale the audience will believe the actor dead, until they see him take his bow at the end.'

'And your mistress does not mind that you lose so much time on this?'

'She did not.'

'*Did* not?' he tried to coax her.

'My lady is dead.'

'Then I am most sorry for you. How did she pass?'

'Plague,' she told him, 'not so very long ago.' And she gave him a look that questioned how he did not know of this.

He pretended to be thinking on the matter. 'What was her name?'

'Lady Celia Vernon.'

'I did know of this lady,' he said as if just realising, 'and you were of her household?' Will pointed to the sprig of herbs pinned to her sleeve. 'This is why you wear rosemary,' he said, 'to remember her by.'

'To mourn her.'

'And the memento mori?' He indicated the ring she also wore, which had a small cross fashioned upon it. 'For Lady Celia also?'

'I mourn no other.'

'I remember such sadness that a lady so well born could be one of the first to die. Were you with her till the end?' She nodded slowly. 'You were brave to tend her, but were the only one from her old household so had the stronger bond.'

'Not the only one,' she corrected him, as he hoped she would, 'but the only woman.' And she told him about Isaac, a sturdy farm worker, and Daniel, a teacher. He mused that it was unusual for them all to have come to London like they did.

'Her mother had told Celia the match with Sir Thomas Vernon must happen. She consented to the marriage with conditions. I was one of them, so were Isaac and Daniel. Celia's mother planned to sell her house and we might have starved otherwise.'

'What use is a farm labourer in London?'

'Isaac has arms like sides of beef and a chest like a barrel. If you saw him coming you would walk the other way... if you didn't know him.'

'And if you did know him?'

'As gentle as a lamb.' She smiled. 'Loyal too.'

'So he would obey his master?'

'He would never think to question a man whose household he belonged to. Given a task, he would do it.'

'What tasks was he given by Sir Thomas?'

'Simple ones,' she told him. 'Stand there and keep silent, which is easy for a mute.'

Will understood. 'He was used to frighten people?'

'If perchance you owed money to a man like Sir Thomas, then one look at the big ox by his side would have you imagining all kinds of things, and you would pay.'

Isaac's size meant he did not actually have to break bones, merely look as if he would, if called upon to do so. Nor would he be able to speak of this afterwards, so could never damn Sir Thomas Vernon to a magistrate.

Isaac was dumb but was he also stupid? Did he understand what he was being made to do and, if he was as gentle as Rosalind claimed, would he not be troubled by it? Isaac might not be able to speak but he could hear what was said, while Sir Thomas used him to bend another man's will to his own. Small wonder he wasted no time in leaving the household once his mistress was laid to rest. Most likely, he found a farm to work on, in return for food and lodgings. His strength would appeal to anyone who needed hard work done fast. Will would waste no time looking for him, though. The big man could be anywhere now and, even if Will did find him, Isaac would not be able to answer any of his questions.

'And this other man? The teacher, Daniel?'

Rosalind explained that Celia valued learning. 'If her mother permitted it, why shouldn't her husband, when he claimed to love her?'

'Claimed to?' She fell silent then and he did not pursue the matter. Instead, he asked, 'And when your poor lady died, did you have to prepare her for burial yourself?'

'It would not have been done, if not by my hand. I cleaned the body and placed the shroud over her. I owed her in death at least as much love as I afforded her in life.'

'Tell me, did she show the marks that usually come with the plague? I have never seen a victim.'

'Her body did show the signs I have heard spoken of.'

'Black marks? Like bruises?'

'They were like bruises, yes.' She seemed uneasy.

'But they were not bruises?' he persisted.

'If they were, they did not cause her death. It was the plague. The physician said so.'

If they were?

'You said no one would draw near for fear of infection.'

'He came to the house and to her room.'

'He came inside the room and examined her closely? A brave physician indeed.'

'He stood by the threshold. My lady was dead by then. She was beyond his care.'

'But he would have wanted to be sure of the cause of her death.'

'I told him she'd had a high fever and voided her stomach. Towards the end, she was no longer herself and became confused.'

'What about?'

'Where she was... sometimes who I was. Celia told me she was exhausted no matter how long she slept. There were swellings under her arms too, and on her neck and legs. He said it was plague and he did not need to examine her more closely.'

'Those swellings,' he asked, 'were they most certainly caused by plague? They were not lumps or bruises from a beating, perhaps?' And when she did not contradict him, he continued, 'And the other symptoms you describe, could they not have been a result of poison?'

'Poison?' The question seemed to alarm her. 'By whose hand?'

'The same hand that gave her the bruises.' She did not reply to that but instead looked down at her feet.

Will realised he had asked Rosalind a multitude of questions for someone who was meant to hold little more than a passing interest in the fate of her mistress, though she did not seem unduly suspicious. Perhaps she was simply used to answering questions from those she considered to be above her station and never challenged it.

'Forgive me,' he said, 'I admit to a dreadful fascination with the plague. I wish to know all about it, to avoid becoming one of its victims, you understand.'

She nodded almost imperceptibly, so he took this as leave to ask her more about her mistress. 'Did anyone else in Lady Celia's house contract the disease?'

'Not before I left it and none since that I have heard of.'

'How was your leaving allowed? Watchmen board up any house with plague.'

'My lady was stricken early. No one was appointed to watch the house or keep it locked back then.'

'Lady Celia contracted plague before anyone else and still, even now, there are not so very many cases yet. Did she come into contact with anyone the others in her household did not?'

'No, sir,' she answered quickly.

'Sailors returned from abroad, a person known later to have it? Did she visit anyone in the days before her death?'

She shook her head. 'I know of no one.'

'Then how did she become infected?'

'God's will?' He must have looked unconvinced by that. 'A bite from a rat perhaps or she brushed up against someone in the market? They say the miasma is worse there because there are so many people.'

'Yet none of her servants were infected.'

'I kept them from her.' And Rosalind explained how they left food by the door while she mixed medicines in Celia's room.

'What of her husband?'

She seemed to stiffen then, before telling Will how Sir Thomas left for another house in the country, as soon as he learned his wife was sick. 'He said he could not die of plague, for she had yet to provide him with an heir and his name would die along with him.'

'Brave of you to stay,' he observed. 'The servants too.'

'Not all stayed. Those that did go knew starvation was as likely to take them as plague.'

'But even you, who cared for Celia, did not contract it?'

'God spared me. I do not claim to deserve that but do not question it.'

'What happened to the body? There were no plague pits then.'

'She is buried in St Leonard's.' This was their local church in Shoreditch. Rosalind told Will that Celia was laid to rest in the furthest corner of the churchyard, where a small stone bears her name.

'Did many mourn?'

'Some came but none stood close to the body or even the grave.' Then she added, 'Nor near me either, once they learned I prepared her. I had to get Isaac to carry her out to the cart then put her in the ground. He was always loyal to his lady and placed his simple soul in God's hands, so was not afraid.'

'Was there a feast for the mourners after?'

'A paltry one. Only cakes and ale.'

'That's poor fare for a lady.'

'Thrift,' she snorted. 'A final indignity that the wake was so meagre.'

'Her husband made it so?' They both knew the answer to that question, so he moved on. 'Celia died when exactly?'

'On the fourth day in August.'

'One of the earliest cases in the whole of London then.' Will remembered the first reports of plague close to the river at the beginning of August. 'Possibly *the* earliest.'

'If you say it,' she conceded.

His thoughts turned to events immediately following Celia's funeral. 'Why did you leave that house?'

'It filled me with a great sadness to be in the house without my lady. I left the day after the burial.'

'Of your own free will?' he asked. 'You were not thrown out of your lady's home by her husband, who returned on word of his wife's passing?' She shot him a glance and he realised he should not have admitted to knowing of this. 'It was talked of in the marketplace. A woman was thrown out of the house. I did not realise it was you.'

'I would have gone anyway.'

'But he was angry at you that day.'

'At God, at the world... and all in it, including me.'

'Yet you were the only one he put out of his house?'

'I was the only one left from my lady's household. Isaac went on the day she was buried, his heart broken.'

'His future must be uncertain.'

'He is a big man and strong,' she said, 'also mute. Who would not want that in a labourer? Plague will take many men before it's done. There will be places for Isaac to fill.'

'And the teacher?' He wanted to hear her account of him.

'Already gone,' she said simply.

'He left freely to take up another position or was asked to leave?'

'I understand he was told to leave.'

'But not by your lady?'

'No.'

'By her husband?'

'Yes.'

'The man who also threw you onto the streets,' he probed, 'on the day after his wife's funeral.'

'He said I was bad luck.'

'He blamed you for his wife's death?'

'He was angry because I neither healed her nor fell sick myself. He said I must be a witch.'

'And are you?' he asked her, as amiably as if enquiring about the weather.

'I am not,' she said quietly.

'What manner of man puts a woman out on the street the day after his wife's funeral?' Will could only imagine how it must have felt to be a young woman cast out like that with nowhere to go.

'As I said, he was angry.'

'At God and the world and everyone in it,' he recalled. 'Including you?'

'Especially me.'

'And your first thought was to go to Master Burbage?'

'Not my first, but I felt it the best place to seek shelter with such little warning.'

'You had no money for an inn?'

'A woman on her own staying at an inn? How would that look? I doubt even a locked door would have protected me.'

Will did indeed know how that would have looked to a certain kind of man. 'But you felt able to trust Master Burbage?'

'I had mended his costumes and been alone with him before. He never took advantage of it.'

'He is a good man,' confirmed Will. 'And he gave you shelter without question?'

'There were questions,' she corrected him, 'and I answered them with the truth: that my lady was dead, had been buried the day before and her husband put me out of their house in anger, so I had nowhere else to lie that night.'

'Did he ask why the husband put you out?'

'No.'

Will was satisfied. 'I thought that he would not.'

'He chose charity,' she said, 'and let me stay. There was room enough for me in the attiring room.' She mimicked James Burbage's booming voice then: '*You will need to make me new costumes, Rosalind, for I will soon have a new play from William Shakespeare. You do not know his name now but one day all of London shall.*'

'He said that?' He could scarcely believe it but neither did he think her a liar.

'He did.'

'But not to me.'

'If he told you how good your play was, you might expect to receive more for the next one.'

'How well you know our game.' He was impressed that she shared the learned Marlowe's opinion.

'Men are simple enough to understand,' she told him. 'If you wish for a puzzle that's harder to solve then look to a woman.'

Chapter Twenty-Four

'The miserable have no other medicine
But only hope'
— Measure for Measure

When Will reported back to James Burbage, he found the older man preoccupied with the plague.

'Today I met a lady who is married to a physician. She told me of a prevention that works better than all of the others. Take a handful of sage, some rue, elder and briar leaves, mulch and strain with a quart of white wine, then add ginger, as well as treacle, and be sure to drink it each morning and evening. I have a mind to ask Rosalind to make up a batch large enough for the whole company.'

'Can we afford enough for the whole company?'

James Burbage thought for a time, then said in a low whisper, 'Perhaps just enough for the three of us to start with then. She can make it into a physic for us.'

'Do you know the quantities?'

'It was a handful of the leaves,' he said vaguely, though it seemed to Will that the whole thing was mostly leaves, 'and a spoonful of the treacle' – he frowned – 'or two. Rosalind will know. She understands these things.'

Was there anything Rosalind could not do? While James continued to talk of this new cure, Will found himself momentarily lost in a daydream of her, one in which the fair Rosalind was standing by a kitchen hearth, smiling at him when he came home to her. If only he was a free man. But it wasn't just Anne preventing it, there were the children too, and he wondered what it would be like if he could divide himself into two? One man could live dutifully at home in Stratford, as a husband and father, and another in London with his beautiful, dark lady. Two? He would like to divide himself into three, so that the third version of himself could spend every hour of the day writing all of the plays he had a mind to complete. If only he didn't need sleep. Then maybe he could get half as much done as he would like, before death finally dragged him off.

'Rosalind made up young Ed most fair,' he told James. 'He was indeed a better girl. Her cloth too was of good quality and will make most impressive costumes. I think she will need some money from you to buy more, so she may commence the work.' They discussed the amount James was willing to give her and Will managed to increase his opening offer on Rosalind's behalf, which he was glad about.

'I will get word to her,' James told him.

'Should I do that small service for you?'

James narrowed his eyes at Will. 'It is surely too small a service to distract the great writer William Shakespeare from the play he is writing for me.' Then he asked pointedly, 'He *is* writing it for me?'

'Of course. I shall write many plays for you. There will be histories, tragedies, melodramas and comedies. You shall see.'

But James was unimpressed. 'The groundlings know you for a history man. They won't accept a comedy from your quill.'

'Why not?'

'You must always give your audience what they expect. Your name is a promise that they will be delivered a certain form of entertainment. They will want mad kings railing in the wilderness. If, instead, you give them comedy, you will confound them and they may never come back.'

'But I wish to be a writer of all things.'

'No one can write history, tragedy and comedy. It has never been done, nor ever will be, and I shall not encourage it. Stick with what you know.'

'Mad kings?' he scoffed.

'And queens and earls and great dukes.'

'I know more of the world than this.'

'But who will pay to see it?' asked James.

'Everyone.'

'That is easy for you to say when you are not the one putting his living at risk.'

'Must a man be so constrained?'

'Is it so lowly an occupation to write histories for me when it pays you two pounds a play?' James sighed. 'You still wish to become a partner one day? Are you not happy with your life? When I first met you, you wanted to become an actor and did so, in time. Then you grew restless again and wanted to be a writer. When I permitted that too, did you already have an eye on owning part of my company?'

'Is ambition a crime now? Why must I be only one thing? An actor plays many parts, why can't a man?'

James surveyed Will carefully then, as if he was trying to get the measure of him. 'Do you wish to be a great man or a contented one, Will?'

'I hope one day I might be both.'

'That is not possible,' James told him firmly. 'Contented men do not need to be great, for they are already happy. Only the discontented desire greatness, for they believe it will bring them happiness.' He smiled ruefully. 'They are wrong about that, of course.'

'Can that really be true?'

'I have seen great men at court and none of them appear happy. Think on it, Will. Why do you desire greatness?'

'I wish to improve my life, my wealth and standing. I would elevate my children, so they may have no fear of poverty and can marry well.' When James Burbage laughed, he asked, 'You mock me for this?'

'I mock your choice of profession. If you wanted those things, why not become a lawyer, even a teacher? A soldier fighting wars in the low countries has a better chance of keeping hold of some coin than an actor or writer. The theatre has been shut for weeks! If the plague hits London hard it will stay closed for months. I will have to make a tiny sum cover all our expenses until we get arses back on seats, and I have no way of knowing when that will be. I *would* sell a stake in the company,' he admitted, 'but a man would have to be mad to invest now and that drives down the price.'

'You would sell a stake in it for less than before, now that the theatres are closing?'

'I might.'

'How much would this madman need then?'

'Fifty pounds.'

'You told me it would be fifty even before our theatre closed, and there were many arses on seats then!'

'I knew it wouldn't last! When things are bad in the theatre, you have to be ever cautious with your money. When things go well in the theatre, you have to be ever cautious with your money, in preparation for the day when they are bad again. I have seen us closed for riots, plagues, or on the whim of the Master of the Revels. A more troublesome and less secure way to earn a living I cannot begin to imagine. If God were to grant me my time again, I would start a tavern or brothel instead. At least they stay open, for now.'

'Not if the plague increases. They will be ordered shut.'

'The ones that can afford it will pay the watch to look for other rule breakers.'

' 'Tis true,' observed Will, 'there will be rules for most of us but different ones for the rich.'

'It has always been that way.'

'And ever will be,' he conceded. 'Would you really open a tavern or brothel instead? I do not believe it is all about money with you, Master Burbage.' He waved his hand at the theatre around them.

'I can still get lost in the story of a play,' James agreed, 'but only when the theatre is full and so is my purse. If I can't afford to pay the actors, musicians, scene setters, costumers and the damned writer then it is hard for me to enjoy the performance. It is funny how those same actors soon refuse to act if their own purse stays empty, along with their bellies. You have lofty ideals about the power of words, but you cannot eat them.'

But one day, I'll make you eat yours, old man, thought Will.

Chapter Twenty-Five

'Love looks not with the eyes, but with the mind;
And therefore is wing'd Cupid painted blind'
— A Midsummer Night's Dream

The more Will thought about the manner and timing of Celia Vernon's death, the more he began to believe it might not have been the plague that killed her. He kept coming back to her having been stricken so early and no one else in her street dying back then, let alone in her household.

When Will heard Rosalind was coming to the theatre again, to collect half her payment for costumes in advance, he made sure to meet her on her way out. She was going to London Bridge to buy from a cloth merchant and Will offered to accompany her there, explaining how he often walked along the river because 'ideas come to me easier than when I stare at parchment in my rooms.'

'I am told you no longer sleep in the attiring room,' he said as they walked. 'Where else do you pass the night?'

'Are you my husband, Master Shakespeare?' It seemed an odd question. 'My father or brother perhaps?'

'No.' He was bemused.

'Then what right do you have to enquire of it?'

'I meant no insult, Rosalind. In truth, I hoped you had somewhere safe to stay during the hours of darkness.'

'Then you need not worry. There is a widow who takes in, for a night at a time, but only women. That way she keeps from harm and so do her guests.'

'As long as you are safe, I shall ask no more.'

Her tone softened then. 'I thank you for it.' Did she mean she thanked him for caring about her or for not asking more? Both perhaps.

As they walked, he again asked of her former mistress, Celia, with the excuse that he wished to write a play about a woman betrothed in marriage by her father, who was most unhappy about the arrangement. 'When her mother told Celia she was to be married, she was not pleased by this news?'

'Would you have been happy? If you were promised to a man like Thomas Vernon?'

'Perhaps not,' he conceded lightly. 'How did you first gain a place in your lady's former household?'

'They told me I was found in the road next to the body of my mother. It was thought she had walked a long way, looking for work most likely. I was weak, hungry and not expected to live but Celia's mother took me in as an act of Christian charity. They fed and kept me for the night, and I lived through it. I stayed the next and the next and grew stronger. Soon, my presence in the house was accepted and I grew up there. Being the same age as Celia, though of lower birth, I became her companion as well as servant. There were not enough men on the farm. I reasoned they would be more likely to keep me if I became skilled at as many of the chores as possible, and they did.'

'And when Celia was pledged to Sir Thomas, he agreed to take you?'

'Not at first, but he wanted to be joined to her noble family. He told me I was an extra mouth to feed.'

'Could he not afford that?' The knight seemed prosperous enough but he recalled Henry Wriothesley telling him of the man's excessive spending.

'Money was always a point of dispute between them. He felt disappointed.'

'With her dowry?'

'He said it should have been larger for a woman of noble name, even if her branch of the family had been ill served by fortune, as he put it. He told her he should have asked for more to take her and a pair of lubberworts.' It seemed a strange word to describe Rosalind, who was surely neither lazy nor stupid, but perhaps he meant the tutor who, unlike Rosalind, would not have contributed to the running of the household. 'He thought I was an influence on his wife too. He said she should have no master but him.'

'*Were* you an influence on his wife?'

'I was an ear she poured unhappy words into.'

'And she was unhappy, not just chastised by her husband in the normal manner?'

'His form of chastisement was to seek fault in everything and always to find it. What she did or said, what she did not do or say. If he ailed, was recovering from too much drink, had lost money in a bad business venture or the weather outside was not to his liking, then he made all of this her fault.'

'I see. And what of Daniel, the tutor? How did he treat him, as one man to another? Better or worse?'

'Far worse.' She seemed surprised he had to ask. 'In the end.'

'How so?'

'You have not heard what happened to poor Daniel? I thought all of London would know by now.'

'I heard of it,' he admitted, 'and wondered if it were true.' He had also wondered if Rosalind would ever tell him about it or whether she, or perhaps Celia, loved the former teacher.

'It was true.'

'Sir Thomas kept you, though, for a while at least?'

'He allowed her to keep me, because he wanted something from me.'

'He liked the look of you,' said Will, as if it was obvious.

She almost snorted at that. 'I made his beer. He called me his ale-wife.'

'A phrase usually saved for widows.'

'I am no widow,' she responded, 'and he used to say I would never be married, for no one would have me.'

'That was a lie.' She did not react to his compliment and Will flushed. 'He had no one to make ale for him?' he asked quickly. Will would have thought that Sir Thomas Vernon, like most men he knew, would place a high value on the beer brewed at his home.

'When we arrived, the house was run by Goneril, an old servant. She was lazy and forgot about the grains when she mashed them. She left them to sit too long in the water before the wort is boiled.' He was beginning to question if there was anything Rosalind couldn't do.

'I made his shirts too and mended them.'

'Not his wife?'

'Celia did not have the eye for it. I was happy to do anything to make her master happier with her, but then he did love her less, and finally not at all.'

'So, you brew beer, make shirts, sew costumes and paint faces? You possess many skills, Rosalind.'

'A man can make his way prosperously through this world with only one, but a woman needs many simply to survive. I can tend the land, milk cows and goats, keep a house, cook, make medicines from herbs that will cure all but the worst of ailments, even deliver a baby, if the birth is not too difficult. I can read and write, speak some Latin and a little Greek, thanks to Daniel. I can dance a galliard too, but when I try to sing, birds leave the trees in fright.' He laughed at that, as she concluded, 'But none of that matters to most men.'

It matters to me, thought Will. 'When Celia's tutor taught her at her former home, were you always there?'

'I was permitted to attend the lessons once my chores were complete.'

'But Celia did no work,' he clarified, 'as befitted her position.'

'She was taught to run a household but outside work was left to others. Her mother did not want her skin to darken in the sun nor her hands to callus. She would be less likely to gain a gentle husband then.' She laughed bitterly at the irony of this, for Celia's husband had been far from gentle.

'So, you attended what portion of her lessons with Daniel. Half of them? Less than half?'

'Less than.'

'She saw far more of this teacher, who was a handsome young man, than you did?'

'He is still young,' she said harshly. 'But no longer handsome.'

'Sir Thomas caused that, during a fight, I understand.' She scoffed at that. 'You thought it an unfair match?'

'A teacher against a soldier?' She shook her head. 'I doubt it was a fight at all.'

'What quarrel did Sir Thomas have with Daniel?'

She shrugged. 'That he was in his house at all when Sir Thomas wished him gone.'

'Was he impudent?'

Her anger increased. 'Is it impudent to question a man when he beats his wife so hard and for such little reason?'

'In chastising Sir Thomas, did Daniel perhaps reveal a greater truth? That her teacher was in love with her?'

Rosalind flared then and Will expected angry words to spill from her, but instead they came haltingly as if she was unsure. 'I... he... might have held my lady in high regard but he never... that is to say, she would not have encouraged any act between them that might leave a husband...'

'Filled with jealous doubts about his good wife's conduct while he was not at home? Did he fear being made a cuckold in his absence?'

'I suspect he was scared of many things. He did not have cause to doubt Celia and Daniel.'

'Because she would never have encouraged any improper act from him?'

'Just so.'

'Not even a kiss?'

He watched Rosalind intently then to see if she was aware of this rumour, and it was clear by her flushed complexion and the way her eyes evaded his when she answered that she was.

'I saw no kiss,' she told him.

'Others did,' he countered.

'Others? What others? Where are they? Gossiping whoremongers one and all,' she declared angrily.

'Very like,' he agreed, 'and perhaps the same ones who claimed Celia was already married or promised to another before Sir Thomas came a-wooing.'

'As ridiculous a notion as any other I have heard from the gossips in the marketplace.' But when he did not immediately agree, she said most assuredly, 'I know nothing of Celia being secretly wed or promised to another man before Thomas. If he lives, then where is he?'

'A man is said to have kissed Celia in a dark corner of the theatre. Surely that came to her husband's attention?'

'It would be a brave man who'd bring word of it to him,' she said, sneering at the idea.

'Did he beat her for it?'

'He never needed a reason to beat her but she did not kiss a man at the theatre nor was kissed by one. It is a lie!'

'But who would start such a slander? Did she have enemies in her house?'

'She had no friends, other than Daniel, Isaac and I.'

'The servants did not take to her?'

'Goneril lost status once my lady became mistress of the house and all the other servants went down in station.'

'And your presence complicated the matter further.' Will could easily see how the arrival of a new wife and her well-educated companion would throw the order of a household out of balance, especially when the servants had their own ideas about how to do things. 'But would this be reason enough for one of them to start a rumour that could lead to a woman being beaten and a man maimed?'

'When people start evil rumours, do you think they consider the consequences or could ever guess what might become of those they slander? No, they want revenge and talk carelessly.' She was most probably right about that. A servant who is slighted might not see much beyond their own grievance. They could have started that rumour without thought as to how quickly or widely it would spread.

There was an alternative. Rosalind might very well be convinced of her lady's virtue, but Celia was an unhappy wife, who could have weakened if a handsome young man paid her attention, by taking her to the theatre perhaps; then she could have been caught unawares when he leaned in for a kiss. Perhaps she fought him off or even welcomed it? Rosalind might not have been able to imagine such a thing of her closest companion, but Will could easily picture that dark corner of a balcony now, where perhaps a few seconds of comfort were stolen, with little thought for the consequences. In truth, only two people knew if that kiss really happened and one of them was dead. Will needed to find the man most likely to have given Celia that kiss, and who better to have introduced her to a new and illicit pleasure than her teacher?

Chapter Twenty-Six

'Hear my soul speak:
The very instant that I saw you, did
My heart fly to your service'
— The Tempest

When Will first tried to seek out the teacher, he was hard to find. There had been much talk of the fight, with its cruel and bloody conclusion, but little thought wasted on the fate of its victim. There were those who considered Sir Thomas a monster, whom God would surely punish with torments at least equal to those of his disfigured victim, but others thought the fault lay entirely with the younger man. He had beguiled his way into Sir Thomas's house to provide learning to a lady who needed none. Most agreed, education was wasted on a woman, doubly so on one already married. Sir Thomas was seen as unimaginably tolerant to allow it under his roof for so long, whatever the terms of the marriage bargain.

It was widely accepted that the teacher was the mystery man seen kissing Celia after a performance at the theatre. Her husband refused to take her there and had forbidden her to see plays unaccompanied. When Sir Thomas realised the other man had intentions towards his wife and had already stolen a kiss, some said he was lucky to escape with his life.

'That's what you get for tupping another man's ewe,' said one man, when Will raised the teacher's name in the tavern.

'He won't be doing that again, will he?' laughed another. 'No woman would have him now.'

Eventually, Will picked up word that Daniel had found a new position somewhere, albeit a far lowlier one. This was little more than an act of charity, allowing the ruined teacher to earn his food and shelter in return for helping some children with their letters and assisting the man of the house with his labours. 'I wouldn't give that creature a place by my hearth,' the source of this information shuddered. 'He would fright the children half to death, for he has no face.'

Will was able to discover Daniel's whereabouts and went to the house that very afternoon. It was far enough from Sir Thomas Vernon's home to avoid an accidental meeting in the street between him and his victim.

Will introduced himself to the mistress of the house as a fellow teacher and she regarded him with suspicion, as well she might, in case he was one of Sir Thomas's men come to finish Daniel off. He had anticipated this but her fear of him was heightened because her husband was away on some errand. Her three young children peered out at Will from behind their mother. Will had deliberately arrived at the house unarmed, which was always a risk in London's streets, but one he was prepared to take, to avoid frightening the family into refusing him entry. Will appeased the woman's fears further by presenting her with gifts of bread, eggs and cheese for his 'friend', which would be shared with the family.

'He's out back,' she told Will, accepting the food gingerly.

He expected her to call out, to warn Daniel that a friend was come, but instead she told her eldest child, a boy of about nine years, to lead Will through the tiny house and out into a shared yard. The boy pointed to a man chopping wood with his back to Will, before he ran quickly back into the house.

'Daniel Russell?' Will called.

At the sound of his name, Daniel ceased chopping wood and his body straightened but he did not turn, just stood there, as if listening for the sound of a closer approach, but Will did not move any nearer. Daniel turned at last and the sight that greeted Will was every bit as shocking as he had feared. Most of the schoolteacher's face was obscured by a piece of black cloth, large enough to cover his mouth and most of the space where his nose had been. Though the material was dark, it was stained by oozing matter that still escaped from his open wound. Daniel's mutilated face was a flattened, misshaped aberration. Only his eyes were visible above the bandage and they peered at Will intently. Almost everything else was covered by the soiled mask, save for the top of the jagged hole where his nose had been. The material had slipped enough to show part of his gaping wound.

Will swallowed hard and forced a smile, but when he offered a greeting, his voice cracked and the words sounded higher than normal. The other man had to have noticed his revulsion but must have grown used to it in strangers by now.

'My master is away,' was all he said instead, his voice distorted by his mask and injuries.

'It is not your master I am here to see.'

The man stared at him for what felt like a full minute before he put down his axe and spread his arms wide. 'If you have come to finish me, then do it and have done with.' He sounded as if he neither cared nor would resist.

'I am come unarmed and with no ill intent.'

'Then who sent you?'

'I am here to speak with you about the Lady Celia but I am no agent of her husband.'

'I can think of no other reason for any man to come near me, but you speak of Celia. Have you not heard that she is gone?'

'I have.'

'Then who are you and why are you here?'

Will had been expecting his questions and had thought about the best way to answer them. Now, for no clear reason, he decided to mimic the words and even the tone of Robert Cecil, though this was not without risk. 'My name is unimportant but you may consider me an agent of the crown,' he said with as much formality as he could muster, while sincerely hoping he would not be challenged on the matter. He suspected that pretending to be an emissary of the queen would be an offence punishable by torture and possibly even death, but he could think of no other way to convince the man to answer his questions.

'And what would an agent of the queen want from me? I am but half a man and the woman you enquire of is dead. She died of the plague.'

'Did she?'

'Did she not?' He sounded genuinely surprised by Will's question.

'That is what I am here to conclude. Now, if you will answer my questions, I can be on my way.'

He seemed to accept this. 'Ask them then.'

'Why did Celia's husband quarrel with you?'

'He never did like me, nor my presence in his house, from the beginning.'

'Because you were close to Celia?'

'That and an expense to him. Thomas said I was a drain on his household. He claimed to have been confounded by Celia. Her reluctance to marry led him to give way on the matter of her household. He said as much to me and more to Celia.'

'He took four of you, when all he actually wanted was a bride?'

'But he got a bargain. Isaac is strong as an ox and Rosalind could cook, clean and brew beer. They repaid the price of their food and lodging a thousand times over, and he knew that but would not admit it.'

'You on the other hand are a teacher whose presence in his home he resented?'

'I brought no talent with me,' he said flatly, 'just the knowledge acquired from my own studies, which I passed to his wife. I had hoped I would find myself in a home where learning might be regarded as a virtue, but Sir Thomas cares not for book learning nor any lesson that does not improve his fortunes in business. He has no interest in Greek, Latin, philosophy or history, and to him, music, plays, poetry, all have no value.'

Will privately placed another black mark against Sir Thomas's name. 'Why then did he allow you to carry on tutoring his wife?'

'Celia had a written agreement with his mark on it before she consented to be his wife.'

'Did you not consider leaving, since he resented you so?'

'And go where? I knew of no other households that wanted a teacher and if there were some, I had no letters of introduction nor friends at court. I would likely have starved for want of a position.'

'But you defied him anyway?'

'One night, he beat Celia so badly she did not rise in the morning. He was drunk on sack again and angry at Celia for being less than he hoped she would be.'

'In what way?'

'In every way. She was neither fair nor wise but too handsome to be allowed to roam the streets alone, even in daylight, for he did not trust her to stay true to him. She was too educated to listen to her husband or obey him, and the fault for that was mine, as well as hers. She brought her own money to the marriage but not enough, and the land he was promised was not to his liking, for it was prone to flooding. He pronounced her ugly but when he wanted her, she was not quick enough nor joyous enough in the yielding. Rosalind was a bad companion for her too and I was worse.'

'What did you say to him that caused him to fly into a rage?'

'That morning, when Rosalind described the condition of her mistress, beaten all over and sick in bed from her injuries, I told him that God would judge him if he struck her like that again. He grabbed me then and threw me into the street.'

'Is that when the fight began?'

'It was no fight. If you have heard it was, then the teller of the tale was not there. No man who witnessed it could have described it so.'

'He attacked you then?'

'The first blow came from behind and I fell to the ground. He never allowed me back up. He struck me with blow after blow and I was powerless to prevent them, having neither the strength nor the skill to fight him off. I wish I could say that I gave a good account of myself. That, being in a quarrel I did not seek, I was at least able to make my opponent regret he had started it.' He shook his head sadly. 'I don't believe I landed a single blow of any consequence. I could hear the voices of people in the street urging him to leave me be, but he was determined to destroy me and he did.'

'You see this?' He pointed to the bandage. 'He used his teeth to tear my flesh from me. What manner of man is able to do such a thing, while God looks down upon him?' Recalling the act made him shake now, as if the assault upon him had happened anew. 'I cannot describe the pain and terror I felt. He chewed the flesh he had torn from my face then spat it onto the ground and stamped his boot upon it to grind it into the earth. He did that so no physician could ever have hoped to sew it back on.'

'And he did this to you for such a small offence, chastising him about the treatment of his wife?'

'Aye, 'twas all.'

'And you yourself never laid a hand upon his wife?'

'Never. If men are saying that, then it is a lie he has put about to explain his cruelty. I could not and would not have done so.'

'But you did love her?' Will asked.

'Who told you that?' His eyes betrayed his alarm.

'It is obvious. You came with her to London, instead of seeking out another position elsewhere, even though she was a married woman and there was no future for you. Her mother could have written you letters of introduction but you chose to follow Celia, blindly.'

'I did love her once,' he admitted, 'but she was the ruin of me.'

'Surely that was her husband. Do you blame Celia for your injury?'

'My injury?' He scoffed at the lightness of the word. 'Do I limp? Am I lacking the use of a hand? That would be an injury. He turned me into a monster. I was a teacher yet now I am so malformed children throw stones at me in the street and dogs bark at me as I pass by. I am an abomination and though I still walk on God's earth, it is as if I am in hell already.' He waved his hand at the house. 'If it were not for this good lady and her husband's charity, I would have starved to death on the streets. There are many days when I would that I had.'

'And yet you live still,' Will reminded him. 'You have purpose, with three young children to teach. There is a warm house to lay your head by its hearth at the end of each day. That's more than can be said for many in London. It's more than can be said for Celia. Do you blame her still?'

'Yes!' he said angrily. 'For bewitching me, for making me love her when I could never have her! For turning me into a fool, who challenged a man full of evil, and all to defend Celia. I lost everything because of her!' Tears formed in his eyes and he wiped them angrily away before letting out a loud wail of frustration. The exertion of this seemed to take all of his energy and much of his anger with it and his body slumped.

'No.' He shook his head to contradict himself. 'I do not blame her. Not fair, sweet and kind Celia, who could no more sin against me than I could against her. The memory of the years I spent in her company is all that sustains me now and I mourn her loss each day. I blame myself, not her, for my foolishness in setting my eye on a woman above my state, even if I did nothing about that, except follow her once she was wed. That was a folly I have repented over and over. I did love her but never shamed her or myself with any act that ought not pass between a pupil and her teacher.'

'Not even a kiss?'

'It was not I.'

'Yet you have heard it said that she was kissed? Who by, then?'

'I do not believe it happened.'

Will realised that, even now, Daniel did not wish to entertain the notion of his beloved Celia being kissed by another.

'But you attended plays with her?' Will did not know this for sure but thought it likely. Celia would have had to attend them with someone, if she did not wish to draw attention to her person or risk being grabbed by a member of the crowd.

'Once or twice.'

'Which is it?'

'Three times then.'

'But you still deny the kiss? Why, when it can be the only explanation?'

'Because it did not happen, upon my honour and hers.'

'And you never declared your love to her, not once?'

He seemed torn between telling the truth of what had happened between himself and Celia, even to a stranger, and the wisdom of keeping his own counsel. 'I wrote it down once, when we were younger and before she was promised to any man.'

'You wrote her love poetry? How did she receive it?'

'Not well,' he admitted, 'nor badly. I hoped... I know not what I hoped for.' It was as if he was trying to recall the thoughts and motives of a much younger man in a more innocent time. 'Perhaps, for her to return my love and then for some miracle that might see us bound together as man and wife, though I must have surely known even then that it would never be possible.'

'Did she return your love?'

'She expressly told me she had no love for me other than that owed to a respected teacher and perhaps a friend or brother. Her words were gentle but took all my hopes with them. I expected she would ask me to leave her house, or her mother would.'

That seemed the likeliest course. 'Celia did not tell her?'

'She burned my declaration of love. Her mother found the scraps of parchment in the hearth and I said it was workings we had finished with. She believed I was without sin where her daughter was concerned, though a thousand times in my mind I had imagined being with her in a way only a husband could. God saw my thoughts then and punished me for them. I accepted a position in her new household, so I could remain close to her. That was a sin,' he admitted, 'if only in thought. God tempted me and I failed. He placed me near the cruellest man in London, who left me with a reminder of my vanity and sinful nature. I was not content with all that a bounteous God had given me – food, shelter, a position and some knowledge – so He punished me for it. I see that now and am ashamed.'

'Did you have any contact with Celia after you left?'

'And have her see me like this?' He shook his head. 'I could not have borne her pity or disgust.'

'What of others in her household? Rosalind or Isaac?'

He snorted. 'Isaac is poor company: he is mute. As for Rosalind, I know she saw me for who I truly am and considered me a fool for ever believing Celia could love me.'

'So, the next you heard of Celia was when news of her death reached you?'

'A lady dying of plague when there was said to be none in London? That travelled quickly. I think I knew it was Celia, even before I heard her name uttered. I know not why but always thought she might not be long in this world.'

'Because of her husband?'

'I thought marriage to him might kill her before long but it was plague that took her.' A deep sadness seemed to weigh on Daniel then and Will decided to end his questions before he distressed the man further. He offered sympathy, both for the loss of his lady and reduced position, then bid Daniel farewell. But the man seemed lost in his own thoughts, so Will walked quietly away. He was almost back in the house before the teacher realised he was about to leave.

'Good sir!' he called and Will turned back to him. 'Do not attempt to scorn or confound Sir Thomas Vernon, nor get between him and what he considers his. It will not end well for you.' And before Will could reply, Daniel reached behind his own head and unfastened the material of the mask he wore, then let it slide away. Will was confronted by a sight so awful he wanted to tear his own eyes from it but could not, thanks to the grim fascination he felt for the terrible injury. The edges of a ragged, torn and fleshy, imperfect circle of skin were made slippery by the matter escaping from a hole where Daniel's nose had once been.

Chapter Twenty-Seven

'The first thing we do, let's kill all the lawyers.'
— Henry VI

Will was badly shaken by his visit to Celia's former teacher. He knew he would never be able to banish the vision of the hole in the man's face from his memory and prayed he would never fall as low as Daniel had. He could not imagine how the man went from the start of each day to its end. He resolved not to talk of it to the others when he returned to the theatre, claiming only to have spent the morning writing. This seemed to please James Burbage at least, who broke free from the stage, where he was in the process of granting new musicians the opportunity to perform in a bid to join his company once the theatre reopened. 'Continue, Richard.' He instructed his son, who gave a nervous young lute player a signal to begin.

'I have learned a little of this Sir Thomas Vernon,' James told Will, as he led him away from the stage, though they stayed close enough to hear as the music began.

'What type of man is he?' asked Will, though he was sure he knew already.

'The kind with a name and coat of arms but only a little money,' he replied, 'and a Latin motto that discredits him to all who hear it. *Homo Homini Lupus* – a man is a wolf to another man.'

'That is Sir Thomas's motto? Sounds more like a warning.'

'Then perhaps you should heed it and stay away from him. He is not a good nor a godly man and known to cheat those he enters into business with. I am acquainted with a Lincoln's Inn lawyer who has some knowledge of Sir Thomas. He is a most litigious man, a complainant who is himself most complained against.' He explained how this lawyer dealt with a case against Sir Thomas from Celia's mother, pertaining to their marriage. 'I think he did not mourn his lost wife long.'

'Why would he not mourn the loss of her good name, if not the lady herself?'

'Because her name alone did not bring him favour from the queen. He thought he was marrying a close relative of the Earl of Southampton, but she was in fact a lowly member of that family, impoverished by Wriothesley standards and not at all known by the queen.' A thought seemed to strike him then. 'It would seem that Celia's mother did to Sir Thomas what he himself may have done to so many others: sold him something of less value than he paid for it.'

The lute player had seemed nervous at first, but his skills were no longer in doubt. He was filling the theatre with a delicate, pleasing sound and the notes he had chosen were welcome as they lightened Will's mood.

'Is it not usual for the groom's family to receive a dowry and not the other way around?'

James explained that Lady Celia was marrying beneath her position, so something had to be done to encourage this. Celia did come with a dowry of a little land and a small sum of money but it was her status he most desired. 'He needed a wife to run his household and provide him with an heir,' said James. 'And he already had some money, so why not aim for a lady with a name and be elevated?' It was agreed that he would pay her mother a sum to make up for the difference in their positions and settle her in her old age, but the case came about because he withheld the largest part of it. 'He complained his wife was not the woman he had been promised.'

'He claimed Celia was not pure?'

'There was talk of that but as for who started it?' He shrugged. 'Celia was assumed a maiden when they were wed. Afterwards he said she was a cold and reluctant wife, unable to give him a child. He claimed an heir to be a condition of the payment he had promised her mother.' James had been told that Celia's mother petitioned the queen but it became one of many claims lost in a long line of disputes, suits and calumnies daily argued over in Her Majesty's court. Most of them never even reached her. A woman in particular could wait years for her grievance to be heard. 'When Celia died, the point became of no importance and this reversed dowry was never paid.'

Richard Burbage had heard enough of the lute player to satisfy him. Whatever was spoken between them seemed to satisfy the young man who nodded his thanks before leaving. Now Richard called a cornet player forward to take his place upon the stage.

'I heard another story about Sir Thomas Vernon,' James told him. 'He was a soldier before he became a merchant. When he thought it to his advantage, he would join the campaign of a powerful lord. He fought as an officer under Robert Devereaux, the Earl of Essex, who was the queen's favourite.' James told Will how they had struggled to break the siege of Rouen, and Sir Thomas had suggested killing plague dogs then firing them into the city from a catapult. This was a new kind of warfare that could kill an enemy without ever having to meet them in battle or even seeing their faces. But, the idea was not well received by the Earl of Essex, who yearned for the glory of battle and despised the notion of deliberately killing men with a disease. With his service no longer desired, Sir Thomas had left the campaign.

'How does one recognise a plague dog?' wondered Will. 'Or catch one without getting the plague?'

'I have no idea,' admitted James Burbage, 'but that was his plan and the earl liked it not.'

The cornet player had barely begun before Richard stopped him, to give new words of instruction before letting him play once more, but the sound he produced was not of the required standard for a company whose plays were always filled with music from lutes and cornets, viols, fifes and spinets. It was not long before Richard stopped the man again. After his third attempt to fashion a pleasing tune, Richard lost patience with the cornet player and banished him from the stage. James had winced at the sound he made and did not disapprove of his son's actions.

'Speaking of earls,' he said, 'I have information that might be of even greater interest to you, Will. It concerns Henry Wriothesley, the Earl of Southampton. With the queen gone, I have lately been in discussion with men left behind at court, disguising my interest in him. Instead of "What know you of the Earl of Southampton?", I cloak my question thus: "That Henry Wriothesley is a confirmed favourite of the queen, is he not?" The man I asked this of replied, "So he is, for now," and then, thanks to my feigned curiosity, he told me things about the earl, not least the reason Robert Cecil hates him so.'

'Because the earl is a recusant?'

'Not so.'

'They are enemies,' said Will helplessly, 'this much I do know.'

'It was not always so,' replied Burbage. 'Once they were like brothers. They even grew up under the same roof, though there is ten years between them.'

Another young man emerged then carrying a bandora. He addressed Richard Burbage confidently then began to play the stringed instrument for him, creating a deeper sound than the lute player, which was no less pleasing to the ear.

James nodded in recognition of the musician's skill then continued. 'When Wriothesley was eight years old and Robert Cecil eighteen, young Henry's father died, so he went to live at Cecil House on the Strand. For four years, he was under the care of Robert's father, William Cecil, who hired the finest tutors for the lad and sent him to Cambridge when he was twelve. He had an eye on the boy's future.' Robert Cecil's father must have viewed the money he spent on young Henry as an investment.

James explained how William Cecil also had a daughter, Anne, who in turn had a daughter herself. He had arranged a match between young Henry and his granddaughter, Elizabeth, whose father was Edward de Vere, the Earl of Oxford. 'All was well.' Then James frowned. 'But Henry Wriothesley liked her not.'

'This I have heard,' Will confirmed, 'the not liking her and wanting to be rid of this future bride. But I confess I did not know her familial tie to Robert Cecil.' A public spurning of his niece would certainly explain Robert Cecil's hatred of Wriothesley.

The bandora player was singing now, as he plucked the strings of his instrument. It was a popular ballad and his voice fine enough to ensure he would be called upon to perform with their company once the need arose again.

'Could the Earl of Southampton resist a match made by such powerful men, so close to the queen?' he asked.

'I would have said no, but resist it he did and made his opposition to the marriage most clear to Her Majesty.'

'What was her mind?'

'She has favoured Henry Wriothesley before. He jousted at the Accession Day festivities and did well. She called him gentle and fair.' Will thought of Robert Cecil then, who was neither. He must have watched his former 'brother' jousting to earn the good opinion of the queen and been jealous. James Burbage continued, 'But the queen did not wish him to escape the union, else other men would think they can wriggle from a marriage she herself has blessed. She told Wriothesley that if he wanted to be free of this arrangement, he must pay an enormous sum.'

'How much?'

'Five thousand pounds.' Will could scarcely imagine such a figure. 'The queen must have thought this too high a price, even for the Earl of Southampton, but pay it he will.' Will recalled Henry Wriothesley's confidence that he could win over the queen but had assumed he would use flattery, not gold, to get his desired outcome.

'He has such a fortune?' he asked.

'He has eleven thousand a year.'

'You could buy half the world with that.'

The bandora player finished his song and Richard spoke to him enthusiastically before he left the stage.

'Five thousand can get him out of the marriage,' said James, 'but he has slighted the Cecils and no amount of money will save him from their vengeance.'

'Is that what this is really about? Robert Cecil wants to destroy Henry Wriothesley because the man embarrassed his father?'

'His sister and niece too,' added Burbage. 'And by extension, himself.'

'I thought he feared a Catholic plot.'

'He does, every day, and likely there are many to fear. But how happy he would be if he could link Henry Wriothesley to one of them and damn the man in the bargain.'

Chapter Twenty-Eight

'If I be waspish, best beware my sting.'
— The Taming of the Shrew

Goneril was old. Too old and frail to be running a household, and he wondered why Sir Thomas Vernon had kept her on so long, when he was hardly known for his charity.

She seemed neither surprised nor alarmed to find Will at her door. The rooms she occupied were larger than he had expected for one who had spent her life in the service of others and could surely have amassed little money.

' 'Twas my father's house,' she explained as she let him in, 'left to me and let out while I worked for Sir Thomas. I knew this day would come and sought to cushion my old age.' Had she invented this inheritance, to explain her relative prosperity for a house servant?

She asked Will why he was bothering to visit a woman of her age and teased him with 'unless you have come courting'. That was followed by a hearty laugh that turned into a cough. She sat down then, having over-exerted herself.

Will explained he was there because he was writing a new play and that seemed to excite her. 'I likes the plays,' she said. 'The bloodier and bawdier the better, but the theatre is shut.'

'It will reopen one day and I wish to write as bloody and bawdy a play as London has ever seen, but I will need your help. I want to fright my audience with a ghost and have heard there is one at the house you worked in.'

'A ghost at Sir Thomas's house? I worked there years and ne'er saw one.'

'When did you leave?' he asked her then. 'Was that before his wife's passing?'

She shook her head. 'Weeks after. I have not long been settled here. It will see me out.'

'Then you did not witness her restless spirit haunting the yard?' he asked earnestly. 'Or standing mournfully by a window?'

'I did not.' She seemed surprised he could have imagined such a thing.

Will did not want to admit to having seen the ghost himself. 'There have been reports, sightings, from neighbours. They have seen the ghostly figure of a young woman who looked very much like Lady Celia, walking in the yard. Sometimes she appears at the window and seems tormented.'

'There's always young women that works there,' she told him. 'Sir Thomas likes them young.'

'But do those servants dress in his dead wife's clothes? This spirit wore Lady Celia's shawl and hooded cloak.'

Goneril seemed to be seriously contemplating the likelihood of Celia's spirit having risen from the grave, but then she did a strange thing. Her face suddenly softened and she laughed. 'Lady Celia become a ghost? That was no tormented spirit!' And she laughed so hard at this he thought she might choke, before finally clearing her throat and exclaiming, ' 'Twas his whore!' He had to wait till her laughter subsided entirely before she explained.

'Sir Thomas brought that girl into the house weeks ago. She is called Viola. He said she is his ward, the daughter of a man he knew in business who had passed, and perhaps she was but now she lives there, in a room right next to his, if you understand my meaning. She is very young too and a pale and pretty little thing. Now she wears his wife's clothes. At least they don't go to waste.'

'You think Sir Thomas has an impure relationship with his own ward?'

'I know he plans to.'

'How so?'

'He aims to marry her.'

'How old is she?'

'But thirteen. I think he waits for her to turn fourteen, then her birthday will become her wedding day.' She seemed to find that amusing.

If Will had a low opinion of Sir Thomas Vernon before, it was even more reduced now. He had taken a young girl in after her father's passing, supposedly to protect her, and now he would have her for himself.

'The girl has an inheritance,' she explained. 'Sir Thomas was granted a portion of it to pay for her keep, but she still has the majority.'

'Which will go to her husband when she weds,' he realised. 'Sir Thomas aims to have it all, through marriage.'

'He likely needs it. There was money stolen. A goodly sum, but not enough to ruin him. Money falls into his lap, though he spends it twice as quickly.'

'Someone stole his money?'

'Lady Celia's money,' she clarified, 'that she brought with her to the marriage.'

'How much?'

'There was a whisper it was ten or twelve pounds, perhaps more.' She shrugged. 'Twenty maybe.'

'When did this happen?'

'A month before she died. Two perhaps.'

'The thief broke into the house?'

'Crept in more like. Front door was left unlocked because there was always someone in the house. No one thought a thief so brazen to walk in and take from a man like Sir Thomas.'

'Because he was feared?' Her silence told him the truth of that. 'How did he react to the theft?'

'Went into a fury the like of which I had not seen before and I have known him angry many times.'

'Did he blame members of his household?'

'Not for the theft but for allowing it. The door should have been locked and we should have kept a wary eye on things instead of letting a thief in. That is what he said.'

'Were you worried he might dismiss you?'

'Not I. I did him good service and for many a year.'

'Then why did he let you go later?'

'I am old and tired. We could both see that. He paid me to leave, with some of what I would have earned had I stayed, and I have my own money.' He took it she meant the house in part but he was still unsure how she could live so comfortably now, having earned a servant's pay for so long. Then he thought of her words about rendering Thomas Vernon 'good service' and wondered if there was more to it than just tending to his house. Had she helped him in some way to commit acts that were against the law or simply practised discretion that he then rewarded? Or was there more to it even than that?

'When Celia arrived, did you take to his new wife?' She shrugged as if it was of no consequence, so he took this to mean she did not. 'It was a stormy marriage, I hear.'

'There were arguments right enough.'

'What caused them?' he asked.

'She talked back to him. It wasn't proper but I suppose, being a lady, she was used to getting her way and had been spoiled. He never should have married her.'

'You think he regretted the match?'

'The whole house heard him. He would shout and she would call back at him,' she said, in wonder at the wife's nerve. 'And he would strike her. Then he would tell her of his regret.'

'For hitting her?'

She shook her head. 'For marrying her. He would say he could have married anyone but was stuck in the bad bargain he made for her.'

'Was he not a poor master to his wife? He did beat her.'

'Most husbands beat their wives,' she said. 'That's why I never took one.' She thought more on the matter. 'He was perhaps a little too eager to stop her wilfulness with a slap.'

'Even from the beginning?'

'I remember the screams on their wedding night,' recalled the old woman, half amused, 'and it weren't just from the tearing of her maidenhead.'

'You seem to hold no great sympathy for your lady.'

'Celia wasn't my lady. She was his.'

'And you were his loyal servant, though your position would have been reduced once she ran his household.'

'Her and her companion, that cursed Rosalind.' Then, almost under her breath, she added, 'I swear she is a witch.'

'It must have been a relief when the lady died then,' he observed, 'and Rosalind left soon after.'

'She didn't leave. Sir Thomas threw her out when he no longer had to put up with her.' He noticed she did not deny it was a relief that Celia had died.

'Were you in the house when Celia passed?'

'Where else would I be? I cleaned, I washed and I cooked. Just like I always done before they arrived.'

'You cooked the meals?'

'Who else would do it, with the Lady Celia ailing and Rosalind tending to her the whole time? We would have starved otherwise.'

'But Lady Celia was too weak for food, was she not?'

'I made her broth. She could manage that, judging by the empty bowls.'

Was there more here than a cook's pride that her food had been eaten? Celia had taken ill and showed symptoms of plague even though no one else had. Once she could no longer eat the same food as the rest of the household, Celia had lived off a broth made by a woman with no love for her. Celia then continued to ail and, soon after, she died. As he sat before the old woman who had shown no sympathy for her mistress, Will had to wonder if this was the work of the plague or something closer to home.

Chapter Twenty-Nine

'Suspicion always haunts the guilty mind;
The thief doth fear each bush an officer.'
— *Henry VI*

A large man entered the tavern, closely followed by a second. Will, who was seated alone, waiting for Richard Burbage and the comedic actor William Kempe to join him for supper, noticed their menacing presence immediately. They looked around the room and one of them spoke to the other. Behind them, another man entered and he was followed by a fourth whose bearing, and the manner in which he was dressed, marked him out as their leader. Then, to Will's alarm, the first two men advanced on his table. They did not speak but, without invitation, sat down either side of him, hemming him in. Will could not leave the table, nor rise or try to draw his sword. The other two men sat down directly opposite. If the first three men appeared threatening, it was nothing in comparison to the look on the face of the fourth man, who faced Will now. He managed to exude anger, contempt and mortal threat in his gaze alone. When he spoke, his voice was a low growl. 'I have heard you have been making enquiries about me.'

Though Will had only seen him briefly and from a distance through Miranda's window, this had to be Sir Thomas Vernon, the man Will had indeed been enquiring about all over this corner of London. At least one of those he questioned had reported it back.

'Not I, sir.' Will lacked the wit under pressure to offer anything bar a denial, but he could tell by the look on Sir Thomas's face that he was not believed.

'I know you have,' his accuser told him. 'Deny it again and Sam will put his dagger in you.' The man on Will's right drew his dagger and placed it on the table, so he could see its sharp point. He kept his hand on its hilt so Will could not attempt to take it, though he was certainly not foolish enough to try. The tavern was a rough place and the other men here made a point of minding their own business. It would be but the work of a moment to stab Will and leave the place before anyone cried out in alarm.

'Forgive me, are you by chance Sir Thomas Vernon?' Will feigned comprehension then.

'I am,' he said, 'and you are Master William Shakespeare. I know your name and what you are about but what am I to you or you to me? I've never set eyes on you before. Name your quarrel.'

'I have no quarrel with you, sir.'

Sir Thomas gestured towards his man, who swept the dagger from the table and brought it swiftly towards Will, moving so fast Will thought the man intended to stab him there and then. Instead, keeping it low and using the table to cloak it, he pressed the dagger against Will's side hard enough for him to feel its point through his clothing. 'Speak now or he will stick you here and leave you to bleed.'

'I did make enquiries' – and Will raised his hands, palms out, in an appeal for calm – 'but meant no ill of it.' He was desperately trying to work out what Sir Thomas knew about those enquiries. Will did not want to be caught in a lie by a man of his violent nature.

'Then what *did* you mean of it? Tell me quickly.'

With that, Sam pressed the point of the dagger more firmly against him. Will spoke swiftly, knowing that if he did not take care, these words could be his last. 'I have a little money and thought to make it grow. I was told you were someone who understood trade and knew merchants, whereas I do not. I thought you might welcome some coin, for a partnership in your next venture.'

Sir Thomas seemed doubtful. 'Who told you that?'

'I feel sure it was Ingram Frizer.' It was a desperate gamble but of all the people he could imagine knowing of Sir Thomas Vernon's character, Frizer seemed the most likely.

There was silence then while Sir Thomas regarded Will. 'Frizer, eh? When was this?'

'Some weeks ago. I decided to proceed but cautiously. I did not wish to approach a man on a matter of business unless he is vouched for by another.'

Sir Thomas regarded Will for what felt like a long time but could have only been seconds. All the while, Will looked his interrogator in the eye, attempting to convey that he was an honest man of some means, while the knife was still weighed in the other man's hands and could be thrust into him at any moment.

Finally, Sir Thomas spoke. 'That was shrewd. Many a man in London is parted from his money by phantoms who disappear. He never sees them or his coin again. But tell me what you learned of me.'

Will had discovered little about Sir Thomas as a man of business, and what he had heard was not good, but he needed an answer, so invented one. 'That you will not be easily deceived by another and, once in a bargain, will most often get the better of the deal. This is how you prosper.'

'That I do,' he assured Will. 'So why allow you to prosper too, upon my back?'

'To make your profits twice. First from your own dealings, then again from a fair portion of the return I enjoy.'

'And how much will you bring?'

'I have fifteen pounds and wish to commit a goodly amount of it.' A lie is always easier to convey when it contains a measure of truth. Will did not have fifteen pounds, only six, though it did not really matter for he was certainly never going to let Sir Thomas see a penny of it.

'Fifteen pounds?'

'Aye.'

'Why risk such a sum? I can tell from your apparel you are a man of low birth. When you are scared, as you are now, your voice betrays your base origins. You sound like the second son of a country innkeeper.'

'My father was a glove maker and yes, I am a man of low birth, but wish to improve my station by the acquiring of property and a coat of arms. I will raise myself.'

'Is that all?'

'I want to buy a share in a new theatre company.' Will had decided to continue to wrap his lies in as much of the truth as possible, to make them more convincing. 'I am tired of acting and writing for a groat here and a groat there, while patrons and theatre owners prosper from my talents.'

'How do I know you have more than a penny to your name?'

'It is my share.'

'In what?'

'A tour of players.' And Will explained he had been allowed to invest his modest earnings as an actor and playmaker into one of James Burbage's touring productions, to help cover the man's costs and reduce his risk should it be cancelled because of plague. 'When the tour proved a success, I gained a share of the profits and used that to make a little more, by lending out what I had to the other players. As soon as their purses are full, most is gone on ale and whores before the week is out, then they need more for victuals or a place to lay their heads. I expect a sum to be added to the loan, against the risk of them running off or dying.'

'Usury then.' Thomas Vernon seemed neither shocked nor disapproving of this, though it was illegal to charge interest on a loan. 'You're a money lender? So that's how you make your coin?' Sir Thomas gave the man with the dagger the merest look. On his unspoken command, the blade was put back in his belt. 'We shall talk more on this but for now I have separate business.'

The other men rose in unison with him and they left the tavern. When they were gone, Will let out a deep sigh of relief.

Chapter Thirty

'There is an upstart crow, beautified with our feathers, that, with his Tygers
heart wrapt in a Players hide, supposes he is as well
able to bumbast out a blanke verse as the best of you.'
— Robert Greene on William Shakespeare

Having barely survived his first encounter with Sir Thomas Vernon, Will was in no mood for merry moments over supper with Richard Burbage and William Kempe. He would not have stayed, in fact, had he not already left his friend to dine alone once before, on the night he was abducted by Robert Poley.

'You did not ask the girl her name,' Richard reminded Will as the pretty serving girl left them, 'so you could tell her what it means.'

'I have grown tired of that game.' It seemed foolish to him now that Rosalind thought it so.

'What is the matter, Will? I can see your troubles writ large across your face.'

Kempe in turn adopted a tone of cheerful chastisement. 'Whatever they are, you think too much on them. We are all just meat for the worms in any case.'

'I was thinking about Robert Greene.' This was not entirely a lie, for he often thought of Greene and his bitter words.

'Talking of meat for the worms,' said Kempe. 'God rest the miserable old dog.'

'He was not that old.'

'Some men are born old.'

'He called me an upstart and a jack of all trades,' Will reminded them.

'In his pamphlet,' recalled Richard. 'Because you are an actor who dared to write a play.'

'Fuck Robert Greene with a rusty mace,' Kempe declared. 'He was jealous.'

'Of a man who didn't go to his beloved Cambridge? I doubt that.'

'Of a better writer than he ever was or could hope to be,' said Richard.

'His "Groat's worth of wit" is not worth a fart, let alone a groat,' said Kempe. 'And I would not have given him one of mine for it. He died penniless. When a man is jealous of another, he is not angry at that man but at himself and his own failure.'

'There is some truth in this, I think,' Will admitted. 'He was thirty-four when he passed. That's not old.'

'Many don't live as long.'

'If I am spared to be Greene's age, I have less than five years. That's not long enough.'

'For what?'

'To write everything I have a mind to, and to become the man I wish to be.'

'None of us ever become the men we wish to be,' Kempe told him.

'Now there is a dark thought,' said Will.

'You plucked it from me with your melancholy. I don't know why we drink with you when you can turn a simple pleasure into a long, bleak search for meaning.' Kempe mimicked Will then: 'What's the point of anything? Why ever do we choose to go on?'

'I don't know who you are playing there, William, but that was not me.'

'It did sound like you,' teased Richard.

'Drink then!' Kempe urged Will, mocking him with the voice of a frail old man. 'For there is little time left and soon we will be under the soil.' That at least made Will laugh at his own folly.

—

When Will next encountered Rosalind at the theatre, he took a great interest in the first costume she had made, commenting on its fine stitching and the way it would make its wearer look 'most kingly'.

'James Burbage tells me you will soon finish your play about King Richard III,' she said.

'James is at court,' he observed, parrying the questions about his play, because King Richard was no nearer fleshed out in his mind than the play he was supposed to be writing about him. 'The queen has returned and he wants her blessing for a Christmas play.' He could have added, *and I might be the one to write it*, though there was stiff competition for that honour from Marlowe, Kyd and Nashe, all of whom would be eager to put their name to it.

'Then I will leave the costume here and will away.'

He offered to walk with her, because the streets of Shoreditch were dangerous even in daylight. 'Full of whores, robbers and cutpurses.'

'They will get naught from me,' she said, 'for I have little.' But Rosalind agreed he could walk part of the way to her lodgings, though she was still reluctant to reveal its location. Along the way, they discussed the process of making a costume, then he asked her how she came to meet James Burbage and gain his trust. Like many Londoners, she loved a play and admitted to enjoying his *Henry VI*, but had noticed some of the costumes were threadbare. She sought out James Burbage while the theatre was empty and he allowed her to mend some. After that, she came to him with ideas for new costumes.

'And your lady did not mind this?'

'I did it in the evenings when the chores were complete.'

'I had a mind to ask you more about Lady Celia.'

'For your play?'

He chose to ignore the suspicion in her voice. 'How did her illness first reveal itself?'

'It began as a weakness. Celia was not strong enough to carry what normally would not have troubled her. Then she fell into exhaustion and could barely get herself to her bed without me steadying her.'

'And she purged?' She lowered her head, perhaps embarrassed to admit her lady's vomiting and diarrhoea to him, though they both knew these were common enough symptoms of the plague. 'Was there a fever?'

'Her brow burned to the touch.'

'What did her husband do when he first found she might have plague?'

'He went out and killed every dog and cat he saw, in case they carried the disease.'

'Physicians doubt the truth in that,' he said.

'They will tell you it is miasma and the air is indeed foul in London.' Then she observed, 'But people still die in villages, where the air is clean.'

Will knew it was accepted by most learned men that bad air was to blame for carrying the plague. People pressed oranges stuffed with cloves to their noses, to mask the foul smells of London and keep out its deadly miasma.

'I cannot account for that,' he admitted. Rosalind had a sharp mind for a young woman who had not seen so very much of the world. He also hoped she might not question the judgement of learned men so freely to others, which could be dangerous.

'How did you treat Celia?' he asked her then.

'I burned dried rosemary in a bowl for its smoke and bay leaves in a chafing dish close to her bed, to clear the air of infection. I fetched some boiled thyme from an apothecary for her cough.'

'She coughed? I did not think that a symptom of plague.'

'You have seen many plague sufferers, Master Shakespeare?' The question was a rebuke.

'No, but still...' His words trailed away. Though she had to be almost ten years younger than him, when Rosalind called him 'Master Shakespeare' it felt like an admonishment from one of his old school teachers.

'Well then,' she said, 'my lady had a cough.'

'But how was Celia infected and none other?' he probed.

'I would say it was God's will but why would God want to take Celia, except...'

'Except?'

She looked as if she had gone too far. 'I don't know.'

'You were about to give me a reason why God might have taken her. Was it to punish her for something?' Could it have been the kiss Rosalind ardently denied took place?

'She was as blameless as a newborn.'

'What then?' He thought he knew. 'To spare her, perhaps, from the troubles of this world?' Their eyes locked for a moment and he saw understanding in hers.

'Perhaps.'

'Sir Thomas is a cruel man. Being wed to him would be a purgatory.'

She thought on this for a time before announcing, 'That it was,' in a soft voice filled with sadness.

'And you would know, for no one was closer to your lady than you,' he said, 'except her husband of course.'

'I was closer than he, she was a sister to me.' Then she questioned him. 'You take a great interest in the events of my humble life. Men woo women with less effort.'

'I confess I am interested in your life, Rosalind. Since it started by the road when you were little more than a babe in arms, it could be a play.'

'Do you always ask ladies questions so you can write plays about them? Or do you use your plays as a reason to ask ladies questions?' He laughed lightly at this but she wasn't done. 'You have asked me many questions about Celia.'

'Have I?'

'You think because you ask me of other things that I do not notice when your questioning always comes back to the manner of her death?'

'I admit to being most curious about that.'

'Then why do I feel you ask me about her for some other reason than curiosity?'

Will could have denied this. He sensed, though, that the only way Rosalind would permit him to spend more time with her would be to take her into his confidence. But that was not without risk. The Earl of Southampton had ordered him never to reveal his role in this affair to anyone and Will had believed him when he called himself a 'vengeful lord'.

Rosalind was looking at him now, while he hesitated, waiting for an answer, and in that moment, as he stared back into those dark eyes, Will found he could deny her nothing.

He told her everything then.

Chapter Thirty-One

'O time! thou must untangle this, not I;
It is too hard a knot for me to untie!'
— Twelfth Night

'Celia never mentioned this great lord,' Rosalind told him when he was done.

'They had not seen one another since they were children, but Henry Wriothesley did love her once as kin.'

'And he wants to know the truth about Celia, her marriage and her death?' she asked quietly.

'He does.'

'Then I shall help you.'

'Tell me this then, Rosalind, when you were with your lady at the end, did you ever leave her room?'

'I stayed with Celia.'

'She was never alone? You never left once, not even for the church or marketplace?'

She thought for a moment. 'I did leave to pray for her. Celia led a blameless life and I hoped that if I reminded God, He might spare her.'

'Could you not have prayed for her at home?'

'I wanted to be closer to God and thought my prayers more likely to be heard in church.'

'You prayed for a miracle then? And when your prayers were not answered?'

'She died anyway.'

'Were you angry at God?'

Her answer was measured. 'When wicked men still walk this earth, while Celia lies cold in the ground, it teaches me that God lets the people of the world do what they will, for good or ill. Innocent children die every day. He does not give them miracles, why would he grant one for Celia?'

Will had often felt the same way about his own inconsequential prayers. Why would God listen to him, when there were so many more deserving souls than he, praying for their salvation every night?

'You were gone at prayer for how long?'

'No more than thirty minutes.'

'Why leave her at all, when she was so gravely ill?'

'Celia had begun to improve. Her colour was better for a time and she slept. I took that opportunity to thank God for his mercy and pray for her full recovery.'

'And when you returned?'

'She worsened while I was away. I had been foolish to think she might be recovering and felt bad for leaving her on her own, even for a little while.'

'So her condition had improved but when you returned she began to ail once more and in less than half an hour.'

'Yes.'

'Did you inform anyone in the household that you were leaving for church?'

'Of course. I called into the kitchen but did not enter in case I was infected, and I made sure to go to church while there was no service.'

'Who heard you?'

'I know not who but did receive an answer. Someone called back from the kitchen.'

'A man or a woman?'

'It was a woman's voice.'

'The former housekeeper perhaps? Or some other servant?'

'I know not.'

'But whoever it was would know you were to be gone for some time, with the lady Celia alone in her room?'

'That is why I called out, in case Celia woke and was distressed. They could at least call to her that I would return soon.'

'You were gone long enough for someone to enter Celia's room.'

'Since she carried plague, they would likely stay apart from her.'

'No one would attend to her if she was stricken with plague,' he agreed. 'But what if she was not, and there was one man or woman in the house who knew this?'

'I do not understand.'

'What if Celia merely showed the signs of plague yet did not have it?' And her face told him she had no idea what he was getting at. 'What if instead someone was slowly poisoning Celia?'

'But why?' she asked.

'Any number of reasons. Being slighted by a new mistress with a lowered status in the household perhaps?'

'You think the housekeeper or some other servant would kill for that?'

'People have killed for less. But let's consider an alternative. That Celia was poisoned by her husband, using the hand of another.' Rosalind seemed about to rebuff the idea but instead looked at him deeply, as if to judge whether he was in earnest. 'You said she seemed to improve and this after two, perhaps three days of purging and voiding, with you as her constant companion. Don't you see? If a poisoner was at work, placing something in her food, they might not succeed if it was forced quickly from her stomach or she was too ill to eat.'

'Celia ate little towards the end,' Rosalind agreed. 'Her food was barely touched.'

'And yet she seemed better, until you left her for but half an hour and, upon returning, found her in a worse state. If someone came into that room while you were gone and administered poison, from a drink perhaps?'

'I know it is possible but surely fantastical?'

'You must try to imagine it and worse. Your lady may well have been the victim of a most foul murder.'

Chapter Thirty-Two

'Many a good hanging prevents a bad marriage'
— Twelfth Night

There was an interlude during this episode when Will could have almost forgotten he was caught between three men with far more power than him. A lull in proceedings, when weeks passed without incident and the Earl of Southampton stayed on his estate and did not summon any poets to his side. Perhaps he had spent too much of his fortune to evade his marriage and had less coin to feed drunken playmakers. As a consequence of this, Sir Robert Cecil did not order Robert Poley to drag Will across London to be interrogated again. He must have been too busy uncovering papist plots elsewhere. Will even managed to avoid Sir Thomas Vernon for the most part, only running into him twice when they both happened to be in the same taverns in Shoreditch. Each time, he told Sir Thomas he needed a little longer to bring in the necessary funds. The man did not take this in good humour but at least allowed Will to leave unharmed.

Will spent much of this time writing and less of it asking about Lady Celia's death, for who had he not already questioned about it? Without proof, he was reluctant to incriminate anyone, even her husband. He realised that, if summoned by the earl, he would have to tell him that Celia most probably did die of plague. He suspected foul play and retained a deep antipathy towards Sir Thomas Vernon, as well as the members of his household who had treated Lady Celia and Rosalind with such disdain, but he did not have enough to damn them all. Even Rosalind would not condemn the man as a murderer.

He still saw Rosalind regularly as she brought each piece of her work to the theatre to gain James Burbage's approval. It was Burbage's aim to have his whole company fitted with the best costumes once the theatres reopened. This was a necessary expense, if he hoped to present the queen with a Christmas play. His actors could hardly gain Her Majesty's favour and patronage if they stood before her in threadbare costumes.

Will and Rosalind had fallen into the habit of walking together following her visits and she had begun to talk more freely about her life in Thomas Vernon's household, now that she knew he had good reason to ask her about it.

'Do you think he wanted rid of her?' he asked her of Sir Thomas.

'He made no secret of his disappointment in his marriage.'

'And if Celia had not contracted the plague?'

'She would have died anyway, for he treated her most ill.'

'You think he might have beaten her so severely, she would have passed because of it?'

'That was likely, or… it hurts me to say it.'

'You owe Celia a true and honest account of her life,' Will insisted.

Reluctantly, as if he had to drag every word from her, she said, 'Once she talked of… and it was only talk…'

'Of killing him?'

'God, no.'

'Killing herself then?' He had only offered up murder so she could strike that notion down, leaving her with only one other, which was just as shocking. 'She talked of self-slaughter?'

Rosalind nodded grimly. 'She told me if he continued to treat her so basely she would throw herself into the river and drown.'

He did not know what to say after this, but finally settled on: 'That would have ended her troubles.'

'It was just talk and only when he had robbed her of her true mind with his harsh treatment of her.'

'Do you think she would have done it?'

'In truth? I know not.'

'But it was possible?'

'For her to commit such a terrible sin against herself and God? Her husband confounded her at every turn and she could not see how to take much more of it.'

'And yet she did not need to take her own life for the plague took it instead. Some would say that was timely, others might be suspicious.'

She rounded on him then. 'Are you accusing me of killing my lady? I could never do such a thing.'

'Even if she urged you to do it?'

'No,' she protested, 'Celia was not poisoned by my hand or another's. She died of plague and I saw it.'

'You did,' he agreed, 'but no one else.'

Her voice trembled when she spoke. 'If you can think that I would kill my lady, even if she begged me to, then you know not I nor her. If the devil himself came in the night and offered me kingdoms full of treasure in return, I would tell him to go back to hell... I could never...'

He held up a hand in supplication. 'I don't believe it was so,' he admitted, 'but had to hear you deny it, and you did, most passionately. I am convinced.'

'You should be,' she told him, 'and shamed too, for ever having suggested it.'

And he did feel shamed. 'Her husband though. There is a man capable of anything.'

'That I do believe.' Reintroducing Sir Thomas seemed to send her fury in a different direction.

'I thought he might have killed your lady,' he said, 'and so did my patron.' He nodded to emphasise the point. 'But you say it was plague, Rosalind, so that answers almost all my questions.'

'*Almost* all?'

'One remains,' he reminded her. 'If she died of plague, how did she get it?'

Chapter Thirty-Three

'Heat not a furnace for your foe so hot
That it do singe yourself'
— Henry VIII

'I have waited long enough for your coin, Master Shakespeare,' Sir Thomas Vernon informed him loudly, his voice carrying in the tavern. 'Either you do not have it or you mock me for a fool.'

It was perhaps inevitable that his patience would run out, but Will had always hoped Sir Thomas would simply move on to another venture. Not so. The man had deliberately sought him out this time, judging by the presence of those burly men from before by his side.

'I do have it.'

'Then you mock me.'

'No.'

'Where is it, then? Do you have it about you? Hand it to me now.'

'I do not. Some of it is loaned out. My debtor needs more time to repay me. I am at the mercy of the borrower.'

'This is usury,' said Sir Thomas contemptuously. 'I should report it.'

'How will that profit you?' This quieted him. 'Have patience and we shall share the spoils from our next enterprise.'

'Give me your debtor's name. I will send someone to him and he will shit your money by nightfall.'

'The man who borrowed from me gave that money to another. Right now, he has none.'

Sir Thomas regarded Will with contempt then. 'There are men in London who have been close companions in my former endeavours and, when they are abroad, it is as if they become mine own eyes and ears. They report back to me, out of loyalty and sometimes fear,' he concluded, 'and they are right to fear me.'

'I do not trifle with you, sir,' said Will.

'But you do. When I demanded to know why you asked about me, you said it was to learn if I might be trusted to increase your paltry fortune. If that be so, then why are all of your questions about my wife?'

Will felt as if he might purge right there in the tavern. Sir Thomas knew the truth of it. Will's life might soon be over, or perhaps he would be mutilated like Daniel. If Will had been able to think of a denial then, he would have quickly spoken it, but he could tell by the look on the man's face that no clever twisting of words would satisfy him.

'Do you think you are the first to come snuffling around me? Do you know what happened to the last man who impugned my name with suspicions about Celia?'

Will knew he was caught now, trapped by a dangerous man with a suspicious nature.

'I do,' he said flatly, and Sir Thomas was at least surprised by that answer. 'He was beaten most violently.'

'And yet here you are, come with the same questions and about to meet the same fate. Tell me who sent you and I will make your beating a little shorter.'

Will reasoned that naming the Earl of Southampton would be as good as passing a sentence of death upon himself. Even a vicious beating would be preferable, if he lived thereafter, but he also knew that Sir Thomas would make that beating considerably worse if he did not cooperate. He might even kill Will. 'It is not just one man,' he lied. 'You have enemies at court.'

'What enemies?' He stiffened at that.

'In truth I know not, only that a body of powerful men are of the suspicion that Sir Thomas Vernon might have had his wife killed to rid himself of her. I was approached by the servant of one such man and ordered to look into the matter.' Will was trying to visualise such a scene in order to make it sound convincing. In his mind's eye he saw Henry Wriothesley's Steward of Matters Domestical talking to him, not about the arrangements for the journey to Place House but instead of suspicions surrounding Sir Thomas. 'I must report back to him and if I do not give my account, it will be assumed that I met my end violently at your hand, sir.'

'I do not believe it.' But Sir Thomas's face said otherwise. 'You claim not to know the identity of the noble who has commanded you to investigate me? It is fantasy!'

'I am permitted to know only that great men have taken a close interest in your affairs. An interest that increased when the last man they sent to enquire about you was brutally beaten. They suspect you are a man of violence and dark intent.' Sir Thomas could scarcely believe what he was hearing. 'Beat me too and it will be confirmed. Then likely the same fate will befall you. Have me killed and expect to be killed...' Then he added the single word, 'Or...'

Sir Thomas's face was a picture of confusion and, for the first time since he had laid eyes upon the other man, fear. He shot Will an urgent glance. 'Or?'

'Convince me,' he said firmly.

'Convince you of what?'

'Your innocence in this matter.'

'Why would I? I have nothing to account for. My wife died of plague.'

'Then convince me of it,' urged Will, 'and I will convince them. Then all will be well.'

Sir Thomas drew his own dagger then and pressed the point against Will's throat. 'Why should I?'

Will had to speak slowly and carefully with the point of the knife pressed against his skin. 'So that these great men will be satisfied. Perhaps even the queen needs to be, if they are whispering to her about you? I am sure she has noticed you at court, Sir Thomas. Kill me and, whether any man sees it or not, all will know you for a murderer and they will become justice.' He used the Earl of Southampton's own phrase.

Sir Thomas stared at Will with a look that was hard to decipher. Was it outrage, frustration, anger or wounded pride he saw in the man's eyes, and what would he do next?

'You will tell them I had naught to do with my wife's death?'

Will shook his head. 'I must account for it for them to believe me. I need your story of what happened. Convince me,' he repeated, 'and I can convince them.'

At that moment, Robert Poley walked into the tavern. 'Poley!' called Will, who had never been happier to see his abductor before now. Vernon put his dagger away as Poley turned, noticed Will surrounded by Sir Thomas Vernon and his men, then walked over to join them.

'What's this?' he demanded.

'Nothing that involves you, Poley,' snarled Vernon. 'Be on your way.'

Poley seemed amused by that. 'Should I quake at the sound of your base voice, Thomas? I will decide what involves me.' Then he demanded, 'What say you?'

'Master Shakespeare seems to believe he has the ear of powerful men, though he will not name them.'

Poley considered the situation for a moment. He looked at Sir Thomas Vernon and each of his men in turn, as if calmly evaluating whether they were a threat to him or not, then he turned to look at Will who stared back at him. Was it possible to say 'I am in danger and need you to trust me and save me from it' with just a look?

Apparently it was.

'He does,' announced Poley. 'So you had best leave him be.'

Whatever history Sir Thomas Vernon and Robert Poley had between them, it was enough for the tension to ease. Sir Thomas gave Poley a curt nod and signalled to the other men to step away, but before he left, he turned back to Will. 'Where and when, then?'

'Come to the theatre tomorrow,' said Will. 'Come early, and come alone.'

'We shall meet,' Sir Thomas assured him. 'And I will give my account.' Then he walked from the building with his men.

Poley watched them go, seemingly unconcerned by their malevolent presence, then he moved closer to Will. 'It's as well you refused to name my master. If you had, I would have let them kill you.' Then he leaned in close. 'But only to save myself the trouble.'

Chapter Thirty-Four

'Thou art a boil,
A plague sore, an embossed carbuncle
In my corrupted blood.'
— *King Lear*

Sir Thomas Vernon did come early, and he came alone. Will hoped for some safety among the players, which was why he had chosen the walls of the theatre to house their meeting. Up on the stage, actors were rehearsing together, for they had heard the company might have to go on tour soon if the plague did not lift. What choice did they have, to avoid running out of money entirely? Will ushered Thomas Vernon to a seat in the lower gallery. Vernon sat stiffly, unaccustomed to doing another man's bidding and far from happy about it but, like every man in England, he knew his place. If there really were men at court asking questions about him, he must have reasoned it was better to deal with Will than be summoned before them.

'Are you here to give me your account of the events leading up to your wife's death?'

'I am,' he said sternly, 'though this be no court of law.'

'The men I will report it to already sit in judgement on you, Sir Thomas,' Will reminded him.

'Well then,' he said impatiently, 'give me your questions.'

'I am lately of the opinion that Lady Celia may not have perished of plague.'

Sir Thomas immediately went on the attack. 'You want to know what killed my wife, if not the plague? I was not there. Who was it told everyone Celia contracted it? Who tended to her in her final hours and frightened the rest of the household away while she lay dying? Her companion, Rosalind. That's who. I did not feed my wife nor hold a

186

cup to her parched lips. That was Rosalind. It was not I who leaned in to hear her final breaths, but Rosalind. Who washed her body once her spirit left it and prepared Celia for burial? Not I. Ask the fair lady Rosalind what she did in those final hours that hastened my wife to her grave. Ask her! I was not there!'

'No,' agreed Will, 'as soon as you learnt your wife was sick, you fled.'

Sir Thomas gave Will a murderous look then. 'I did what any man would do. I left my wife in the care of a woman she trusted, then took myself away. It is my duty to live long enough to provide an heir. I kept myself safe to keep others safe.'

Will nodded slowly as if Thomas had made a reasonable point. 'Yet took none other with you to the country house. You alone departed. The servants were retained and your home stayed open. All were free to come and go as they pleased.'

'I gave orders...' he said weakly.

'Then they were not obeyed, which is strange for a man with such a fearsome reputation, but you were no longer there to see that they were.'

'I wish I had stayed. If I had, that *witch* might not have killed my wife and robbed me of my heir.'

'You think Rosalind killed Celia? Why did you not say so at the time?'

'I thought plague killed Celia but your persuasive words have lately convinced me otherwise. If not plague, then it must have been Rosalind. None other came so close. Who else could have poisoned her to make it look like plague?'

'You,' said Will simply. 'You could have administered poison to your wife easily, by putting something into her food or drink.'

'I wasn't there!' he roared, loudly enough for one or two of the players to look their way. Then, in a quieter voice, he continued, 'She took three days to die. I had been gone two by then. What poison does that?'

'I am no apothecary,' admitted Will, 'yet I know of poisons that course through the body slowly, conquering that territory an inch at a time and prolonging their victim's pain.'

'What know you of poison?' he snorted.

'I write plays that tell of murder most foul. Sometimes I am forced to seek knowledge of such matters from dark corners of the city. Henbane might do it or hemlock. Belladonna can kill or you can make a paste from almonds and stir it into food. Some of these poisons rot the organs of the body for days before the victims die.'

'I don't know of these things.'

'Some other could possess that knowledge. I myself cannot smelt metal but can easily buy a dagger from one who can. All that's needed is coin.'

'You think I am a man who could kill a woman?' he asked angrily.

'If that woman wronged you, then perhaps. It was said your wife was seen at the theatre with another man. Some say he even kissed her there.'

Sir Thomas did not seem shocked to hear this. 'What does it matter now? Celia is dead.'

'Did she not bring shame upon you?'

'She brought shame on herself. What did I care?'

'You might have cared if men called you cuckold behind your back because another man placed horns upon your head.'

'I care not what other men think or say or do. Good luck to any man who tried to put fire in her. I never could. Celia was cold to my touch and ever frigid in the marriage bed and it was not from want of my skill. I can make a whore claw my back and moan while I'm tupping her.'

'I hear they do that,' said Will dismissively. 'Though sometimes it costs extra.'

Sir Thomas ignored the jibe. 'Why would I kill my wife before I even had an heir?'

'To get another and a second dowry. Celia brought a parcel of land to your marriage but you were heard to say it was less fertile than you had hoped.'

'I said that some of it floods, 'twas all. I meant nothing by it.'

'You deny you were unhappy with your match, disappointed with your dowry and loathed your wife?'

'I did not hate my wife.' By denying one accusation, he seemed to confirm the others.

'But did seek to replace her,' probed Will. 'When you looked to the Lady Viola, a girl much younger than your wife, who you made your ward, at least to begin with.'

'An act of charity, by God! I had done business with her father and swore to take care of her when he was gone, for he knew how little time he had remaining.'

'And you knew how little time your wife had?'

'Not true, not so.'

'You placed the girl in your home to get a slice of her inheritance.'

'A small consideration that scarcely covers the cost of keeping her.'

'Imprisoning her, you mean, so that none would know of her, still less be able to court her. If you convinced her to marry you instead, the dowry would not be a fraction of her father's estate, but its whole. All that was hers would become yours.'

'That is not so.' He waved a hand dismissively but his lack of eloquence, or even anger, convinced Will that it was. 'I only sought to do right by her. To save her from those that might confound or rob her. I have been as good a guardian to her as any father.'

'Is it normal for fathers to wed their daughters in this parish?' His face told Will that Sir Thomas did not expect him to know of this. 'Even a man like you must abide by the customs of the realm. You cannot marry in secret. They have to cry the banns and this they have done for two weeks now. Do you deny it?'

Sir Thomas turned defiant then. 'I deny nothing. Viola was my friend's daughter, she is my ward and I protected her. I will continue to do this when she is my wife.'

'And with her father dead, who better to consent to this match than her guardian?' He smiled grimly. 'Also you.'

'The church has no objection.'

'What of the girl?'

'She is humble and obedient, as a daughter should be, as a wife would be.'

'She is but thirteen years. I doubt she would know how to refuse you anything.'

'The banns will be cried again this coming Sunday,' he said defiantly. 'We will marry thereafter. Call murder at me if you like but everyone knows my wife died of plague. None will believe it.'

'Married again within a year.' Will shook his head. 'That will be talked of.'

'Widows often marry in this parish before a year is out. No one will care.'

'Women do. What choice do they have to avoid starving? You, though, will not starve. Your haste is unseemly.'

'I need an heir! This girl is ripe and will be fruitful. Viola will not resist me. She will do her duty to her husband and to God. She will atone for the sins of Eve by giving me children and there is nothing you nor any other man can do to prevent it.'

Though it turned Will's stomach, Thomas Vernon was probably right. The girl was too young, but if her guardian gave his permission for her to marry, then it would likely happen, even if he was also the groom.

Will decided to allay his growing fury by questioning Sir Thomas on another matter. 'When Celia's money was taken, what did you do?'

If he was surprised that Will knew of this, he masked it well. 'What could I do? I yelled that we had been robbed.'

'Your house was secure and yet the thief got in.'

'The door was left open.'

'And he was not seen nor heard?'

'He was not.'

'Even when the strong box was broken into. Did no one hear the hammering?'

'There is hammering every day in Shoreditch. The house behind ours was not there a year ago. No one takes heed of hammering in London.'

'So, some cunning thief made off with money from your wife's estate and you did nothing?'

'I did not do *nothing*. I alerted everyone around. We went out with clubs to look for a thief and found none. No one was spending any of that coin in the taverns round here.'

'What about your own house, did you question the servants?'

'I did but none had the money. They would not dare steal from me.' He seemed very sure of that.

'And no one left their position in your household, either before or just after the loss?'

'No one.'

'Did your wife wonder where the money might have gone?'

'She was insolent enough to accuse me of the theft and I beat her for it.' Then he scoffed. 'As if I would steal what was mine already. I could have taken her money and used it as I pleased. I had no need to break into her strong box.'

'You might have,' Will offered, 'if she would not open it for you.'

'She would have opened it if I commanded her to, but I did not.'

'Not even when you went out to play at dice?'

'I have my own money for that and all my pleasures. I did not need hers.'

'Was anything else taken?'

'Nothing.'

'Did you not think that odd? It is a puzzle, is it not?'

'I did chastise her for it.'

'You chastised your wife for being robbed?'

'It was not my doing, so the fault must lie with her. What had she done for God to punish her so? Naught was taken from me.'

'Because you are such a good Christian?' retorted Will.

'I do as I do, and she did as she did. I was not robbed nor taken by plague. If she had been a better woman and wife, she might still be here.'

'Taken by the plague? But none other in the house.'

'Celia stayed in her room away from others. Only Rosalind and Isaac from her former household came near her.'

'The mute?'

'Aye. He knew no other life but by her side.'

'Why did you take him?'

'Because she asked me to or he would have starved when the farm and house were sold, and I wished her to be my wife.' He shrugged. 'He had strong shoulders, so could work.'

'And where is he now?'

'Gone. Left after her burial.'

'Did that anger you?'

'It's no concern of mine whether he starves or not and a simple enough task to replace him. There's plenty will work a long day now just for food and a roof over their head.'

'Why do you think he left?'

'Because he couldn't bear it any more without Celia.'

'But you could?'

He seemed to flare at this but then Sir Thomas brought his temper back under control. 'Celia was neither kind to me, nor wifely. She didn't deserve the life I gave her.' He said this both proudly and resentfully.

'We can both agree on that, Sir Thomas.'

Chapter Thirty-Five

'...yet do I fear thy nature;
It is too full o' the milk of human kindness'
— Macbeth

It was to her credit, and Will's frustration, that Rosalind continued to deny the likelihood that Sir Thomas Vernon might have poisoned his wife.

'He is not a good man,' she admitted, as they walked by the river together, 'but is he a murderer? I think not.'

They kept some distance from the ships docked by the Thames, to avoid contact with foreign sailors, but Will still swore the riverside was safer to walk than the city's streets. The air was cleaner here, with less miasma.

'Your heart is too good for this world, Rosalind, and your sweet nature denies evil. I have no proof that Sir Thomas killed his wife but how strange it was for her to be one of the first to be taken by plague, and the only one for a time.'

'Wondrous strange,' Rosalind admitted.

'Did nothing unusual happen in the days leading up to her death? Did she go nowhere, nor meet anyone?' Rosalind's brow furrowed slightly. 'What troubles you?'

'Sir Thomas sent a man to the house,' she recalled. 'I had not thought of this before but you made me recall it. 'Twas but a few days before my lady took ill. He was a foreigner, from the low countries. Flemish, I think.'

'What was his business?'

'He traded in cloth.'

'Did Sir Thomas not often bring men to his house?'

'Many times. He said men were more jovial if they were fed and poured drink, which led to a better bargain for him.'

'So why remark upon this man, if his presence was not so strange?'

'Because Sir Thomas insisted that Celia fetch the food and wait upon the man most attentively.'

'He wished his wife to serve, not his servants? Why?'

'He said she should dazzle the man with her beauty, so that he might be more likely to invest in their venture.'

'Some men are foolish enough to be blinded by beauty and lose all sense,' he told her, 'but didn't Sir Thomas tell his wife she was no beauty?'

'Yet still he thought her fair enough for this work. The foreigner's eyes followed her whenever she walked across the room and once, when she drew too close, he pulled my lady onto his lap.'

'In front of Sir Thomas? Was he not enraged?'

'Sir Thomas was not there,' she said.

'He was absent, while this Flemish merchant was a guest in his house? Was this not odd?'

'It did seem so, but a lot of his behaviour was unusual. He came and went at all hours, and his moods changed like the tides. Inviting a man to his home then absenting himself was perhaps not so strange for Sir Thomas. Celia pushed the man from her and escaped his embrace. She said it was nothing and blamed herself for drawing too close to him and providing him with temptation.'

'Did she tell her husband?'

'He would have either blamed his wife or beaten the man, which did not encourage her to inform him of what happened. The foreigner finished his meal and left with barely a word.'

'What was his name?'

'Janssens,' she told him without hesitation. It was a common enough name for a man from the lowlands.

'Was there anything else of note about this Janssens?'

'Oh yes,' she said. 'That is why I mentioned him. He did not look well.'

Will gazed at Rosalind then and wondered if she might have solved the puzzle for him. 'This man was sick?'

'I think now that he might have been,' she answered. 'He was sweating even though it was a mild evening but not a warm one. Then, not long after the meal, he purged himself. We thought this brought on by an excess of wine, for there was naught wrong with the meat and no one else fell ill after.'

'But now you wonder if it could have been plague?' He was wondering that too. 'Celia might have caught it from this Flemish man?'

'He was not long off a ship from the lowlands and could have brought it with him. That is usually how it begins in London, is it not?'

'Often, yes. He could have passed it to Celia as she served him or when he dragged her onto his knee.'

'I never thought of it before,' she admitted, 'but you kept asking how she could have caught it when no one else did. Then I remembered that Flemish gentleman who dealt in cloth.'

'Was this the first time Sir Thomas invited a man to his home but was not present himself?' She agreed it was. 'And he left instructions that in his absence his wife alone should tend to the man personally?'

'We wondered perhaps if the merchant might consider himself more important if the lady of the house did this for him,' she explained. 'Or perhaps it was the custom in his country? I know not how they do things in other lands.'

'Sir Thomas could have known the man was ill when he invited him to his home.' It struck him then. 'He was a plague dog!' But Celia did not understand. 'Thomas was absent that night, yet sent a foreigner to dine at his home, someone who was clearly sick, a man base enough to drag Celia onto his knee and, not long afterwards, she fell ill then died.'

'You think this was deliberate?'

'I am saying it may well have been.'

'But he could have infected the whole household.'

'Would Sir Thomas Vernon care about the lives of others?' he asked her bluntly.

'Perhaps not, but his own life?' She thought for a moment. 'He did not return thereafter. I had to send a man to find him and tell him Celia was ill, most likely with plague. He sent word back most promptly, saying he would quit London for the country because he had to think of his heirs.'

'What if that was his plan all along?' Will asked. 'What became of this man, Janssens?'

'I never saw him again. Gone back to the lowlands, I imagine.'

'Or perished here,' he said. 'If Sir Thomas saw signs of sickness in this merchant then sent him to dine with Celia,' he mused, 'then he might as well have sent his wife a vial of poison and bid her drink it.' He took Rosalind's silence as an acceptance that this could at least have been possible. 'Yet no one looked into the matter further. Everyone too frightened of the plague to linger long in a house that had seen it,' he speculated. 'And you still say she never gave him cause? By being untrue with another man?'

'Never.'

'You knew nothing of a secret love she may have had?'

'Other than her husband, you mean?'

'We have already agreed it was unlikely she loved her husband.'

'That does not make her a whore,' snapped Rosalind. 'She was married under God and would have taken that vow to her grave.'

'Would have or did?' He softened his tone then, before she grew angry. 'There was no one who might have been assumed a secret love of Celia then, even if they were both entirely innocent of wrongdoing?'

'It would scarce be a secret love if I knew about it,' she retorted.

'Do ladies have secrets when they are as close as you were?'

'You would be surprised by what is hidden in the hearts of women. If Celia loved another man, I knew naught of it.'

'Whom then did she admire, if only from afar? Was there no one?'

She hesitated for a moment before answering. 'I can think of only one man she admitted to admiring, and that was chaste enough. 'Twas only for his talents. Nothing more.'

'Who?'

'An actor. One of your company, in fact.'

'Name him then.' Though Will felt sure he knew the answer already.

'Your friend,' she told him. 'Richard Burbage.'

Chapter Thirty-Six

'Friendship is constant in all other things
Save in the office and affairs of love'
— Much Ado About Nothing

Richard Burbage was practising the long soliloquy from *Henry VI*, so he would be able to recall every line while on tour. He was just finishing it as Will joined him on the stage.

'Did you ever hear a story about the Lady Celia?' he enquired of Richard, without any greeting or feigned interest in other matters.

'Aside from her being a goodly young woman who died of the plague?'

'That she attended a play.' Will waited to see if his friend would take on the appearance of a guilty man.

'Most do attend plays, Will, and many of them are women.'

'But while Celia was attending this play, she was kissed.'

'Kissed? Kissed where?'

'In the balcony and on the lips.'

'I had not heard that.'

'Strange, since half of London knows it.'

'Then I belong to the second half that knew it not.' He smiled, then the smile became a frown. 'Why are you asking me about this?'

'Because it goes to the heart of the matter concerning her husband, Sir Thomas Vernon, and his treatment of her. Some believe his wife made him a cuckold that day and it gave him cause to want her dead.'

'Surely it was the other man who made him a cuckold, by seducing his wife.' He seemed to find this notion amusing.

'Some say she was kissed by her lover straight after the performance,' said Will, 'and that lover was an actor.'

Richard's face creased, as he finally understood the accusation Will was making. 'You surely do not think that I… the woman was married, was she not?'

'They often are, Richard. To speak plainly, I know of your phil-andering.'

'That is wondrous, coming from you!' protested Richard. 'I am not married, remember, and you are, lest you forget it… again!'

'But I did not kiss her,' Will said. 'And Celia told her closest companion she admired you.'

'Her closest companion?' he scoffed. 'You mean the fair Lady Rosalind?'

'I can think of none other in our company handsome enough, grand enough, yet wretched enough to attempt such a thing in the dark corner of an empty balcony once the audience has dispersed.'

'If they had dispersed, how could anyone know of it?' Richard demanded.

'They had not all gone. One stayed and saw you there.'

'No, he did not, for it was not I.'

'I did not say that it was a he.'

'A he or a she, it matters not, because, I say again, 'twas not I.' He seemed uncomfortable and Will seized on this.

'You, sir, are a liar.'

'And you, sir, shall be struck, if you repeat that slander.' Richard was angry now. 'Is this how you turn against a friend, when a woman enters your heart and wobbles your head? Have you lost all reason? Think on it!' Then he lowered his voice. 'If I was the type of man who had, on occasion, diminished his honour by finding himself alone with a woman who was already wed, do you really think I would kiss her in the balcony of the theatre my father built? My father who is always there and liable to see, then fly into a savage fury and beat me all the way down to the riverbank? Of course not! I am one thing, if nothing else: discreet. Now take your accusations and launch them like arrows at another, for I am not the man you seek!'

Will's fury instantly abated then. Richard's earliest protestation that he would not kiss a married lady was ridiculous; but this defence, that he would not risk the wrath of his formidable father, rang perfectly true.

'Good then,' he said simply. And when Richard said nothing in reply, 'So it was not you. Then I am satisfied and shall ask no more.' The further silence that met his words showed Will he had badly miscalculated. 'Come, Richard, are we not friends?'

'Do friends quarrel as much as we do?' Richard replied resentfully.

'No,' Will said finally, 'they do not.' And he nodded thoughtfully at his own observation. 'Brothers do, however,' he told Richard, 'and you are mine.' He held out a hand. 'Come.'

'Come where?' snapped Richard.

'Ale awaits us.'

Chapter Thirty-Seven

'Come not between the dragon and his wrath.'
— King Lear

It seemed to Will that he had established sound reasons why Sir Thomas Vernon might have wanted his wife dead. Firstly, he had married Celia for her family name and was disappointed when this brought him no advantage. He had not taken to the lady and their marriage was an unhappy one that he had wished he could undo. When asked to take in a ward, whose money would pass to her future husband, he saw an opportunity, but Sir Thomas could only marry Viola if he was a widower. That was reason enough to kill his wife, whether the rumours of her cuckolding him were true or not.

Celia was tended by her loyal companion, Rosalind, when she took ill, who swore her lady died of plague, but Rosalind had never treated anyone else with the disease and might not recognise the difference between its physical symptoms and bruises left from a husband's beating. Could Celia's other symptoms have been caused by a deadly poison that coursed through her blood? Who better to administer it than Sir Thomas's long-serving housekeeper Goneril, a woman with no love for Celia, who had been slighted by the arrival of a new mistress and her companion?

But what if Goneril had not taken so strongly against her mistress to kill her on her master's instructions? Could Sir Thomas instead have put something in his wife's food before leaving for his country house? Then there was the Flemish merchant he sent to have dinner with his wife, likely knowing the man was sick, while insisting Celia alone tended to the foreigner. This was Sir Thomas's plague dog idea in human form and it was no less deadly. No one wanted to be near a plague death, providing the perfect cover. Will wondered how many more might secretly die by someone else's hand before this epidemic was through. If you wanted to commit murder in London, plague was the perfect accomplice.

–

Rosalind continued to doubt that even a man as vile as Thomas Vernon could be blamed for her lady's death. Will admired her for ignoring her own prejudices against him but thought it naïve to discount the possibility.

She had finally trusted Will enough to reveal the whereabouts of her lodging house and Will walked there that morning, telling himself he had more questions to ask her about Celia, but he knew that was not the real reason. He wanted to spend more time with his dark lady. His questions that day would have to be invented, to become the excuse he needed to justify his visit. Was this proof that he loved her? Had he ever felt this way before now? Not since he was a youth, who had longed to know his Anne, in every sense of the word. There had been many flirtations since then. Some led to assignations he kept secret from his estranged wife, but had he spent as many of his waking hours thinking on any of them? Had he ever known a woman as fair as Rosalind? Was she not the embodiment of the dark lady he wrote and dreamed about, with her raven hair, deep brown eyes and even the light tan of her skin? It was as if God Himself had created Rosalind from a plan that had always been buried somewhere deep in Will's mind. Was there anything he was not entirely enamoured of? Her voice, the curve of her body, her sharp mind and mischievous humour, the sweet smell of her when she drew near? Will even liked the way she was bold enough to chastise him. Could he somehow fashion a world for himself with her by his side? He was determined to create one.

But not today. 'Rosalind is gone,' the widow told him.

'Gone? Gone where?'

'They roused her from her bed, and she was taken.' Tears stopped the words of the widow at Rosalind's rooming house, and Will had to urge her to tell him what had happened.

'What do you mean, woman? Who has taken her?'

The widow composed herself long enough to explain. 'They led her away to the Clink and will keep her there with the thieves, the drunks and the harlots. It is a calumny and I do fear for her safety.'

'Of what is she accused?' he demanded.

'Of witchcraft,' she said. 'And they say she will burn.'

-

Will wasted no time in crossing the river and went straight to Bankside in Southwark, to the site of the notorious Clink prison. There was at least a separate jail for the women but even that contained the very worst of London life. Will knew he would be unable to secure Rosalind's release if someone had sworn out a warrant against her, but he might at least be able to pay for her to have her own cell, with enough to eat and drink. A prisoner could live in less terrible conditions if they had money to pay their jailers; if not, they would be cast into 'the hole' along with the worst kind.

Rosalind's jailers would not let him see her. He had anticipated this, so offered a bribe. He was told she was a most dangerous prisoner indeed, for she was a witch. They even had to keep her apart from other prisoners, in case she took command of them with spells and urged them to rise up against their guards. This would keep her safe, but Will was alarmed by their conviction that she was so dangerous. They took his money in the end, in exchange for no more than a quarter of an hour with Rosalind.

He was let into her bare, windowless cell, which was lit by a solitary candle. Rosalind sat on the cold stone floor, still manacled. 'What need is there of chains when the door is bolted?' he demanded of the jailer. 'There is no window to fly from.'

'She could melt through the walls and be away,' argued the jailer.

'If she could do that, would chains stop her?'

The two men looked at each other directly until the guard must have decided he did not want to argue the point further or lacked the ability to do so. He took keys from his belt, undid Rosalind's manacles and left the room, locking it behind them.

'Are you harmed?' he asked her urgently as he helped Rosalind to her feet.

'No,' she replied softly, rubbing her wrists.

He led her to the hard bed by the wall and bid her sit. 'I have but little time,' he explained, and vowed to do all he could to free her. 'Who has accused you of witchcraft?'

'Who else but my former master, Sir Thomas Vernon. Your questions enraged him into repeating his accusations that I practised witchcraft against him, after he put me out. This time he does not only mention it in the marketplace but swears out a warrant against me. I shall stand trial for cursing him and making him fall from his horse. It seems such a small matter but, I am told, is enough to see me killed for it.'

'I shall not stand for this. I will protest.'

'An actor and playmaker, protesting against the word of a knight of the realm? What chance will I have?'

'Then I will summon good and learned men to come to your defence,' he insisted.

'I know none.'

'I must know some,' he said, though his world was almost entirely populated by actors, writers and villains. 'I will not give up,' he insisted. 'There must be something that can be done to have you spared.'

'If there is, let it be done quick,' urged Rosalind. 'I am to go before the magistrate at the assizes the day after tomorrow. If I am condemned on the word of Sir Thomas, I will die soon after. My jailer has told me to confess, then they might show mercy and I will not be burned. They will hang me instead from the Tyburn tree.'

'I will not let this stand!' Will protested.

She looked defeated then. 'For this I thank you, Will, but I fear there is nothing you can do.'

—

This was all Will's fault, and he knew it. Sir Thomas Vernon would not have cried witch at Rosalind had he not asked the man questions about Celia; he would not have wasted any thought on his wife's former companion had she not been the most likely source of Will's information. He was desperate now to help Rosalind escape her cruel fate.

Did Sir Thomas have them followed perhaps, so one of his men could report that Will Shakespeare spends much time with Rosalind Rivere, formerly of your household? Did he do this now to silence her or to cause Will distress in his revenge? Will's strong questioning of him had left Sir Thomas angry and frustrated. Poley's testimony, that Will was indeed backed by powerful, anonymous men at court, had given Sir Thomas pause. He could not yet act against Will but Rosalind was unprotected. She would soon be accused in court of witchcraft. There would be a short trial, in which Sir Thomas's word would be worth far more than her own, for she was both a woman and of lower birth. If found guilty, she would be hanged before a crowd in front of the three-sided gallows commonly known as the Tyburn tree.

If only Will had powerful friends or knew someone with more authority who could speak out in her defence, but Robert Cecil would not trouble himself, nor the Earl of Southampton. The earl had already warned Will he could never be seen to be involved in anything concerning his late cousin Celia.

Who then? He needed someone who could appear on Rosalind's behalf and discredit Sir Thomas Vernon's foolish claims.

Will thought some more, dredging back through his time in London, in a desperate attempt to come up with someone he had met at court or in Shoreditch who might serve Rosalind's cause.

Finally, he settled on one man. He alone might do it.

Chapter Thirty-Eight

'But love is blind and lovers cannot see
The pretty follies that themselves commit'
— The Merchant of Venice

'Why me?' protested the doctor, who had been surprised to be followed down the street and halted by Will, who breathlessly explained that he needed the help of Edward Jorden.

'You are a man of science and reason,' Will stated. Will had sought out his near-neighbour because he was a notable physician and the perfect man to argue against Rosalind's accuser. He then offered to buy him supper, the better to have him grant this favour in return. Jorden accepted the meal, although he was less than convinced that he could help Will.

'You know that in matters of this nature it is more often superstition that wins the argument,' he told Will over supper. 'A man who feels himself wronged by a woman need only point his finger and cry *witch* for her to be taken away and examined.'

'And a confession might be extracted through false promises of mercy or release,' said Will. 'If that fails, there are tortures that would break a man and should never be used on a gentle lady.'

'If a man has but the flimsiest evidence of unnatural powers being used against him, the woman will likely be condemned as a witch,' Jorden observed. 'Tell me, though, is this woman a healer or a midwife?'

'She has been both at times, when called upon.'

'Then she is twice condemned. They will say she has powers that come not from God.'

'How so, when healing can bring only good?'

'There are still those who are suspicious of physicians and all medicines,' he explained, 'for they prevent the will of God.'

'Then you yourself could be accused of sorcery.'

'I have been.' He smiled indulgently, for this was a charge that had done him no harm, since he was not a woman.

'You would not think her a witch,' Will assured him.

'I believe there are witches in this world but it would be strange for them to pass their lives peacefully in London, curing the sick.'

Will could see a small light of hope. 'Then you will speak at her hearing, as a man of reason?'

He blanched at this. 'That I cannot do.'

'But you are no more convinced she is a witch than I am and without your help, I fear Rosalind will hang.'

'I don't know this woman, Will. How can I vouch for someone I have never spoken to, least of all examined?'

'Must you see her?'

'Would you stand in public and declaim the good character of a stranger accused of a crime?'

'But she is under arrest and may not see anyone.'

'Then I know not how I can be of service to you in this matter, or her.'

'I have money. I could pay you.'

Jorden stiffened. 'You offer me money to give an opinion I do not truthfully hold about a woman I have never spoken with?'

'I meant no offence.' It was clear Will had caused that offence, nonetheless. 'I truly beg your pardon, Doctor Jorden. I fear I am not in my normal mind. My worry for this lady has made a beast of my reason.'

'This lady is dear to you?'

It was the first time Will had been asked to confess this to another man. He had not long admitted it even to himself. 'She is.'

'Then do not waste your money on me.' At first Will did not understand Jorden's point and assumed he was still offended or did not care about Rosalind's fate, but that was not what the doctor meant at all. 'It will find a better use *elsewhere*,' he added significantly, and Will understood then that the doctor was guiding him in a manner subtle enough to be denied later. 'I will see thee anon,' he concluded, and Will took it to mean they would meet again when the deed was done.

Will needed no further urging. He went home, retrieved some of his money and took it with him to parley with Rosalind's jailer.

–

That evening, he returned to the Clink with Edward Jorden. The physician was permitted to see Rosalind for one hour by the man Will had bribed. He explained the presence of the doctor to Rosalind, then Jorden suggested he wait outside while she was examined. Will reluctantly agreed and left the room, wondering why Rosalind seemed so unmoved by the presence of the doctor. Had she given up hope already or was she one of those superstitious people who had little faith in men of reason? Will felt quite helpless as he waited outside for the doctor to reappear. Jorden was with her for just short of the hour before he finally emerged.

'Well?' Will demanded.

'Let us leave here,' suggested the doctor quietly. He steered Will away from the jailer and guards before venturing his opinion and Will was forced to be patient a little longer until they were on the street outside.

'How found you the Lady Rosalind?'

Jorden frowned, and took what felt like an eternity to give Will his thoughts. 'That woman,' he declared, 'is no witch.'

'Oh, merciful Lord,' said Will, as if the court itself had just delivered the same verdict.

'She is merely a creature of high spirit, possessing a forceful, near-manly nature and a will that has not yet been bent to a master's, and I intend to prove it.'

Chapter Thirty-Nine

'Do you not know I am a woman? When I think, I must speak.'
— As You Like It

The magistrate had to speak loudly at first, to silence the spectators who had filled the gallery. They had all taken time out of their day to come and gawk at the witch and were packed in tight. Will's eyes left them and settled on a malevolent presence to one side of the courtroom. Sir Thomas Vernon was sitting alone with a grim look on his face, as if determined to get his revenge on Rosalind and, by extension, Will.

Rosalind was led into court with a manacle on each wrist. She appeared tired and dirty from her time in the cell and there was a look of resignation on her face.

'Rosalind Rivere, you stand accused of mischief following anger,' the magistrate told her, 'in that you did cast charms against one Sir Thomas Vernon, in revenge for him threatening to expel you from his house.'

She scoffed at that. 'I am accused of being a witch. Call it what it is.' Will's relief that she still had some fight left in her was tempered by the effect Rosalind's defiance might have on the magistrate overseeing her case. He was right to be fearful, for the man did not like her tone.

'Then I shall,' he told her. 'Are you a witch, Rosalind? Confess it now and mercy could still be shown to you. It is not too late,' he warned her, 'but soon will be.'

'Since when did the practice of a little low magic make a woman a witch?' she asked defiantly. 'I will answer that. As soon as she becomes troublesome to a man.' There were a few women in the public gallery who laughed quietly at that, for they knew the truth of it.

'What is this low magic of which you speak?' The magistrate sounded shocked, as if Rosalind had just confessed her crimes.

'Turning herbs into medicine or making them into a poultice. That's no more than any apothecary would do,' she said, 'though, being a man, he would charge you double.' There was more mirth from the crowd at this further truth, from women and men both.

'And what trouble did you cause this man who has accused you?'

'I bore witness to his unchristian treatment of his wife. He would not wish that to be made public.'

Will watched Sir Thomas as he stared malevolently at Rosalind.

'What form of ill treatment did she receive at his hand?' asked the magistrate.

'He beat her.'

'A lot of men chastise their wives,' the magistrate said firmly, 'often with good cause.'

'Can they then not leave the house for a week?' she asked and there were gasps and murmurs from the public gallery at that. 'Until the bruises finally fade?'

'A week?' Even the magistrate seemed a little shocked by this and he glanced at Thomas Vernon, as if newly appraising him. Sir Thomas was stone-faced, as if he had not even heard the accusation against him.

'You think I magnify the sin and Celia healed in a day or less?' she asked. 'It was not often that way.'

'And for what sins did Sir Thomas beat his wife?' It was clear the magistrate thought there must have been good reason for it.

'For naught and for all. He beat her for speaking when she shouldn't and not speaking when he thought she should. She was beaten for not running the household well enough or spending too much time in the management of it. She was too familiar with his friends or not familiar enough. He beat her when he was drunk, recovering from the drink or sober afterwards. He beat her for breathing.'

The magistrate considered this for a time before stating, 'Yet we only have your word on the matter, or is there another here present who can bear witness to these acts you have described?' He looked around the room, but no one spoke.

'There is no one here today,' she conceded, 'but if you were to ask the current or former members of his household—'

'There is no one here *today*' – he cut her off – 'and *today* is what concerns us. Now, I ask you again, why would Sir Thomas Vernon, a knight of this realm, name you for a witch, if you were not one?'

'Because he hates me.'

'And why would he hate you?'

'It is as I said, for seeing everything he did to my lady in her lifetime, and now he wishes to silence me.'

'Something he has singularly failed to do.' That caused some laughter, which the magistrate did not seek to stifle, adding, 'I doubt any man could achieve that.' He was playing to the gallery now and Will worried that Rosalind was too outspoken for this man who sat in judgement of her. Will wished she would appear meek, but he knew Rosalind would be unable to.

'You were in his household for a year or more but only now does he name you a witch. Do you claim he hated you from the beginning?'

'I was an extra mouth to feed. He would remind me of this daily but I worked hard and stopped his complaints. Then one day, I stepped between him and my mistress during a beating. His final blow struck me instead of her and I fell hard upon the floor. I thought he might kill us both then, but the sight must have shamed him, for he stopped, then left his house in a violent rage.'

The public gallery greeted this account in silence and the magistrate did not challenge it. 'But why would he call you a witch?'

'He fell from his horse that very night.'

The magistrate was reading from a statement now. 'Sir Thomas claims the fall onto hard ground could have killed him, and that this was in revenge for your own *fall*, when you slipped and lost your footing because you came between a man and his property, by which he means his wife.'

'I did not fall. He felled me with a blow. By his account, I cursed him as he left his house. This is a lie. He says it is the only explanation for why a rider of such accomplishment could possibly have slid from his horse.'

'It reared up in the street and threw him,' the magistrate quoted from Vernon's testimony, 'as if the devil himself had pulled on its tail.'

'That's your "mischief following anger" that I am accused of? I would have done it too, if I had the power.' There were gasps from the gallery at this assertion and Will closed his eyes. Why would she say something so damning?

'You should not speak such a thing,' the magistrate said, confirming his fears, 'for it will be used against you.'

'If I really had that power, then why would I let him fall so hard yet land so soft, without so much as a broken bone? He wasn't even injured, save for bruises and his hurt pride, but claims I almost killed him. I was nearly banished from the house after that but the marks on my face would have told a story he didn't want telling.'

'He put you out anyway in the end, once the Lady Celia had passed.'

'He did.'

'What did you do then?'

'Sought out Master James Burbage at the Theatre, confessed my plight and begged to sleep there, in exchange for work as a seamstress. We both benefited from the arrangement, and I slept in the attiring room.'

The magistrate did not seem to be listening to her answer. Instead, he read out another statement: 'His housekeeper, Goneril, claims you said Sir Thomas should die.'

'I said no such thing,' protested Rosalind.

'Why would this lady lie about it?'

'Because her own position was made less important by my arrival and that of my lady. We ran the house together.'

'Making her burden less,' he observed. 'So why would she complain?' He did not wait for an answer, continuing, 'Then what did you say, if not that?'

'That if he did not die, Celia surely would.' There were gasps from the public gallery at this and she had to speak louder to be heard. 'Which is not the same as planning his death nor even wishing it upon him. It was clear to me that if God did not take Celia's husband before the year was out, then He would take her instead and Thomas Vernon's hands would be the instruments He would use.' This caused a further and louder reaction from the gallery but Will could not tell whether they believed her and were outraged at Sir Thomas or were siding even further against her as a liar.

The magistrate held up a hand to demand silence. 'So, you did not urge your friend to kill her husband?'

'Not I, sir.'

'Nor for her to leave him?'

'And go where?' She snorted. 'What can a woman do on her own without a man? Nothing. She is considered worthless without a husband.'

The magistrate considered this and declared, 'I think I have heard enough.' He then went on to explain that Sir Thomas would not be testifying against the accused woman since he had outlined his accusations in written statements already in the magistrate's possession.

Will began to panic then. He had expected Sir Thomas to appear before the court and to list, possibly at some length, his grievances against Rosalind before declaring her a witch. If there were no other witnesses against her then there might be very little time left in this case, but Edward Jorden was nowhere to be seen. Had he forgotten the trial was today, forsaking Rosalind in her hour of greatest need?

Will's worst fears were confirmed when the magistrate asked the room, 'Is there anyone else who wishes to appear before this court to offer testimony, either in support of the woman, Rosalind, or against her, before a verdict?'

Will scanned the room again for Edward Jorden, in case he was standing in the public gallery, ready to get to his feet and declare his presence, but he could not see the man. Without him, the verdict would surely go against Rosalind. Nothing she offered in her defence so far was convincing enough for an acquittal and Sir Thomas's written words would be considered of far higher value than her spoken ones.

'Anyone?' asked the magistrate and he paused. Still, no one stood or spoke in reply. 'Very well...'

But before the magistrate could finish, Will found himself getting to his feet and calling out, 'There is!'

This caught the magistrate by surprise. 'And who are you, sir?'

Will gave the court his name and occupation. He could tell by the frown on the other man's face that his status as an actor and writer was not enough to lend weight to any opinion he might have had.

'By what authority do you stand and speak in this court?' he asked dismissively.

'It is not I that will speak on Rosalind's behalf.' He needed to engage with the court as slowly as possible, to give Edward Jorden the chance to make it there in time, but he knew he would not be able to talk forever and that very soon the magistrate would tire of this and call a halt.

'Who then?' He looked round the court as if expecting someone to declare themselves.

'A man of high renown,' Will began, 'someone who, if it please, can offer an opinion about this accused lady that will entirely convince you of her innocence. You might rightly be asking me why and how I know this?' He paused, looked towards the door and, seeing no one, continued. 'This witness is a man of such learning that to discount his opinion would be to commit an act of gross folly. Consider how rare it is to hear words spoken in defence of an innocent woman—'

'We will be the judge of that,' interrupted the magistrate, meaning her innocence.

'—by one of such high reputation that he is known, not just in London, or indeed merely in England but throughout the continent, as a man of deep learning of both a scientific and medical nature. This man has studied at universities, he has visited the wisest, most learned men in not just one but several countries in Europe and has shared his knowledge with the greatest minds in Christendom.'

'And who is this man?' asked the magistrate.

'I am speaking of none other than the world renowned, highly respected physician' – a glance at the door in case he should walk in at just that moment and hear his name, but still no one was there – 'Doctor Edward Jorden.'

'I have never heard of the fellow.'

'But you will!' declared Will with full bombast. 'For he is the one of the brightest and best young minds this country has ever produced. One day he shall be considered the foremost—'

'Yes, yes' – the magistrate waved his hand impatiently to silence Will – 'but where is he?'

Will took a deep breath. 'Not yet here,' he admitted.

'Then it is of no consequence how acclaimed this man is. For if he is not here, he cannot be heard.' Then he added, 'And that is scientific fact.' His smile indicated he expected laughter from the gallery but he received none.

'Indeed sir, but he is coming.'

'And so is nightfall. Must we wait indefinitely for him?'

'I beseech you, do please wait,' Will urged him. 'But only for a time.'

'How much time?' the magistrate enquired.

'I do not know.' This prompted a sigh from the magistrate. 'But I do know that his words will be worth waiting for. This is an opportunity for us all to listen to a man of—'

'Yes, yes.' More waving of the hand and the same words to silence Will. 'You have already given a most eloquent, if overlong, introduction to this physician, but if he does not arrive anon then I will not delay the court for him, when I have only your word he will appear at all. I ask you now, again, is he here?'

'No, in truth, he is not.'

'Then I cannot—'

'Is a lady's life worth nothing?' Will roared in desperation at the gallery, silencing its mutterings and shocking the magistrate. 'Must we condemn this poor, wretched woman as a witch, when waiting for mere minutes will provide us with eloquent testimony that would prove her innocent of all charges against her? Can we not sacrifice a few moments of our time, so that she may not give up her young life for no reason?' He was appealing directly to the gallery and they responded with supportive noises, seemingly in no hurry to leave. Clearly they were enjoying this entertainment. Rosalind meanwhile was watching proceedings with a face that betrayed no emotion.

The magistrate was not impressed, 'I cannot halt the business of this court in order to wait for a phantom to appear.'

'But appear he shall!'

'He may or he may not, but we cannot wait longer.'

'Just five more minutes.'

'No.'

'Not five? Then two. You can spare two.'

'I cannot,' he told Will resolutely, just as the door opened.

'He is here!' Will roared, and the gallery cried out as one as Edward Jorden walked into the room, taken aback by the loud greeting he received. 'Will you not hear him now?'

Chapter Forty

'Boldness be my friend!
Arm me, audacity, from head to foot!'
— *Cymbeline*

The crowd would have been in uproar if the magistrate had failed to permit Edward Jorden to appear before them after such an eloquent and weighty introduction by Will. They were all now eagerly waiting to hear what he had to say in defence of the accused woman. The magistrate bid Jorden to come forward then and stand where he could be more easily examined by the court.

Edward Jorden seemed to cast an air of scholarly authority upon proceedings, as he outlined his credentials, describing himself as a man of reason and of learning. He had studied extensively in this country and abroad, he told the magistrate, particularly in Italy, and had a degree from Padua. His university education meant he preferred science to ancient superstition, though he obviously acknowledged the existence of both God and magic.

Will urgently scanned the faces of those in attendance to try and gauge whether they were impressed or suspicious of the man's know-ledge. There were many in England who distrusted learning and espe-cially the words of those with expertise in a particular field. They preferred to get their views from the collective superstitions of friends or neighbours, no more learned than they were. Ignorance was a comfort to them and trusting completely in God a less bothersome way to live a short, simple, often brutal life, without bothering to consider opinions contrary to their own.

Will could not tell how the gallery were receiving Jorden's words but at least the magistrate was listening. He was leaning forward and regarding the doctor seriously, as if he was a man worthy of attention.

The magistrate was clearly worried the doctor's learning might prejudice him against what all men knew to be true. 'You cannot deny the existence of witches, surely?'

'I do not deny it,' he said. 'All I say is, there are witches and then there are ordinary women who upset their neighbours and are denounced as witches. Not every midwife, potion-maker or spinster is a witch, but many are accused of the crime without proof.'

'What proof is needed?' asked the magistrate. 'If you argue with a woman then fall ill, are you not bewitched? If you anger them and see your good fortune melt away, your crops ruined or your barn burned down, are you not the victim of charms? That is proof.'

'Maybe you left your pipe burning in your barn and it fell into the straw, the day after your quarrel with your neighbour. It need not always be witchcraft.'

'If it feels like witchcraft then it is witchcraft,' argued the magistrate.

'I lack your certainty.'

'A man cannot be undecided in this world. He should come down on one side or the other and, having chosen his course, must stay on it or be damned. There is no room for doubt.'

'Then allow me to remove it, in this case. With your permission, I have some questions of my own for Sir Thomas Vernon, if he is here?'

The magistrate seemed more intrigued than hostile. 'He is here,' he said, 'and since a woman's life depends on it, I will allow your questions.'

'Why should I answer his questions?' snapped Sir Thomas, but this was the wrong approach.

'Because I wish it,' the magistrate told him, 'and there is an end to the matter.'

Reluctantly Sir Thomas stood and faced the doctor.

'You accuse this lady of being a witch?' Jorden began.

'I accuse her of being more of a witch than a lady.' This brought some laughter from the men in the gallery.

'Then what is her familiar?'

'How say you?' he asked as if confused by the question.

'I ask again, what is her familiar?'

Sir Thomas thought for a moment and Will wondered if he was weighing up the risk of telling a lie by inventing one on the spot, but he must have decided against it. 'She has none,' he said quietly.

'Really?' Feigned surprise from the doctor. ' 'Tis strange. Everyone knows that a witch must have a familiar.' He glanced towards the magistrate, adding, 'Is this not so?' and the magistrate obliged by nodding sagely. 'That is, a creature gifted to her by the devil or another witch, to be her attendant in her evildoing.' He let that thought be digested by his audience. 'But she has none you say: no cat, no dog, no rat?'

'None, sir.'

'Then she cannot be a witch,' he proclaimed and the gathered people in the gallery were most attendant now. 'So says Reginald Scot, who in 1584 wrote *The Discoverie of Witchcraft*, a most scholarly and learned work on the subject. He further stated that witches are "commonly old, lame, bleary-eyed, pale, fowl and full of wrinkles". He goes on to describe witches as lean and deformed, showing melancholy in their faces, to the horror of all that see them. He states that these miserable wretches are so odious unto all their neighbours, and to be feared.' He let that sink in. 'Now then, let's take a look at this supposed witch, Rosalind.' He turned theatrically to view her, as if for the first time, then he gasped, 'Is she not hideous?' This brought everyone in the court to laughter.

'In no form does she resemble a witch. In her manner too she is the opposite of an evil doer. She cures the sick and brings new life into the world. This woman is no witch.' He repeated the words he had used on Will to such good effect: 'I have examined her thoroughly and found no malice or evil intent within her. It is true she has a high spirit and a leaning towards hysteria but this is a common trait in both unbroken horses and unmarried women and we don't hang either.' There was some mirth in the room at that. 'They are yet to bend to their master's will but both wives and horses benefit from time and a good man's attentions.' The gallery enjoyed that. There was laughter from both men and women at this. The doctor appeared momentarily confused by their reaction for he was quite serious and had not intended to amuse. 'It is a common enough condition,' he stated firmly.

'You are saying it is an actual malady?' asked the magistrate. 'For which there is a cure?'

'It is. I have studied it extensively with other learned men. I intend to write a book on the matter, in fact, for it is too little understood.'

'Then what is the cause?' demanded the magistrate.

'*Passio Hysterica*,' he proclaimed, 'or the "suffocation of the mother" as it translates, though in this instance it means the womb, which is where this affliction starts.'

'The condition occurs before the woman is even born?' asked the judge.

'You misunderstand me, sir,' Jorden said in a tone that made it clear this was not his fault. 'It starts with *her* womb.' And he pointed at the Lady Rosalind.

'*Her* womb?'

'Yes,' he explained. 'It wanders.'

'You mean the condition moves around the body?'

'The womb itself does,' the doctor said confidently. 'In unmarried women, yes. They become restless and hysteria naturally follows. What Sir Thomas Vernon took as a malevolence from within her was merely a congestion of humours around the womb, which causes it to wander. This is a well-known condition, recognised as far back as ancient Greece, when the physician Hippocrates noted that both maidens and widows are more likely to experience hysteria than married women because they do not receive the benefit of marriage.'

'Do you mean...?' The magistrate could not find the words.

'She is currently deprived of marital activity,' Jorden clarified.

The gallery was greatly amused by that and even though Will was preoccupied with Rosalind's fate, he made note of it for the stage. Bawdy humour that might not be tolerated in a small gathering quickly wins over a crowd.

'I see.' The magistrate seemed uncomfortable. 'Is there a treatment for this condition?' he asked quickly, as if keen to move on. 'Or a cure?'

'Why, yes,' said Jorden, 'the cure is simple: a wedding' – laughter went through the gallery like a wave – 'and the treatment is found in the marriage bed.' Now the laughter was unrestrained.

'Enough!' the magistrate bellowed at the gallery. 'We have had enough!' And as if to illustrate his point, he quickly threw out the entire case against Rosalind.

Chapter Forty-One

'Come live with me and be my love'
— *'The Passionate Shepherd to His Love'* – Christopher Marlowe

Will and Edward Jorden left the hearing together, along with the acquitted Rosalind. Will was concerned for her safety now that Sir Thomas had been confounded by the magistrate. He would surely look for another way to harm her. Will's own life would be in peril too, since he had brought the man who saved Rosalind. Sir Thomas would be unlikely to bear that public humiliation, whether Will had the protection of powerful men or not.

Jorden had tethered his scientific knowledge of this wandering womb condition to the view that what Rosalind really needed to cure her ills was the attentions of a man. This was both a widely held and a bawdy argument to set before a public gallery and had swayed the magistrate.

Rosalind was strangely muted. She did offer her thanks to both Will and the doctor but said little else. Will could not help feeling disappointed, even a little aggrieved. Perhaps she was exhausted from her ordeal.

Will thanked the doctor with all of his heart and Jorden bade them both farewell. When he was gone, Will suggested they go back to the theatre. A night in the attiring room might be safer for Rosalind than walking the streets to her lodgings. She agreed and Will took a chance then, suggesting they wait a while in his rooms first, to lessen the chance of accidentally stumbling upon Sir Thomas or his men.

'What ails thee, Rosalind?' he asked her as soon as they were inside. 'Are you not overjoyed?'

'Overjoyed?' She seemed confused.

'This morning you had an appointment with the Tyburn tree. Now you are a free woman.'

'Am I? I am told not to leave London for a time, in case another man accuses me of witchcraft and I should be summoned before the magistrate again. I am innocent but hardly free,' she protested. 'I do thank you for your care towards me, though, Master Shakespeare, and for the time and money you gave to free me.'

'Yet you seem ill pleased. I thought you might be happier.'

'You think I should be happy?' she asked in disbelief.

'Now that your ordeal is at an end.'

'It is not at an end.'

'Sir Thomas cannot bring that case against you again. It has been heard and dismissed, thanks to Doctor Jorden's testimony.'

'His shaming of me, you mean?'

'This morning you were marked as a witch.'

'But now I am a woman whose womb wanders because I am in want of a tupping. I am free from a cell but marked as one with a hysterical nature, a malady that can only be cured by a man. I am nothing without a husband, it seems. Worse than nothing, in fact. I am dangerous to men until one among them can tame me, like a wild mare.' It was rare for Will to discover he was short of words but, just then, he could find none to placate her. 'You believe that too,' she said.

'I believe that we are all in want of another. A man needs a woman, a woman requires a man.'

'Where is your woman then?'

'We are separated by my work and a hundred miles.'

'So, if a man needs a woman, how do you yourself not require one, or do you take whores?'

'I do not.'

'You bridle at that,' she noted. 'Is it the idea of it or the money you object to parting with?'

'I did not object to parting with my money when it helped you,' he snapped.

She sat down heavily on his bed and then lay back on it. 'You'd better take me then, for I have no money to repay you. But will it be just the once or am I to be yours for a while? I confess I do not know how much I am worth.'

'Don't speak of that even as a jest. It demeans you and shames me. I have no use for whores.'

She sat up. 'Then what kind of woman *do* you use? Do you only deflower virgins or pass afternoons with grateful widows? Which would be the more respectable pursuit, I wonder?'

'Why do you insist on taunting me when I am your only friend?'

'If you are my only friend, then who else am I to taunt?' She stood then and let out a sigh. 'I do not seek to hurt you, Master Shakespeare. You have been far kinder to me than most. But I have never met a man who did a good thing without expectation of payment of some kind or another.'

'I seek nothing more than your good opinion of me. Is that so dark a motive?'

'It depends upon how you will use that good opinion. Will it be traded later for something else? You wish to own me perhaps?'

'I have no need of a slave.'

'A wife is as much owned by her husband as any slave but I assume yours has no more plans to die soon than I do, though of course none of us know when death might call, what with the plague in town.'

'If I were an unmarried man, I confess I would see you as a fine wife, for me or a more fortunate other, but I am wed already and can no sooner marry you than the queen.'

'Careful, Will. You should not mention the queen and marriage. She will assume you mean to tame her. Why do you think she has avoided it all this time? She prefers to rule than be ruled by a husband, and who could blame her, when she sees what happens to other women who take a man?'

'Can we stop this talk of marriage?' he pleaded.

'If it troubles you to be reminded of it. If you do not seek it, then what *do* you want from me, with my good opinion of you secured?'

'Nothing.'

'So if I were to thank you for your help but tell you I must be away, we would be done? I am under no obligation to you, save for the coin you used to bribe the doctor into my jail?'

'Forget the coin,' he snapped. 'I do not wish to be repaid the bribe money. You did not ask it of me, and I spent it from my own purse without your foreknowledge.'

'Then I do thank you.' And she waited for him to speak but he did not. 'And we need never see one another again beyond this day?'

In answer, he stepped away from the door to allow her to leave, which she made to do, but as she reached it, he said, 'Unless?'

'Unless?' She turned back to face him.

'You wish it?'

'In what way could I benefit from a continued dalliance with a married man, when tongues are already wagging about me all over London?'

'Not a dalliance. A friendship, of sorts.'

'A friendship, of sorts,' she repeated, as if she was genuinely contemplating the idea. 'Between a man and a woman? Would it be like that between two men?'

'Very like,' he assured her.

'Would we go hunting together, hawking, drinking, whoring? No, you object to whores, though they at least understand what they are agreeing to.'

'I have no need for you to go hunting or drinking with me. I meant I could be a friend to you, as I think I have proven this day already. I could support you.'

'In what way support me?'

'In every way.'

'You would tell the gossips to quiet themselves, for I am a lady of virtue, convince James Burbage to pay me extra for costumes and to make up more of his actors?'

'If you wish it so.'

'Or support me in other ways?' She sounded suspicious and this made Will nervous. As always, when in that state, he used too many words.

'Rosalind, I have of late given much thought to your reduced circumstances. You are a lady undone by cruel fate, cast out of a home where once you had a position, even if you lacked security and contentment there. Spurred on by your kind and gentle heart and thanks to my own improved position of late, I thought to try and aid you. My sonnet "Venus and Adonis" will be published soon and should bring in a good sum. There are rooms next to mine that are empty and can be let. They are dry and warm and better than the attiring room or lodgings with a lowly widow. I feel sure they would be to your liking. If I recommend you, the owner would have no objection to a lady such as yourself taking them.'

Her face betrayed no feelings on the matter. She simply asked, 'And what is the cost of these rooms?'

'That can be agreed and I will act as your agent in this matter.'

'And what if, even with you as my agent, the rent proves too high?'

'Then I will pay it,' he said firmly, 'and gladly.'

'And what would you expect from me in return?'

'My reward would come in the knowledge that you are sheltered and safe with a roof above your head.'

'Safe from *all* men?' Her tone told him she did not believe this.

He bridled then. 'If by that, you mean you would not feel safe from me, then I take it badly, for all I offer you is my charity.'

'You think I need charity?'

'Charity meaning love,' he amended his words. 'We all need both love and charity at times. I have benefited from the charity of others and will continue to do so through my patrons. I simply wish to share my good fortune.'

'You are offering me charity?' she asked. 'Or love? Which is it?' And her voice was so calm he could not hope to detect the answer she might have preferred.

'Both.'

'I see,' she said, 'or think that I do. You have such feelings of Christian charity for me that you are willing to install me in rooms next to yours and even pay the rent. For how long? A day, a week, a year?'

'For however long it is needed.'

'And when would you tire of that arrangement, if I were to show you no love in return?'

'Why do you think you would show me no love? Would not your heart soften towards me if I helped you in a time of great need? That is all I ask, no more.'

'A moment ago you pledged you wanted nothing in return, now you say you need my heart to soften towards you or we won't have a bargain. What will you ask for next, I wonder?'

'Lady, you twist my words like a lawyer,' he protested. 'Then add meanings to them that I did not intend.'

'I know your meaning true enough. You will set me up in rooms next to yours. Why not across town instead? I know the reason. How long before word gets out that the poet Shakespeare keeps a woman in his lodgings and all of London knows it?'

'They are not my rooms,' he protested.

'They might as well be. You could knock down a wall or make a door between them and it would make no difference to my reputation or yours.'

'I am offering to help you, not install you as my mistress.'

'At least there would be some honesty in that bargain!'

'Lady, I am insulted!'

'No, sir, you insult me!' she snapped. 'And in doing so, you try to keep your good name but surrender mine. You even lie to yourself! You say this has nothing to do with the usual run of things when a man sets a woman up in rooms. At least have the courage to call it what it is: a generous offer to become your whore, though I can imagine it would be a less costly arrangement than paying for one by the hour.'

'I sought only to...' But what had he sought and how to explain it to Rosalind?

'You sought only to put me in your debt then keep me at your mercy. How long before you opened my door and crept to my bed? I would lie there knowing that if I did not permit it, I could be on the street the next morning.'

'That is not... I swear I would never...' But he had indeed hoped she might think better of him for this act of generosity than she did now. Perhaps then, over time, she would yield willingly to his advances, but he never imagined they were as clumsy and unwanted as she had just painted them. Now he had made an enemy of her. What a fool he was.

'Do not swear or promise me anything, Master Shakespeare. Look inside your heart instead, then ask yourself what you truly expected from me, in return for your charity. Confess your sins, if only to thine self.' Then she made to leave but not before turning on him one last time. 'A whore by any other name is still a whore.'

'Wait!' he called but the door was already open. 'Wait, Rosalind. Damn it, woman, wait. Hear me out, by God!' He had not intended it to become a roar and she was clearly unimpressed by it, though she did stop and turn back to him.

'I do not expect you to become my whore.' He made an effort to sound calmer. 'I merely wish to help you. That is all.' Having said his piece he sat down on the bed and must have looked defeated then, because she stepped back into his room and closed the door again.

'And you would risk your reputation by tying it to mine, even though it is disgraced? You would feed and house me, at some expense, but want nothing in return? Really, come now, Will, you sell yourself cheaper than those whores you look down upon. I would respect you more if you told me the truth. What then should I give you in return?'

'I do not know.' He was done now and just wanted this quarrel to be over.

'But you do know. Say it, Will. I would rather you did.'

'That is not something to be said, for saying cheapens it. I would rather let it take its natural course and then perhaps, in time, if you were to will it, a love of sorts might grow between us.' He looked at her hopefully then, but she soon scorned him.

'A love without marriage?' she asked. 'But not a love without tupping?'

'Do you have to say it so?'

'You are against me saying it, but want me to do it? When? Today, tonight? A week from now or a month? You would not wait a year,' she said calmly. 'No man would. How many months would I get, before you took what I had yet to give freely?'

'That is not what I want! I could never harm nor deceive you, Rosalind. I want only to love you but I am trapped in my marriage, so cannot make you my bride. I was young when I met Anne and she with child. We had to be married. Why do you turn the one thing I *can* give you into something coarse and shameful?'

'Because it is, because it would be! You would ruin me with your love, Will. As soon as the first man or woman in the street cast a scornful word about me being Shakespeare's whore, it would destroy what little reputation I had left.'

'Would that be so bad when on your own admission you have already fallen so low?' Instantly, Will checked himself but it was too late. He could tell by the look of shock on her face. 'I did not mean—'

'Since I am so base and low, I shall leave here, Master Shakespeare, before you are seen with me and cast out by gentle folk, who might think you prefer the company of witches and whores.' He gave her a despairing look but she was not done. 'And in the future, be careful how freely you give your heart,' she cautioned, 'lest, like my womb, it begins to wander.'

Chapter Forty-Two

'…wise men know well enough what monsters you make of them.'
— Hamlet

Will spent the following days in a torment. He was torn between the desolation that follows an end to all hope and the sweet memory of a love he was not yet able to give up on. If he went to her, if he pleaded with Rosalind for another chance to explain himself, would she perhaps alter her poor view of him? Did she miss his company at all? He decided to give this love one last chance.

Rosalind was back living with the widow in her rooming house and, when she received Will, the fire had gone from her eyes. He was permitted to enter and sit in a small kitchen while she stood, as if ready to leave the room if she heard anything that might aggrieve her. Will began tentatively, by apologising for his rough, uncivil words and the clumsiness of his offer of rooms. He explained this had been born not from lust but out of love for her.

'You have a wife, Will. Have you forgotten her?'

'I have not forgotten her.'

'Do you not love her then?'

He tried to explain his feelings about Anne to this woman who had completely bewitched him. 'How often have I been told I am hardly a gentleman or scarcely a gentleman, sometimes barely a gentleman? And yet, Anne embarrasses me. There, I have said it, and I know it makes me as bad as all those men I despise for looking down upon me, but I can deny it no longer. She embarrasses me: with her lack of curiosity, learning or letters, her superstitions and the way she puts every unjust thing down to God's will. She embarrasses me,' he said it again for emphasis, 'or she would if she were with me and that is perhaps why she is not.'

'What of her feelings?' asked Rosalind. 'Have you thought of them or do they not matter? Is she not embarrassed by you?'

'I have not given her cause. She can walk Stratford with her head up, knowing her husband is close to becoming a success in London and a good portion of what he earns is sent back to her there. She will not starve.'

'Good then. She will not starve. That's a fine thing,' she snapped. 'I thought a playmaker must daily don another man's shoes in order to understand him.'

'He must,' he agreed.

'Then walk for a time in hers,' she urged him. 'Her husband is gone for much of the year. In London, yes, and something of a success too, writing his sonnets and plays and performing on the stage, but what else is he up to? Where, nightly, does he lay his head and next to whom? If she does not have these thoughts herself, she knows others will and they'll talk of it too, behind her back. You don't care what they say, for you are a man and not there often. She is not here because she embarrasses you, while you turn her into a fool.'

'Anne's no fool,' he protested.

'Her neighbours will say she is. There's that Will Shakespeare, away in London, drinking and whoring away the money he earns from those libidinous plays he writes. I've heard he has a mistress or two, or so *they* say.'

'Who are *they*?'

'It does not matter. *They* will say it. It is always *they* who say it. It was *they* who said Celia broke her vows, it was *they* who saw her kissed by another man at the theatre while her husband was gone, and *they* who said she did not die of plague but was killed. *They* see everything and are never idle, always busy telling others what *they* have seen or heard.'

'I care not what *they* think,' he protested. 'Only how I feel.'

'You do love me then?' she asked him gently.

'I think that I do, yes.'

Rosalind did a strange thing then. She stepped forward, reached out her hand and placed the palm over his, which was resting on the table, squeezing it softly. 'You only *think* that you do?'

'I know it, fair Rosalind.'

She took her hand away then. 'You think me fair?'

'Most beautiful.'

'And yet you think me a whore?'

'No, not so. You are gentle, kind and virtuous.'

'Yet you would have me?'

'I merely state my love for you. As for anything else, that would be for you to decide.'

'But not marriage, for you have a wife.'

'Who could never understand a man such as I,' he said. 'But you could.'

'You think because I can watch and admire your plays, could read your sonnets and talk of them with you, that I understand you. Are you and the plays and poems the same thing?'

'They come from a part of me, I believe, yes.'

'Do you think yourself an honourable man?'

'I do not think I am a dishonourable man.'

'Your wife might not agree. And I believe you would kill the very thing you wish to own.'

'How so?'

'You state you love me, in part, for my virtue and yet would take it from me. Then you would tire of me, having taken that which you value most.'

'You talk of taking, not giving, of virtue stolen, not surrendered.'

'Surrendered?'

'Traded then, for love.'

'Oh well, traded then, so be it. Let's clasp hands and call it a bargain!' And she adopted a manly pose, one leg out in front of the other and an arm extended to offer a firm handshake.

'That is not what I meant.'

'I think it *is* what you meant. You would offer me love but not marriage, lust without God's blessing. You would tup me, then tire of me and cast me aside. I would be left with nothing more than I came to you with, and a little less than before. There would be no marriage contract, no protection in law, only disgrace and ruin. Men like you would watch me pass by and say, "There goes Will Shakespeare's whore."' He recoiled at that image. 'Tell me it would not be so, if you dare?' And her tone made him realise that if he did, her fury would increase.

'In truth, I cannot dispute it might be so…'

'It would be.'

'…*if* I did discard you, but know this: my love for thee is an eternal thing, like the stars.'

'Pity me for believing that and it proved less lasting.'

'I know not what else to say…'

'There's a thing,' she mocked him. 'A man lost for words, a play-maker too, struck dumb by a simple woman's reasoning. You want all from me and I would live with fear of the day I became too old, too plain or too constant in your life and then you would love another.'

'I swear it would not be so.'

'Do not swear to me, Will. You swore oaths to your wife, before God, on your wedding day, and how long did they last?'

'Tell me then,' he pleaded, 'how I can return to the life I had before I met you, Rosalind, because I cannot sleep nor eat for thinking of you.'

'You will sleep when you are tired and eat when you are hungry. All that will pass, else you will starve to death and they will say, "There lies poor Will, the first man ever to die of love."'

'And now you mock me. I thought you kinder than that.'

'Well, I am angry.'

'Then why did you give me hope?'

'You think I led you down this path, with you pleading to get me into your bed? I did no such thing.'

'When I say that I do love thee and always will, do you not think it so?'

'I believe you think it so,' she said, 'and I think you believe it true. But for how long, Will? What happens when I am less fair, yet cost the same to keep? Who will prevent you from casting me aside? The church?' She shook her head. 'They would call me strumpet and say I may as well continue to be one, on the street or in a bawdy house. I'd be ruined and you would continue much as before.'

'I am not that type of man,' he protested.

'Then what type are you? The kind that takes a wife because he has to, having already given her a child? The type that leaves her, yet sends her enough money to get by? The type that forgets her, except to say I love her not and we should never have been together? Are you that type of man? If past is prologue, then if I lie with you, I am doomed.'

'I thought we had a bond.'

'One of friendship, perhaps; a respect for one another, possibly; a sense of some chaste affection between us, once, before you brought me to your rooms and broke it into pieces.'

'You are saying there is no world in which we can be more than that? I beg you to think on it more, Rosalind, before I go mad.'

'Then go mad!' she commanded, and in her anger and exasperation, she finally broke and with a shout, told him the truth: 'For I am bound to another!'

Her words landed like a blow and Will was shocked into silence, until finally he demanded, 'You are promised to another man? Who? You have never spoken of anyone. Do you invent him to turn me away from you now? Do not trifle with my affections, Rosalind. I beg you.'

'Will, understand this. There can never be anything more between us, not in this life nor the next.'

'Why?'

'Because I am already wed.'

Chapter Forty-Three

'…how bitter a thing it is to look into happiness
through another man's eyes!'
— As You Like It

Will stared at Rosalind for close to a full minute, to see whether she might be lying or if this was some bad jest. 'You wear no wedding band.'

'Master Burbage would not have me work for him if he knew I was meant to be keeping house for a husband. He would find another girl to sew his costumes and bid me have babies instead.'

'Keeping house? You have no house. You sleep here or in the attiring room.'

'I have no house *yet*. My husband is away securing one.'

'If you are truly married, then how long?'

'These past three months,' she said, without hesitation.

'Not long after you were cast out of Thomas Vernon's house? Can it be true?'

'It can,' she said. 'It is.' And there was such finality in those four small words that Will could no longer deny the verity of them.

'Then where is your husband and where was he when you were brought before a magistrate?'

'Abroad,' she told him. 'With no way to get word to him.'

'You did not think to mention in court that you had a husband?'

'Would it have made any difference if I had when I could not produce this husband? I was to be condemned anyway, before your doctor spoke on my behalf.'

'You are truly married then?'

'In front of God and a minister.'

'Where?'

'The Church of St Leonard's.'

'Who is this man you married?' He still found it impossible to believe she had a husband and had never even mentioned him.

'John Makepeace. He is a soldier, a captain who did good service in the lowlands, but that life is over.'

'Where did he fight?' If she hesitated to answer, she might have invented this captain.

'Breda, Zutphen and Deventer. He helped take them from the Spanish last year. More recently, he fought at Coevorden, where he was wounded and took ill, so returned home for a time.'

'That is how you met him?'

'His sister asked me to tend to his wound and treat the fever that came with it.'

'And he made a full recovery?'

'Thanks to God.'

'And you, Rosalind, I have no doubt.' When she said nothing, he asked, 'Should he not be with you? You have not long been wed.'

'He has matters to conclude in the lowlands and is owed money but will return soon. He is done with soldiering. We are to take on the lease of a farm.'

'Does it not trouble you to be wed to a man who has most likely killed other men?' Had she perhaps traded one rough master for another?

'There is violence in the hearts of all men, I think,' she said easily.

'Then you saved him from his.'

—

Though Rosalind's explanation seemed true, he had to be certain.

The next day, he walked to the Church of St Leonard's to speak to its minister, a man he knew well enough. This was his own church, though he did not go as conscientiously as he would have done in Stratford, where he would have been fined for non-attendance. In London, no one noticed if you missed church on Sunday or, if they did, they might assume you had died of some malady during the week. This was why he had not heard of Rosalind's marriage.

Will had not seen the minister in some time, having neglected God of late for more worldly matters. When he walked into the church, the old man came to greet him but he was not faring well. The minister walked with a heavy limp and both of his eyes were cloudy now, one so bad it looked like a pond frosted over in winter. It would be a wonder if he could see anything through it at all, but with his better eye he was able to recognise Will. As he reached his wayward parishioner, Will reached out an arm to steady him.

'I am not blind,' he said, as if reading the other man's thoughts. 'I manage perfectly well with one good eye.'

It seemed optimistic to describe his other eye as good. 'I have a doctor for a neighbour,' Will told him. 'I could ask him to examine your deficient eye.'

'And he will tell me what I know already. That I am old and my affliction is *cataracta*. A doctor examined me before and said it can only be cured with the knife. He wants to cut open my...' He pointed to his eye but struggled to describe the process.

'The... eyeball?' suggested Will.

'Yes, how clever, it is a ball inside, one assumes, so yes, the eyeball. He told me to take fennel and drink wine to preserve my eyesight, but he cannot cure me without the knife. He wants to peel my eye like an apple. I asked him what promise he can make that the pain would be worth it. He told me none. I sought assurance that I would not die from his cure and he said I must place myself in God's hands. I told him I listened for the voice of God every day and he has yet to tell me to pluck out mine own eye or let someone else take a slice from it, so I will go blind if I must.' He shook his head. 'For now, I can see what I need to see. I can make out shapes clear enough; and when those shapes speak, I know them to be men or women.' He smiled at that. 'If they bark instead, I know them to be dogs. The smell of my food leads me to it and I find my way to my bed at night. I have all that I need.'

Then he asked Will what he could do to help him. Will explained he had questions about a wedding and gave the bride's name. 'Do you remember this marriage ceremony?' he asked, still hoping that Rosalind had invented her nuptials.

Since such things were already a matter of public record, the minister did not feel the need to keep anything from him. 'Between Rosalind Rivere, of this parish, and a certain Captain John Makepeace, not long returned from fighting the Spanish in the lowlands? Yes.' He narrowed his eyes at Will in case the question was an accusation concerning his memory. 'I recall all of the weddings I sanctify before God.'

'But was there anything unusual about this one?'

'The wedding or the marriage?'

'Either,' he said, then, 'both.'

The minister thought about this for a moment that seemed to stretch out in front of them, before concluding hesitantly, 'Not so unusual, these days.'

'But a little unusual, perhaps?' He was coaxing the man, sure there was something there.

'In what capacity are you asking me this, Master Shakespeare?'

Will had already determined to bluster through with a vague notion of some unofficial authority. 'As a friend of one close to the crown,' he said sternly.

The minister did not seem remotely troubled by this. 'The queen has expressed her interest in a marriage I conducted?' He chuckled. 'How thrilling for an old man. I would be happy to present myself, to put her mind at rest.' He smiled mischievously at the notion. Will assumed he would be told to leave and never trouble the old man again, but instead the minister said, 'It was an ill-attended and somewhat hasty marriage.'

'Did you not cry the banns?' The custom was for the church to announce the couple's intention to marry on three consecutive Sundays or holy days, to make the matter public and ensure no one had any objection to their union, as well as encouraging attendance from those close to the bride and groom.

'No.'

'Why not?'

'Because they secured a marriage bond.' This meant their impending marriage would only have had to be announced once, in a reading of the banns, but it necessitated a sworn statement, denying any pre-contracts elsewhere, in order to satisfy the bishop. Only then would permission to marry be granted. It would also have brought the ceremony forward by a week or two.

'We see this more and more often now the city has increased in size. People crowded in together forget their morals and duty unto God. They rut like animals, even before their union has been consecrated, but I am bound to overlook it, if they are to be saved from sin and joined by God, for the sake of the children. It is likely the woman was already with child. That is the usual reason.'

'I understand.' Will still felt the shame of his own marriage bond when Anne, eight years his senior, fell pregnant because he too had forgotten his morals, and he did not have an overpopulated London to blame for it. His father had almost thrown him onto the street for his sinning. Eventually, he granted permission for the marriage bond, which Will needed, as he was only eighteen. His father had told him what a damned fool he was, having to marry so young.

'This woman was not with child,' said Will. 'At least there is no child now.'

'Perhaps it was lost before it entered the world,' said the minister, 'or… it is not uncommon for a woman to deceive a man in such matters, if she is already dishonoured by him and fears no one else will take her. "I am with child," she might say, "you must marry me." This is followed later by a further lie, that "the baby did not fully grow inside me", and there is naught to be done about it by then. *Let not man therefore put asunder, that which God hath coupled together,*' he said, quoting Matthew.

'And not many attended this wedding?'

'She has no family and was estranged from the household of her former lady.'

'What of her husband?'

'Not long returned from the low countries and had no one with him, save for his sister.'

'Then who else witnessed the ceremony?'

'A big man who left that household also. I remembered him carrying the Lady Celia's body from the cart when she passed. He stood witness to Rosalind's wedding, but I never saw him again.' So Isaac had not left on the day of Celia's burial, as had been commonly understood. He was still in London when Rosalind was married. 'She told me he left to work in Norfolk but I thought that strange. It is a very long way for a labourer to go for work.' He mused. 'Perhaps he knew a family there.'

Rosalind had claimed not to know what happened to Isaac or where the mute went when he left Celia's household. Either she was lying to the minister about that, for no reason he could imagine, or she was lying to Will.

'Did anyone else attend?'

'Two maids but I would be surprised if they knew the couple. Their language was coarse and they were soon gone. I think they took some coins from the bride.'

'You do not object to paid witnesses?'

'It's a small fault and understandable if there is no one else to stand with them. Many more will marry like that if the plague really is in London.'

'It is.'

'Then God have mercy on us all. I remember the misery it brought, ten years ago now, making orphans and widows in every street.'

Ten years ago, he thought. James Burbage had told Will the theatres had closed in 1582 as well and, back then, they had stayed shut for months.

Chapter Forty-Four

'...there is nothing either good or bad, but thinking makes it so.'
— Hamlet

When Richard Burbage came to see Will in his rooms, he found his friend in low spirits.

'I have not seen you in days, Will. I worried you'd been taken by the plague. You do realise even death would not spare you from delivering my father's play?' Will felt he was only half-joking about that.

'Alive or dead, it makes no difference. The play is unfinished and shall remain so.'

'But you are always writing,' he protested. 'Surely you must have produced something?'

'I have produced all of this.' He waved his arm towards a pile of scrolls, stacked high, that Richard had not noticed because his back was to them as he walked in. Richard turned then and his mouth fell open.

'But there is enough here for a dozen plays!'

'Six,' Will corrected him.

'Six plays? You have been working on six plays?' Will nodded but his friend did not seem to believe it possible. 'However could you expect to finish one, if you are writing another five? There is so much of it!'

'I have too many hours. Before the theatres were closed, a play would begin at two of the clock and end at five with a jig. I have been gifted those three hours each day and am determined not to be idle. Now you see what I make of them.'

Richard marvelled at Will's industry. 'Would it not be better to use all of your time to finish just one, instead of dabbling with so many?'

'Yes,' Will said, exasperated. 'Clearly it would.'

'Then, knowing this, why not haul in a whale, instead of a net full of sprats?'

'You are not a writer, Richard, and be thankful for it. I have no lack of ideas. They flow like wine into a cup but then, at some stage, I start to question whether an idea has real merit. I then move on to the next, contained within the play I have yet to start, convincing myself it is superior in every way to the old one. Alas, when I am two thirds in, it happens again and I put that work to the side and commence another play, and so on, possibly unto the end of time,' he said glumly. 'Or at least my time in this world.'

'This is a form of madness. Recognise it for what it is, Will, and heal thyself.'

'I thought so too. It was obvious to me I was losing my mind. I went to Marlowe then Kyd and told them both of my affliction. I was convinced they would brand me as crazed, bewitched or bedevilled. Do you know what they said?' Richard shook his head. 'That it is always the way. Marlowe said that while you are writing a play there is no more enticing prospect to deflect you from it than the one you want to write next. He said it is because, at that point, it is entirely perfect in your mind, and you have yet to take up your quill and ruin it.'

'Marlowe said that?'

'He did. I then asked Kyd how to resolve this and he told me it is a malady without a cure. I would have to live with it, the way men learn to live with the pox, by keeping the disease and its symptoms to myself, unless with a fellow sufferer who might understand my torment, for no other would care to hear of it. He said I would bore them and he was right. Nightly I bore myself with my inability to complete a play by going over it again and again in my mind. To finish it is to admit it is done and will be performed, despite its manifold imperfections.'

'There is no such thing as a perfect play, Will,' Richard told him. 'God Himself could not write one where every word dances from an actor's tongue and lands upon the ear of a groundling like the song of an angel.'

'In truth, I know that.'

'So, finish one or be damned, man! You know it is the thing to do.'

'But which one?' He picked up a parchment. 'This?' He showed it to his friend, then picked up a second. 'This one perhaps?' Then a third.

'Or this? I have so much I want to say but am confounded by overlong and maddeningly complex stories, so I abandon them and start again.'

'And you have done this six times?' Richard said, appalled. 'Yet not completed a single play?'

Will's anguished face told Richard the truth of this. 'What will become of me if I cannot cure myself of this affliction?'

'You do not need to worry about your future,' Richard assured him.

'Do I not?'

'If my father discovers he has paid two pounds for a play and instead receives six unfinished ones, he will murder you. You know his rage, Will. It is like a tempest!'

'And knowing that has made me doubt even more the value of my words.'

'What are these six plays about?'

'So many things,' he said helplessly. 'The folly of a great old man with too many daughters, the jealousy of a husband, a wronged prince, murder, betrayal, revenge, storms, mistaken identities, star-crossed lovers...'

'Stop! This is too much for six plays let alone a single story. Dear God. Is at least one of them about King Richard?'

'Yes.'

'Thank heaven. And is that play long enough to salvage it from the wreckage of your shipwrecked mind?'

'Perhaps.'

'Perhaps?' Richard's frustration was clear. 'Have you written King Richard as a villain at least, a foul and wicked spider who weaves plots against all those around him before he seizes the throne?'

'There is... some of that,' Will conceded.

'*Some* of that? Pray there is much of it... or the queen will have your head removed. Her own grandfather took the throne from Richard. Be clear that he had good cause, then remind everyone he saved the nation from an evil tyrant.'

'I shall.'

'And how have you written him? Is he a cripple, a limping, God-cursed, hunch-backed varlet?'

'He is... he will be... It's just...'

'It's just what?'

'I can usually understand a man when I write about him, but not King Richard.'

' 'Tis simple,' his friend told him. 'He had a foul devil inside that drove him to such acts even the worst of men would baulk at, like the murder of those poor boy princes, his own nephews, by God.'

'The groundlings will want to know what made him,' said Will. 'He was a loyal brother to a king once and uncle to the princes he dispatched. As Duke of Gloucester, he was beloved by the people. King Edward favoured him and he served his brother well in battle. Why was he not content with his place by a new king's side? Why risk everything when it proved the ruin of him?'

'Does it matter?'

'It is everything. For therein lies the man and, without that knowledge, I cannot find him,' Will confessed.

'He did it to preserve his position.'

'You would kill Cuthbert's children to preserve yours?'

'No, but my brother's children may not give me orders. It would likely gall me if they could.'

'You would have them murdered then, to prevent this slight?'

Will could tell Richard Burbage had not given this much thought before. 'Some say the Woodvilles wanted him dead,' he suggested.

'The queen's family may have wanted him gone but would they really execute the brother of their dead king, uncle to the princes? Could he not simply have gone back to his lands for a life of contentment? There could have been peace while the young king ruled with a regent. Instead, Richard made himself king then lost everything. Why? Until I know, it is impossible to place words into King Richard's mouth.'

'No one knows, Will, nor ever shall, for he has been dead a hundred years or more. Five hundred groundlings won't care a fig for it either. Show them he is evil at the beginning and punish him for his wickedness at the end. Put a few clever speeches in between for your favourite actors to declaim. Now, *that* I know you can do, having done it before.'

'Would it were that simple.'

–

When James Burbage returned from Whitehall that afternoon, he was in a state of distress. 'The whole court is in outrage because of some heresy,' he told Richard and Will. 'A dangerous libel has been nailed to the Stranger Church on Broad Street, more than fifty lines threatening Dutch immigrants and warning them to quit the country. Since they are Protestants, this offends the queen and her agents will not be calmed until they have punished a culprit most brutally. They are too excitable to still their tongues even in front of the ladies of the court. It is an ill time and we must all have a care. Men will swing for this.'

'Why would any man risk his life to libel the Dutch?' asked Richard.

'Because they prosper here. It is the usual lament of the Englishman,' said James Burbage, 'bemoaning the arrival of foreigners, who steal his trade and coin from him, whilst living better over here in God's England than in their own country. There are men who will never accept that others work harder or are wiser than they are. Instead, they rail against all foreigners, yet there are as many cheats, thieves and vagabonds born and raised here as in any other country. And it is not the heretical words that matter most but the name signed beneath them: *Tamburlaine*. They will think it writ by Marlowe.'

Will thought that ridiculous. 'If Marlowe truly wrote this, why would he name the character from his own play? Wouldn't suspicion immediately fall upon him?'

'Unless he was clever and reasoned that men would think it could not be him?' said Richard.

'Then he failed, for every man at court thinks it could be,' countered his father.

'And I say again, why draw attention to himself like this?' asked Will.

'Who knows what Marlowe is thinking?' asked James. 'I doubt even he does, when he has been at the wine. Let us imagine it is not him then. Who could it be? You?' Will gave him a look. 'Not you, which means there are now scarcely half a dozen men in the whole of England who could have written it.' He corrected himself: 'And some of them are already dead.'

'Some follower of Marlowe's perhaps?' suggested Richard. 'Who has misunderstood the meaning behind his plays?'

'If it is a follower of Marlowe, then Kit will be judged for that other man's actions,' James told him.

'How can he be?' protested Will. 'What if someone saw *Henry VI* and thought a monarch anointed by God should be brought down, even though that was never my intention?'

'Well, Will, I tell you plain, if someone tried to kill the queen and cited your play as the reason, you would likely swing for it, even if you had never met the man. The world is neither fair nor just. Marlowe will be judged for the actions of his followers whether he shrugged the matter away or not.'

'But it's only words, not revolt.'

'It is sedition and treason!' barked James. 'Words encourage others more than deeds.'

William Kempe ran into the theatre then. Rightly famous for his comic roles, he looked deadly serious now and was short of breath. 'Kyd has been arrested,' he blurted.

'Kit, arrested?' asked James.

Kempe took a deep breath and shook his head. 'Not *Kit* Marlowe,' he managed, 'Thomas *Kyd*. *He* has been arrested.' Then he added, 'And they mean to stretch him.'

Chapter Forty-Five

'...it is not enough to speak, but to speak true.'
— A Midsummer Night's Dream

'Thomas Kyd will be racked?' Will was horrified. 'How do you know of it?'

'They said it loud enough for all the world to hear,' said Kempe, 'while they dragged Thomas from his rooms.'

'Why was he even arrested?' asked Richard. 'He did not write *Tamburlaine.*'

'Someone will have denounced him,' explained his father wearily. 'It does not matter who, only that they did.'

Will fumed. 'Then God help him, but what good will torturing him do? Thomas did not write those words!'

'Are you certain, Will?' asked James. 'Then who did? The libels on the pamphlets were written in blank verse. Few men are capable of it and one of those has already been dragged to the Tower. To end his pain, Thomas will either confess, whether he did it or not, or more likely implicate others.' Then he fixed his eye on Will and asked, 'Have you ever given Kyd cause to speak ill of you?'

Will hesitated for a moment. 'No good cause.'

'What do you mean by that, Will? This is no trivial matter. A man who is racked will denounce God, his closest friends, wife and children if he has to, let alone his enemies. If you are one of them, then you should run and do it now.'

'Run where? And live off what, rainwater and air?'

'At least you *will* live,' Richard told him.

'I have a bed and friends or family in but two places in England, Richard: London and Stratford. They know they would find me quick enough at one or the other. But in truth, I have no reason to run. I had but a small quarrel with Thomas.'

'A small quarrel?' James Burbage looked aghast. 'What was the cause?'

'His last play.'

'*Arden of Faversham*? You did not like it and you told him so?' James asked, as if Will had lost his mind.

'No.' Will shook his head. 'I helped him with it.'

'You helped him write it?' Richard did not understand.

'We all help each other when we are stuck for words. Thomas was confounded by the middle section. I offered help and he accepted, happily I thought.'

'So, you wrote parts of it?'

'A small amount, to help him build a bridge between the parts he had already written.'

'I had not heard that,' said Richard.

'Nor did anyone else.'

James Burbage understood. 'Now I see the cause. You were unacknowledged.'

'Unacknowledged, unpaid and unthanked.'

'Why not paid or thanked?'

Will waved his hand. 'I did not do it for money but to aid a fellow writer who could not find his words. He gained my sympathy, for I have had days like that. I did not expect payment. I would have liked acknowledgement, and I did expect to be thanked,' he said with a sigh, 'but it seemed he resented the very thing he needed from me.'

'Your words,' said James Burbage. 'He would have preferred them all to be his own?'

Will nodded. 'You understand writers.'

'They are a lot like actors.' He did not make this sound like a compliment. 'And you quarrelled over this?'

'More that there was a distance between us thereafter.'

'A rift then. Oh, Will, you had better hope that when Cecil's men stretch Kyd, it is not your name he calls out to save himself.'

'Why would he?'

'Isn't it obvious? To silence the one man who can claim a portion of his latest work and rid himself of a talented rival in the bargain. With you gone, it would be easier for him to sell his work or gain a patron.'

'I feel sure he won't.' But as soon as he had uttered those words, he began to doubt them. Thomas Kyd had acted in the manner Burbage described, seeming to resent Will because not all of the words of *Arden of Faversham* were his own. He could only hope that old Burbage's intuition, gained from years of observing writers, as well as courtiers plotting against one another, would not hold true where Thomas Kyd was concerned. Surely he would not betray Will simply because he was a rival? But then, who could tell what a man might say when he was stretched upon the rack?

'Can you imagine what it is like to have your joints pulled until they tear?' James Burbage was clearly thinking the same thing. 'Even without your rift, Kyd would sell you for a moment's peace. Let us pray he does not think to do so.'

'They would not believe him, surely?'

'If he says you wrote the libel, they will believe it, Will. I told you that fewer than six men in the whole of England could have written that verse, and you are one of them.'

Chapter Forty-Six

'...ambition's debt is paid.'
— Julius Caesar

Will had not been sleeping overlong and never well. That night, he barely slept at all. When he was not thinking about Rosalind and her tragic mistress, Celia, his attention switched to Henry Wriothesley, the Earl of Southampton, who still expected Will to report to him on his cousin's death. Then his thoughts would turn to Sir Robert Cecil, who awaited a denunciation of Wriothesley from Will, so he could destroy the earl. Sir Thomas Vernon was still at large too and newly aggrieved at Will for saving Rosalind from the rope, yet the singularly violent former soldier was not even the most dangerous man he knew, nor even the third most. Added to that list now was his friend and fellow playmaker Thomas Kyd, who would be able to end Will's life, or prolong it through torture, simply by mentioning the name Shakespeare to his inquisitors.

Somehow Will was supposed to sleep, wake refreshed, eat, walk, breathe and write, with all of this peril hanging over him. He found himself longingly wishing for a return to a simpler time when all he really concerned himself with was his inability to finish a play. Now that he understood what real anguish was, Will was not sure how he would be able to get through the coming days without weeping over his lot. His situation failed to improve when James Burbage returned to the theatre from another visit to court, designed to learn more about the aftermath of the Dutch Church Libel.

'There is new evidence against Thomas Kyd.' The older Burbage looked shaken. 'They searched his rooms and found heretical writings.'

'Dear God, no.' The torture Thomas Kyd had already endured would be as nothing compared to that which would follow. With actual evidence of heresy, things would be far graver for the man. Before, there was only the knowledge that Kyd was one of several men who might possibly have conjured up some blank verse on a wall. Now the queen's men had damning proof that Kyd might be against God and, by extension, the queen.

'How did he answer for this?'

'The only way he could. They were not his. They belonged to another. Someone who had used his rooms before.'

Richard Burbage shot his friend a look and his father spotted it. James asked him then. 'Where did you write the words for that middle section of Thomas Kyd's *Arden of Faversham*, Will?' he asked urgently. 'In your rooms or his?'

Will knew how dismayed they would be by his answer.

'His.'

–

They waited nervously for more news throughout the rest of that day and most of the next, until James Burbage resolved to ride back down to Whitehall again to flush out the truth. He was late returning. Was there a simple explanation for this or had he been indiscreet with his enquiries? Was he detained too, to prevent him from warning Will? Men could arrive at any moment to arrest him. Would Robert Cecil protect him then or seek to harm Will for his failure as a spy? He knew that guilt or innocence would not matter, only how long it would be before he was forced to confess under torture. Would they burn him afterwards like poor Anne Askew?

A horse was already saddled with provisions enough for a long ride. If James did return and the news was bad, Will would have no choice but to take flight immediately, but where would he go? How long could he survive in England as a wanted man? Who would dare shelter a heretic? If they put a bounty on his head, someone would surely turn him in.

As the hours passed and still James Burbage did not return, Will's thoughts kept returning to his fate. Would his friend really betray him? According to Richard Burbage, you would denounce those closest to you on the rack. Why not whisper the name Shakespeare then, if that put an end to your pain?

James Burbage was barely through the theatre door before they were both on their feet. There were no greetings, only looks that showed him they had waited too long for his news from court. Will was ready to mount his horse in an instant if he had to.

The older man looked quickly about him to ensure there were no ears close enough to pick up what he was about to say. 'I came directly.'

'What news?' urged Richard.

James's voice was almost a whisper. 'As we feared, Thomas Kyd did indeed betray a friend.' Will felt his heart jump.

'Who?' demanded Richard.

'Marlowe.'

'Thomas sold Kit to them?' Will could not believe it. He had no time even to feel relieved. He was safe for now but at a terrible cost. 'Thomas was closer to no man more than he!'

James was contemptuous of Will's scorn. 'They stretched Kyd until his limbs were torn and pulled from their joints, Will, and they kept on demanding a name. It had to be one of a handful of men who could have written that verse. It could have been yours that he uttered but, by chance, you were not the only friend of Kyd's to visit his rooms. Marlowe lodged there with him for a time. He had no way of knowing then the cost he would pay for that roof over his head. Kyd swore the heretical papers were Marlowe's.'

'Maybe they were,' said Richard.

'Perhaps, but you know Kit,' Will said. 'He doesn't believe half of what he says.'

'Yet says it anyway,' Richard observed.

'To provoke,' Will reminded him, 'to draw out enemies of the queen, to move them into the open.'

'Or to side with them,' suggested James. 'You cannot be sure it isn't so.'

Will had to admit this, if only to himself. 'What will happen to Kit now?'

'The Privy Council has called for him. He must come to them and answer for this, but he has not yet been arrested and has friends at court.'

'They will help him?'

'They cannot.' James Burbage shook his head. 'And will admit no association with him now, but they won't want Marlowe stretched either. If he is placed upon the rack and they tear him, who knows what he will say or who he will denounce? No, they will want him gone.'

'Dead?' asked Richard.

'I doubt they would mind too much whether he was alive or dead, but I meant gone abroad. The low countries or Italy perhaps. Somewhere his voice can no longer be heard by the groundlings, who they fear might rise up in their thousands if he tells them to.'

'He would never say that and nor would they rise up,' said Will. 'It is a fiction.'

'*We* know that but the queen does not. If someone close to Her Majesty tells her it is likely to happen, she may believe what she is told. Marlowe must leave the country.'

'Then we shall help him,' said Will.

'No,' James replied firmly. 'He needs different friends for that.'

'What manner of friends?'

'Rough men who will do his bidding even if he is disgraced, as long as he gives them enough coin. They will find a ship's captain willing to take him abroad. Marlowe does not require help from us. He already knows such men.'

Will instantly thought of Robert Poley, a regular companion of Marlowe's who Will himself had cause to fear. Better to call a man like that friend than foe, and he found himself relieved that Marlowe was on such good terms with the spymaster's creature. The argument in the tavern with his companions, Frizer and Skeres, was surely forgotten by now. These men made up an unlikely group, with Marlowe at their centre, but their common bond was a taste for intrigue and a shared experience of spycraft. If anyone could get Kit safely out of the country, they could.

'My father is right, Will,' said Richard. 'If there is a man of the theatre who knows better how to carry himself away from trouble than Kit, then I have yet to meet him.'

'But trouble follows Kit wherever he goes. Strife is his constant companion.'

'And yet he still lives,' said Richard. 'Christopher Marlowe cannot die; not yet awhile. There is too much poetry and fight left in him.'

'You think he will return?'

'Certainly,' Richard assured him.

'I fear that day may not come for a while,' said James with a frown. 'If it comes at all.'

Chapter Forty-Seven

'I'll be revenged on the whole pack of you.'
— *Twelfth Night*

For days, the Dutch Church Libel haunted Lord Strange's Men and the other acting companies. They listened intently for news and every whisper or rumour was pounced upon and quickly relayed to their fellow players, while the fates of Kyd and Marlowe hung in the balance. Everyone's livelihood, as well as their lives, depended upon the decisions made by the Privy Council on behalf of the queen. Some believed the acting companies might be broken up forever.

Thomas Kyd was eventually released and there was a ghoulish fascination as to how he would manage following his torture. Some were less sympathetic than others, since he had been the one to give up Marlowe, who had been ordered to attend the Privy Council daily until they could make sufficient time to question him. Will thought it odd that Thomas Kyd had been arrested, detained and tortured immediately, in order to wrestle the name of Marlowe from him, who by contrast was allowed to move freely around until the Privy Council were ready for him. Perhaps he really was being protected by influential friends. Had not the mighty Robert Cecil himself once used Kit as an agent of his will? Was he responsible for the delay, which might allow Marlowe to take flight.

'I think your father is right,' said Will, as he ate a supper of meat pasties with Richard Burbage. 'Words are more dangerous than deeds these days.'

'These were,' agreed Richard. 'Both heretical and blasphemous, according to Kyd, who nearly died because he shared lodgings with the man who wrote them.'

'You have been to see him?'

'I have,' admitted Richard, 'and wish I had not, for he is much changed, though perhaps lucky to be alive. Those writings...' he lowered his voice then, '...held the most dangerous heresies. That there is no God or, if there was, He is dead. Also that Jesus lay with John the Baptist and there are numerous other blasphemies pertaining to the Apostles.'

'Did Kit really write them?' asked Will.

'Thomas swears he did.'

'Has he gone mad?'

'Perhaps he always was and we did not see it.'

—

Will found Marlowe outside his rooms, arriving just in time to see him leaving in some haste. A few of his possessions had been bundled into a canvas drawstring bag and, as he turned to go, he almost collided with Will.

'You're leaving?' Will was both sad and relieved, for no good could come from Marlowe staying in London.

'I must.' There was a look of resignation on his face. 'I have heard what they did to poor Thomas. I am told he is broken. I know he would never have given me up otherwise.'

'Where will you go?'

Marlowe gave him a warning look. 'Abroad. It is better if you do not know where.' Then he confided, 'For now, I'll stay at Eleanor Bull's rooming house in Deptford, until I can slip out of the country.'

'Do you need anything, Kit? Money? Someone to find a ship's captain willing to...'

Marlowe stopped him with a raised hand and a half smile. He seemed amused or perhaps touched at the notion of Will helping him. 'I have money, and friends who have helped me quit England before.'

James Burbage had told Will as much. It seemed there was little more to be said between them. 'Until we meet again then.'

He offered his hand and Marlowe took it. 'That may be some time. I wish that I could stay in England, Will, but it is too perilous here for me now.' Then he turned Will's own words back on him. 'Even for a man who embraces danger and marches towards it like a familiar friend.'

'I meant nothing of that. I know you are no fool, Kit. You even talked yourself out of the clutches of the Privy Council.'

'They let me go,' he said with a grin, 'for they do not wish to hear what I might say about them in front of others.'

It was true then. Marlowe really did know enough to damage powerful men and they had grown to fear him. Will was not sure if this was necessarily a good thing, but was pleased Kit was removing himself from harm and would be safe for a time at least.

'You should be happy, Will.'

'How can I take any joy from your departure?'

'Because I will be gone but London will still need plays.' Marlowe smiled at him. 'And you are the only man fit to write them.'

'Not so.'

'I have heard your words and there is such poetry in them. I even confess I was made envious by a line or two.' Then he laughed. 'Me, the great Marlowe!' and Will laughed too because he knew England's finest poet was mocking himself this time.

'I shall miss you. London shall miss you and the groundlings will mourn your flight.'

'Then I place them in your care till I return and, while I am gone, let me be your muse. Come, embrace me.' And Will did just that. When Marlowe broke free, he announced with some ceremony, 'I pass the torch to you, my friend. Keep the flame of our poetry alive for both of us until I return once again to these shores.'

'I will. I swear it.'

—

Richard Burbage usually greeted his friend and his father with a smile, a jest or a playful insult, but when he walked into the tavern that evening he did none of those things.

'What fresh calamity have you brought news of?' Will asked.

'It concerns Raleigh. They talk about him in the streets. He has been arrested too.'

'On what charge? Treason?'

'I know not, though some say it is to do with a papist plot. He has been taken to the Tower this very morning and is held there.'

'By God, Cecil is bringing everyone down!' snapped James Burbage. 'You could be next, Will. You should prepare yourself for that.'

First Kyd, then Marlowe, now Raleigh. 'I shall.' He promised and meant it but how could he escape Robert Cecil's men when it seemed they were everywhere?

'I will away to court again,' James told them, 'to see what I can learn. If Raleigh is arrested for heresy or treason then you must flee London, Will, for you are known to have been in his company at Place House and Henry Wriothesley is a friend of his and Marlowe's. Both their lives will be forfeit if Cecil has his way.'

James left them both then, without even finishing his ale.

Richard said, 'Do not think more on it, Will. Raleigh has been in and out of the queen's favour these past ten years or more. This will likely be a storm that passes.' The words were optimistic but, great actor though he was, Richard Burbage's face told a different story.

They drank, for there was little else to do while they waited for more news. Neither man could get beyond a melancholy mood into cheerful drunkenness, for too much now was at stake. In the end they gave up and went back to the theatre, to wait there for James Burbage to return with news of Raleigh's fate and perhaps more arrests.

When James did walk into the theatre he looked solemn, but when he realised Richard and Will were both gazing at him intently, he actually laughed. 'Raleigh was arrested, that much is true,' he told them, then he smiled. 'But not for sedition or heresy, nor treason either.' He started chuckling to himself then but neither Will nor Richard could see how the arrest of Raleigh could be in any way amusing.

'Out with it, Father.' Richard's face showed his indignation that James could find this in the slightest bit funny.

James waved a hand dismissively, determined to tell the tale his way. 'The queen used to favour Raleigh greatly. He is handsome and an adventurer, which puts him above more noble and landed men, who have never drawn a sword in anger nor left their country. Anyway, she liked him. Some even dared to say he did her good service, of some form or another, though not I.' The implication that Raleigh might have talked himself into the queen's bedchamber was not lost on either of them. 'But' – and Burbage paused for dramatic effect – 'he is now jailed... for tupping her lady in waiting!' And he couldn't help himself, he laughed in relief as much as good humour. 'Worse, the queen discovered he secretly married the woman, one Elizabeth Throckmorton, more than a year ago, without asking Her Majesty's permission. Now they are both sent to the Tower and will remain there until her anger with them has abated. That might be a while.'

'So, there is no Catholic plot against the queen uncovered?' asked Will.

'There is none involving Sir Walter. Unless he hoped Her Majesty might die of jealousy.'

Chapter Forty-Eight

'Cry "Havoc", and let slip the dogs of war'
— Julius Caesar

A few more days passed and Will's mood brightened further with each one that did not lead to his arrest. Raleigh's imprisonment was down to the queen's jealousy and not Robert Cecil's vindictive nature, and Marlowe had probably already left England by now. With little point in pursuing the recently married Rosalind further and no new information on the fate of Celia Vernon, he even busied himself with writing, which went passably well for once. He walked into the tavern that night in a more optimistic mood than usual, but it was soon dashed.

The place was almost full, with many of the drinkers from his own company. He was surprised to see members of the Admiral's Men there too, unaware of any planned gathering. Even more surprising, the place was uncommonly quiet.

'What has happened?' he asked no man in particular but their faces showed that nobody wanted to be the one to tell him.

Richard Burbage got to his feet then, with an anguished look on his face, but all he managed was 'Will...' before his words, for once, failed him.

His father, James, spoke up instead. 'I will tell you plain, Will, for no amount of honey could sweeten these words.' He paused for a second to allow Will to prepare himself. 'It's Marlowe.'

'He is arrested?'

'Dead!'

'Dead? No! This cannot be.' In his shock, Will was convinced James had to have been mistaken. No one could kill Christopher Marlowe. Why would they? *How* could they? He was too young and vital to be marked for an early death, as well as too brilliant.

'He took flight to the lowlands,' Will protested, but then he saw the look in James's eyes, glanced again at Richard to check the truth of the matter and saw no contradiction. This was why the men had all assembled here and it explained their solemnity, for there was nothing good now that could ever be said of it. 'Dead how?'

'They are saying it was a brawl at Bull's tavern in Deptford,' Richard told him quietly, 'but there were only four men in the room and one of them was Kit. The other three were his *friends*.' Richard spat the word.

'That place was no tavern.' He knew Eleanor Bull's rooming house. Marlowe had told him he planned to wait there a while, until he could meet with some unnamed associates and agree the manner of his flight from England.

'Even so, food and drink was had and there was a bill to be paid,' explained James patiently. 'The argument was about that reckoning.'

'What happened?' Will demanded.

'It is said Kit snatched another man's dagger and wounded him. That man then wrestled his dagger back from Kit and stabbed him in the eye with it. He died in a moment.'

Despite Will's shock on hearing this account, he immediately disputed it. 'Kit has his own dagger and would not need to snatch one from another. If he *had* done this, then it would be a brave or foolish man who tried to wrestle the blade from his hand. Could *you* manage such a thing if Kit's blood was up?'

Will wondered how James could possibly have heard so much detail of the killing so soon and realised the three men with Marlowe must have put their account about, to absolve themselves from blame. 'They are saying it was self-defence?'

'Aye,' said James, then added softly, 'so the others claim.'

'Which others? Who did this foul deed?'

'Nicholas Skeres was one…' Richard began.

Will snorted his derision. 'An actor, on and off the stage, who will talk you out of your money, then come at you with the point of his dagger when you dare demand it back!'

'Ingram Frizer,' Richard continued.

'Another who has played many parts, all of them villains.' The men were all watching Will now and, though no one contradicted him, they did not voice their approval either. These were dangerous words, but he did not care. Will continued unabated. 'His patron is Thomas Walsingham, cousin to the late and most great Francis, the queen's assassin, though he never once stuck the knife in himself.'

'Keep your voice low, Will,' warned James, drawing Will's attention to strangers sitting at the tavern's edges and in its corners, who were not members of either acting company. Any one of them could have been a spy. Perhaps they all were. 'Do you wish to be the next poet found dead in a tavern?'

'I told you, that house is no tavern!' he said just as loudly. 'Who was the third man?'

Richard hesitated. He could see Will was now attracting curious and unwelcome looks from several rough-looking men.

'Who was it?' demanded Will, loudly enough to alarm Richard into answering before he drew more attention to them both.

'It was Robert Poley.'

Will remembered Poley's threatening words to him. '*How easy it would be to say you came at me with your dagger drawn, so I had no choice but to plunge my own into your throat. They would see me pardoned for it too.*' It was no surprise that Marlowe's former friend, a man who had pressed a dagger against Will before now, should be there too. He had as good as confessed to the murder of Marlowe in advance, though his threats at that time were directed at Will. 'Well, there's the proof! None more needed than the company Kit kept on the day he died. Murderers all!'

'Quiet yourself, Will,' hissed James, truly alarmed now. 'It is dangerous.'

'Dangerous, is it?' Will's eyes challenged the room and everyone in it. 'Will they kill us all? Soon, there will be no one left to write their plays and they will have to find some new entertainment!'

Some of the men continued to stare at Will but none stood or reacted to the challenge. Perhaps the killing of Marlowe was so shocking that no one wanted to draw attention to himself after it, or possibly they reasoned that Will wasn't worth the effort.

All of Will's energy seemed to leave him then and he sat down with Richard, quiet and sullen now.

'Who killed him?'

'Does it matter?' asked James Burbage.

'Does it matter? It matters very much. Who struck the blow?'

'Frizer,' James told him, 'but they were all three there, Will.'

He meant they were all involved. James was privately admitting that he did not believe the account that was already being put about, concerning this 'brawl in a tavern', when it was neither a brawl nor took place in a tavern.

Will was picturing the scene in his mind's eye. Marlowe suddenly grabbed by two men, Poley and Skeres, his supposed friends, there to help him escape London. There would have been one either side of him, clasping his arms and pinning them down, so he could not wrench free nor get up from his seat. The third man, Ingram Frizer, coming at Kit and thrusting a dagger into his eye, killing him instantly and silencing him forever.

'Have they been arrested?' Will asked.

'Questioned but released. It is put about that Frizer was defending himself when he struck the mortal blow.'

'With his own knife?' Will was outraged. 'If he was really injured by Kit, he had managed to seize back his dagger and did not have to kill the man who supposedly attacked him. The account is not believable.' No one argued against that. 'This was no tavern brawl about a bill. It was a reckoning of another kind. This was about words and Marlowe's had power. Oh, I do not mean the ones his actors spoke. Powerful men did not want to see Marlowe put on trial. He would be allowed to speak, to answer the charges against him. If he was condemned to hang in front of crowds, even his last words could be dangerous. They were scared of Kit's fame and eloquence and saw hidden meanings in his work.'

'He had powerful enemies,' Richard agreed.

'And a most powerful patron too,' James reminded him.

'You think Henry Wriothesley is behind this?' Will could scarce believe he might have ordered Marlowe's death. 'Why would he want Kit dead?'

'I meant his other patron,' said James, his voice low. 'Who stood to lose everything if Kit confessed to the Dutch Church Libel under torture or examination? Who is supposed to be responsible for the queen's safety and yet might have engaged the services of a man now accused of heresy, blasphemy, atheism, even treason? What would happen to him, if he was known to have employed such a man, in the supposed defence of the realm? He would be brought down. It would be the end of him.'

'Robert Cecil,' Will confirmed.

'The man who used Marlowe's talents as a spy in the low countries, the same man who keeps Robert Poley on a leash.'

'How simple it would be to lure him to his death,' observed Will, 'with the promise of escape and salvation provided by his friends, on the orders of a man he trusted. Kit walked straight into a trap.'

'Robert Cecil has tortured and broken Kyd and most likely ordered the murder of Marlowe,' James said. 'What do you think he will do to you, Will?'

Chapter Forty-Nine

'…let grief
Convert to anger; blunt not the heart, enrage it.'
— Macbeth .

The men of both companies raised their drinks again and again, to toast Marlowe's life, his memory, poetry and plays. Before long, they were all quite drunk.

Will looked to the door just as a hunched figure dragged himself through it, hobbling unsteadily until he reached the nearest table, where he sat down heavily, a grimace of pain etched upon his face. Thomas Kyd looked a decade older than the last time Will had seen him. He was damaged, broken, and Will sensed he was not long for this world.

'Kyd is finished,' said James quietly. 'He has no patron nor will ever have another. Who would risk the queen's displeasure? No players will perform his works.' Then he placed his hand on Will's shoulder and grasped it firmly. 'And now Marlowe is gone.'

'The finest poet of our time. Or any other.'

'The finest of *his* time,' said James emphatically. 'And that time is done.' Then he wondered, as if to himself, 'But who will replace him?'

Will bridled. 'It is too soon, Burbage.'

'Is it? I'll wager I am not the first to muse on this. Mourn Kit as you should but do not allow your flame to be extinguished just because his was. You didn't stick that dagger in his eye and nor did I. Life is for the living.'

Kyd did not glance over at their group and they kept their distance from him. If spies were indeed everywhere, then no one wanted to be seen to be in league with the disgraced and ruined Kyd. Since he had also been the one to give up his former friend Marlowe, he was now reviled by many who knew them both. Will felt differently about it, for he had been shown the rack by Robert Cecil and thought himself most fortunate not to have been tortured on it too.

Kyd sat and drank alone but ate nothing. He had to delve deep into his purse to find enough coin even to do that. He managed to pay the girl for bringing him ale but it seemed he could not afford supper. He looked as if he had not eaten well in a while.

Will overheard one of their company say unkindly, 'Thomas dines with Duke Humphrey tonight.' It was a phrase often used by poor gentlefolk when they could not afford to eat. Instead, they would pass the dinner hour walking near the tomb of Humphrey, Duke of Gloucester, in Old St Paul's, because of a well-known tale of a man who was once locked in Humphrey's tomb and missed dinner.

On hearing this, Will beckoned the serving girl to him and, in a low voice no one else could hear, gave her instructions while he pressed coins into her hand, before ordering more ale for himself and his friends in a louder voice, which met with their approval.

Thomas Kyd was surprised when the girl came to him later bearing another pot of ale, some bread, cheese and a plate of hot stew. He eyed the food hungrily but shook his head at her mistake because this feast could not be for him. The girl explained its origins and left him to eat. As soon as she departed, Thomas Kyd looked around the tavern, perplexed by the identity of his mysterious benefactor. Only one pair of eyes was fixed upon his. Will caught the man's gaze, not to make a show of Kyd or seek his thanks, but simply to acknowledge his one-time friend and collaborator, so that he did not feel entirely alone in the world. Will could see the emotion in Kyd's eyes. The broken, hungry man nodded once in recognition but must have known the risk Will had taken with his act of kindness. He immediately broke the connection between them and turned back to the food, to avoid drawing unwanted attention to the man who had paid for it.

The tavern filled up over time but none of the newer arrivals who knew Kyd acknowledged his presence, save one who cursed him to his face before moving on. Kyd kept his head bowed low and left as soon as his meal was done. Will did not realise it then, but he would never see the man again.

There was still a certain solemnity, even a melancholy, to the night's drinking. They told tales of simpler days, when Marlowe and the now absent Kyd were at their pomp and seen as bright young stars in a firmament that was losing its finest poets almost daily. Will could not help wondering if he would be next. He barely had time to let that thought settle when there was a great roar from the doorway.

'Where is William Shakespeare?' Sir Thomas Vernon's fury would have made Will run from the tavern, if he had not been blocking its only exit.

Sir Thomas saw him and roared again, 'There he is!' He raised his sword and started towards him. Will knew then that it was his fate to meet destiny at the point of a rapier, just as he had always feared. Sir Thomas barged others to one side and was almost upon Will before anyone had time to react. He would have plunged his blade into him too, if he had not been quickly and decisively met by several members of the company, who grabbed at Sir Thomas's arms and restrained him, his sword hanging uselessly from his clasped hand. 'Unhand me!' he demanded of them while staring straight ahead at Will. 'Fight me, Will Shakespeare, fight me, damn you!' he roared. Will clasped his own sword then, not to fight Vernon in a duel but simply to defend himself, in case the man managed to wriggle free from the grip of his fellow actors.

'Hold hard!' Another roar then, which silenced everyone and seemed to fill the room with its depth and ferocity. It was Richard Burbage, who had seemingly come from nowhere and was now standing between Sir Thomas and Will. He raised his own sword and ordered the men who were struggling to contain Sir Thomas in his fury to let him go.

This they did, stepping quickly away in case he swatted at them with his sword. 'Get out of my way, boy,' he told Richard Burbage, 'and let me at the man behind you.'

'One more step and this boy will run you through,' Richard promised him.

'Ha! You're an actor too. I can tell by the look of you, you fop! Heed this last warning and get out of my way or I will walk over your body to reach the man who hides behind you.'

'Step away Richard,' Will urged him. He did not want to fight a man who had known war but nor did he wish to see his friend, who was quite drunk, killed by his enemy. 'This is not your quarrel.'

'I believe it is,' said Richard with a calmness bordering on arrogance. 'This rogue called me boy. The man in me will teach him a lesson.'

But Richard Burbage knew only how to fight on a stage, thought Will, not in a street or tavern, where death was the most likely result. Sir Thomas Vernon was a dangerous and vicious opponent who would do anything required to rid himself of the nuisance standing between him and his quarry.

Before Will could speak again, Sir Thomas made a lunge for Richard, who managed to parry the blow and step to one side. The crowd around them drew back to clear space and watch the duel. The two men began to circle one another warily. Will had never seen his friend look so tense or determined before. Normally, he was as relaxed as if the sword were a part of him, but this was no exhibition match before a play: it was a fight to the death.

Sir Thomas pressed forward again and thrust out his sword but Richard parried early, turning his defence into a counter-attacking move. Sir Thomas appeared surprised by his skill but quickly attacked again and, once more, Richard parried then advanced, forcing Thomas backwards until he almost fell against a table. Angrily, he let out a roar and swatted his blade at Richard, who parried and went backwards, but then came a swift deluge of blows from a now angered Thomas and, one after another, they landed against Richard's sword as he frantically retreated, parried and retreated again. Will could not imagine how he was managing to stave off the speed and ferocity of the attack, but it was clear Richard was losing the duel and that the other man's momentum would soon be decisive. Sir Thomas knew it too and with another roar he sent thrust after thrust of his rapier at Richard who was now pinned back against a table at the other end of the room. He came at him to deliver the final blow and, as he did this, Richard stepped deftly to one side, dodged the thrust from the blade and let his opponent's momentum take it past him. Sir Thomas could not stop and suddenly found himself in a perilous position, with his sword beyond his opponent, while he himself was now within striking distance. Richard spun round then and used his left hand to grab the hilt of Vernon's sword, pinning it uselessly to the table. Then he struck a mighty backwards blow with his right elbow, which crashed into Sir Thomas Vernon's face at full force, breaking his nose with a crack everyone heard. Sir Thomas was forced to release his grip on the sword as he was propelled backwards. This was a street-fighting turn from Richard, not a stage move. Both Sir Thomas and Will had underestimated Richard Burbage's skill and his brutality. The actor spun round to face his opponent once more and, as Sir Thomas tried to get round and past him to retrieve his rapier, Richard jabbed his own sword forward till its point pressed against the other man's chest and lightly pierced the skin. Sir Thomas cried out in pain and frustration but ceased his fight. He stood there, helpless, with the point of Richard's sword against him.

'Do you yield?' Richard demanded and Sir Thomas looked as if he would rather die, so Richard drew his sword back to strike the fatal blow.

'I yield,' he said quickly and Richard relented.

The assembled company whooped and applauded Richard Burbage's skill, while Sir Thomas Vernon simply stood there, with blood coming from his nose and some staining his shirt where the point of Richard's sword had cut him.

'I was exhausted!' he shouted, an excuse no one believed, but he went on. 'Attacked in the street by another this very evening, a man I never met before nor e'er had quarrel with. He tried to kill me, but I dispatched him.'

'A fantastical tale,' said Richard, 'but nothing to do with us.'

'It has everything to do with him.' And Vernon jabbed a finger at Will, who had only just recovered from the relief of seeing his friend survive a frenzied attack and prevail. 'He set that man about me, or instructed great men to do so.'

'My friend here is a poet and has no authority over great men.'

'You are mistaken,' Will told Sir Thomas, though he could not truthfully be sure about that. Had this other assailant been sent prematurely by the Earl of Southampton to avenge Celia's death? He seemed far from the men with clubs and cudgels Henry Wriothesley had once mentioned. And if he had sent a man to kill Sir Thomas with a rapier, why not pick one who was sure to succeed, not fail and die in the attempt?

'I know it was you, by gad,' he told Will before turning to the entire company. 'And if you were gentlemen, instead of vermin and varlets all, you would give him up to me now and I would take him from here.'

'So you could stab him in the gutter?' asked James Burbage, who also looked like a man who had been through a great ordeal during his son's fight. 'That is not the act of a gentleman.'

'So fight me then!' Sir Thomas roared at Will in response to James Burbage's accusation.

'Then you would be humiliated again,' said Richard, 'for Will is twice the swordsman you are and he would run you through.'

It was not true, of course, but Sir Thomas did not know that. 'Give me my sword!' he demanded.

'I will not. You surrendered it to me, now I shall hang it from my wall as a monument.'

'By God!' Vernon roared. 'There was a time when a man such as I could have called the constable and the watch, then all you players would be locked up for daring to challenge me!' He emphasised the word 'players', as if it meant vermin and, like many ignorant men, he seemed to long for a mythical, golden age that had somehow passed. 'You think you are better than I, because you have a disloyal, popish patron?' It was dangerous to slander the likes of Lord Strange in public, let alone shout it in a crowded tavern. 'A just king would condemn you all!' And he shook his head at the injustice of their world. 'This is what happens when men are ruled by women!' he roared in exasperation before finally storming from the tavern, minus his sword.

Will was quick to thank his friend for risking his life. 'I have fought with a rapier often enough,' said Will. 'But only on stage. I am not sure I have the stomach for it elsewhere.'

'I know you feared dying by the sword,' Richard explained. 'I worried your hand might shake if you thought this some act of fate, designed to take your life for stealing Knell's.' He placed a hand on Will's shoulder. 'And what is the point of constantly studying the art of fencing, if I cannot put my skills to the test, even if he was no real match for me? God, I enjoyed that!'

Before Will could thank him again, James Burbage congratulated his son on a duel well won and Will could see the relief in the older man's eyes. Then he turned to Will. 'I have known men like Sir Thomas

Vernon before. He will not stop and I tell you plainly, Will, it is not just your life that hangs in the balance now. None of us will be safe while that man is free to roam abroad, especially my son, who took his sword from him in front of everyone. Sir Thomas will not allow a humiliation like that to go unpunished. You know what you must do.'

Chapter Fifty

'And from that torment I will free myself,
Or hew my way out with a bloody axe.'
— Henry VI

Henry Wriothesley's London home, Southampton Place, sat on Chancery Lane. It was quiet that afternoon. The earl was not hosting half of London nor entertaining its poets, which suited Will's purpose. Aside from his servants, he was alone, though he informed Will that he would be away to Greenwich soon, since the queen was returned and the court moved there. This was Wriothesley's way of telling Will to be quick about his business.

'I will speak plain then,' Will told him, glad that the earl lacked the time to interrogate him too deeply on the matter. 'I have discovered the true fate of your fair cousin, Lady Celia.'

'Well then, did she in fact die of plague, as I was told, or was she poisoned, as I surmised?'

'Both.'

'Both?' The earl appeared baffled. 'How could it be both?'

'It is quite simple. Celia died of plague. That is the true and correct manner of her death, as reported by the physician that attended her house and the woman who tended Celia in her final hours.'

'Then how could she have been poisoned, man?'

'It was not done with a vial poured into food or drink, rather she was deliberately infected.' Will told the earl how Sir Thomas Vernon had invited a Flemish merchant to dinner, though he himself was not present. 'He made sure his wife and she alone waited upon the man's needs, placing herself near him during dinner. A servant told me the man arrived looking unwell, that he had a fever and did sweat, even though the night was mild, and voided his stomach after the meal.

Before leaving, he pulled Celia onto his lap and she had to struggle to break free from him.'

'He was drunk?'

'Not so, according to this servant. The man was sick.' He did not name Rosalind, hoping to keep her out of it.

'You think my cousin contracted plague from this foreigner? But how is this anything other than ill fortune?'

'Because Sir Thomas knew him to be sick when he invited the fellow to his home. Note how he absented himself and ensured none but his wife waited on the foreigner.'

'That is most strange,' admitted Wriothesley. 'But is it proof?'

'The merchant was from a ship known to have plague on board. Sir Thomas knew this and invited him anyway. He must have seen the man's condition and recognised the symptoms from his time serving abroad in the army. There is more.'

'Go on.'

'When part of a force laying siege to a town, Sir Thomas Vernon urged his commander to use plague dogs.' And Will explained the notion of catapulting dead animals infected with plague over a city's walls to infect its inhabitants. 'His commander was appalled and told him it was expressly against the law of arms.'

'That was a most dishonourable act to urge upon his commander,' Henry Wriothesley concluded. 'The man is a vile and contemptible rogue. But tell me, what reason would Sir Thomas have to end his wife's life? For I confess I know of none.'

'A dowry,' said Will, 'or rather an inheritance.' And he told the earl how Sir Thomas had taken in his thirteen-year-old ward, Viola, with the intention of making her his bride. 'This is something Sir Thomas could not do while married,' Will concluded, 'so he resolved to become a widower.'

'By God, I see it all now.' The earl seemed convinced, perhaps because he wished to be. 'You have done me a good service, Shakespeare, and will be rewarded in time. When you leave here, do not speak of this to anyone.'

'What shall become of Sir Thomas Vernon?' asked Will.

The earl made a promise then: 'Nothing shall become of him.'

Will understood his meaning.

Chapter Fifty-One

'You told a lie, an odious, damned lie'
— Othello

He kept to the same route, walking to his supper at the same tavern at the exact time each evening, making sure to wear his sword and carry his dagger whenever he ventured abroad, glancing back over his shoulder from time to time as he went. Will instinctively felt it would not be long now. Sir Thomas Vernon had his spies who would surely alert him to Will's movements. There were narrow, dark streets aplenty between his home and the inn and Will constantly braced himself for the attack that would surely come. Aside from his sword, he was as vulnerable as any man who ventured into London's streets after dark, where robbery and murder was commonplace enough to attract little comment. If he was killed here, he wouldn't be the first, nor even the first that month.

It happened on the fourth night and, as Will fully expected, it was Thomas Vernon himself who stepped from a dark corner to block his path, in a tight street with little light aside from the torch he carried in his left hand, while his right rested on the hilt of a new sword, ready to draw it.

'Shakespeare!' he called and Will immediately halted some ten or so yards from the man, before glancing around and about him, to see if there was anybody coming up from behind. There was no sign of anyone else. Vernon wanted to finish Will off himself. The man's injured pride would not have allowed him to pay others to run Will through. He had to do the deed alone. Will had guessed as much. 'I hope you enjoyed my humiliation at the hands of your actor friend. He will pay for it anon but first let him mourn the death of the man he tried to save. Say a prayer, then draw your sword,' Sir Thomas ordered as he drew his own.

Will did just that, his hand shaking a little as he adopted a defensive posture.

'Put up your swords, friends!' The voice was jovial enough and it had come from behind Will, who glanced back to see the rough-looking man it belonged to, while ensuring he never turned his back fully on Sir Thomas.

'This quarrel does not concern you!' barked Sir Thomas, who was not going to let the presence of the man and his three companions prevent his revenge. They continued to walk towards him, even though he was blocking their way, just as he had blocked Will's.

'But let us pass first,' the man urged. 'Then we will be gone.'

Sir Thomas grunted, lowered his sword, then stepped to one side to let them go, the quicker to be rid of them. 'Make haste.'

'Oh, we will,' he said, and the four men moved quickly onwards until they drew level with Sir Thomas, whereupon the man who had spoken moved with both speed and dexterity, pulling a cosh out from under his cloak, then smashing it with ferocity against the side of Sir Thomas Vernon's head. Vernon cried out and fell hard to the floor, letting go of the torch and his sword in the process, which clattered against the cobbles. One of the other men kicked the sword to one side, even as Sir Thomas tried to scramble towards it. They were on him in an instant then and Will watched as they dragged him back along the ground towards them, a look of panic, fear and great alarm drawn upon his face.

'No,' was all he had time to say before the blows from their clubs began to rain down upon him. Will watched it all unfold, frozen by a combination of relief and horror, as the four men Henry Wriothesley had paid to guard him from a distance set about their work enthusiastically. Will had agreed to set himself up as bait and walk the same route at the same time each evening until Sir Thomas attempted to exact his revenge. They had wasted no time in catching up with him, once Sir Thomas had called his name. Now they were setting about the man without mercy. Blow after blow came down on his limbs, body and skull, while one of the men then used his free hand to press his face down into the mud. His muted cries of pain were pitiful and short-lived. Within moments, the only movement left in him was the twitching as more, quite unnecessary blows were added to the ones that had already finished him off. Even from where he stood, Will could tell he was quite dead.

The broken body of Sir Thomas lay in the muddy street, looking like one more victim of the plague, if it wasn't for the blood oozing from his skull and puddling at his attackers' feet. The man who had spoken stopped then and took Sir Thomas's purse, then he and the others all backed away from the body. He straightened and turned to Will, breathless from his exertion and with a mad look in his eye.

'Master Shakespeare?' he called and Will started, so wild did he look from the blood lust in him. Oh God, was Will to be next? Did the earl want rid of him too, to ensure his silence? But instead of attacking Will, he asked him, 'Are you satisfied?'

Will did not comprehend at first and it took him a moment to realise the villain wanted to know if Will was happy with his murderous work. He instinctively glanced down at the lifeless body of Thomas Vernon and answered, 'I am.'

'And will you tell your master you are?'

'I will.'

'Then after, never more speak of this night?'

'I swear it.'

'Good. Then we will away, for this will out.'

–

The theatre was busier that day, with men learning their lines and others rehearsing them, while acrobats tumbled across the pit and William Kempe stood off to one side, practising a new jig with comedic moves that would send the audience home at the end of a play with smiles upon their faces. Others occupied themselves with music, in the hope that they would be called upon once more to play those instruments in front of a crowd when the plague lifted. On the stage, there was a run-through of a sword fight that would appear in their next production. On closer viewing, it had a suspicious similarity to the recent duel between Richard Burbage and Sir Thomas Vernon. All of Shoreditch had heard how Richard had publicly disarmed the man and broken his nose, so the company had decided to re-enact the fight, in the certain hope that this would get even more arses on seats, once the theatre finally reopened.

Their work was cut short, however, when several armed men of the watch arrived, accompanied by the constable. 'I am here on the queen's business!' he told the assembled players, who stopped what they were doing to listen. 'To enquire upon a grave matter that happened scarcely a mile from these very walls. Sir Thomas Vernon is dead.'

Will felt an immediate physical sensation of shock from their appearance at the theatre, combined with a feeling of intense relief that the constable had not immediately marched up and blamed him for Sir Thomas's murder. His nemesis was dead right enough and that meant both he and Richard Burbage, as well as Rosalind, would be safe, but only if Will was not implicated in the matter now. Just what did the constable and the men of the watch know about Sir Thomas and his dealings with the company, to bring them here, and how would they link the dead man to the players?

'Sir Thomas is dead?' asked Richard Burbage.

'The very same.'

'Of the plague?' he asked. 'Or the ague?'

'Neither one,' the constable told him. 'He died at the hands of men.'

'He was murdered?'

'Set upon in the street.'

'Where did this happen?' asked Richard.

'Near the Bull tavern. He was attacked not two streets from his door and beaten most thoroughly.'

'With clubs and cudgels.' Will said it quietly to himself but the constable's ears were sharper than he imagined.

'What say you?'

'Clubs and cudgels,' he repeated, louder this time. 'That is what rough men use, is it not?'

The constable eyed Will suspiciously. 'There is no honour in that,' he said. 'In a quarrel, a man may pull a dagger or sword, but he must give the other fellow a chance to reach for his own. Then it's a fair fight and the outcome in the hands of God. Better to die that way than like a beaten dog in the gutter. They say Sir Thomas had ne'er a bone in his body left unbroken, before the killing blow was landed. What kind of man can beat another person like that without mercy?'

Will thought not of Sir Thomas's killers then, but of the man himself and how he had mercilessly beaten his own wife and mutilated her teacher. 'The kind that deserves no quarter,' he answered.

James Burbage arrived then. 'What's all this?' he demanded of the watch. 'What brings you to my theatre?'

'Sir Thomas Vernon of this parish is dead,' he told Burbage, 'or I should say is killed, for he was struck down by other men. I mean to discover who might have done it. I did hear he had business with some or other of you and quarrelled?'

'Business with us?' asked James. 'What kind of business?'

'The kind that involves money. I am told he had an actor for a partner in some business or other.' Will looked down at the floor but James Burbage laughed.

'An actor? Hah. Whoever said this did not know actors. They never have a penny between them.' And there were some laughs and murmurs of agreement at this from members of the company.

'That same man told me there was an argument the other night between you' – he indicated the members of the company – 'and Sir Thomas. The quarrel saw swords drawn.' He said that uncertainly, as if he was not sure of the trustworthiness of the source of his information.

'That there was,' said James Burbage firmly and without hesitation, as if it was the most natural thing to admit to having had a quarrel with a man who was murdered not long after it. 'An argument, I mean, but no swords were drawn.' Will was impressed by this blatant lie and hoped the men of the watch did not challenge it.

'And what was this argument about?'

'Certain words were spoken,' James said conspiratorially.

'What words?'

'I would rather not say, for they should not be repeated.'

'What do you mean? Out with it, man!'

'It does not surprise me to hear that Sir Thomas is dead,' said James Burbage darkly.

'It does not?'

'No, for in the tavern that night, he did rail against the queen's person.' James appeared newly wounded from describing this behaviour.

This intrigued the constable. 'What did he say against the queen?'

'He questioned the right of Her Majesty to be ruler in her own kingdom.'

The leader of the watch was shocked. 'Is this true?'

Burbage turned and addressed the members of his company who were gathered around him. 'Did we not hear him say, when hearing of some unhappy news or other, and with a snarl upon his lips, that "this is what happens when men are ruled by women"?'

The members of the company all nodded or murmured their agreement, and Richard Burbage added, 'Aye, 'tis true. He did say it.'

James Burbage continued. 'Would I have been a younger, stronger man, I would have run him through myself, for our queen is loved by every man in this company, as is the earl, our patron.'

'The earl?' The constable seemed unaware that the company had an illustrious patron and looked unnerved to learn that it was an earl.

'Lord Strange, a fine and noble man, who was also besmirched by the wretched fellow you found in the gutter.'

The men of the watch all seemed to straighten then, on realising that Sir Thomas had made an enemy of an earl, as well as seemingly every loyal subject of the queen.

'It fills me with shame to admit what a coward I am,' said James, 'and how I lacked the strength to give the scoundrel a lesson.' He held up his hand and it shook from a false ailment he acted out in front of them. 'I am not built for swordplay but I doff my cap to the man who was.'

'It was no sword that killed Sir Thomas.' He repeated the account for James Burbage's benefit, since he had arrived late to the interrogation. 'He was set upon by men with clubs.'

'Beaten to death then? Why, no gentleman of this company would do such a thing. If it were a matter of honour, and it would have been for impugning the queen's good name, then one of our number would have stuck a rapier in him. Look how my son, who is a master swordsman, wears his, and note how Master Shakespeare also has his sword by his side.'

The men did look and took note of it. They must have been wondering why a man with a rapier would risk getting close enough to an enemy to hit him many times with a club, when it would be far simpler and quicker to stab him through the heart instead.

'No, it was rougher men that did this,' Burbage concluded. 'Most likely for coin.'

'His purse *was* taken,' admitted their inquisitor.

'There it is then,' announced Burbage. 'Sir Thomas escaped retribution for his vile slurs against the queen in the tavern, but God saw to it he was punished on another night, by sending him home along a path lined with robbers.'

'That is likely what occurred,' the constable conceded, seemingly content now to have an explanation for Thomas Vernon's death that avoided the need to question the players further, since they had such an important patron. 'We will away and trouble you no more. God save the queen!'

'God save her!' roared James. He looked overcome with the false emotion he had once conjured at will for an audience.

Chapter Fifty-Two

'Cowards die many times before their deaths;
The valiant never taste of death but once.'
— Julius Caesar

'I congratulate you on that performance,' Will told James Burbage after they all departed to the tavern.

'I am out of practice,' James admitted, for it had been a while since he trod the boards of a stage, 'but think it was convincing enough to satisfy a constable.'

'It was indeed.'

'I only wish I could thank the man that rid this world and us of Sir Thomas Vernon.' He said this significantly, but Will met his words silently. 'Yet your face tells me you are still not at peace.'

'My troubles are far from ended,' Will told him. 'Word has been sent to me that I must soon report to Sir Robert Cecil. Tomorrow in fact.' He had been woken by the messenger that morning, whose loud rapping upon his door had Will fearing the watch had come early, to drag him away for Thomas Vernon's murder.

'And what will you tell him about the Earl of Southampton?'

'I know not.'

'You must tell him what he wishes to hear,' urged James. 'Surely 'tis clear?'

It was with a great deal of trepidation that Will took himself to Robert Cecil's London home the next day. This was not quite as grand as the Earl of Southampton's but still a great house, filled with the trappings of a wealth largely given to him by Her Majesty, and a far warmer place to meet than the Tower. In the entranceway was a huge portrait of his father, William Cecil, and they admired it together for a moment.

'Have you read *Christ's Tears Over Jerusalem?*' Cecil enquired lightly, as if he was asking Will something of small importance.

'I have little time for pamphlets.' Will hoped to avoid being pressed about the contents of Thomas Nashe's latest work, which he had of course read. It was dedicated to Elizabeth Carey and had outraged the authorities far more than his bawdy 'Choise of Valentines' ever could. Will could still picture Nashe, riding with him in that carriage to Place House, then standing so confidently in front of those noble lords and courtly gentlemen as he delivered his bawdy brothel poem dedicated to the Earl of Southampton.

'Its author, Thomas Nashe, of whom you are familiar, declared that unless this kingdom reforms we are destined to follow the path of Jerusalem and fall to the Turks or some other heathen.' Robert Cecil shook his head at the depravity of the world. 'He has been given time in Newgate Prison to reflect upon the seriousness of his words, where he shall remain until Her Majesty deems him sufficiently penitent.' Then he added, 'That may not be soon.'

He was still looking at the portrait of the older Cecil, who was depicted wearing the rich, velvet robes of a Knight of the Garter. He had the same piercing eyes of his son. 'My father can always detect a lie. They used to say Walsingham could smell one. I myself cannot. I rely upon my ability to read something in a man's face when I question him. You, sir, seem nervous to me, which makes me wonder what you are hiding.'

'All men quail in front of great power, I think.' Robert Cecil laughed at that. He appeared dismissive but Will could tell he was flattered too, which had been his aim. 'A man who has the ear of the queen would surely make all other men afraid? I wish I were braver, but understand enough of this world to know my fate rests entirely with you.'

Cecil couldn't help but let a thin smile play on his lips. He could read another man's face but so too could Will. Cecil clearly enjoyed the reminder of his power to destroy other men. 'I am merely Her Majesty's loyal servant,' he began, 'but the queen's power does reside in me. I do God's work and hers, but no man who loves the queen has anything to fear.'

'Then I know my lord will find no fault in me.'

'Have you been with Henry Wriothesley since our last meeting?' asked Cecil.

Been with? Was Cecil being deliberately provocative? Will admitted he had, while noting how Cecil avoided using Southampton's title, referring to him only as Henry Wriothesley. It was as if he had already been stripped of everything by the man enquiring of him.

'Tell me everything,' Cecil ordered.

Will began a long and carefully worded answer, while Cecil listened so intently that Will felt sure he would pounce on a single loose word. He understood Robert Cecil now or thought he did. Knowledge was his power and information its currency, something to be amassed, traded and hoarded, like wealth.

Will gave a partial description of everything that had occurred, from the moment the Earl of Southampton enlisted his help to solve the mystery of the death of his cousin. He spoke honestly about those events while giving away nothing, having removed any part that might prove damning to the earl or his reputation. In particular, he avoided planting any notion that Wriothesley might have 'become justice', passing off his interest in the fate of Celia as merely that of a concerned but slightly distant relative.

After a time, Cecil asked him, 'Did he love this girl?' He seemed surprised, either that Southampton could love a lowly young woman or perhaps any woman at all. Had he dismissed the earl as a sodomite or did he believe that, like Narcissus, he loved only himself? It was also possible that Cecil may have been incapable of love and might struggle to recognise it in others.

'He held a sentimental attachment to her, from an innocent time in my lord's life, when they were but children.' Will did not want Cecil to believe Wriothesley's affection for Celia had in any way contributed to the demise of the earl's arranged marriage with Cecil's niece.

'And he thought her murdered?'

'He thought her dead of the plague,' explained Will, 'but wanted to be certain of it.'

'Why did he doubt this?'

'Because my lady was the first to die in her street and, for a time, the only one.'

'And, having looked into it, what did you say to him on the matter?'

'That she did indeed contract the plague, from a Flemish merchant who dined at her home. Celia fell ill soon after. She did not venture outside again nor have contact with anyone else in her household, so was the only one afflicted.'

'It is a sad end for a lady to be the only one of her household taken by plague,' Cecil observed. 'She had no children?'

'None,' confirmed Will.

'And her husband? You told Wriothesley he was innocent of wrong-doing in the matter?'

'I told my lord it was the plague.'

'And he accepted this?'

'It was the news he had expected.'

'Then why question it?'

'To prove the matter beyond doubt and put his mind to rest.'

Robert Cecil seemed to be weighing this up. 'There was talk of this woman, Celia. She was Sir Thomas Vernon's wife but was seen with another man at the theatre.' Did Robert Cecil know everything that happened in London? It seemed so, especially if it touched on anyone with the slightest presence at court. 'She was intimate with another man?' probed Cecil.

'There was talk,' Will admitted, 'as my lord said.'

'Only talk or more to it? Was she close to another man even after marriage?' He seemed shocked, which was unusual in one who had seen so much of life. 'Was it this foreigner?'

Once more, Will deliberately chose a variation on the truth. 'Prior to her marriage, the lady held some affection for a teacher who came with her from her old household.'

'And Sir Thomas permitted this?'

'It was a condition of the marriage.' Cecil shook his head in wonder at the oddness of such an arrangement. 'In time, there was a quarrel and Sir Thomas put the teacher out of the house. There was a brawl in the street.'

'I hope Sir Thomas thrashed him for his impudence.'

'He did,' confirmed Will and Cecil smiled approvingly at this. 'Then he bit off the man's nose.'

'Merciful heaven!' It was an unusual choice of words for a torturer, but then he spoiled the effect by laughing heartily at the other man's fate. 'I can see why a sentimental man such as Henry Wriothesley might think a man capable of mutilating another might be given to murderous rages against his wife.'

'I can state the truth of the matter clearly, my lord. Sir Thomas did not kill his wife.'

Cecil seemed to accept this. 'And yet someone did kill Sir Thomas.' He knew of this too, already. 'Some might call this ill fortune... or fate... Others might persuade themselves it was connected to her death in some way. Foolish men might consider it justice of a kind.'

'It was none of those things.'

'Explain yourself.'

'It is not uncommon for an honest man in London to be dispatched by a robber or a fellow he quarrelled with in a tavern over the smallest of slights. Sir Thomas fought almost every day.' This was an exaggeration but designed to paint the truth of the man's character. 'It was surely only a matter of time before he met someone more than his equal.'

'He fought that often? Was he as rough a man as that?'

'My lord, he bit off a man's nose and jested about it afterwards.'

Cecil did not argue the point. 'So, the lady is dead and her husband had naught to do with it. The husband is dead and Henry Wriothesley had naught to do with it?'

'My lord.' Will nodded his assent.

Robert Cecil leaned forward then, tiring of the matter. 'And what of Henry Wriothesley's friends? What of Raleigh and Lord Strange, Lord Stanley and others? Tell me, are they all innocent men too? Don't say that it is so, for I do not believe it.'

Will hesitated. 'Speak!' commanded Cecil. 'And speak well, for I must show the queen how loyal these subjects of hers truly are.'

'Where to begin?' Will was delaying the inevitable, while hoping to navigate the difficulty of failing to betray his patron, while satisfying his newer master, Cecil.

Cecil grew impatient. 'What happens when they are together in the same room at Place House?'

How could Will tell Robert Cecil that he had failed to ingratiate himself enough with the earl to be invited back to his country home for a second time? His only knowledge of the earl's hospitality and secret symposiums had been confined to that one visit to Place House, though he had not given Cecil every detail of that weekend and could perhaps mine that single experience again.

'You wish me to tell all?' Will asked. 'You desire me to include even the indelicate moments?'

'I especially want you to include the indelicate moments.'

'They are served victuals by young women dressed as Amazons, with their breasts bared, and listen to bawdy poems.'

Robert Cecil stared at Will for a moment, then he erupted. 'I care naught for lewd sonnets amongst men! Nor do I wish to hear of bare-breasted Amazons! What of atheism?' he demanded, then he grew eager. 'Did the earl recite the atheist's prayer? Did he incite another to read it aloud in their presence?'

'My lord, he did not.'

'Did he speak heretical views? Did he wish the queen dead or deposed? Did he hope that another monarch be found to seize her crown, one with a Catholic faith?'

'He did not.'

'Did he ever express the treasonous wish that England be invaded by her enemies and overrun? Did he call for the French or Spanish to come to our shores with an army? Would he welcome them, if they were intent on toppling the queen? Did he say this at all, even if it seemed in jest?'

'He did not.'

'Did he rail against our pursuit of priests and the bringing down of treacherous families that shelter them? Does he talk of holding mass in secret in his house? Does a priest attend him there? Did he boast of secret rooms to hide him when our men call?'

'He did not.'

This was too much for Cecil, who roared, 'He did not! He did not! He did not!' back at Will so sharply that he flinched. Cecil's voice seemed to fill the room, spittle flew from his lips and landed on Will's face. Cecil's own face was red now in his fury. 'Do you consider me a fool? I know he is a heretic! I know he is a recusant! I know he is a traitor and I know he is a sodomite!' He lowered his voice then until his next words were almost a whisper. 'I know it. I simply require you to swear it. You can provide me with evidence of the earl's treachery and if you do not, Master Shakespeare, I will take it most unkindly. I will take it most unkindly indeed!'

Chapter Fifty-Three

'All the infections that the sun sucks up
From bogs, fens, flats, on Prosper fall and make him
By inch-meal a disease!'
— The Tempest

Will managed to get very drunk that night. When he thought back later on the events of those most recent days, he was unsure how he was able to bear them. Marlowe's death and Kyd's breaking under torture hit him hard. The killing of Sir Thomas Vernon and his own narrow avoidance of death at that same man's rapier happened while his mind was already in a turmoil, from his doomed wooing of Rosalind. Robert Cecil's deadly threats on top of all this proved too much to endure, so Will went deep into his cups and drank, then drank some more.

In the morning, he could not recall the walk home, though he must have borne it or he would not have been lying there upon his bed, his clothes still on him, his head as sore as if he had been struck a blow from one of those clubs wielded by Southampton's men. He felt sick in his stomach and blamed himself for the folly of drinking far in excess of a sensible measure. When his headache eventually lifted, Will left his rooms in search of food but could eat little. He wrote nothing that day and found that by evening he felt no better. In fact, he was somehow in a worse condition than he had been that morning. What could be ailing him, apart from the after-effects of the drink, as well as a bruised and heavy heart?

He decided to return home and retire to his bed early, the better to sleep off the symptoms that ailed him so persistently and had become progressively worse throughout the day. He even felt a little feverish and his brow was definitely hot to the touch.

As he walked back to his lodgings, Will began to feel weak and dizzy. He told himself to keep going until he reached his door. He opened it, took a step inside, then his legs suddenly gave way and he fell heavily to the ground, leaving his door still open.

-

'I found him like this,' the landlord's servant told Rosalind. Will could just make out her voice, which seemed to come to him as if in a dream.

'And left him here?' Rosalind chastised her. 'Did you not think to pick him up?'

Why had the girl brought Rosalind here? He could hear their words, but it was as if he was still drunk or drugged perhaps. They seemed far away and he could neither speak nor summon the energy to pick himself off the floor.

'I could not,' the girl protested.

'Did you even try?'

'I came to fetch *you*,' the girl said pointedly, as if it was Rosalind's business what happened to Will and not hers. 'I thought he had plague.'

'I know what the plague looks like. This is not plague.' She bent low to check on Will and placed her cool hand upon his hot forehead. It felt like the touch of an angel. 'This is a fever of the ague,' Rosalind decided, 'most likely from contact with the river. Help me pick him up.' But when she turned back, the servant was already gone. 'Foolish girl.'

She managed to pull Will up into a sitting position and this caused him to stir. He opened his eyes, mumbled something unintelligible, but managed to comply with Rosalind as she attempted to haul him to his feet. He even stood unsteadily for a moment as she supported him, before he staggered backwards then fell onto his bed, his legs still trailing to the floor. Rosalind grabbed him by the boots and swung his legs onto the bed but that caused the upper part of his body to slide, and he almost fell from the bed. Rosalind quickly wrapped her arms around Will and held onto him tightly to prevent this. Her body was pressed firmly against his and her warm breath touched his cheek. Even in his fever, he was aware of the sweet smell of her, like lavender, and it was the last thing he was conscious of before passing out again.

\-

'Drink this warm wine,' she told him and Will moved, dreamlike, into a seated position, though he barely had the strength to lean forward, even with her help. He managed a sip or two before falling weakly back onto his bed. He was under a sheet, his boots had been taken from him and his shirt was soaked in sweat from the fever. Will closed his eyes and passed out once more.

Later, and he was not sure if minutes or hours had passed by then, he felt something damp on his forehead, a wet cloth or a poultice, which cooled his fever. Then, sometime after this, he was aware of her touch again. This time she loosened his shirt and spread something on his bare chest with her hands. It smelt of sweet herbs and he realised it was an unction or salve of some sort.

Rosalind's voice, which seemed to come to him from a distance, assured him that all would be well in time and that she would stay with him until his fever broke. He doubted it could be true, as he felt sure he must die from this malady and that it must certainly be plague, but he drew some comfort from her words. He was vaguely aware of Rosalind sitting in his chair a little way from his bed, a constant, calming presence as he drifted in and out of sleep, his body racked with fever.

While he half slept and sweated, tossed and turned on his bed, Will's thoughts were altered by the fever. He was an acute observer of people and much of what he saw and heard stayed with him long afterwards. It had always been this way and he had what he termed a writer's memory. He could recall phrases and pieces of conversation perfectly, sometimes from years before. In his earlier days, this was a habit born of curiosity about others that was then encouraged further by his desire to become a writer of plays. It necessitated the close study of how men spoke to one another. Forced into this dormant state while he battled his fever, Will's half-awake and half-sleeping mind was free to wander. Without consciously willing it to do so, it began to revisit the most recent events of his past, in particular his quest for the truth concerning Lady Celia

Vernon's death, which had left Will with a deep but imprecise, nagging sense of unease.

His prodigious memory, stimulated by that burning fever, made him recall the words of others now, as if spoken anew. He had listened carefully to so many people of late, hoping that what they told him would, like so many threads, combine to create something whole, which would then supply him with the entire truth of what had happened to Celia, leaving him with more than just suspicions of her husband's guilt, but this had eluded Will. He began to toss and turn on his bed, speaking unintelligibly, while his fever raged on.

Something innocuous that Richard Burbage had said to him during their sword fight on stage came back to him first. '*Make it real or at least make it seem so. Show me the naked truth in this, even if it is only for a play. Convince me.*'

Then Rosalind spoke to him, as if she was standing next to Will and not sitting silently in a chair close to his bed: '*You would be surprised by what is hidden in the hearts of women.*'

In his mind's eye he replied to her now, just as he had before, his lips even moving silently. '*No one was closer to your lady than you,*' he said, '*except her husband, of course.*'

'*I was closer than he.*'

Then she added, '*If you wish for a puzzle harder to solve then look to a woman.*'

He recalled Sir Thomas Vernon next, telling Will how he had quit London once his wife contracted plague but had left the mute Isaac behind to protect her. '*He knew no other life but by her side.*'

Rosalind spoke to him again then, just as she had done before: '*She did not kiss a man at the theatre nor was kissed by one. It is a lie!*' Then she swore, '*I know nothing of Celia being secretly wed or promised to another man before Thomas and have never seen nor heard of this former husband the gossips talk of. If he lives, then where is he?*' Rosalind had said this to Will before he had known of her own marriage. He had even doubted the ceremony had taken place, until it was confirmed by the old vicar, who assured him, '*I can see shapes clear enough, and if those shapes speak, I know them to be men or women.*'

Rosalind again spoke just as before, when she told the court during her trial how impossible it was for poor Celia to ever leave her husband.

'*What can a woman do on her own without a man? Nothing. She is considered worthless without a husband.*'

Then she spoke again. '*Sir Thomas sent a man to the house. I had not thought of it before but your question made me recall it. 'Twas but a few days before my lady took ill.*'

Then, just before the truth of it all finally reached him, he remembered his own prophetic words, which came back to torment Will now in his fever. '*Some men are foolish enough to be blinded by beauty and lose all sense.*' It was what he had once told Rosalind and he was right about that. Oh, what a fool he had been.

Chapter Fifty-Four

'Our doubts are traitors
And make us lose the good we oft might win
By fearing to attempt.'
— Measure for Measure

When Will finally woke, some hours later, Rosalind was still sitting in the chair by his bed. He managed to say her name and she got up, poured some wine and came to him, bringing it to his lips. He drank a little, gratefully.

She pressed a cool hand against his cheek then his forehead. 'Your fever has broken. It took its time but all will be well now. I was worried about you, though.'

'Were you?' he croaked, his mouth still dry.

'It has been two days, Will,' she explained.

He could scarcely believe that. 'You stayed?'

The certainty that had come to him from within his feverish dreams seemed to evaporate now that he was looking at the real Rosalind, not some phantom from a scene they had played out between them weeks earlier. He was no longer sure if he was thinking like a man with full reason. Surely the doubts he'd had were caused by the malaise which had just left him. The truth he was sure he had uncovered, while he sweated and called out in his fever, was so outlandish it could not actually be, could it? Either way, he had no proof of any of it. The only thing he could reasonably be certain about was the presence of Rosalind in his room. He would have most probably died here alone, had it not been for her care.

'Are you really wed, Rosalind, or did I dream that in my fever?'

'I am.'

'Then you risk a damaged reputation being here.'

'If my husband cared overmuch about my reputation, he would not be my husband. He takes me for all in all.' Then she said, 'Your landlord's servant thinks me your whore, which is lucky for you, or she would not have gone to the market looking for me. Gertrude sent her to my rooming house.'

'Why did you come, when I have been such a fool in all my dealings with you?'

'Not all,' she assured him, 'and I am thankful for your help when I was before the magistrate. My anger was directed at other men that day, not you, though you were the closest at the time.'

'Thank you for saving me then,' he said.

'You saved me first.'

'I thought I was dying of plague.'

'Ague,' she corrected him, 'and you won't die of that, at least not today. You spend too much of your time down by the river, Will. They say the sun sucks up foul vapours from the water there, which causes the ague. You are fortunate to have survived it.'

'Then God has spared me so I can beg your pardon, Lady Rosalind.'

'What crime have you done unto me now,' she said lightly, 'without my knowing?'

'No new crime but one for which I am truly humbled. When I offered you rooms here, it was a folly born from love. Men are oft governed by desire and perform low acts for that most powerful of mistresses.'

'And yet women, for the most part, are governed by men. Would it were the other way around.'

'Women should govern men?'

'We have a queen and does she not govern you all? Is she not fit to? Oh, look how you quail when you hear that. I am not your inquisitor, Master Shakespeare, nor a spy from the court or an agent of the Privy Council, just a lowly woman who oft looks upon lowly men and wonders what profit it brings either of us to be ruled by them.'

'Is your husband lowly?'

'In the eyes of some. He is a captain, which is lowly if you are an earl but lofty to a farm boy. He is neither rich nor poor, base nor noble, but he is a goodly man, a kind man and would no more beat me than he would a babe in arms.'

'And is he truly finished with war?'

'He is and will soon come on a ship from the lowlands to claim our farm. He aims to be a husbandman, since he owns no land himself but can afford to rent it.' Lowlier than both was the labourer, who toiled upon another's land from dawn to sunset for a groat a day. That silver coin was worth just four pence and nearly all of it needed to buy bread, butter and ale. If Rosalind's husband could afford to rent the farm and perhaps even buy it one day, then he would better himself and she was far less likely to starve. Will was glad of that at least.

Chapter Fifty-Five

'An untimely ague
Stay'd me a prisoner in my chamber'
— Henry VIII

The next day, he received a visit from Richard Burbage, who explained he had been to Will's rooms before now but had been refused entry by Rosalind due to the risk of infection.

'Since she was most diligent in her care of you, I let her turn me away. It is good to see you up from your bed, also at your writing.' For Will was still holding his quill when he let Richard in. 'Is there anything you need to help you in your recovery? Anything at all?'

'I need you to find me some rough men, Richard,' Will said determinedly, and when his friend questioned this with a look, Will explained. 'They must be base enough to complete a task no Christian man would ever agree to.' Then he added, 'But not so low I cannot rely on their discretion, for there must be a trust of sorts in this transaction.'

'What in hell's name are you planning, Will? Murder?'

'Not murder, but it were better you did not hear more of the matter. I only ask whether you know of such men.'

Richard thought for a time, while regarding his friend uneasily, before finally announcing, 'I believe that I do.'

–

Will chose the quietest tavern in Shoreditch and arranged with Richard Burbage to meet the men at an hour when most others would be away from it. They were to introduce themselves by stating that they were there to help him devise a scene for a play, a ruse that did not seem so convincing once Will surveyed these two new recruits to his conspiracy.

One was a big, fierce-looking man and the other had a face ravaged by scars from smallpox. You would not want to meet either man on your way home in the dark, but Richard had assured Will that they were both known as 'honest, dishonest men', in that they were biddable and buyable but not treacherous. They would take your coin in return for a service but would not steal it from you nor betray you to the watch. Both men believed their reputations depended upon it, while they committed their crimes with a clear conscience.

They joined Will at a corner table and drank ale with him, while he explained the service he needed from them. They listened silently at first, then there was some discussion about the timing of the act and the price they would accept for it, which seemed more than reasonable to Will under the circumstances.

'Then we will do this service for you, sir,' the big man told him. 'Though we will be rightly damned for it,' he added with resignation.

–

Will had not been back to the theatre since his illness. He arrived there to find James Burbage eager to pass on news from court.

'There was a drama fit for the stage at Whitehall today. Your inquisitor, Robert Cecil, came to see the queen.'

'On what business?'

'The business of state as he described it, but the queen was not in the right humour to listen to him. She had been enjoying the company of her ladies and the tall, handsome men of the court, who know how to flatter her. He chose the wrong moment to disturb her with news of yet more papist plots.'

'She berated him then?' asked Will. 'In front of the whole court?' If the queen upbraided him publicly it would have a devastating effect on a man like Robert Cecil. Though Will had never witnessed her fury in person, it was legendary.

'Much worse than that,' said James, and Will wondered how anything could be. 'She mocked him.'

Will could not imagine a man as serious as Robert Cecil being mocked by anyone, even the monarch. 'How so?'

'*Little man*, she called him.' Then he mimicked the queen's voice. '*It is not the place of little men to question their mighty queen and you, sir, are a pygmy.*'

'How did he respond?'

'With but two words, spoken softly.' And he bowed to Will, as if he was Robert Cecil bowing before the queen who had just torn his heart open in front of all present. '"Your Majesty," he said and then he left. I'm told the laughter of the whole court followed him from the room.'

Will could picture the look of shock and hurt on Robert Cecil's face, as the woman he had sworn to protect with his life turned on him. She was the provider of all he had or ever would be and could rob him of it all in an instant: his money, palace, rank and titles, even his head. Will knew that none of them would matter as much to Robert Cecil as the one thing he craved more than anything else: power. Not even his head.

Without the queen's favour he would be nothing, just a small, ugly, powerless creature of no consequence. This time of treachery and intrigue, chaos and plotting was almost designed for Robert Cecil. Protecting Elizabeth from her many enemies, real or imagined, was his destiny. But if she ever stopped believing in Cecil's ability to keep her from harm, he would find no other place in a court filled with beautiful, fashionable women and handsome, charming men, for Elizabeth would have no need of him then.

It hit him so abruptly he almost started. Suddenly, Will understood the man entirely.

'What is it, Will?' asked Richard Burbage and Will was suddenly wrenched from his thoughts and remembered he was not alone. 'You looked as if you were in another place.'

'That's a writer's look,' said James, who had seen such distraction before. 'No doubt he has thought of something to put in his play.'

'I have found him!' said Will suddenly. 'I have found him!' And he hastened away, back to his rooms.

–

He had agreed to meet the men again the next day, at the same table in the same tavern, and Will half expected they would not return. Worse, they might arrive with the constable and betray him as a villain. When they did come, they were alone but grim-faced. The larger man spoke for them both, just as before.

'We carried out the task you gave us.'

'And what did you discover?' asked Will eagerly.

'It was not there.'

'You are certain?'

He snorted. 'We went deep enough. He will tell you the same.' He jerked his head towards his companion, who remained silent but gave a little nod to show his agreement. The big fellow must have expected to be challenged by Will further but, when he was not, he said, 'Many would be confounded by that news, but you are no more surprised than if I told you the rain fell outside while we were gone.'

'In truth, I paid you to prove what I already knew,' admitted Will, 'or thought I did. The service you performed was a good one and its price stands. The coin is earned.' He handed the money over to the men.

'Then we will drink to you tonight, good sir, and question you no further,' said the big man, as he took Will's money, 'nor ever speak of that night's work to any man.'

Chapter Fifty-Six

'Men at some time are masters of their fates'
— Julius Caesar

It was one of those brothels that had more boys than girls. As soon as Will heard a whisper that Henry Wriothesley was at large in the city, he sought him out there, for it was one of only a handful of places where the Earl of Southampton might choose to pass an evening. He could have had any number of boys or girls brought to his home, but perhaps he wanted to keep those worlds separate, or was it that he simply enjoyed being in this nest of vipers?

If Wriothesley was surprised to see him, he managed to sound untroubled, despite the presence of a half-dressed boy sitting either side of him. 'Did I summon you, Will?' he asked. 'I have no remembrance of it.'

Will shook his head. 'I reasoned I would find you here or in one of the other houses.'

'You have the nerve to look for me when not sent for. I should have you thrown into the street for your impudence.' One of his men stiffened then, as if in readiness to do just that.

'I fear I already know what would happen to me then. Clubs and cudgels.'

The earl's anger increased. 'Do you have something to say to me in the presence of these men?'

'*Not* in the presence of these men.'

The earl's curiosity must have outweighed his anger. He rose and indicated a darker corner of the room. Before Will could follow him there, he was pressed to the wall by burly hands who searched his person, removing the sword and dagger, which were passed to another man. 'I can be on you in an instant,' he was warned by the man who had searched him, but Will had no intention of attacking the earl. Instead, he walked to that dark corner and sat at his table.

'Tell me,' demanded Wriothesley impatiently.

'We were questioned by a constable and men of the watch.'

'And what did they seek?'

'An explanation for the death of one Thomas Vernon.'

'Then what did you give them?'

'Nothing,' he said, and explained how James Burbage had conjured a tale involving Sir Thomas Vernon showing disrespect to the queen, and the providence of his demise soon after at the hands of robbers. Wriothesley seemed satisfied by this. 'But there is more to tell, my lord.' Will steeled himself then, for this was a gamble. 'Lately, I have attracted the interest of a most powerful man who holds a lofty position at court.' This immediately sparked the earl's interest, which peaked when Will added, 'I believe him to be your enemy.'

'Why would you imagine that?'

'He seeks your downfall and wishes to disgrace you in the eyes of the queen. Even telling you this puts me under threat of a sentence of death by his hand.'

'Robert Cecil,' Wriothesley said then, as if he knew it could be no other.

'The same.'

'Then why tell me?' He was clearly suspicious. 'If it puts your life at risk? You have no loyalty to me, other than as your hoped-for patron.'

'Because he wishes to use me as the instrument of your destruction.'

'Forgive me, Shakespeare, but how could he possibly use a man as lowly as you to achieve that?'

'By recruiting me as his spy.'

Neither man spoke for a time, while the earl considered this statement and pondered its true meaning. Then he asked, 'When did he do this?'

'After the night in the tavern when you first invited me to your home. I was brought to him then by another agent of the crown, one Robert Poley.'

'And did you agree to this commission?' he asked abruptly. 'To spy upon me?'

'I did.' Wriothesley looked as if he could not believe Will was admitting this to him so openly. 'At the time I felt I had no choice. He made that much clear.'

'At the time? And now?'

'My thoughts are the same.'

'So, you agreed to spy on me and report back to him? On what?'

'On whether I heard or witnessed in your house any heresy, popery, blasphemy, atheism, sodomy... Anything that would sour the queen's good opinion of you.'

'That is what he sought,' said the earl, 'but what did you give him?'

'Nothing,' said Will, 'as yet.'

'I assume that Cecil would very much desire to hear all about the School of Atheists, as Raleigh likes to mischievously call my little symposiums?'

'He would.'

'And of other matters that occurred in my house during that same weekend?'

'He wishes to know everything, but also...'

'Yes?'

'He would like me to invent plots and conspiracies, heresies and blasphemies, whether I heard them or not.'

'So he can persuade the queen to have me brought to the block for treason,' observed Wriothesley.

'I do believe it so, my lord.'

'Why not do it then and have done with? He would reward you.'

'Perhaps I do not wish to serve Robert Cecil. I doubt he is a good man.'

The earl scoffed, 'I very much doubt that I am.' Then he said, 'Why tell me about it at all? Why not go back to Cecil and say you saw nothing at my house, except the Earl of Southampton constantly clutching his prayer book, offering up thanks to God for his merciful sparing of Her Majesty from her many heretical enemies?'

'I fear he will not believe it. He would then most certainly break me on the rack.'

'For not giving him what he most desires?' The earl smiled grimly. 'And all because I wronged his niece by not marrying her.'

'That is not the only reason.'

'What else could it be?'

'Jealousy, my lord. I believe Robert Cecil envies you.'

Wriothesley considered this. 'I think you are right about that, Shakespeare. I am richer than he, grander, more fair, and in the queen's favour... usually.' He brought the fingertips of both hands together then and leaned forward. 'What will you tell him then?'

'I know not,' he admitted, 'but I am a writer, so perhaps I shall invent something.'

'Perhaps? Why perhaps?'

'Though I very much want to help my lord, I know it will place me in grave danger.'

'And at the thought of the rack, your nerve fails you?' Wriothesley nodded slowly, as if he understood. 'How might we restore your courage?'

'A great patron like yourself understands what a poet needs in order to thrive.'

'A sum large enough to buy an artist his leisure?' asked the earl. 'To shield him from the concerns of the common man? Enough for food, lodgings and ale and perhaps some other essential needs.' He let his eye wander around the walls of the brothel. 'I gave as much to poor Kit before he was taken. I could perhaps award you his stipend.'

'That would be very much welcomed' – and the earl smiled, until Will added, 'if the circumstances were normal. But mine are not. Soon, I shall greatly anger an agent of the queen and might be broken for it, like Thomas Kyd.'

'I have not seen Kyd. How does he manage?'

'Not well, my lord.'

Wriothesley sighed. 'You know it would be far cheaper for me to pay some other men with clubs and cudgels to turn on you for a groat.'

'You could do that,' acknowledged Will. 'But if I were killed, your enemy would believe it was because you were hiding something from him.'

'How so? You could easily die at the hand of another without it falling on me. You could be stabbed in a tavern brawl.'

'Like Kit?'

'Like Kit, yes.'

'No one close to Marlowe really believes he was killed in a brawl and Cecil would know I died by your hand.'

'How will he know that?'

'Because I told him it would be so.'

'You told an agent of the queen that, if anything happens to you, it will be my doing?' Will nodded slowly, hoping the earl would believe this lie. 'I should have you whipped for that impertinence alone. By God, you had better stay alive, Will Shakespeare, for if you do not, I will come down to hell myself, drag you from it and kill you all over again.' He stared into the fire then and seemed to be making an effort to calm himself before continuing.

'How much?' he asked. 'To persuade Robert Cecil to hunt elsewhere?'

'I would say that to a man of your wealth and stature, who has so much to lose if he fell out of grace with the queen, fifty pounds might not seem like such a fantastical sum.'

'Fifty pounds! Do you know how many sonnets and plays I could have dedicated to me for that amount?'

'That would be included in our bargain. There will be fulsome praise of my noble lord in the dedication of my sonnets, for being my most generous patron.'

'What could a man like you possibly spend fifty pounds on?' He clearly couldn't conceive of anything.

'A share in a new theatre company. And I promise you this, my lord: I will deliver to you a body of plays the like of which has never been seen before. Say the word now and they will burst forth onto the paper in a trice. Many of them are half-finished already.'

'I do like your work, Master Shakespeare, but thought not to pay so much for it,' he said sullenly.

'That is not all you are paying for. For your money, you will receive my silence and discretion, my never-ending gratitude and loyalty to you and you alone, as well as a performance like no other.' And when Wriothesley raised a quizzical eyebrow at that, Will explained: 'One from me, that will satisfy Robert Cecil that you are a wronged and innocent man.'

'That will be a performance I should like to witness, for he trusts no man and believes few. You will have to be a very good actor indeed.'

Will greeted this observation with a steely look. 'You expect me to give you fifty pounds, to protect me from an enemy I might be able to confound on my own, just by retaining the queen's favour?'

'You might,' admitted Will, 'but you are not always at court and Cecil is. He has the queen's ear and whispers lies into it constantly. The risk you take is great when the fear of it can be cured with not such a very large sum.'

'It's large enough.' He shook his head. 'That's not enough, Shakespeare. What else will you give me?'

'Eternity,' said Will with a confidence he had not found within him until that moment. 'A remembrance in men's hearts and minds that will outlive us all. Fame beyond this life to follow you into the next.'

They locked eyes then and Wriothesley regarded Will with something bordering on wonder. Presently, the earl said, 'I will be your patron, Will, and you will get your fifty pounds, *if* you survive your audience with Robert Cecil, but you must never speak of the true reason for my generosity to anyone.' Then he said, 'I'd rather they called us sodomites than found out the truth: that a lowly, ill-born man such as you has wrung this much coin from one as grand as I, with threats.'

'I am an actor and you are a young and handsome lord,' observed Will. 'They will call us sodomites anyway.'

Chapter Fifty-Seven

'Money buys lands, and wives are sold by fate.'
— *The Merry Wives of Windsor*

Shortly after Will had recovered from his ague, Rosalind finally left London to be with her husband. Under normal circumstances, Will would have likely never seen her again. But the unproven allegation of witchcraft against her and the sudden, violent death of Sir Thomas Vernon meant she briefly fell under suspicion after his murder, though few believed she could have cast a spell powerful enough to bewitch men to attack him so violently. James Burbage's account of Sir Thomas's loud and treasonous utterances in the tavern had removed sympathy for the man, and the manner of his death helped too. His purse having been taken put robbery as the most likely cause of death and not witchcraft. But still, Rosalind was required to notify the constable if she left London and inform him of her whereabouts, so she gave him the name of a farm in Norfolk. Will acquired it too, upon the payment of a small bribe to the man.

Will set off from London and travelled to the nearest town, lodging overnight in a tavern before arriving in the afternoon. Claiming to be the administrator of a will of which Rosalind was a beneficiary, he also paid for the information he needed. This was usually the best way to overcome any lingering suspicions about the character of the person asking the questions, and he soon had the location of the farm.

He rode out there the next morning. It consisted of a stone cottage, a wooden barn and several enclosed fields on which livestock grazed. She may not have been prosperous by the standards of the households she had lived in once, but Rosalind was better off than many.

Will noticed a horse tethered by the barn and a tall, muscular man nearby sharpening a scythe. He regarded Will suspiciously but did not utter a word as he rode by. Presently he reached the farmhouse, which had two windows at the front, though one was shuttered, even in daylight. Will banged on the door.

'Lady Rosalind,' he said when she answered.

'Will?' Rosalind looked surprised to see him, as well she might have been.

'You have a good-sized farm,' he observed.

'It serves us. We can make our living here.' He noticed she did not immediately ask him why he was here, nor did she invite him in.

'You have a lease. Must have cost what...?' He made a show of thinking on the matter.

'Four pounds a year,' she told him. 'It's an old lease and land is less expensive out here. My husband did well to find it.'

'Then he summoned you here,' he said. 'And yet the lease is not in his name, but yours.'

'How is that your business?' she snapped. He had wondered how long it would take.

'I meant nothing of it. I was merely commending you on your choice of land and husband. He must have a good eye for a farm. He trusts his new wife too, if he places it all in her name.'

'It's warm out,' she observed. 'Can I pour you a cup of ale?'

'Before I leave?' She still hadn't asked him why he had chosen to visit her. 'That would be Christian of you.' And as she went to fetch it, he followed her into the house, uninvited.

Rosalind's home was small but lacked for nothing. 'You will lately be used to much grander places, Master Shakespeare.'

'There's many a great reckoning in a little room.'

'A great reckoning? I don't understand.'

'It's time to settle matters, Rosalind,' he told her. 'To resolve all. Is the captain here?'

'My husband? No, he is not.'

'I saw a horse outside when I rode up.'

'That is not...'

Will shushed her then. 'Let us not add a new layer of lies atop the others. Words can kill when they are used carelessly.' He stood by her hearth and watched as she poured ale into a cup for him. 'You've not asked me why I am here?'

She finished pouring the ale with a steady hand and gave it to him. 'I assumed it was about Celia. It always was with you, wasn't it?'

'Not always,' he corrected her, and they looked at each other intently.

'But it is today?' she offered and he nodded once.

'Her husband is dead,' he said, 'but then you know that and were likely questioned about it.'

'Word did reach me of it,' she admitted, 'even his poor, late wife would not have grieved for him.'

'Not when he beat her so.'

'Beat her and killed her,' she reminded him. 'So everyone says. So *you* said.'

'I did say that,' he admitted, 'and whispered it into a great man's ear. But what if I were to admit to you now that I was deceived?'

'Deceived? But if not Sir Thomas, then who could have killed her?'

'Who indeed? It would have to be someone close to her, someone who would benefit greatly from her removal from this world.' She shot him a fierce look then but did not dare to challenge him, just as he had expected.

For a moment they both remained silent, while they stared at one another, each waiting for the other to speak. Will did not quite accuse her of murder, while Rosalind for her part did not choose to respond to the unspoken accusation with her customary outraged fury.

In the end, it was Will who grew tired of the game. He aimed his next comment not at Rosalind but at the closed door of the nearest room to them, the one he had noticed on his way in, because it had a shutter across its window, even in daylight. He called loud enough for his voice to pass through it.

'Will you not come out now, Celia?'

Rosalind flinched.

'Come now!' he shouted louder. 'Or I will fetch a magistrate and you can tell your story to him instead!'

For a second or two, he actually questioned if he might be calling into an empty room. But if Rosalind thought he had gone mad, as he shouted for a woman to rise from the dead and join them, she held her tongue. 'Come out, Celia,' he called, 'else I will leave here thinking Rosalind killed you for the money for her new farm. Would you prefer me to give that account to half of London?'

There was a moment of absolute silence, while Will stared at the door and Rosalind gazed down at the floor. Neither of them spoke. The fear that her closest companion could be hanged as a murderess must have broken the spell. The latch finally moved, the door opened, and Will found himself staring at a ghost, yet her cheeks had as much colour in them as his and her eyes were very much alive now, with fear.

'You seem well, Celia,' Will said, 'for a dead woman.'

It was the first time Will had seen her but this could only have been Celia. She was perhaps fair of face but looked for all the world more like a boy than a girl, for there was little that Will would have considered womanly about her still. Her hair had been shorn short and close cropped at the sides, and there was even stubble on her chin. Horsehair, he assumed, applied by Rosalind each morning to aid her disguise. Her manly attire was as you would have expected for a former soldier turned farmer. The illusion was heightened by her naturally slim figure. Either she lacked breasts worth speaking of or they were bound to ensure they could never give her away. Her hips were disguised by a long, baggy shirt for working in the fields and, save for a smoother, paler complexion, she looked for all the world like a young, fresh-faced man. There were boys in his own company of players who looked more passably female than Celia, even without make-up.

'Master Shakespeare.' Her voice was naturally deeper than Rosalind's, or was it from recent habit? 'You do not give up, do you?' Celia exchanged a look with Rosalind and told her, 'It's all right.' Though her voice seemed to crack as she said it. 'We always knew it was likely to happen.' Then she turned to Will and asked, 'Spare her, for my sake?' and when he remained impassive, she implored him, 'Then spare her, for your sake. You did love her once, did you not?'

Before he could answer, Rosalind rushed towards Celia and pulled her lady to her in an embrace. 'No! You cannot leave me!'

Celia comforted her then. 'What choice is there, my love?' She glanced at their unwanted guest. 'Would you kill him to keep us safe? Then the next man who came looking for him… and the one who came to find that man?' She shook her head. 'It is over. We had our time together and it was wondrous. That's how I can bear to go back and face them all.'

She turned again to Will. 'Would you let her be? Please, I beg of you. This was all me, all of it.'

'Wait.' He could hear the desperation in Rosalind's voice now. 'What would it take for you to leave us both here then ride away and forget about us?' she asked. 'There is still some money.'

Celia shook her head. 'You will need that. If the crops fail or—'

'I need you more,' said Rosalind. 'What do you want, Master Shakespeare? What would it take for you to let us be?'

'I'll start with more ale.' Will raised the cup to his lips and drank deeply, finishing the last of the draught he had been given and setting it down empty on the table. 'And I want what I always want. The story.'

'The story?' asked Celia.

'Your story and another cup of ale while you tell it. Afterwards I will decide what's to be done. There needs to be a reckoning here.'

The two women exchanged nervous glances then Rosalind reached for his cup and filled it anew.

'I pray thee have mercy and let me account for this,' said Celia as he took his ale. 'Rosalind had naught to do with it.'

'She had everything to do with it. She is your *wife*, is she not? Thanks to a half-blind cleric in a darkened church. Did you really think you could fool everyone like that?'

Celia looked close to tears, but Rosalind was defiant. 'We did fool everyone.'

'Then the question is how? Come now, for the truth is out and you must account for it.'

'We brought witnesses, gave them drink and coin beforehand and made sure they did not see Celia until they reached the church. I dressed her in a man's clothes, with a hat and cape, then disguised her like your actors when they play women, only in reverse. If I can beguile a thousand watchful souls in a theatre, I can fool an old blind man in a church.'

'But you can't hide from God,' Will said. 'Celia was already married to Sir Thomas Vernon.'

'You think God wanted me to die at the hands of that man?' snapped Celia. 'Would that be His will?' She forced herself to return to a calmer state before continuing. 'Thomas could not hide his true nature, even as he played the lover. He thought I would elevate him, being a

Wriothesley, so he bought me and secured my mother's position, but a man cannot take a woman's name to soften his. It only works the other way around.

'I tried to be a good wife, as if that would have been compensation enough, until I learned whatever I did would get me a beating. He liked me not, though had me anyway. I would have yielded out of wifely duty, but he preferred to take what otherwise would have been given.'

'I heard her screams in the night,' said Rosalind, 'and for the first time in my life wished that I were a man, so I could kill him for her.'

'You did kill him for her,' Will told her. 'It was your deception that led to his death.' He turned back to Celia. 'I said your husband did for you, not the plague. You were its only victim and he had fixed his eyes on another, richer wife. There was little enough proof but my word was sufficient for an earl who once loved you as kin, Celia. Your cousin did not have to wield the clubs and cudgels himself, only hire rough men to do his bidding, and now a man is dead because of you both.'

'It would rather seem, Master Shakespeare, that a man is dead because of you.' Celia let those words crash against him like a wave, before continuing. 'I wished to be free of my husband but did not plot to kill him, though the thought entered my mind.'

'Along with the fear of being burned for it,' he chided.

'That too, but I did not want to offend God by killing one of His creatures, however base. It would have been easy enough, though. We both know the right things to put in a man's meal to ensure it is his last.'

'They would have suspected you for that.'

'My husband had enemies.'

'And deserved them, but if he died in his own home they would not have had to look long or far to find his killer.'

'It matters not,' said Rosalind, 'for we devised a different plan, one that involved life not death, escape instead of endless unjust punishments. Killing Thomas only came into the matter when you appeared, Will. We knew your questions and all of your wild imaginings would lead you to Celia eventually, unless you were deflected from that course, so we confounded you with a different story, and laid out another trail for you to follow.'

'One which ended with her husband suspected of Celia's murder.'

'We only wanted Celia believed to be dead and she was. You were the first to suspect him of murder, an accusation that would have been hard to prove. But you did not need proof,' she reminded him, 'only the sureness in your heart that he was not a good man and you were doing a noble thing.'

'The best intentions pave the way to hell,' he admitted.

'That is sometimes true,' said Celia, 'and I believe your intentions were noble enough, though you were always blinded by your love for Rosalind.'

He turned to Rosalind then. 'I did love thee... once.' He brought his hand up to his forehead and kneaded it wearily with his fingertips. 'Now you have left me in a form of hell, with a man's death on my conscience.'

Rosalind laughed bitterly. 'He committed enough crimes to swing a dozen times, had he not been a knight of the realm, protected by a small place at court.' Rosalind sat down then and regarded Will with less hostility and what appeared to be sadness. 'With Thomas gone, we thought your quest for truth was over. In the end, none of it mattered anyway, for you found your way to us in any case. Was that God's will too, do you suppose?'

'I arrived too late for Sir Thomas, who lies cold in his grave.'

'And you accuse us of that? Blame yourself!'

'I do, and the worst of it is, I would have killed him with my own hand to protect you, Rosalind... I did, in fact.'

'Blame Celia's cousin instead, the man who ordered his death, or you could blame the men who beat him with clubs, wretches so base they would kill a man for a handful of coins to drink away in a tavern. Perhaps the earl and those fellows will be punished by God in the next life.'

'You could still be punished in this one.'

'What is our crime?' asked Rosalind. 'We have committed some perhaps, but not murder. If you bring us back to London, we will at least be allowed to speak, and speak we shall.' She meant it as a threat.

'And when women speak up in London, it always goes well for them.'

'They would call us witches,' admitted Celia, 'who cast spells and bewitched you and the earl into doing our bidding. They would hang us for it and the earl would be pardoned by the queen.'

'But would she pardon you, Will?' asked Rosalind. 'A low-born writer of plays? Would our deaths be enough to quell their anger, do you suppose? They killed Marlowe and tortured Kyd. What do you think they would do to you?'

'If you were to keep our secret unto death, we will keep yours,' Celia offered. 'Then our sins would be weighed by the only fair judge and, if punishment be ours, it would last an eternity. Can you honestly say that Thomas would not have fallen foul of some other rough men eventually and ended his days lying in a darkened street, whether you were involved or no?'

'Your husband was a vile and base man but did he really deserve to die like that, left lying in filth?'

Rosalind took a defiant step towards Will and hissed, 'You did not hear her screams and, in front of God, I tell you this: I wish I could have heard his.'

'Rosalind!' Celia turned her name into a warning and Rosalind ceased.

'What's to be done about this?' he asked them both then.

'What do you wish to be done?' asked Celia. 'If you bid me come back to London with you to answer for this, then I will go.'

'No!' protested Rosalind. 'Let the sin be on my head.'

'On mine alone,' said Celia, who looked panicked now.

'It should be on both of them,' he told them sternly, 'and mine too.'

'Then we will all go,' said Celia, 'and Thomas shall have revenge upon us from beyond the grave.'

'It is decided then.'

Chapter Fifty-Eight

'Is this her fault or mine?
The tempter or the tempted, who sins most?'
– Measure for Measure

Neither woman moved then, nor did either of them speak any more in their defence. He could see they were resigned to their fate now. Will regarded them both for a moment and suddenly found himself quite exhausted. He sat down heavily on a stool. 'And if, instead, I left you this day and resolved to forget I had ever seen you here, how would you propose to live?'

The two women exchanged hopeful glances. 'We have enough to pay four years on the lease,' Rosalind assured him. She meant the money they had taken from Celia's meagre dowry. 'If the farm doesn't earn enough by then, we were fools to even start this, but it will. I know it.'

'But you would never be able to leave here.'

'I have no desire to leave,' said Celia. 'I am saddened by the condition of England and have no wish to experience the ways of men any more. We are done with London and the rest of the world can drown in blood and tears. You look at our farm and see a jail. I see an Eden. I am happy here with Rosalind' – she took her companion's hand in hers – 'and she is happy with me.' Rosalind squeezed Celia's hand and held onto it.

'Who kissed you at the theatre?' he asked then. 'Was it Rosalind?'

'That was just a giddy trick,' said Celia dismissively. 'We were playing at man and wife when Thomas was gone. It was a game. He would not take me to the theatre nor allow me to go on my own, so Rosalind had me make her up like one of your actors and, though it took a while, we fooled everyone when we walked into the theatre. No one thought her anything less than a man.'

'It *was* a giddy trick,' agreed Rosalind, 'but it was the start of this too.' He wondered if she meant the beginning of their uncommon relationship, or the moment when the notion of how to free Celia from marriage to Thomas Vernon took hold. Most likely both.

'You lie together as man and woman then?' he asked.

'It is the same but not the same,' Rosalind answered enigmatically.

'God *will* judge you,' he said then. 'For everything.' Then he sighed and stood up. 'But I myself cannot. I know nothing of love… in this or any other form.'

'A poet who knows nothing of love?' asked Celia. 'How can that be?'

He didn't want to answer that question but instead asked, 'Will you not miss children?'

'Do you miss *yours*?' asked Celia.

'Yes, but I have learned to live without them.'

'Then so must I. It shall be easier for me since they are not born.'

'Nor can be,' he said, 'unless you have found a way to fool a midwife.'

'The Lord shall not bless this union with children,' said Rosalind, 'and we will not burden anyone else with our secret.'

'Who else knows, save you and I? The man who tills your fields?'

'Isaac cares not how we live, for he loves us both,' said Rosalind. 'He has a dry roof and a warm hearth, with food and ale once his work is done. He cares naught for all else.'

'And is mute in any case,' Will observed.

'He is silent,' agreed Celia, 'but not stupid, though many mistake him for an idiot.'

'He helped you fool everyone at the burial.' Celia's presence was proof enough of that. Will did not admit he had paid two honest villains to dig up that grave and find it empty of a body, just as he had suspected. 'He must have, but how?'

'The cart we took her in was covered with sackcloth. He placed Celia on it and drew the cloth over her. She was in her shroud, which I pierced near the mouth so she could breathe. When he got to the churchyard he went to the other side of the cart, lifted the sackcloth and took out a different shroud wrapped tightly around a bundle of sticks, blankets and stones to give it some weight. It resembled Celia's shape and no one wanted to draw near. They stood back and watched as Isaac carried her to the grave.'

'You buried a bundle of sticks,' he said.

'We buried Celia,' Rosalind told him, 'and that day, the captain was reborn.'

'And this Captain John Makepeace? Is he real and lives somewhere still or did you invent him like one of my characters?'

Rosalind explained. 'Captain Makepeace took ill when he came back to London from the lowlands. A doctor bled him but said he could do nothing more and urged his sister to pray to God for his recovery. She learned I had some skill tending the sick and came to me quite desperate. She had already lost her husband the year before and was raising children on her own. I could not see how to cure him, if a doctor could not. I thought him beyond my help and he believed it too. He told me he was going to die and his suffering would end, but he feared for his sister and her children in case they starved. That was on his conscience, for he had nothing to give them.'

'He was stricken with plague?' asked Will.

'Brought it back from the lowlands. I knew if he had it, there would be more like him, walking round London passing it to others.'

'He could have passed it to you.'

'I confess I almost left, but he would have died alone and I'd already had contact with him. I remember thinking that if I fell ill with plague, it was meant to be, since Celia and I were both in a wretched state by then. I couldn't see how we could sink lower, except in death. So I stayed with him, knowing he would likely last no more than a day or two. He kept saying he had turned his back on God and cared not a jot for the church. He had seen men torn apart in war and said it didn't matter what happened to your body. He had looked into dead men's eyes and had seen neither life nor soul there, once they were gone. He scoffed at the idea of a Christian burial. I would have been shocked by that once, but it was then that the idea came to me and I offered him a way to ease his mind. He heard me out then clasped my arm hard and urged me "let this be".'

'He consented to your plan?' asked Will.

'He did.'

'He let Celia become him after death, so she could be wed to you in disguise in that church, married by a half-blind old man in the dark.' She nodded at this. 'And you did that before God?'

'When my lady was beaten half to death, where was God?' asked Rosalind. 'When her husband tried to force himself upon me when he was drunk, God stayed silent. When Thomas tore a man's face with his own teeth, God looked away. If He allowed all of that, I doubted He would intervene at a wedding.'

'And the sister knew? She stood witness.'

'I gave her money for his name. She mourned her brother but it was a comfort that he bought her family bread and four walls with a warm hearth. She came to the church with us and swore Celia was her brother.'

'His name was in the parish records?'

'When he came back from the wars, he was returning home but he had been gone a long time. I had to use all of my skill to make Celia look like him, but he was slight and thin, as she is. His pale face had some beard on it, but I fixed that with horsehair, her hair was cut shorter and put up under a cap, her breasts bound and her womanly figure, such as it is, disguised in manly clothes. It was much easier than you would imagine. She barely had to speak, except to consent to wed the lady Rosalind and one of the groom's guests was his own sister. The other guests were a loyal, mute man and a couple of paid passers-by to bulk out the wedding party. If the minister had not been half-blind, I never would have had the idea.'

'The captain and his sister both knew you would deceive a minister into marrying one woman to another?' Will asked. 'They did not think this an abomination?'

'The sin was not on their heads, only ours. He had no love left for God after all that he had seen. It troubled the sister, though, and I could not have been sure about her right up until the end, but she silenced her conscience by saying "this is better than death for my children". She would repeat that like a prayer: "This is better than death for my children."'

'And after this wedding, Celia quit London?'

'With Isaac.'

'But she left you behind. So she could pretend to be you when they leased the farm in your name.'

'It took longer than we thought to find one and lease it. All that while I was trapped in London.'

'No wonder you could not summon your husband when you were arrested. And what about the money you stole, to pay Captain Makepeace and his sister, then lease this farm?'

'That was Celia's. It was hers to take. We did not steal it.'

'In the eyes of the law, it was her husband's property, as was she.'

'Yes,' she said, 'the law, which is written by men to enrich men, but Sir Thomas Vernon was a bad husband. If Celia had stayed another six months, he would have killed her and been hanged for it. She left that marriage no richer than when she walked into it.'

'What happened to the real captain's body?'

'I gave his sister coin for a funeral.'

'Under whose name?' Will knew that a man could hardly die and be buried then marry days later in the same parish.

'Her husband. He died a year before, killed fighting in the lowlands, and was buried there.'

'No one saw the body?'

'It was wrapped in a woollen shroud and we made it known how he died. No one wants to examine a body infected with plague.'

'The physician saw Celia in her room, from the doorway,' he remembered then. 'How did you give her the appearance of death?'

'Atropa Belladonna,' Rosalind answered.

'Deadly nightshade? They say even a small amount will kill a man.'

'Mix a few drops with another measure of leopard's bane, then soften it with certain herbs and it is enough to put a body beyond life but still a step from death.'

'But the risk...' He couldn't imagine such an act. 'You could have died,' he told Celia. 'If the wrong quantities—'

Rosalind interrupted him. 'I took great care to use the right quantities.'

'I was prepared for the possibility of death,' Celia told him, 'and pardoned Rosalind before her work began, in case my blood proved too weak to survive the potion she made. Better death than the life I had.'

'And this potion?' he asked. 'It stopped your heart, halted your breath, left you lifeless but not dead?'

'No potion could do that,' Rosalind told him. 'This one merely gives the appearance of death. Her skin turned pale, she slept deeply, almost without breath, her heart slowed and the pulse could barely be detected. It was still there but no one dared come close enough to check.'

'From a distance, she looked as if in death,' he observed. 'Your cousin, Henry Wriothesley, did love you, Celia, but believes you dead. Does he not deserve to know the truth?'

'My cousin might have loved me once,' said Celia, 'but had not given me a thought since my girlhood. He could have helped my mother, spared our family from shame and the most unfortunate of circumstances, even found me a better husband, yet he did nothing. Henry only remembered me once he thought I was in my grave. It was as if my husband had broken an old toy that once belonged to him. That is all this has ever been about.'

'And now he is satisfied his honour has been upheld and a form of justice done,' added Rosalind. 'Say no more on this matter and he will be content.'

'Oh, I have far more to say on this matter,' Will told her. 'When did you realise my interest in Celia was more than as a subject for a play?'

'From the beginning,' she confirmed and he realised just how much of a fool he had been. 'Your knowledge of Celia was too great and your questions too eager. You invited the answers I gave you.'

'You used that to your advantage,' he said. 'You lied to me.'

'I planted seeds and watched them grow. I merely told you what you hoped to hear. I even denied that my lady could possibly have been murdered. I told you many times she died of plague, but I could see in your eyes you did not wish it to be so. You thought that because you had to drag it from me, it must be the truth.' She was right about that too. What he took to be her reluctance to suspect anything was really an act on her part. 'You wanted a plot to kill her, so I gave you just enough to put one together and let your writer's imagination do the rest.'

'To deflect my suspicions from you?'

'From us both,' said Celia.

'You so wanted to be right about Thomas,' Rosalind told him. 'You were convinced he killed Celia. You could have told your patron that Celia died not by the hand of man but from plague, and that would have been the end of it, but you pressed me then questioned others, and would not let this lie.

'Did anything unusual happen before her death – remember how you asked me that? I knew then I had to fetch you an answer so that you would not suspect Celia might still be alive. It needed to fit your idea, your invention of a man murdering his wife. That's when I remembered the foreigner.'

'Remembered? Invented, you mean?'

'He was real enough,' she recalled. 'He visited our house and Thomas made Celia bring him food and wine but it was me he dragged upon his knee, not the wife of his host and, mercifully, he was not sick. He did not sweat or have a fever, nor did he purge himself after the meal. That part was invention, but you thought it true, because you cannot imagine a world in which a woman could lie to a man as clever as you and make him believe her.'

'I was the more deceived,' he admitted.

'You pointed the finger of blame at Thomas Vernon. You had no proof but whispered persuasively into your patron's ear. Rough men did the rest, but you killed him.'

'And how many commandments have you broken?' he retorted, though he had little strength left for this argument and already felt sick to his stomach, because she was right. Will was as responsible for his murder as the men who wielded the clubs.

'You wore your grief for Celia not lightly,' he told Rosalind. 'How did you act in such a convincing manner when you had no training? You were never apprenticed to the craft.'

'I thought of how I would feel if she really were dead, then imagined it to be true. I told myself I would never see Celia again. In convincing my mind of it' – she made a fist and pressed it to her heart – 'I felt as if it were real.'

'Thinking on it made it so?' He pondered before conceding, 'There is method in this.' And he resolved to try the technique in his own acting.

'And I had seen the players so many times. I imagined myself among them, up on the stage, a silenced crowd moved by my every word.'

'Yet no woman has ever acted, for it is forbidden.'

'A woman learns to act much sooner than a player,' she told him, 'and we play many parts before we are done. Dutiful' – she bowed. 'Modest,' she added, and lowered her head but raised her eyes as an innocent girl might. 'The scold' – and she frowned and wagged a finger, as if her husband had just walked in after spending all of his day's earnings on ale. 'The mother' – and she looked down at her now folded arms and rocked an imaginary baby that lay there – 'and the coquette.' She turned her face slightly to one side then raised her eyes until they locked onto his invitingly. My God, she was impressive and, despite himself, Will still found he looked upon her with, if not love, then something close to admiration, for Rosalind had all the talents.

'What a piece of work is a woman,' he told her then. 'And how many more layers they have to them than a man.'

–

He left them soon after, with the grim realisation that he would never see Rosalind again. Isaac watched him leave and if the big man looked wary of Will, he need not have been. He had no intention of exposing her new life with the supposedly dead woman. What they did when they lay together, and how they did it, might still be something of a mystery to him, but he had heard of such things before and accepted them to be true. Celia, Rosalind and Isaac were a family of sorts, and he hoped and believed that they could thrive.

As Will rode away from the farm, down an empty country lane, a great sadness enveloped him, along with a deep sense of loneliness. He gave voice to James Burbage's words then, even though there was no one else there to hear them. 'A great man or a contented man?' he asked himself, before declaring, 'A great man then.'

Chapter Fifty-Nine

'The fool doth think he is wise, but the wise man knows himself to be a fool.'
— *As You Like It*

It took Will two days to return to London. He spent his time thereafter locked away alone in his rooms in Shoreditch, trying not to think about his reckoning with Robert Cecil, which could not be postponed much longer. When he was not eating, drinking or sleeping, he was writing. He counted the days in candle lengths and went out only for provisions. London's streets were eerily quiet now and few ventured abroad if they had no desperate need to, though he noticed there were fewer bodies in the streets. Either the plague was taking fewer victims by now or the men on the death carts were becoming more accomplished at their work. The rich had all fled the city long ago for country homes with sweeter air, but Will refused to leave until he had finished his play and he worked on it tirelessly.

When it was finally done, he delivered it to Richard Burbage and told his friend he was heading home at last, though Will was tired before he even set out on the journey to Stratford and his friend noticed this.

'Are you well now, Will?' he cautioned. 'Fully well, I mean?'

'Well enough. Give your father my new play and make sure that he reads it.'

'He will read your play,' Richard assured him. 'He has been waiting for it.' He took the play and regarded its title suspiciously. '*As You Like It*? Is this the history play he asked for?'

'This is… something else,' Will said hesitantly. And when Richard looked aghast, he said, 'A comedy… perhaps.'

Richard frowned. 'Then it were better *you* gave it to him, for he will swing his sword at me. Why should I be maimed for your madness?'

'If he but reads this, he will find there is method in my madness. It is good, Richard. I am almost sure of it.'

'*Almost* sure?'

'I am a writer. We never know for certain and always doubt what we have set down. That is the way of things but I think there is something here, within.' And he nodded at the manuscript.

Richard sighed. 'I know what he will say. That now is not the time for comedy. When the plague passes and the theatres open again, people will not want to laugh. They will still be mourning ten thousand dead.'

'Then they will need to laugh more than ever. We all will.'

Richard seemed unconvinced. 'What's it about?'

'You know I hate that question.'

'I know all writers do.'

'It's about life, everything,' Will began.

'Is there a shipwreck? You know he likes a shipwreck.'

'There is no shipwreck.'

Richard sighed deeply, but Will told him, 'There's some disguise, mistaken identity and love of both kinds: requited and unrequited.'

'And a happy resolution?'

'Of sorts.'

'Please give us that at least.' Richard sighed again.

'You sigh like a young girl in love with a boy from the wrong family.'

'And you are the cause of my sighs, Will. I don't doubt this will be good but he asked you for a history and you present him with a comedy. My father will not want to put money into this. It is as uncertain a gamble as dice.'

'What if it fills his theatre every day for a month?'

'What if it doesn't? Will you pay the actors and everyone else who comes looking for their money, because they built or stitched something used upon his stage? No, of course not. The risk is all his.'

'Is money all he cares about?'

'No, Will, but without money no one is paid and everyone starves, including the writer!'

'I did not write this for money. I wrote it because…' He realised he did not want to explain why. 'It was necessary.'

'Why? Did God guide your hand, or the devil perhaps, like Faustus? Tell me that and I will try to convince him not to run you through.' Richard shook his head. 'He will think this a bad play, Will.'

'Then he is a fool, for this is not a bad play!'

'It *is* a bad play,' argued Richard, 'because it is *not* the play he asked for! My father is no fool, Will. He built a theatre, much of it with his own hands! Do you know what it takes to manage a company? Of course you don't. All you have to concern yourself with is your writing. If you think you are above him, then you are wrong. Your plays would be nothing without his stage or those that sit before it. If you cannot see that, then you will never be half the man James Burbage is.'

Though he knew Richard to be right on his point about the stage, Will was too angry to concede it. Instead, he shouted back at his friend: 'Why is it never about the art with him and always about the arses?'

'Because the arses pay for the art!'

Richard stormed away then, still clutching Will's new play.

Chapter Sixty

'I do love nothing in the world so well as you:
is not that strange?'
— *Much Ado About Nothing*

With the theatres still closed, his new play delivered and a little money
to his name, it was time for Will to make the journey home, to settle
debts and tend to his family.

It was good to see his bright young boy Hamnet again, and his sweet,
loving daughters, Susanna and Judith, were always a consolation to Will
when he felt at odds with the world. Anne asked him no questions
about his life in London without her and gave no hint of any suspicions
she might have had about how he spent his time there. She professed
herself happy to see him returned safe and well from London, despite
the plague, which she had heard ravaged the city, but when she turned
in for the night, she made not for the second best bed, where they had
lain since they were first married, but instead slept with the children.
He had been gone too long this time and they were almost strangers.
It was then Will realised that his wife knew he had not been true. Of
course she did. Just as his friend, Richard Burbage, had said she must.
With the gaining of this knowledge, it was clear that whether he liked
it or not, their marriage was already done.

He spent a week with Anne and the children until he began, as he
always did, to yearn for the company of his theatrical friends once
more. Anne though was not poor company herself nor anywhere near
as unintelligent or superstitious as he had described her to Rosalind.
Will realised he had dealt her harshly then and he felt the shame of this

keenly. In reality, Anne knew and understood many things: about the seasons and nature, herbs, plants and farming, tending to animals and the weather. She always knew the latest word from the pulpit, of which she held a more critical and enquiring view than he had given her credit for; and, thanks to the gossip in the marketplace, she also knew who was doing what to whom and why. Her intelligence was of a rough kind, and it came from the street and the fields, not the classroom, but was no lesser for it. She reminded him of Rosalind, in fact. They were quite alike in that regard, with only their years between them, and he realised this might even be why he had loved them both.

Will found that he could while away a pleasant evening or two in Anne's company, but it was not the same as being in a tavern with Richard Burbage or the other members of their troupe. It had been more than seven years since he had first left home to join the company and they were his people now. He missed their bawdy and bitter wit, their merry japes, as well as the earnest talk of their craft. He even missed the actors' vanity, when they would come to him separately to plead for an extra line or two, a stronger entrance or more dramatic exit, even a death scene of sufficient length to show their talents to the groundlings, so they would be loved by them for a time.

When he told Anne that he must return to London, to write more plays before the theatres reopened, she seemed resigned and did not object. 'Do what you must, husband,' she said, not unkindly. 'We are grown used to your absences and must muddle along without you. We will see you again anon.'

He left enough coin with Anne to ensure they would want for naught, then set out on the journey back to London.

Chapter Sixty-One

'If money go before, all ways do lie open.'
— The Marry Wives of Windsor

'Master Burbage,' called Will and both men turned to face him. 'Master *Richard* Burbage,' he clarified and the younger man straightened, while the theatre owner watched Will passively as he climbed up onto the stage to join them there.

'We quarrelled,' Will began.

'We did.' Richard folded his arms, as if recalling the moment anew.

'And I was in the wrong. Not for the first time, nor likely the last.' Richard's furrowed brow told Will he was not expecting this. 'I present myself here now to humbly beg your forgiveness and beseech you to forget my foolish words. I am a poet and we are sometimes governed by an excess of feeling, but I have lately had time to reflect on what I said and I now know the truth of the matter.'

'That you are a fool with neither wit nor sense?' asked Richard.

'More or less that,' Will admitted, and despite himself, Richard let a half smile form on his lips.

Will glanced at James now, who returned his gaze. 'Much of what you foretold has come to pass,' Will acknowledged. James Burbage's countenance was blank and he resisted the temptation to tell Will that he was right all along. 'Also, my plays would be nothing without your stage.' And he bowed as low as dignity would allow.

'They would not.' It seemed he was going to enjoy humbling Will but then he lowered his voice to a more pleasing level. 'Nor would my stage be of much use without a play, Will Shakespeare.' He smiled tightly. 'And you have written a new one.'

'You have read *As You Like It*?'

'I read your play,' James Burbage acknowledged. 'Master Shakespeare has written a comedy,' he told his son, even though Richard knew that already, 'though I asked him for a historical. Mark me well, writers do what they will and never listen.'

'But was it any good?' Richard pressed his father.

'It was... a puzzle.' And his manner did not give away any of his private thoughts as to its worth. 'It tells the story of two young women,' he told Richard before switching his gaze back to Will. '*Celia* and *Rosalind*.' He smiled indulgently at that. 'Both ladies of a court in the Forest of Arden.'

He turned back to his son and began to explain the plot. 'Rosalind has to flee her wicked uncle's court, for he has overthrown her father,' James began, but then he started to laugh, 'disguised as a young man, Ganymede, accompanied by her cousin Celia, who also pretends to be someone she is not: a poor lady, in fact. They live in a forest together and meet Orlando there. Rosalind falls in love with him, though he thinks her to be a boy. He has already seen Ganymede when she was Rosalind and is also in love with her but does not recognise her in this disguise. She... he – as Ganymede, if you are still with me – offers to cure him of his love for Rosalind by counselling him against it and she does this by pretending to be *his* Rosalind and acting out his courtship with Orlando, as Ganymede, while also of course secretly being the very same Rosalind he is in love with.' He laughed at the sheer complexity of it all, as well as its potential for comedy.

'I can scarcely keep up,' said Richard, laughing too.

'And there is poor Phoebe too,' said James, 'who also falls in love with Rosalind, while she is disguised as Ganymede, thinking her to be a man.' He chuckled. 'Our young boys would have great sport and many merry moments acting this out: boys playing girls, disguised as boys.'

'It's genius, Will,' concluded Richard, laughing.

'It's absurd, ridiculous and an absolute folly.' James grinned. 'I adored it.'

'Good then.' Will's mood had brightened considerably. 'So, you will put it on?'

James Burbage's smile vanished. 'Alas, I cannot.'

'What? Why not?' demanded Will.

'It is not yet ready for an audience and no audience is ready for it. I said I would accept new, Master Shakespeare, but not that new. I also said I wanted a history not a comedy. There are too many newly dead in London for those that remain to be laughing at players on the stage.'

'Maybe those that remain need something to laugh about,' argued Richard to Will's relief. 'To soften their grief.'

'Perchance they will,' conceded his father. 'One day but not yet a while. It's too early, so this play is too much of a gamble. I could lose everything.' Then he said, 'Soon I will need another history play, a different one.' Then he smiled, which made Will suspicious.

'What are you concealing from me?'

'The plague has lifted and they reopened the theatres while you were gone.' This was very encouraging news and Will had not expected it, but his new-found hopes were dashed soon after. 'Richard persuaded me to give our audience your Harry the Sixth again, blank verse and all.' James looked stern then. 'Takings were not as I would have imagined.'

Will felt a great sickness in his heart then. He had hoped that his play would finally find its audience and they would come to see it, but it seemed *Henry VI* had been forgotten by the groundlings while the theatres were closed. All that effort, all of those hours of writing and rewriting, and for what? Now he discovered the take was not what Burbage had hoped for and the play would surely die, along with his career as a writer. He would be an actor for the rest of his days and not even a prosperous one, certainly never a leading man like Richard. Will's ambitions were all folly, turned to dust.

'I had hoped for an audience of four hundred to cover costs,' added James.

Oh God, it was lower even than that.

James Burbage reached for the scrap of paper he had written the day's take on and read it to Will, as if to hammer the point home. The humiliation was too much to bear. After this, Will might as well throw himself in the Thames. He would do it too, if he could trust himself to get even that right. With his luck, he would merely be fished out with a cold.

'The takings for *Henry VI* by William Shakespeare, performed on 3 September 1593, having been all accounted for, amounted to...' His tone could not have been more sombre until, wholly unexpectedly, he broke into a grin, then a broader one and finally a laugh. 'Three pounds and sixteen shillings!'

Will's eyes widened in pleasure and shock. 'Three pounds?' he cried. 'And sixteen shillings!'

'That's a lot of arses, Will.' Richard was smiling at him then.

'Over two thousand,' James confirmed.

'More than *Doctor Faustus*.' Will said this with wonder.

'You have had more arses than Faustus,' Richard said, grinning. 'Now that is an achievement.'

'Don't be vulgar, Dick,' reprimanded his father. 'Now then, Will, that should inspire you. Go away and finish your *Richard III*, then write me another history and I will give you another two pounds. What say you?'

Before Will could answer, his friend interrupted. 'He will want three.'

His father rounded on him. 'Why speak you at all? He would have taken two as a fair price, which it is!'

'He would not,' argued Richard. 'Will is no fool. He knows his value, you have just told him it' – and he gestured at the record of the *Henry VI* takings, still in his father's hand – 'and his price.'

'Three is not fair,' James persisted.

'Then he will write his play for someone else,' said Richard, with a calmness that disquieted his father.

'Don't tell him to do that,' James scolded him, as if he hoped Will might not hear the advice.

'He knows already. Give him three pounds, Father, or watch him take the play to Philip Henslowe and see it performed by the Admiral's Men, who will open at the Rose before the biggest crowd in London, with Edward Alleyn in the lead role.' He said that last part with a level of sadness that did not seem feigned.

'Damn it, Richard! Are you two in league? A pox on Philip Henslowe and a pox on the Admiral's Men! Will would not do that to me, he would not do that to *us*. Would you, Will?' asked Burbage, though now unsure. 'Henslowe is a fraud and a charlatan.'

'A fraud with Edward Alleyn in his pocket,' Richard reminded him. 'They say Alleyn will marry Henslowe's step-daughter this very year.

Can you truly afford to give Alleyn the words of the finest living poet in London, Father?'

James Burbage stayed silent for a time and appeared to be pondering his best option, while liking none of them. Will knew he did not want to part with more money for an, as yet unwritten, play but he would also be reluctant to see it possibly fall into the hands of his wealthier rival and make *him* the toast of all London instead.

He braced himself, calmed his temper and turned to Will. 'Three pounds and all's well that ends well, then?' And when Will did not answer immediately, he added, 'Don't dare say otherwise!'

'I don't want three pounds,' said Will wearily.

'Then what on God's earth *do* you want?'

'To be your partner.'

James shook his head. 'One day, perhaps, when you have written thirty plays and earned enough to buy your share in the company. For now, write me a play about the hunchback King Richard that I have oft spoken to you about. It will keep the queen happy too, for it was her grandfather who sent that monster to his grave. Write it well and we might even be asked to perform it before her at Christmas. Get it to me in a few weeks and I'll give you three pounds for that one. What say you?'

'Is that your final word?'

'It is.'

'No.'

'No? What do you mean no? Who else are you writing for, damn you?'

'No one.'

'Then take my coin, Will.'

Will sighed wearily and then said, 'I'll write your play but I don't want your three pounds. I want a share.'

'In the company? Have you lost your senses? That's worth a lot more than three pounds. I turned down an offer of forty pounds to buy in last year!'

'Then I will give you fifty,' said Will. 'Minus three for the next play, and that's *my* final word.'

James laughed then, but bitterly. 'Do you have fifty pounds, Will? I think not!'

'I have it,' Will announced, 'or will soon.' And he said this with such quiet determination that James was silenced.

'Where did you get it, Will?' asked Richard but James stopped him.

'I care not from whence it came nor how he came about it. Our new venture with the Lord Chamberlain is short of coin and we lack merchants prosperous enough to buy in. Plagues are costly. A new partner who brings money, *as well as a play about Richard III,*' he added pointedly, '*might* be welcomed.'

'Then it's a bargain,' agreed Will.

'Good.' James spat on his palm and they clasped hands to seal the deal. 'Bring my money and the play and you will be elevated to a partner in the Lord Chamberlain's Men, sharing all costs and profits henceforth. We will make a gentleman out of you yet, Will. That's what you want, yes? Perhaps in time we might even put on your *As You Like It.*' And he laughed. 'A woman playing at being a man, who is loved by another woman and a man who both think her to be a man and a woman at the same time? That is a devilishly funny idea. However did you come up with it?'

Will thought for a moment then said quietly, 'I stole it.'

James had lost patience now and said, 'Please, I beg you, go back to your rooms, take up your quill and write my history of King Richard.'

'It is done,' Will said.

James looked as if he did not understand. 'You've written it?'

'Yes. I have been writing your play for months and finished it anon.'

'My history? You have completed it as well as the comedy? Is this possible?'

'It is possible to work on more than one play,' said Will flatly. 'I work on several at a time.'

James looked to his son in confusion, who told him, 'I have seen this. Will has plays in his rooms that are part finished. I urged him to complete this one for you, Father.'

'Good then,' he told his son and turned back to Will. 'It is truly finished?'

'It is.' He reached into his bag and produced the play.

James Burbage snatched the manuscript from Will's outstretched hand, peered at it and read the title. '*Richard III,*' he confirmed excitedly, then he left the two friends alone and walked across the stage to scrutinise it, as if he would not truly believe it was finished until he had read a few of its pages.

'When did you find the time to do all this, Will?' asked Richard.

'While I was in Stratford with Anne and the children.'

'You always told me you could not write while they were with you.'

'I was wrong about that. When I needed to, I could shut out the sound of the children, just as I must ignore the noise from London's streets. As soon as I found him, my Richard became as flesh to me. Finishing the play then took but a week. In truth, I was always writing it.' He pointed to his head to show that he did not need a quill and paper to compose words.

'You are two people, Will Shakespeare. One lives his life like any man, while the other is locked away somewhere in a corner of your mind.' Richard shook his head while he tried to find the most apt word and he settled on 'scratching'.

Will allowed himself a low chuckle at Richard's recalling of his father's word for his writing. 'Aye,' he said, 'scratching,' and he mimed the action of it with his hand, 'always scratching.'

When James eventually returned to them, he was reciting lines from the opening scene of Will's play. 'Listen to this.' It was as if he couldn't help himself and wanted to share them even with their author, who knew them already. Instantly, he became Richard, with his hunched back, head angled upwards and to one side, voice deeper and more sinister. '*I, that am not shaped for sportive tricks, nor made to court an amorous looking glass; I, that am rudely stamped and want love's majesty to strut before a wanton ambling nymph; I, that am curtailed of this fair proportion, cheated of feature by dissembling nature, deformed, unfinished, sent before my time into this breathing world, scarce half made up, and that so lamely and unfashionable that dogs bark at me as I halt by them.*'

He looked at Will then. 'That is good, Will. That is *very* good.'

'I thank you.'

'There are fine lines here for you, son, if you can learn to speak them hunched over.' And he continued to mimic the effects of a crooked back as he handed the play to Richard. 'Look here,' and he pointed towards the page.

Richard took the play, glanced at Will, then he too read aloud, delivering its opening line. '*Now is the winter of our discontent made glorious summer by this son of York.* That's a good phrase, Will.'

'No, no, not that part.' James was dismissive. 'That bit is good enough but not as memorable as this.' And he took the play back, turned it to show the section he had meant for his son to read, then returned it to Richard's grasp, while stabbing a bony finger at the relevant words.

Richard recited once more. '*And therefore, since I cannot prove a lover to entertain these fair well-spoken days, I am determined to prove a villain and hate the idle pleasures of these days.*'

'That's it,' said James triumphantly, 'that is our Richard: a man so deformed and ugly in body and mind that he cannot enjoy a time of peace and leisure, with wine in his glass and a woman on his lap, but must always be hatching plots instead for his amusement, to set men against men and condemn women to widowhood.'

Richard looked at his friend in something close to wonder. 'You found him. Your Richard.'

'It came to me in a moment. Who he is and why, what formed him over time and the impulse that pushed him forward through this world. A damaged and bitter man, fighting for his corner of it. It was all there, right in front of me. I just could not see it.' He meant of course that Robert Cecil was his example and Richard understood this. How incredible that the man Will had been tasked to write about, the villain he could not hope to understand until recently, had suffered from the same condition as his interrogator, Robert Cecil, whose own back was twisted and body malformed. He privately recalled the jealousy of Cecil then and his humiliating upbraiding by the queen, as well as the malignant hatred he held for the taller, fairer and more blessed Henry Wriothesley. Will thought of the harm he intended to do to a man who had once been like a brother to him and how like King Richard he was, who murdered his own brother's children. Cecil's stature was smaller than Henry Wriothesley in every way: in height, in court, in the eyes of the queen, and Will was certain much of his enmity towards the other man stemmed from it.

He did not want to explain this now, for fear of putting James Burbage off the play, in case he worried it might offend the man of state his King Richard subtly mirrored.

'I thought this king was just a vessel of the devil, but now,' James chuckled, 'I am starting to understand and perhaps even pity the man he became.'

'You must,' said Will. 'How can we care what happens to a character unless we understand them, even as they are dragged to their doom? That which he can never have, even when he is king, undoes him in the end, for he cannot find contentment, only chaos and death.'

'I am away to read the rest,' said James. 'I'll read your comedy again too' – he waved a hand dismissively. 'London is not ready for it yet, but perhaps one day it shall be.'

Chapter Sixty-Two

'When the hurly-burly's done,
When the battle's lost and won.'
— Macbeth

With his play about King Richard finished and an agreement to become a partner in the newly formed Lord Chamberlain's Men reached, Will could put off his final reckoning with Robert Cecil no longer. He needed Henry Wriothesley's fifty pounds and could only get it if he defended the earl against his most bitter enemy, but how to do that without forfeiting his own life?

The queen's inquisitor agreed to meet him at the same plain house where he first demanded Will spy on the earl and report back to him. Cecil's wishes had not altered but now he was prepared to accept lies instead of truth, as long as they achieved the same goals.

'What have you to say to me about Henry Wriothesley?' he demanded.

Will had been dreading this moment. 'Nothing.'

'Nothing will come of nothing,' Cecil told him. 'Except most cruel torture. So speak and spare me no detail about his treachery.'

'I cannot,' said Will, 'for there is no treason.'

'What is this defiance? Have you forgot yourself? I could have you racked,' Cecil reminded him, 'like that blasphemer, Thomas Kyd.' And a great feeling of fear begin to grip Will then. 'Or I could put you in a windowless hole and forget about you, until you went mad. On my word, you could be found guilty of treason. I could have you hanged, drawn and quartered!'

Will tried to speak but his mouth was too dry. He had to stop, swallow, breathe, then try again. When he looked back on this moment, as he often would, Will wondered how he managed to find the words he needed, but somehow, despite the terrible images of the cruel fates Cecil had conjured for him, they came to Will, at the very height of his terror.

He straightened and looked Cecil directly in the eye. 'But if you were to do that, my lord, then who would write the queen's Christmas play?'

'Her Christmas play? What of it?'

'Robert Greene is dead, Christopher Marlowe is dead, Thomas Kyd finished, Thomas Nashe in jail.'

Cecil scowled on hearing Nashe's name. 'That purveyor of filth.' He seemed to think on it now. 'You are the only one who is not jailed, broken or dead, is that it? There is no one else?' He scoffed at that notion.

'No one even scarce good enough. Of course, you know Her Majesty well. Perhaps she has the patience to sit through hours of an inferior play while keeping her good humour. If so, my argument is false.' He could tell by the look of exasperation on Cecil's face that his interrogator's superior knowledge of the queen supported Will's notion. Her Majesty would not tolerate anything of length that did not engage and amuse her, for she hated to waste time. This might provoke a fury in her. Then she might very well turn her wrath against Cecil and ask why, thanks to him, there was no one left in England who could deliver a better play.

There was a long pause while Cecil considered this.

Finally, he spoke. 'How fortunate you are, Master Shakespeare, being a man of such low birth that you are of no consequence to anyone.' It was the first time Will had ever felt grateful for his lowly status. 'And yet the queen herself has heard mention of your name, thanks to your *Henry VI* and now, as you say, there is a scarcity of poets.' He sneered the word, as if being a poet was as lowly a profession as any gentleman could find himself in. 'I tell you plain that I intended to rack you.' There was anger in his expression and frustration too, but this quickly dissolved, until he appeared to become resigned, for once, by the limitations of his power. Will could read this resignation in Cecil's face almost immediately. The man had a violent temper when roused but he was no fool. All that he had came from the queen and he was dependent on her continued good humour. Will's point was accepted and Cecil's inclination to torture or execute the playmaker died along with it. Instead, he lowered his gaze to the papers on his table.

There was a moment's silence, and when Cecil did speak again, he did it without looking up at Will. Instead, he kept his eyes firmly on more weighty matters of state that were already occupying him. 'Fortune favours you further,' he said. 'Henry Wriothesley, who, not long ago, was held in scorn by the queen for ending his marriage contract without her blessing, is now back in Her Majesty's favour.' Then he added, 'For the time being.' And Will could tell how much this rankled with Cecil. 'Having paid five thousand pounds, it seems he is something of a favourite with her once more,' he admitted, 'because he is fair and knows how to whisper honeyed words into her ear to gain the queen's favour.' He sneered then. 'But all fair things age, wither and die. Wriothesley was once out of the queen's favour, now none may speak against him,' he said bitterly, concluding, 'until such time as he is disgraced once more, which he shall be, for the man cannot help himself. It is in his nature. Then my time will surely come.' He spoke as if to himself, then looked up, as if suddenly remembering Will was in the room. 'So, you wish to write the queen's Christmas play, Master Shakespeare?'

'It would be the singular honour of my life.'

'And what would you give her?'

'A great historical play, of the life and terrible times of King Richard III. A man who usurped the throne, murdered his own nephews and was only prevented from plunging the kingdom into complete tyranny when he was brought down by Henry, the queen's own grandfather, whose selfless and heroic intervention led to the founding of the most glorious dynasty this country has ever known, thanks to God's will.'

Cecil seemed taken aback by the passion of Will's proposal. The playmaker was used to capturing James Burbage's attention with a handful of hastily spoken words, but Cecil looked impressed. 'She would enjoy that, I think, and the queen does love a good play. So, Greene, Marlowe, Kyd and Nashe are all gone,' he concluded. 'The way is clear for you now. If you were to write one and it is well received, you would become known at court and might befriend men with influence. I could make use of you then. Remember, though, that the Master of the Revels will not be the only one who examines your plays from now on. I will pore over every word.' He enunciated the final sentence slowly and clearly, like an actor about to make his final exit from the stage as the end of a play draws near. It sounded like a threat, because it was one.

Will bowed low before him and made his own exit soon after.

As he walked out of Robert Cecil's rooms, having conducted an unlikely, possibly even brilliant escape from his inquisitor, Will had much to think about. He would be more cautious from now on and mindful of everything he wrote. Upset the queen and they could jail you, lop off your ears, stretch or even burn you. Was there anything more dangerous in these darkest of times than words?

Will was left with a feeling of intense relief at having survived his encounter with Cecil. Somehow, he had managed to outwit the most dangerous man in the kingdom, at least for the time being. Will would never take Cecil for granted though. If he was careless just once, a grim fate at the inquisitor's hands would await him.

He thought about Cecil's parting words then, and how he planned to scour every line of Will's work, searching for hidden meaning. He was struck by the sheer folly of wasting hours like that, examining every word of a play, looking to find some significance there that the writer had most probably never intended. A play was meant to be performed and watched by an audience, not read and certainly never studied to excess, until every ounce of enjoyment of it is killed in the process. Surely, only a complete fool would attempt an act of such folly.

Afterword

The historical events that form the background to this work of fiction occurred between 1592 and 1593. These include an epidemic of the plague in London that caused the deaths of 15,000 people, the exodus of Elizabeth I's court from the capital, the Dutch Church Libel, the suspicious death of Christopher Marlowe, the torture of Thomas Kyd and jailing of Nashe and Raleigh. The Lord Chamberlain's Men were formed in 1594, with Will Shakespeare as one of their founding partners.

Christopher Marlowe's death, on 30 May 1593, is still widely assumed to be the result of a tavern brawl he was responsible for, even though it did not take place in a tavern and the men he was with were government agents. William Shakespeare deliberately evoked the memory of Marlowe in *As You Like It*, when he included the line 'When a man's verses cannot be understood... it strikes a man more dead than a great reckoning in a little room'.

Thomas Kyd died broken and penniless in 1594, just one year after his friend, Christopher Marlowe.

Thomas Nashe was soon released from prison and lived until 1601. He died at the age of thirty-four.

Lord Ferdinando Stanley, patron of Lord Strange's Men, under suspicion due to a tenuous claim to the throne, died suddenly on 16 April 1594, at the age of thirty-five. It is widely believed he was poisoned, though at the time, some blamed witchcraft.

In 1603, the eminent physician Edward Jorden, Shakespeare's neighbour, wrote a book about hysteria in women, called *A Briefe Discourse of a Disease Called the Suffocation of the Mother*. As an expert witness, he offered his wandering womb theory in numerous trials where women were accused of being witches. He was not always successful.

337

Walter Raleigh was released by the queen after a few months in the Tower but was eventually executed in 1618 by her successor, King James I.

The Earl of Southampton was in and out of Queen Elizabeth's favour for the remaining years of her reign. He was eventually imprisoned and only released upon her death. Scholars still wonder if he and Shakespeare were lovers.

Sir Robert Cecil had scoliosis, the same condition that afflicted King Richard III. He kept his pre-eminent position as the queen's spymaster up to and beyond her death, retaining it under James I, who made him the Earl of Salisbury and referred to Cecil as 'my little beagle'. Overworked by the new king, he died in 1612, at the age of forty-eight.

When Richard Burbage finally died, in 1619, twenty-six years after the events described here, he was acknowledged as the finest actor of his generation. One of his most poignant epitaphs is the shortest: 'Exit Burbage.'

William Shakespeare's only son, Hamnet, died at the age of eleven in 1596 but his daughters, Susanna and Judith, outlived him. Will went on to write a total of thirty-nine plays, which together make up the most illustrious and regularly performed body of work in the history of the dramatic arts. He seems to have been fascinated with the idea of characters cross dressing in order to hide their true identities and employed this device in no fewer than seven of his plays: *Twelfth Night*, *The Merchant of Venice*, *Cymbeline*, *The Merry Wives of Windsor*, *The Taming of the Shrew*, *The Two Gentlemen of Verona* and *As You Like It*.

Will finally left London for good when the Globe Theatre, which became the home of the Lord Chamberlain's Men, burned to the ground in 1613, after a spark from a stage cannon accidentally set fire to its thatch during a performance of *All Is True*, his final play. Will enjoyed a prosperous retirement in Stratford, with Anne and his daughters. He died in 1616 at the age of fifty-two. Some say it was ague that finished him off.

More than four hundred years after his death, William Shakespeare is still considered England's greatest dramatist. His works are performed far more widely than even the great Christopher Marlowe's.

Acknowledgements

This book has been a labour of love, so I would like to thank everyone at Canelo for publishing *A Serpent In The Garden*. A special thank you goes to my brilliant editor, Kit Nevile, for believing in this story and helping me to make it even better.

I've been writing books for a while now and my amazing literary agent, Phil Patterson, at Marjacq has been with me every step of the way. Thanks for your faith and hard work on my behalf, Phil. I never take it for granted.

The following people have been hugely supportive of my writing, so I'd like to thank Adam Pope, Andy Davis, Nikki Selden, Gareth Chennells, Andrew Local, Stuart Britton, David Shapiro, Peter Day, Tony Frobisher, Katie Charlton, Gemma Sealey, Susan Jackson, Ion Mills, Annette Crossland, Peter Hammans, Emad Akhtar, and Keshini Naidoo.

A big thank you to my wonderful wife, Alison, for all your support and for always believing in me. I couldn't do this without you.

Finally, huge thanks to my lovely daughter Erin, who always cheers me up when the words aren't cooperating and makes all my days brighter.